"Your sister thinks you should marry…"

Bethany's face grew hot. "Husbands don't exactly grow on trees in New Covenant."

"Anyone you chose would be getting a fine wife."

She looked up to study Michael's reflection in the glass, but it wasn't clear enough to let her see what he was thinking. "Are you making me an offer?"

"You would be getting a very poor bargain if I was."

She turned around so she could look into his eyes. "Why do you say that?"

"Because it's the truth."

There was so much pain in his voice and deep in his eyes that she wanted to hold him and promise to make everything better.

She couldn't. "What's wrong, Michael?"

"Nothing that you can fix."

"How do I know that if you can't tell me what troubles you?"

"Trust me. You don't want to know." He turned and walked down the hall and out the back door.

He was so wrong.

Bethany wanted to know everything about Michael Shetler.

After thirty-five years as a nurse, **Patricia Davids** hung up her stethoscope to become a full-time writer. She enjoys spending her free time visiting her grandchildren, doing some long-overdue yard work and traveling to research her story locations. She resides in Wichita, Kansas. Pat always enjoys hearing from her readers. You can visit her online at patriciadavids.com.

Emma Miller lives quietly in her old farmhouse in rural Delaware. Fortunate enough to have been born into a family of strong faith, she grew up on a dairy farm, surrounded by loving parents, siblings, grandparents, aunts, uncles and cousins. Emma was educated in local schools and once taught in an Amish schoolhouse. When she's not caring for her large family, reading and writing are her favorite pastimes.

USA TODAY Bestselling Author

PATRICIA DAVIDS

&

EMMA MILLER

An Amish Match for Christmas

2 Uplifting Stories

An Amish Wife for Christmas and
Her Surprise Christmas Courtship

LOVE INSPIRED
INSPIRATIONAL ROMANCE

LOVE INSPIRED®
INSPIRATIONAL ROMANCE

ISBN-13: 978-1-335-45454-6

An Amish Match for Christmas

Copyright © 2023 by Harlequin Enterprises ULC

An Amish Wife for Christmas
First published in 2018. This edition published in 2023.
Copyright © 2018 by Patricia MacDonald

Her Surprise Christmas Courtship
First published in 2022. This edition published in 2023.
Copyright © 2022 by Emma Miller

Recycling programs for this product may not exist in your area.

This is a work of fiction. Names, characters, places and incidents are either the product of the author's imagination or are used fictitiously. Any resemblance to actual persons, living or dead, businesses, companies, events or locales is entirely coincidental.

For questions and comments about the quality of this book, please contact us at CustomerService@Harlequin.com.

Harlequin Enterprises ULC
22 Adelaide St. West, 41st Floor
Toronto, Ontario M5H 4E3, Canada
www.LoveInspired.com

Printed in U.S.A.

CONTENTS

AN AMISH WIFE
FOR CHRISTMAS

Patricia Davids

This book is dedicated with great admiration to my longtime and dare I say long-suffering editor, Emily Rodmell. I'm sure I have tried your endless patience far more often than any other author, but you have never failed to help me get back on track. During the bleak moments of my personal life and in some weird and crazy times, you have remained confident in my talent and pushed me to write a better book even when I wasn't sure I wanted to go there. Thanks for your faith in me. Here's hoping it isn't misplaced. Onward and upward.

That he would grant you, according to the riches of his glory, to be strengthened with might by his Spirit in the inner man; That Christ may dwell in your hearts by faith; that ye, being rooted and grounded in love, May be able to comprehend with all saints what is the breadth, and length, and depth, and height; And to know the love of Christ, which passeth knowledge, that ye might be filled with all the fullness of God.

—*Ephesians* 3:16–19

Chapter One

"Your brother's behavior reflects badly on you, Bethany, and on our community. Something must be done."

Bethany Martin sat across from Bishop Elmer Schultz at her kitchen table with her head bowed and her hands clasped tightly together in her lap. Her dear friend Gemma Lapp sat beside her. Bethany was grateful for Gemma's moral support.

"We Amish are newcomers here," he continued. "We can't afford to stir ill will among our *Englisch* neighbors. Don't you agree?"

Bethany glanced up and met his intense gaze. She nodded slightly. An imposing man in his midfifties, the bishop had a shaggy gray-and-black beard that reached to the middle of his chest. A potato farmer and owner of a shed building business, he was known for his long and often rambling sermons, but he was a fair man and well liked in their small Amish community. Bethany didn't take his visit lightly. She prepared to defend her brother.

"Ivan isn't a bad boy. It's just that he misses his grandfather. He's angry that God took Elijah from us and he feels guilty. The two of them were very close." Her heart ached for her troubled brother.

"Time will heal this," Gemma added.

The bishop sighed. "Your grandfather Elijah was a fine man, Bethany. I have no doubt that he kept the boy's high spirits in check, but Ivan has quickly put one foot on the slippery slope that leads to serious trouble. He needs a firm hand to guide him and mold him into an upstanding and righteous man."

"I can do that," Bethany assured him. "I've raised Ivan from the time he was five and our sister, Jenny, wasn't much more than a newborn babe." She might be their sister, but she was also the only mother they had ever known. Both mother and father to them after the man who bore that title left his family for the fourth and final time. Bethany's anger surged to the surface but she quickly brought it under control. At least her mother had been spared knowing about his final betrayal. She had been positive he would return to care for his children after she was gone. He hadn't. Bethany brought her attention back to the matter at hand.

Gemma waved one hand. "Ivan is almost fourteen. Boys that age get into mischief."

It was a weak argument and Bethany knew it. Her brother's recent behavior was more than mischief, but she didn't know what to do about it. He seemed to be done listening to her.

The bishop's expression softened. "Bethany, your

grandfather was concerned that you have sacrificed your chance to have a family of your own in order to care for your siblings."

She drew herself up straight. "I don't feel that way. Ivan and Jenny *are* my family."

The bishop laced his fingers together on the table. "I am the spiritual leader of this community and as such I have a duty to oversee the welfare of all my flock. Normally I would leave the discipline of children to their parents. In this case I feel duty bound to step in. Elijah was my dear friend. It was his vision that founded our new community here. It was his desire to see it grow. For that we need the goodwill of our *Englisch* neighbors."

"I'm aware of that. I spent many months helping him search for the best place to settle. New Covenant is as much my dream as it was his." She didn't like the direction the bishop seemed to be going.

"Then you agree that we can't let the reckless actions of one boy ruin what has been created."

"He isn't trying to spoil anything." Bethany was compelled to defend Ivan, but the truth was she didn't know what was wrong with him. Was he acting out because of his grief or was something else going on?

His schoolwork had suffered in the past weeks. His teacher had complained of behavior issues in class. He had been in several scuffles with non-Amish boys earlier in the year but they weren't anything serious. It was his recent secrecy and withdrawal that bothered Bethany the most. How could she help him if she didn't understand what was amiss?

She lifted her chin. "There is no proof that he damaged Greg Janson's tractor or that he is responsible for letting Robert Morris's cattle loose."

Bishop Schultz leveled a stern look at her. "He was seen near both farms at the time and he'd been in fights with both the Janson and Morris boys."

"That's not proof," she insisted.

The bishop pushed back from the table. "I have written to your uncle in Bird-in-Hand."

She frowned. "To Onkel Harvey? Why?"

"Elijah mentioned that Harvey and his family plan to visit you this Christmas."

"That's true. We are expecting them to stay a week as they were unable to come to the funeral."

The bishop rose to his feet. "I have asked your uncle to take Ivan with him when the family returns to Pennsylvania."

Bethany's mouth dropped open. "*Nee*, you can't send Ivan away. This isn't right."

"It was not an easy decision. I know your intentions are *goot* but the boy needs the firm guidance of a man. You are too easy on him."

"Because he's still a little boy." The situation was quickly slipping out of her control. They couldn't take her brother from her. Fear sent her pulse pounding in her temples. "Please, Bishop, you must reconsider."

"I will not."

Bethany pressed both hands to her heart. "I promised my mother before she died that I would keep the family together. I promised her. Don't do this."

The bishop's expression didn't change. Her plea

had fallen on deaf ears. Men were the decision makers in her Amish community. The bishop had the last word even in this family matter.

He took his coat and hat from the pegs by the door and put them on. "Bethany, if you were married I wouldn't have to take this course of action. Your husband would be the one to make such decisions and discipline the boy. With Elijah gone, I see no other choice. I must think of what is best for all, not just for one."

He nodded to her and left. Bethany wanted to cry, to shout at him, to run after him and beg him to change his mind, but she knew it wouldn't do any good.

"I'm sorry." Gemma laid a hand on Bethany's shoulder.

"What am I going to do? There has to be a way to change the bishop's mind."

"Why don't I make us some toast and a cup of coffee. Then we'll put our heads together and come up with a plan."

"We're out of bread and I don't want any coffee."

"What Amish woman runs out of bread?"

"This one. There has been so much to do since Daadi's passing I haven't had time to bake. If Ivan straightens up and starts behaving, if he apologizes to the bishop maybe he'll be allowed to stay. It's five weeks until Christmas. That's enough time to prove he has changed."

"Or you can get married. That will fix everything."

Bethany gave her friend an exasperated look. Gemma knew Bethany's feeling about marriage. It

wasn't for her. "It's unlikely that I could find someone to wed me before Christmas, Gemma."

"If you weren't so particular, maybe not. Jesse
Crump holds you in high regard."

Bethany wrinkled her nose. "Having a conversation with Jesse is like pulling teeth. He's a nice enough
fellow, but he never has anything to say."

"Ack, you're too fussy by far."

"You marry him."

Both Gemma's eyebrows shot up. "Me? Not a
chance. Besides, it isn't my brother that is being sent
away."

Bethany battled her rising panic. "I wish Daadi
were still here. I don't know what to do."

Gemma slipped an arm around Bethany's shoulders and gave her a hug. "If your grandfather was
still alive we wouldn't be having this conversation."

"I know."

Ivan's troubling behavior had started when their
grandfather became ill early in the fall but it had gotten much worse since his death. Her gaze moved to
the closed door leading to her grandfather's workroom. Their grandfather had happily spent hours repairing clocks and antique watches during the long
winter months in his tiny shop. With the door open
she used to hear him humming or muttering depending on how a particular project was progressing.

The workshop hadn't been opened since Ivan found
Elijah slumped over his desk barely breathing. The
boy ran to find help but by the time it arrived Elijah
was gone.

She should have mailed his unfinished works back to their owners before now but she couldn't bear to enter the room. The grief she tried so hard to control would come pouring out when she did.

Tears stung the backs of her eyelids, but she quickly blinked them away. The quiet strength and unquestioning love of her grandfather had seen Bethany through the worst times in her life. It was still hard to accept that she could never turn to him for guidance again.

She drew a deep breath and squared her shoulders. He would tell her prayer and hard work solved problems. Worry and regret never did. There had to be a way to keep her family together and she would find it. Perhaps her uncle would side with her. She would write her own letter to him and plead her case.

She slipped into her coat. "Thank you for coming today, Gemma, but I'd best get the rest of my chores done."

Gemma followed her to the door. "I don't know how you'll manage this farm without Elijah and Ivan."

"One day at a time and with the help of our neighbors if I need it."

"I've never known you to ask for help." Gemma moved to put on her black bonnet and coat.

"I asked you to sit with me when the bishop came today, didn't I?"

Gemma rolled her eyes. "Okay, you have asked for help one time. I wish I knew what to say but I think it is all up to Ivan. I'm surprised he wasn't here this morning."

"He's at school. I didn't want to take him out of class."

The New Covenant Amish community was too small yet to have their own school. The five Amish children in their church, including her brother and sister, attended the nearest public school. It was far from ideal but the teachers and school board had taken great pains to accommodate the needs and customs of the new Amish pupils.

The two women walked outside together. Gemma pulled on her gloves. "Do you want me to come over this evening when you talk to him?"

Bethany shook her head. "*Danki*, but I think it's best I speak to him alone."

"All right. I'll stop by tomorrow and you can tell me all about it." The two women exchanged a hug. Gemma climbed into her buggy and drove away.

Bethany's breath rose as puffs of white mist in the chilly mid-November morning as she crossed the snow-covered yard to the newly completed red barn. It was the latest building to be added to the new community. The bulk of the structure had been raised in a single day with the help of an Amish community from upstate New York. Thirty men had traveled all night by bus and worked feverishly to complete the barn before taking the long bus ride home again that night. Someday the people of New Covenant would return the favor.

Her grandfather had had plans for half a dozen additional structures to attract more Amish families to New Covenant. It had been his dream to form a thriving Amish district in Maine, far from the tourist centers in Pennsylvania. To him, fewer tourists meant less money but more time to spend close to God and family without worldly influences. If only he could have lived to see his dream grow and thrive.

Bethany fed and watered the chickens, gathered the eggs and then fed and watered the geese before heading to the barn. Her mind wasn't on her chores. Her conversation with the bishop replayed in her head as she fed and watered their two horses. Outside the milk cow's stall, Bethany paused and leaned on her pitchfork. "I've got trouble, Clarabelle."

The cow didn't answer her. Bethany pitched a forkful of hay to the family's placid brown-and-white Guernsey and then leaned on the stall door. "The bishop has decided to send Ivan to Bird-in-Hand to live with Onkel Harvey. It's not right. It's not fair. I can't bear the idea of sending my little brother away. It will break his heart and Jenny's, to say nothing of mine. We belong together."

Clarabelle munched a mouthful of hay as she regarded Bethany with soulful deep brown eyes. The bell around her neck clanked softly as she tilted her head to allow Bethany to scratch behind her left ear. Bethany complied. As a confidant, Clarabelle was unassuming and easy to talk to, but she was short on advice.

"Advice is what I need, Clarabelle. The bishop said Ivan could stay if I had a husband. Someone to discipline and guide the boy. I don't believe for a minute that is the solution but I'm getting desperate. Any idea where I can get a husband before Christmas? And please don't suggest Jesse Crump. Jedidiah Zook might be a possibility if he smiled more. Maybe he just needs a wife to make him happier. What do you think?"

"I doubt your cow has the answers you seek but if she does I have a few questions for her about my own problems," a man said in an amused drawl.

Bethany spun around. A stranger stood in the open barn door. He wore a black Amish hat pulled low on his forehead and a dark blue woolen coat with the collar turned up against the cold. He carried a duffel bag over one shoulder and he leaned on a black cane.

The mirth sparkling in his eyes sent a flush of heat to her cheeks. How humiliating. To be caught talking to a cow about matrimonial prospects made her look ridiculous.

She struggled to hide her embarrassment. After looking the man up and down, she stabbed the pitchfork into the hay again and dumped it into Clarabelle's stall. "It's rude to eavesdrop on a private conversation."

"I'm not sure talking to a cow qualifies as a private conversation but I am sorry to intrude." The man put down his duffel bag.

He didn't look sorry. He looked like he was struggling not to laugh at her. At least he was a stranger. Maybe this mortifying episode wouldn't become known in the community. She cringed at the thought of Jedidiah Zook hearing the story. "How can I help you?"

"Mind if I sit here for a minute?" He pointed to a stack of straw bales beside the barn door.

She wanted him to go away but her Amish upbringing prevented her from suggesting it. Any stranger in need deserved her help.

He didn't wait for her reply but limped to the closest bale and sat down with a weary sigh. "The bus driver who dropped me off said New Covenant was a little way along on this road. His idea of a little way does not match mine."

"It's less than half a mile to the highway from my lane."

He rubbed his leg. "That's the farthest I've walked in six months. How much farther do I have to go?"

"You have arrived at the south end of our community."

He tipped his head slightly. "I thought New Covenant was a town."

"It's more a collection of houses strung out on either side of the road right now, but it will be a thriving village one day." She prayed she spoke the truth.

"Glad to hear it. I'm Michael Shetler, by the way." He took off his hat and raked his fingers through his thick dark brown hair.

She considered not giving him her name. The less he knew to repeat the better.

He noticed her hesitation and cleared his throat. "It's rude not to introduce yourself in return."

She arched one eyebrow. "I'm being rude? That's the pot calling the kettle black. I am Bethany Martin," she admitted, hoping she wasn't making a mistake.

"Nice to meet you, Bethany. Once I've had a rest I'll step outside if you want to finish your private conversation." He winked. One corner of his mouth twitched, revealing a dimple in his cheek.

Something about the sparkle in his blue eyes invited her to smile back at him but she firmly resisted the urge. She stabbed the pitchfork into the remaining hay and left it standing upright. "I'm glad I could supply you with some amusement today."

"It's been a long time since I've had something to smile about."

The clatter of hooves outside caught her attention as a horse and wagon pulled up beside the barn and stopped. She caught a glimpse of the driver through the open door. He stood and faced the barn. "Ivan Martin, are you in there? It's Jedidiah Zook. I want to speak to you!"

Her gaze shot to Michael. His grin widened. Her heart sank as he chuckled. "I may not have given Clarabelle enough credit. It seems your preferred beau has arrived. It was Jedidiah Zook you hoped would come courting, right?"

She glared and shook a finger at him. "Don't you dare repeat one word of what you heard in here."

Michael couldn't help teasing her. The high color in her cheeks and the fire in her eyes told him she was no meek Amish maid. He wagged his eyebrows. "Do you need a go-between? Shall I speak on your behalf? I'll be happy to help any way I can."

"If you say anything, I'll… I'll…" She clamped her lips closed. The sheen of unshed tears gathered in her eyes, but she quickly blinked them back and raised her chin.

Teasing was one thing. Upsetting her was another. He held up one hand. "Relax. Your secret is safe with me. If the cow spills the beans, that is not my fault."

"Stay here." Bethany rushed past him out the wide double doors. "*Guder mariye*, Jedidiah. Ivan isn't in here. He's at school. Can I be of any help?"

"Your brother has gone too far this time."

The man's angry voice brought Michael closer to the open door to watch. Bethany faced Jedidiah defiantly with her head up and her hands on her hips. "What has he done?"

"Two thirty-pound bags of potatoes and a ten-pound bag of dried beans are missing from my cellar."

"What makes you think Ivan took them?"

"Because he sold a bag of potatoes to the general store owner just this morning."

She folded her arms in front of her. "That's not proof he took them. Maybe it was one of our sacks that he sold."

"Was it?"

"I'm not sure."

"You tell him I came by and that I'm on my way to report this theft to the bishop. This has gone beyond what can be ignored. It must stop. If you can't control the boy someone else will have to." He lifted the reins, turned the wagon around and headed down the lane.

Michael limped out to stand beside her. "Not a very jolly fellow. Are you sure he's the one?"

She shot him a sour look. "In spite of what you

think you heard earlier, I am not in the market for a husband."

Why wasn't she married already? She was certainly attractive enough. Not that he was in the market for a relationship. He wasn't. He might never be. He sobered at the thought. The men who shot him and robbed the store he had worked may have robbed him of a family, too. He had no idea if his PTSD would get better living in the isolation of northern Maine, but it was his last option.

Bethany brushed past him into the barn, a fierce scowl marring her pretty features. "I need to speak to my brother and get to the bottom of this. You are welcome to rest here."

He was glad he wasn't the brother in question. She went down the aisle and opened the stall door of a black mare with a white blaze. She led the mare out, tied the horse to a hitching post and began to harness her.

"Let me do that for you." He took a step closer.

"I can manage," she snapped.

He took a step back and held one hand up. She didn't need or want his help. In short order she had the harness on and then led the animal outside, where she backed the mare in between the shafts of the buggy parked in a lean-to at the side of the building.

"May I?" he asked, pointing to the buggy. She nodded. He finished securing the traces on one side while she did the other. He buckled the crupper, the loop that went around the mare's tail to keep the harness from sliding forward on the animal, as Bethany finished her side and came to check his work.

"Danki."

She thanked him like it was a chore. Bethany Martin was clearly used to doing things by herself.

Michael realized that he hadn't looked over his shoulder once since hearing Bethany's voice. That had to be some kind of record. He glanced around out of habit but there was nothing sinister in the farmstead and empty snow-covered fields that backed up to wooded hills on either side of the wide valley. All throughout his trip to New Covenant he'd been on edge, expecting danger from every stranger that came close to him. He'd spent most of the bus ride from Philadelphia with sweating palms and tense muscles, expecting another attack or a flashback to overtake him at any second. They never came when he was expecting them.

He rubbed a hand across the back of his neck. For the first time in weeks the knots in his neck and shoulders were missing. Maybe he was getting better. Maybe this move was the right thing, after all. He prayed it was. Nothing here reminded him of the Philadelphia street or the shop where his life had changed so drastically.

Here the air was fresh and clean. The next house was several hundred yards up the road. Nothing crowded him. He could start over here. No one would look at him with pity or worse. He had a job waiting for him in New Covenant and a place to live all thanks to the generosity of a man he'd never met. He needed to get going, but he was reluctant to leave Bethany's company for some reason. Her no-nonsense attitude was comforting. He pushed the thought aside. "I should be on my way. Can you give me directions to Elijah Troyer's farm?"

She shot him a startled look and then glanced away. "This was his farm," she said softly with a quiver in her voice.

"Was? He sold it?" Michael waited impatiently for her to speak.

She kept her gaze averted. "I'm sorry but Elijah Troyer passed away three weeks ago."

Michael drew back with a sharp intake of breath. "He's dead? That can't be."

He fought against the onrush of panic. What about the job? What about the place to live? Were his hopes for a new life dead, too?

Chapter Two

Bethany watched as Michael limped away and sat down on the hay bale inside the barn door. He rubbed his face with both hands. She could see he was deeply affected by the news of her grandfather's death. Sympathy made her soften her tone. "I'm sorry to give you the sad news. Did you know my grandfather well?"

Michael shook his head. "I never met him."

If he didn't know her grandfather, why was he so shaken by his passing? As much as she wanted to stay and find out Michael's connection to Elijah, she had to speak to Ivan as soon as possible. If he had stolen the potatoes and beans as Jedidiah claimed, the items would have to be returned at once, but there had to be some mistake. Her brother wasn't a thief.

Please let it be a mistake, Lord.

The bishop would never reconsider sending Ivan to live with Onkel Harvey if Jedidiah's claim was true.

She slipped the reins through the slot under the winter windshield of the buggy. "I'm sorry you didn't have a chance to meet my grandfather. He was a wonderful man."

"He offered me a job working for him. Is that job still available?"

"I know nothing about such an offer. Are you sure it was my grandfather who promised you work?"

"Elijah Troyer, in New Covenant, Maine. That's what the letter said. Is there another Elijah Troyer in the community?"

"There is not. I don't know what my grandfather had in mind, but I can't afford to hire someone right now."

"I was also told I would have a place to stay. I reckon if there's no job there's no lodging, either?"

Was he talking about the small cabin that sat at the back of her property? Her grandfather had mentioned readying it for a tenant before he became ill, but she didn't know if he had finished the repairs. Besides, she wasn't ready to host a lodger. Nor did she want to leave Michael Shetler like this. He appeared dazed and lost. Her heart went out to him.

"You should speak to our bishop, Elmer Schultz. I'm sure he can help. He won't be at home this time of day, but I can give you a ride to his place of business."

"It seems I don't have much choice. *Danki.*"

Michael slowly climbed into the passenger seat. Bethany walked around the back and got in on the driver's side. She picked up the reins. "The school is about three miles from here."

"I thought we were going to the bishop's place of business."

"We are but I must stop at the school first. I hope you don't mind."

"As long as I don't have to walk three miles I don't mind."

From the corner of her eye Bethany noticed him rubbing his leg frequently. It must pain him a great deal. This close to him she noticed the dark circles under his eyes, as if he hadn't slept well. He was pale, too. She sat silent for the first half mile of their trip but her curiosity about Michael got the better of her. "Where are you from?"

"My family lives in Holmes County, Ohio. My father and brother have a construction business in Sugarcreek."

"Did you work in construction with them?"

"Nee." He didn't elaborate.

"I've heard that's a large Amish community. Do you have a lot of tourists who visit there?"

"We do."

"Like where I am from. Bird-in-Hand, Pennsylvania. My grandfather wanted to start a community that wasn't dependent on tourism. Don't get me wrong, he knew how important the industry is to many Amish who can't make a living farming, but it wasn't the lifestyle he wanted to live."

Michael pulled his coat tighter. "There had to be warmer places to settle."

She chuckled as she looked out over the snow-covered fields that flanked the road. "The coldest part of the winter has yet to come."

"So why here?"

"The price of land and the ability to purchase farms large enough to support big families were more of a consideration than the weather. Plus, we were warmly welcomed by the people here. Many local families have been here for generations. They like the idea that we want to be here and farm for generations, too. A lot of the elders in the community remember farming with horses when they were children. Folks are very independent minded in Maine. They know what hard work is. When someone has to sell farmland they would rather sell it to the Amish because we will live on it and farm it as their grandparents did. They consider it preferable to selling to a large farming corporation intent on grabbing up as much land as possible."

"What do you grow here besides snowdrifts?"

She smiled. "Potatoes. Maine is the third-largest producer of potatoes in the United States. Broccoli grows well in the cool climate as do many other vegetables."

"As long as you don't get an early freeze."

"That's true of farming in Ohio or almost anywhere."

"I guess you're right about that."

The main highway followed the curve of the river and after another mile Fort Craig came into view. Bethany turned off the highway into a residential area at the outskirts of town. The elementary school was located in a cul-de-sac at the end of the street.

As she drew the horse to a stop in front of the school she noticed several of the classes were out at recess. She stepped down from the buggy and caught sight of her sister, Jenny, playing with several other girls on the swings. Jenny spotted her and ran over. "Sister, what are you doing here?"

"I've come to speak to Ivan. Did he get on the bus with you this morning?"

Jenny shook her head. "*Nee*, he said Jeffrey's mom was going to bring him to school."

"And did she?"

"I don't know. Sister, I have *wunderbar goot* news."

Bethany crouched to meet Jenny's gaze. "Have you seen Ivan today?"

Jenny screwed up her face as she concentrated. "I don't think so. You should ask his teacher."

Bethany stood upright. "That's exactly what I plan to do."

"Don't you want to hear my news?"

"In a minute."

Jenny's happy expression faded. Michael got out of the buggy. He took several stiff steps. "I just need to stretch my legs a little."

"Who is that?" Jenny asked in a loud whisper.

Bethany was inpatient to find Ivan but she made the introduction. "This is Michael Shetler. He's a newcomer. This is my sister, Jenny."

He nodded toward her. "I'm pleased to meet you, Jenny. I'd love to hear your news."

"You would?" Jenny asked hopefully.

"Sure. It must be important. You look ready to burst."

Jenny smiled from ear to ear. "I got picked to be

in the community Christmas play. I'm going to be the aerator."

Bethany looked at Michael. He returned her questioning gaze and shook his head slightly. Jenny was bouncing up and down with happiness.

Bethany smiled at her. "That is *wunderbar*. What does the aerator do?"

"I get to tell everyone the Christmas story in English and in Pennsylvania Dutch while the other kids act out the scenes. Ivan is going to sing a song by himself."

From the corner of her eye, Bethany saw Michael rub a hand across his mouth to hide a grin. Bethany was afraid she'd start laughing if she looked at him again. Learning English as a second language was difficult for many Amish children who spoke only Pennsylvania Dutch until they started school. "I'm sure you will make a *goot* narrator if you practice hard."

"I'll practice lots and lots if you help me."

"You know I will."

"I need to have an angel costume, too. I'm going to be an angel aerator."

"Angel *narrator*," Michael corrected her in a gentle tone.

"Narrator," Jenny replied slowly. He nodded and she grinned at him.

Bethany patted her sister's head. "We'll talk about it when you come home from school this evening."

"Okay." Jenny took off to rejoin her friends.

"Cute kid," Michael said, still grinning. "How many siblings do you have?"

"Just Jenny and Ivan. Excuse me while I check on him." Bethany headed through the front doors of the school. She found the eighth-grade room and looked in through the open door. Ivan wasn't in his seat. His best friend, Jeffrey, was missing, too.

A bell sounded in the empty hall, startling her. The boys and girls in the room filed to the back to gather their coats, mittens and hats from hooks before rushing past her to get outside. After the last child exited the room Bethany stepped inside. "Ms. Kenworthy, may I have a word with you?"

The teacher looked up from her desk. "Miss Martin, of course. Do come in. I was just getting ready to write a note to you."

"About Ivan?"

"Yes. I hope he is feeling better. He's missed almost an entire week of school. I have a list of homework assignments for him to complete and hand in when he returns."

Bethany's heart sank. "My brother is not sick at home."

"I see." Ms. Kenworthy opened a desk drawer and pulled out a sheet of notebook paper. "Then I assume you did not write this note?"

Bethany removed her gloves, took the note and quickly scanned it. It informed Ms. Kenworthy that Ivan would be out of school for a week due to his illness. It was signed with her name. Bethany sighed heavily and handed the letter back. "I did not write this. It is not my signature."

Ms. Kenworthy took the letter and replaced it in

the drawer. "I thought it was odd that Jeffrey was the one who delivered it to me and not your sister. Do you know what Ivan has been doing instead of coming to school?"

"I wish I did. He doesn't confide in me these days."

"He was close to his grandfather, wasn't he?"

The understanding in the teacher's eyes allowed Bethany to unburden herself. "They were very close. Since Elijah's death Ivan has refused to talk to me about what's troubling him. He's changed so much. I was hoping he might have confided in you."

"I am deeply sorry for your loss. Elijah was well liked in this community."

"Thank you."

"Your brother's grades were not the best before your grandfather passed away. Since that time, he has earned nothing but Fs for incomplete work. Even when he is here he seems withdrawn until someone speaks to him. Then he's ready to start a fight over nothing. Unless he does extra-credit work and turns in his missing assignments, I'm afraid he is going to flunk the semester. I know that according to your religion this is his last year of education, but I still have to follow state guidelines. That puts me between a rock and a hard place. If he flunks the semester, he'll have to attend summer school."

Bethany shook her head. "Ivan will be needed on the farm this summer. I don't see how we could spare him even a few hours a day."

"In that case he will have to repeat this grade next year. Talk to him. Try to make him see what's at stake." She removed a folder from another drawer. "Give these assignments to him. Hopefully he can finish most of them over the weekend."

"I will. Thank you." Bethany was angry with Ivan for his deceit, but she was more disappointed in herself. Where had she gone wrong? How had she failed him? She tried to be a parent to her siblings but without her grandfather's help she didn't know how to reach Ivan. Maybe letting him return to Pennsylvania would be for the best.

Except that it didn't feel like the right solution. She loved her brother. She couldn't imagine life without his annoying habits, constant teasing and his hearty laugh. She had to make him see that his actions were tearing the family apart.

But she needed to find him first. Clearly Jeffrey was in on whatever Ivan was up to. His parents lived a mile farther up into the woods from her home.

Bethany left the school building and saw Michael sitting on the buggy step. She'd forgotten him. A thin yellow hound lay a few feet away from him. The dog wagged its tail tentatively as it watched him. Michael pulled his gloves off and took something from his pocket. He held it toward the dog. The animal crept a few inches closer.

"Good girl," Michael said, tossing the item at the dog's feet. She snapped it up. At the sound of Bethany approaching, the dog darted for cover between two nearby parked cars.

Bethany stopped beside Michael. The dog grew

bold enough to peek out from between the cars but didn't approach. "I see you made a new friend."

He rose to his feet. "She was sniffing at the trash cans and trying to get them open. I could see she was looking for a meal. I had a little leftover jerky I picked up on the bus ride here. She appears to need it more than I do. Is your brother at school?"

"*Nee*, but that doesn't prove he stole provisions from Jedidiah."

"You're still giving him the benefit of the doubt?"

"Of course. He's my brother."

"I hope your confidence isn't misplaced."

"I pray it's not but I will admit I'm at my wit's end. His teacher says he hasn't been to school all week. His friend gave the teacher a note that was signed with my name that said he was sick at home. I have to find out what's going on. He's left each morning to catch the school bus with his sister and he's walked home with her each evening, yet he hasn't been in school."

"Don't think too badly of him. Boys his age are sometimes impatient to grow up and live their own adventures. Then they make foolish mistakes because they aren't as smart as they think they are."

"Are you speaking from experience?"

"I am. My own."

"How many forged notes did you send to your teacher?"

A wry grin curved his lips. "My teacher happened to be my mother's youngest sister, so none."

"I'm afraid of what the bishop will say when Jedidiah tells his side of the story."

"If the bishop is a reasonable man he'll listen to your side of the story, as well."

She was grateful for his reassurance, but he didn't know how serious the situation was becoming. She held on to the hope that her uncle could be persuaded to let Ivan remain with her. "I will take you to see the bishop now."

"I appreciate that." He moved to open the buggy door for her and took her hand to help her in.

His grip was firm but his hand was soft. His skin lacked the calloused roughness of a man who made his living farming the land or woodworking. It wasn't the hand of a laborer, yet she found his gentle strength oddly comforting.

Perhaps he was a shopkeeper. Her grandfather had had plans to open a small grocery in New Covenant. Maybe that was the job he had promised Michael. It didn't matter. Her grandfather was gone, and she wasn't in a position to continue his work. At least not yet.

She looked up and met Michael's gaze as he continued to hold her hand longer than necessary. There was a profound sadness in the depth of his eyes that she didn't understand. What troubled him? What was he thinking?

Michael stared into Bethany's light blue eyes as the warmth of her touch went all the way to the center of his chest and warmed a place that had been cold for a long time. He studied her face, trying to find out why she triggered such a strong reaction in him.

Her pale blond hair was parted in the middle and worn under a white prayer covering. Her skin was fair with a scattering of freckles across her dainty nose. She was an attractive woman, too attractive for his peace of mind.

He let go of her hand, stepped away and limped around the back of the buggy, letting the pain in his leg remind him of why he had no business thinking about how perfectly her small hand had nestled in his. If things had been different, if he wasn't so damaged he would have enjoyed getting to know her better, but things weren't different. He had to accept that.

He also had more serious things to think about. He needed a job and he needed somewhere to live. Preferably a good distance away from other people in this remote community. His neighbors wouldn't appreciate being awakened in the middle of the night by the screams that sometimes accompanied his nightmares.

Thoughts of his dreams filled him with apprehension as his pulse shot up. He quickly scanned his surroundings. A car drove past the school, the tires crunching on the snow. Children were playing on the playground. He could hear their laughter and shouting. Someone stood at the corner of the school building. He thought it was a woman but he couldn't be sure. The person was bundled in a parka with the hood up. Perhaps a teacher watching the children. He struggled to convince himself that there was nothing sinister here but he couldn't shake the feeling that something bad would happen at any second. His heart began to pound as tightness gripped his chest.

The dog ventured out and came to stand in front of him. He focused on her unusual golden eyes. She looked to be part yellow Labrador retriever and part pointer. Her white-tipped tail wagged slowly. He held out his hand and she sniffed it. It was a shame he didn't have more to feed her. She retreated again and he got in Bethany's buggy.

Inside the small space he started to relax. No one could get behind him now. He glanced at Bethany. She was watching him intently. Could she see how anxious he was? He needed to divert her attention. "Are you waiting for something?"

"Nee." She turned the horse and headed back up the street. The clip-clop of the mare's hooves was muffled by the snow that covered the road. It was the only sound other than the creaking of the buggy. He discovered he would rather hear Bethany's voice.

"What kind of business does the bishop own?"

"Our bishop builds and sells storage sheds as well as farming, but he's thinking of branching out into tiny homes."

"Then he is a progressive fellow?"

"In his business, but our church is a conservative one."

"I noticed a propane tank at your home."

"Our Ordnung allows us to use propane to power business machinery, our refrigerators, washing machines and hot water heaters. We also have running water and indoor bathrooms. We aren't that conservative but our cookstoves and furnaces must use wood or coal."

He glanced out over the dense tree-covered hill-sides and the snowcapped mountains in the distance. "It doesn't look like you'll run out of fuel anytime soon as long as you have a strong fellow to chop and haul it."

"My brother does that for me." Her voice was strained. Worry marked her brow with frown lines.

"How old is he?"

"Almost fourteen. Our mother died when Jenny was born. Our father was gone soon afterward." The undertone of bitterness in her voice surprised him.

"So you were raised by your grandparents."

"My grandfather took us in. He was a widower."

"It must've been hard to be both mother and sister to your younger siblings." He found it easier to talk to Bethany than anyone he'd spoken to since the attack. Maybe it was because she talked to cows. He smiled at the memory.

"I never saw caring for my siblings as a burden." She turned the horse off the street into the parking lot surrounded by various sizes of storage sheds.

A tall, muscular Amish fellow stepped away from a half-finished shed and slipped his hammer into a tool belt that hung on his hips. He didn't sport a beard, so Michael knew he wasn't married. His clothes were tattered and sweat-stained, but his smile was friendly as he greeted them. "*Guder mariye*, Bethany. Need a new shed, do you?"

Bethany opened her door but didn't step out. "Good morning, Jesse. Is Bishop Schultz about?"

"*Nee*, he isn't. He's gone to Unity. Their bishop is

laid up with pneumonia, and Elmer has gone to do the preaching for their service this Sunday and perform a wedding on Tuesday. He won't be back until Wednesday night."

"Have you seen Ivan today?"

"*Nee*, I've not. Who is that with you?"

"Jesse, this is Michael Shetler. He is a newcomer. He came expecting to work for my grandfather. He hadn't heard about Elijah's passing. I thought perhaps the bishop would know of some work and could find a place for him to stay."

Jesse hooked his thumbs under his suspenders. "There is work aplenty here. You're welcome to bunk on my couch until you can find a place, but you'll have to suffer through my cooking. I'm no hand with a skillet."

Michael got out of the buggy and grabbed his duffel bag. He would rather stay somewhere alone, but he didn't have much choice. He forced a smile and a lighthearted reply. "Your cooking can't be worse than mine. You have yourself a boarder until I can find a place of my own. We can work out the rent later."

"No need for that." Jesse moved to take Michael's bag. "Let me get this for you."

Michael handed it over. Jesse nodded toward the building he had been working on. "If you don't mind, I'd like to finish this shed before taking you out to my place."

"I don't mind. I'll give you a hand with it."

Looking at Michael's cane, Jesse raised one eyebrow. "Are you sure?"

"I can still swing a hammer."

"Then your help will be welcome. I'll see you get paid for the work you do."

"Danki."

Michael turned to Bethany. "Looks like your brother has been granted a reprieve if Jedidiah wasn't able to speak to the bishop."

Bethany's eyes brightened. "That's right."

"Oh, Jedidiah was here and spoke to Elmer before he left," Jesse said cheerfully.

Michael watched the hope fade in her eyes and wished there was something he could do to console her.

Chapter Three

Michael watched Bethany drive away with a sharp unexpected sense of loss. She was a lovely woman, but he sensed she was much more than a pretty face. It was obvious that she cared about her family. Anyone who asked a cow for advice had to have a good sense of humor.

He smiled then quickly pushed thoughts of her out of his head. As much as she intrigued him, he was better off not seeing her.

Forming a relationship with Bethany would mean letting her get close. He couldn't risk that. He had jumped at the chance to come to this part of Maine because it was remote and thinly populated but it held an Amish community. He had left his Amish upbringing once with devastating consequences. After the attack he had returned home hopeful that rejoining his faith and family would repair his shattered life. It hadn't worked out that way. He didn't know what more God needed from him.

Michael's plan for his new life was simple. Live and work alone while coming into contact with as few people as possible. He wasn't a loner by nature. He had become a recluse out of necessity. Avoiding people was the only way he felt safe. The only way he could keep his affliction hidden. Staying with Jesse was risky, but he had nowhere else to go. He could only pray he didn't have an episode in front of him.

A doctor in Philadelphia had called it PTSD. Post-traumatic stress disorder, the result of a robbery gone wrong at the jewelry store where he had worked. What it meant was that his life was no longer his own. He lived in near constant fear. When a full-blown flashback hit he relived every detail as his coworkers, his friends, were killed in front of his eyes. The gunshots, the screams, the sirens—he saw it, heard it, felt it all again just as if it were happening to him the first time.

He never knew when a flashback would happen, making it impossible for him to return to work. Even a walk down a city street left him hearing the footsteps of someone following him, waiting to feel the cold, hard barrel of a gun jammed in his back.

He was the one who had let them in. He was the only one who came out alive. Sometimes he felt he should have died with the others, but he couldn't dwell on that thought. God had other plans for him. He just didn't know what they were.

The heavy thudding of his heart and the sweat on his brow warned him that thinking about it was the last thing he should be doing. He took a deep breath.

Concentrate on something else. Think about Bethany asking her cow for advice and the shocked look on her face when she realized he'd heard her conversation. He visualized her in detail as his pulse slowed to a more normal speed.

From the corner of his eye he caught sight of the yellow dog trotting along the edge of the highway in his direction. Did she belong to someone or was she a stray surviving as best she could? Her thin ribs proved she wasn't being cared for if someone did own her. Her chances of surviving the rest of the winter on her own didn't look good. She approached as close as the drive leading into the parking lot. After pacing back and forth a few times she sat down and stared at him.

He turned to Jesse. "Do you know who that dog belongs to?"

Jesse glanced at her and shook his head. "I've seen her around. I think she's a stray."

"Would you happen to have anything I can feed her?"

Jesse laughed. "Are you a softhearted fellow?"

"Is there anything wrong with that if I am?"

"*Nee*, I like animals, too. Maybe more than most people, but I think I'm going to like you, Michael Shetler." Jesse clapped him on the back with his massive hand, almost knocking Michael over. "There's a couple of ham sandwiches in the refrigerator inside the office. You are welcome to them. For you or for the dog. Your choice."

"*Danki.*" Michael walked into a small building with Office in a hand-lettered sign over the door. Inside he found a small refrigerator with a coffeepot sitting on top of it. He took out two of the sandwiches, happy to see they contained thick slices of ham and cheese. After taking a couple of bites from one, he walked out with the rest in his hand. The dog was still sitting in the driveway.

He walked to within a few feet of her and laid the sandwich on the ground. As soon as he moved away she jumped up and gulped down the food. Looking up, she wagged her tail, clearly wanting more.

"Sorry, that's all there is. We are two of a kind, it seems. You needed a handout and so did I. We have Jesse over there to thank for sharing his lunch." Michael chuckled. He had teased Bethany about talking to her cow but here he was talking to a dog. It was too bad Bethany wasn't here to share the joke.

What surprised him was how much he wanted to see her again.

Jeffrey Morgan's home was a little more than a mile farther up the road from Bethany's house. As she pulled in she saw Jeffrey's mother getting out of her car. When she caught sight of Bethany she approached the buggy hesitantly.

"Good afternoon, Mrs. Morgan." Bethany stepped down from the buggy unsure of what to say.

"You are Ivan's mother, aren't you?" The woman remained a few feet away.

"I'm his older sister. Our mother passed away some years ago."

"That's right. Jeffrey told me that. I'm sorry about your grandfather. Jeffrey was fond of him."

"Thank you. Is Jeffrey here?"

"No. He's at school."

"I'm afraid he isn't. I just came from the school. Neither he nor my brother showed up for class today."

Mrs. Morgan looked around fearfully and moved closer to Bethany. "Are you saying that the boys played hooky today?"

"I don't know that word."

"*Hooky?* It means they skipped school without permission."

"Then *ja*, they played hooky."

Mrs. Morgan looked toward the house at the sound of the front door opening. Mr. Morgan stepped out. Jeffrey's mother leaned closer. "Don't tell my husband about this. I will speak to Jeffrey."

Puzzled by her fearful reaction, Bethany nodded. "Please send Ivan home if you see him."

"I will."

Bethany waved to Mr. Morgan. He didn't return the gesture. She got in her buggy and left. Where were those boys and what were they up to?

Bethany arrived home just after noon. She parked the buggy by the barn and stabled her horse. She wasn't any closer to finding her brother or figuring out what he was up to. As she came out of the barn, a car horn sounded. She glanced toward the county road that ran past her lane. Frank Pearson's long white passenger van turned off the blacktop and into her drive. Frank was the pastor of a Mennonite congregation a few miles away. He and her grandfather had become good friends. Frank used to visit weekly for a game of chess and to swap fishing stories.

Frank pulled up beside her and rolled down his window. "Good day, Bethany."

"Hello, Frank. Would you like to come in for some coffee?"

"I'm afraid I don't have time today. I have my bereavement support group meeting in twenty minutes. I just stopped in to see how you're getting along and to invite you and your family to attend one of our meetings when you are ready. It doesn't matter what faith you belong to or even if you are a nonbeliever. We all grieve when we lose loved ones."

"*Danki*, Frank. I don't think it's for me."

"If you change your mind, you're always welcome to join us. Please let me know if you need help with anything. I miss Elijah, but I know my grief is nothing compared to yours. I promised him I'd check in on you."

"Our congregation here is small, but we have been well looked after."

"I'm glad to hear it. I'll stop by again in a few days and stay awhile."

Maybe Frank could reach Ivan. "Why don't you come to dinner on Sunday? I know Ivan and Jenny would enjoy seeing you again. Maybe you can interest Ivan in learning to play chess."

"You know, I believe I will. Your cooking is too good to resist. Thanks for the invite."

"You are always welcome here."

After Frank drove away, Bethany headed for her

front door. The smell of warm yeasty dough rising greeted her as she entered the house. Gemma was busy kneading dough at the table. Bethany pulled off her coat and straightened her prayer *kapp*. "What are you doing here again so soon? I thought you said tomorrow?"

"What does it look like I'm doing?"

"It looks like you are making a mess in my kitchen."

Gemma giggled as she surveyed the stack of bowls, pans and the flour-covered table. "It does, doesn't it?" She punched down the dough in a second bowl and dumped it onto a floured tabletop.

"Why are you baking bread in my kitchen?"

"Because you didn't have any. I realized on my way home this morning that the least I could do for a friend was to remedy that."

"I appreciate the gesture but why not bake it at your home and bring the loaves here."

"I didn't want to mess up my kitchen. I just finished washing the floor." Gemma looked at her and winked. "Where have you been, anyway?"

Should she confide in Gemma about Ivan's recent actions and Jedidiah's accusations? Once more Bethany wished her grandfather were still alive. He would know what to do with the boy. She hung her coat on one of the pegs by the kitchen door. "It's a long story."

Gemma looked up. "Oh?"

Bethany went to the far cabinet and pulled out a cup and saucer. She felt the need of some bracing hot tea. "Jedidiah came by earlier. He accused Ivan of stealing two bags of potatoes and a bag of beans from his cellar."

Gemma spun around, outrage written across her face. "He did what?"

"He said Ivan stole those items and he had proof because Ivan sold some of the potatoes to the grocer this morning."

"I don't believe it. I know Ivan has been difficult at times, but he is not a thief."

Bethany filled her cup with hot water from the teakettle on the back of the stove. "That's what I said. I went to the school to hear Ivan's side of the story."

"And?"

"And he wasn't at school. He hasn't been to school all week. He forged a letter from me telling the teacher that he is out sick." Bethany opened a tea bag, added it to her cup and carried it to the kitchen table, where she sat down.

After a long moment of stunned silence, Gemma came to sit across from her. "You poor thing. Still, that doesn't mean he stole from Jedidiah."

"It doesn't prove he didn't. And it certainly doesn't speak well of his character. Jedidiah went straight to Bishop Schultz with the story. I had hoped to speak with the bishop, too, but he is gone to Unity until Wednesday. I don't know how I'll ever convince him to let Ivan remain with us now. What is wrong with my brother? How have I failed him?"

Had Ivan inherited his father's restlessness and his refusal to shoulder his responsibilities? She prayed that wasn't the case.

Gemma reached across the table and laid a comforting hand on Bethany's arm. "I'm so sorry. I had no idea things had progressed to this degree of seriousness. He's always been a little willful, but this is unacceptable behavior and it is his own doing. Bethany, you did not fail him."

"Danki." Bethany appreciated Gemma's attempt to comfort her.

Gemma returned to the other end of the table and began dividing the dough into bread pans. "You'll simply have to talk to the boy and tell him what the bishop has planned. Perhaps that will convince him to mend his ways."

"I hope you are right. Christmas is only five weeks away. I don't know if a change in Ivan's behavior now will be enough to convince Onkel Harvey and the bishop that he should stay with us. Stealing is a serious offense."

Bethany had lost so many people in her family. She couldn't bear the thought of sending her brother away. She had promised to look after her brother and sister and to keep the family together. It felt like she was breaking that promise and it was tearing her heart to pieces.

"You still have the option to marry. I think Jesse would jump at the chance if you gave him any encouragement."

"I saw him this morning and he didn't appear lovestruck to me."

Gemma laughed. "Did you honestly go see him with marriage in mind?"

"Of course not. I took a stranger to see the bishop at his workplace. The bishop wasn't there but Jesse was."

"What stranger?" Gemma looked intrigued.

"His name is Michael Shetler. He claims my grandfather offered him a job and a place to stay."

"Did he?"

Bethany shrugged. "I never heard Grandfather mention it."

"What's he like? Is he single?"

"He's rude."

"What does that mean? What did he say to you?" Gemma left the bread dough to rise again and returned to her seat, her eyes alight with eagerness. "Tell me."

Bethany blushed at the memory of Michael listening to her conversation with Clarabelle. That was the last time she would speak to any of the farm animals. "He wasn't actually rude. He simply caught me off guard."

"And?"

"When I told him about Elijah's passing he was very upset. I thought the bishop would be the best person to help him find work, so I gave him a ride to the shed factory. Jesse said he would put him to work."

"You took a stranger up in your buggy? Is he old? Is he cute?"

"He walks with a cane."

"So he's old."

"*Nee.* I'd guess he's twenty-five or so. I had the impression it was a recent injury to his leg."

"So he's young. That's *goot*, but is he nice looking?"

Bethany considered the question. "Michael isn't bad looking. He has a rugged attractiveness."

"Michael?" Gemma tipped her head to the side. "He must be single. Is he someone you'd like to know better?"

"I have too much on my mind to spend time thinking about finding a man."

"That's not much of an answer."

"It's the only answer you are going to get. You'll have the chance to see Mr. Shetler for yourself at the church service next Sunday."

"All right. I won't tease you."

Gemma walked over and put on her coat. "Ivan is a good boy at heart. You know that."

Bethany nodded. "I do. Something is wrong, but I don't know what."

"You'll figure it out. You always do. I'm leaving you with a bit of a mess but all you have to do is put the bread in the oven when it's done rising."

"*Danki*, Gemma. I'm blessed to have you as a friend."

"You would do the same for me. Mamm is planning a big Thanksgiving dinner next Thursday. You and the children are invited of course."

"Tell your mother we'd love to come."

"Invite Michael when you see him again."

"I doubt I'll see him before Sunday next and by then it will be too late."

"My *daed* mentioned the other day he needs a bigger garden shed. Maybe I'll go with him to look at the ones the bishop makes. You aren't going to claim you saw Michael first if I decide I like him, are you?"

Bethany shook her head as she smiled at her friend. "He's all yours."

Bethany was waiting at the kitchen table when both children came home. Ivan sniffed the air appreciatively. "Smells good. Can I have a piece of bread with peanut butter? I'm starved."

Bethany clutched her hands together and laid them on the table. "After I have finished speaking to you."

"Told you," Jenny said as she took off her coat and boots.

"Talk about what?" Ivan tried to look innocent. Bethany knew him too well. She wasn't fooled.

"Why don't you start by telling me what you did wrong and why." Bethany was pleased that she sounded calm and in control.

"I don't know what you are talking about." He couldn't meet her gaze.

"You do so," Jenny muttered.

"Stay out of this," Ivan snapped.

"I went to school today. I'm not in trouble," Jenny shot back.

"I'm waiting for an explanation, Ivan." Bethany hoped he would own up to his behavior.

"Okay, I skipped school today. It's no big deal. I can make up the work." His defiant tone made her bristle.

"You will make up the work for today, and Thursday and Wednesday and Tuesday. You will also write a letter of apology to your teacher for your deliberate deception. Is there something else you want to tell me?"

He stared at his shoes. "Like what?"

Bethany shook her head. "Ivan, how could you? Skipping school is bad enough. Forging a letter to your teacher is worse yet, but stealing from our neighbors is terrible. I can't believe you would do such a thing. What has gotten into you?"

"Nothing."

"That is not an answer. Why did you steal beans and potatoes from Jedidiah?"

Ivan shrugged. "He has plenty. The Amish are supposed to share what they have with the less fortunate."

"What makes you less fortunate?"

When he didn't answer Bethany drew a deep breath. "Your behavior has shamed us. Worse than that, your actions have been reported to the bishop."

"So? What does the bishop have to do with this?"

"The bishop is responsible for this community," Bethany said. "Because you have behaved in ways contrary to our teachings, the bishop has decided you need more discipline and guidance than I can give you."

"What does that mean?"

"When Onkel Harvey and his family come to visit for Christmas, you will return to Bird-in-Hand with them."

"What? I don't want to live with Onkel Harvey."

"You should've thought about the consequences before getting into so much trouble."

Jenny, who had been standing quietly beside Ivan,

suddenly spoke up. "You're sending him away? Sister, you promised we would all stay together." She looked ready to cry. "You promised."

"This is out of my hands. The bishop and your uncle have decided what Ivan needs. They feel I have insufficient control over you, Ivan. I'm afraid they are right. Bishop Schultz believes you need the firm guidance of a man. If your grandfather was still alive or if I was married, things would be different."

"That's stupid," Ivan said, glaring at Bethany. "I didn't do anything bad enough to be sent away. It isn't fair."

"None of us wants this. You have time before Christmas to change your behavior and convince them to let you stay. You will return the items you've taken from Jedidiah. He knows that you sold one of the bags of potatoes you took. You must give the money you received for them to Jedidiah. You will have to catch up on all your missed schoolwork and behave politely to Jedidiah and to the bishop. We will pray that your improvement is enough to convince Bishop and Onkel Harvey to let you remain with us."

Ivan glared at her. "Jedidiah Zook is a creep. He's never nice to me, so why should I be nice to him?"

Bethany planted her hands on her hips. "That attitude is exactly what got you into this mess."

Jenny wrapped her arms around her brother's waist. "I don't want you to go away. I'll tell the bishop you'll be good."

"They don't care what we think because we're just kids and we don't count."

"That's enough, Ivan. You and I will go now to speak to Jedidiah and return his belongings this evening."

"I can't."

"What do you mean that you can't?"

He shrugged. "I don't have the stuff or the money anymore. I gave it away."

"Who did you give it to?" Bethany asked.

"I don't have to tell you." He pushed Jenny away and rushed through the house and out the back door. Bethany followed, shouting after him, but he ran into the woods at the back of the property and disappeared from her view.

Jenny began crying. Bethany picked her up to console her. Jenny buried her face in the curve of Bethany's neck. "You can't send him away. You can't. Do something, sister."

"I will try, Jenny. I promise I will try."

Ivan returned an hour later. Not knowing what else to do, Bethany sent him to bed without supper. Jenny barely touched her meal. Bethany didn't have an appetite, either. She wrote out a check to Jedidiah for the value of the stolen items and put it in an envelope with a brief letter of apology. She couldn't face him in person.

After both children were in bed, Bethany stood in front of the door to her grandfather's workshop. He wouldn't be in there but she hoped that she could draw comfort from the things he loved. She pushed open the door.

Moonlight reflecting off the snow outside cast a large rectangle of light through the window. It fell across his desk and empty chair. She walked to the chair and laid her hands on the back of it. The wood was cold beneath her fingers. She closed her eyes and drew a deep breath. The smell of the oils he used, the old leather chair and the cleaning rag that was still lying on the desk brought his beloved face into sharp focus. Tears slipped from beneath her closed eyelids and ran down her cheeks. She wiped them away with both hands.

"I miss you, Daadi. We all miss you. I know you are happy with our Lord in heaven and with Mammi and Mamm. That gives me comfort, but I still miss you." Her voice sounded odd in the empty room.

Opening her eyes, she sat in his chair and lit the lamp. The pieces of a watch lay on the white felt-covered board he worked on. His tiny screwdrivers and tools were lined up neatly in their case. Everything was just as it had been the last time he sat in this chair. The cleaning rag was the only thing out of place. She picked it up to return it to the proper drawer and saw an envelope lying beneath it. It was unopened. The name on the return address caught her attention. It was from Michael Shetler of Sugarcreek, Ohio.

Chapter Four

"Why didn't you tell me that you repair watches?"

Michael looked up from Jesse's table saw. Bethany stood in the workshop's doorway he had left open to take advantage of the unusually warm afternoon. She stood with her hands on her hips and a scowl on her pretty face.

The mutt, lying in the rectangle of sunlight, had already alerted him that someone was coming with a soft woof. She shot outside and around the corner of the building. The sight of Bethany made Michael want to smile. She was every bit as appealing as he remembered, even with a slight frown marring her face.

He pushed away his interest. Jesse had filled in a lot of details about the family last night. Bethany was trying to keep her family together. Jesse said without her grandfather and her brother to work the farm she could lose it. A handsome woman in need of help was trouble and Michael had enough trouble. He positioned the two-by-four length of pine board and made the cut. As the saw blade quit spinning he took the board and added it to the stack on his right. He kept his face carefully blank when he met her gaze. "I didn't think it would make a difference."

"It certainly would have."

"How so? Your grandfather is gone. You said you couldn't afford to hire help."

"You neglected to tell me you had sent the first and last months' rent on the cabin."

He picked up another board and settled it in the slot he had created for the correct length so he didn't have to measure and mark each piece of wood. Bishop Schultz used a diesel generator to supply electricity inside his carpentry shop. The smell of fresh sawdust mixed with diesel fumes that drifted through the open door. Michael squeezed the trigger on the saw and lowered the blade. It sliced through the pine board in two seconds, spewing more sawdust on the growing pile beneath the table.

He tossed the cut wood on the stack and reached for another two-by-four. Bethany crossed the room and took hold of the board before he could position it. "Why didn't you tell me you had already paid the rent?"

"I figured you would mention it if you knew about it. Since you didn't say anything and you already had a crisis to deal with, I thought it could wait for a better time."

"That was very considerate of you. A better time is right now. My grandfather never deposited your check. In fact, he never read your last letter. I only found it yesterday evening."

She let go of his board and reached into a small bag

she carried over her arm. "I have the check here. I've been unable to bring myself to clean out his workshop. For that reason, his agreement with you went undiscovered." She held out the check. He didn't take it.

"Do you know the rest of your grandfather's offer?" He kept his gaze averted.

"Your letter said you agreed to work with him for six months. Was there more?"

"If he considered me skillful enough after that time he would make me a fifty-fifty partner in the business." He looked at her. "I can show you his offer in writing if you want to see it."

"There's no need. I believe you. Are you still willing to do that?"

"How can I be a partner now that he is gone?"

"The business belongs to me but I can't repair watches, so it is worthless except for his tools. I had planned to sell them unless Ivan showed an interest in learning the trade."

"Has he?"

"Not yet."

"How is the boy?" he asked softly.

A wry smile lifted the corner of her mouth. "I wish I knew. Right now he seems mad at the world."

"Boys grow up. He'll come around."

"I pray you are right. I have a proposition for you, Mr. Shetler."

"Call me Michael."

She smiled and nodded once. "Michael. It's similar to the one my grandfather offered you. Work for me for six months. You keep two-thirds of everything you earn during that time. I will keep one-third as rent on the shop, for the use of Grandfather's client list and his tools. If at the end of that time I am satisfied with your skill I will sell you the business or we can continue as partners."

"Who is to decide if my skills are adequate?"

"My grandfather did the majority of his work for a man named George Meyers in Philadelphia. He owns a jewelry shop and watch repair business. If Mr. Meyers is satisfied with the quality of work you do, then that is all the assurance I need."

Michael smiled inwardly. One part of the puzzle had finally been solved. George had started this whole thing. It was certainly like George, to go out of his way for someone who didn't deserve the kindness. Michael wondered how much, if anything, George had shared about his condition with Bethany's grandfather. "I wondered how your grandfather got my name. Now I know."

"I'm afraid I don't follow you."

"I used to work for George Meyers." Up until the night he had let two armed criminals into the business George owned.

"Why did you quit? Is that when you got hurt?"

His heart started pounding like a hammer inside his chest as the onset of a panic attack began. In another minute he would be on the ground gasping for air. He wasn't about to recount the horrors he saw that night to Bethany. He had to get outside. "I don't like to talk about it."

He grabbed an armful of cut wood and pushed past Bethany. "Jesse is going to wonder what's keeping me."

She followed him outside. "I'm sorry if it seemed that I was prying. If you don't want to work for me, I understand, but the cabin is still yours for two months."

"I'll think about the job, but I'll take the cabin." He kept walking. It wasn't that he wanted to be rude but he needed her to leave. His anxiety was rising rapidly.

"The cabin is yours whenever you want."

The yellow dog came around the side of the building and launched herself at him. He sidestepped to keep from being hit with her muddy paws. One of the boards slid out of his arms. "Down."

She dropped to her belly and barked once, then rolled over, inviting him to scratch her muddy stomach.

"I see you still have your friend," Bethany said, humor bubbling beneath her words.

He looked from her to the dog. "I don't have anything to feed you, mutt, unless you eat two-by-fours."

The dog jumped to her feet, picked up the board he had dropped and took off with it in her mouth.

"Hey, bring that back!"

The dog made a sweeping turn and raced back, splashing through puddles of melted snow. She came to a stop and sat in front of him, holding the four-foot length of wood like a prized bone.

"Goot hund." He reached for the board but the dog took off before he touched it. She made a wild run between the sheds lined up at the edge of the property where the snow was still deep.

Bethany burst out laughing. "Good dog, indeed."

He liked the sound of her laughter. The heaviness in his chest dissipated and he grinned. "It seems her previous owner didn't spend much time training her."

"I can see that. She is friendlier since she's had a few meals. She seems to have a lot of puppy in her yet. In a way she reminds me of my brother."

"How so?"

"A lot of potential, but very little focus."

"I'd like to meet this kid."

"I'm sure you will since you'll be living just out our back door."

He frowned. "The cabin is close to your house?"

"Fifty yards, maybe less."

"I assumed it was more secluded."

"It is set back in the woods. We won't bother you if that's what you are worried about."

"I like my privacy." He couldn't very well explain he was worried she'd hear him yelling in the middle of the night.

The dog came trotting back and sat down between them, still holding her trophy. Michael bent to grab the board as Bethany did the same. They smacked heads. His hat flipped off and landed in the snow. The dog dropped the wood, snatched up the hat and took off with it.

Michael held his head and glanced at Bethany. "Are you okay?"

Bethany rubbed her smarting forehead. Maybe it was a sign that she needed some sense knocked into her. She had come to give Michael his money back and had ended up offering him a job instead. The thump on her skull had come too late. "I'm fine."

"Are you sure? Do you want some ice?"

"*Nee*, it won't leave a mark. Will it?" She pulled her hand away.

He bent closer. "I think you're going to have a bump."

"Great."

"I am sorry." He looked down at the dog, now standing a few feet away, still holding his hat. "See what you did to Bethany."

The dog whined and lay down, the picture of dejection. Bethany crouched and offered her hand to the animal. "Don't scold the poor thing. It wasn't her fault. Are you going to keep her?"

"I can't walk away and leave her to fend for herself. Besides, her goofy behavior leaves me smiling more often than not. *Ja*, I will keep her. She seems to have decided she belongs with me."

Bethany knew she should leave but found herself reluctant to go. There was something intriguing about the man. One minute they were discussing his job and the next second he went pale as a sheet and couldn't get away from her fast enough. A few minutes later they were both laughing at the antics of a stray dog. The truth was she liked him. A lot. But she had to find a way to keep her family together. She couldn't allow a distraction to interfere with that.

She took the hat from the dog and handed it to Michael. "I should get going."

"Right." He nodded but didn't move.

She took a few steps toward her buggy but something made her turn around. He was still watching her. "Michael, do you play chess?"

"I enjoy the game. Why?"

"Would you do me a favor?"

"If I can."

"I have a friend of my grandfather coming to supper on Sunday evening. He and Daadi used to play chess every week. I know he misses Daadi and their games. I don't play. If you aren't doing anything, would you like to join us for supper and give Pastor Frank a game or two?"

Hadn't she just decided she didn't need a distraction? Maybe he would say no. "Don't feel obligated just because I asked."

"I need to get moved in. I'm not sure I'll find the time."

"You have to eat."

"Another time maybe."

"Of course." She turned away, more disappointed than she cared to admit.

"Bethany?"

"Ja?" She spun around hopefully.

"I appreciate the job offer. I'll give it some serious thought. Do I get the key to the cabin from you?"

"It isn't locked. You'll find the key hanging on a nail just inside the door. When you come to my place you'll see a wooded ridge behind the house. The cabin is up there. Just follow the lane. Do you have transportation? I can send Ivan to pick you up."

"Jesse has offered me the loan of a pony and cart

until I can send for my horses. Is there someone locally who sells buggies?"

"There's a carriage maker in Unity. I've heard he is reasonable."

"I'll look into it."

"If you change your mind about having supper with us tomorrow night, just show up. There will be plenty to eat."

"Are you a *goot* cook?"

She grinned. "Do you expect a modest Amish woman to brag on herself?"

"I expect a modest Amish woman to tell the truth."

She bobbed her head once. "I could tell you that I'm a very good cook, but I suggest you come to supper and decide for yourself."

After stepping up into her buggy, she looked back and saw he was still watching her. A tingle of pleasure at his interest lifted her spirits. Just as quickly, she dismissed her feeling as foolishness. Her mother's unhappy life spent loving the wrong kind of man had driven home to Bethany just how cruel romantic love could be. She was determined not to suffer the same way. If she married it would be a beneficial arrangement based on sound judgment. Not love. She waved and then drove away. Would Michael come or wouldn't he? She would have to wait an entire day to find out.

Jesse walked past Michael with a load of boards in his arms. "Have you decided to hang on to her or are you going to ignore her and hope she goes away?"

Michael scowled at him. "What does that mean?"

Jesse stopped and gave Michael a funny look. "I was just wondering if you are planning to keep the dog. What did you think I meant?"

Relieved that he wasn't referring to Bethany, Michael decided to share the joke. "Bethany Martin was just here."

Jesse chuckled. "I wouldn't tell a fella to ignore Bethany and hope she goes away, but the same can't be said for some other single women in this community."

Although Jesse hadn't made Bethany's wish list when she had been talking to the cow about walking out with someone, Michael liked the man and thought he would make a decent husband. "Do you have your eye on one maid in particular?"

"Me? *Nee*, I'm not ready to get into harness with any female. They talk too much, and they expect you to talk back to them. I don't have that much to say. I can't imagine a lifetime of staring at a woman who is waiting for me to utter something interesting. If you are looking to go courting, Bethany Martin is a fine woman. You wouldn't be stepping on anyone's toes."

"I'm not interested in courting, but I did wonder why she isn't already married."

"Her grandfather told me that she wants to get her brother and sister raised before she looks to start another family."

"Did you know Elijah well?"

"He was a fine friend. Everyone loved him. He was always laughing, quick with a joke, always ready to lend a helping hand. It didn't matter if you were

Amish or not. There are only twenty adult members in this church, six *youngees* and five *kinder*. We know each other well."

Youngees were unmarried teens in their running around time or *rumspringa*. The potential marriage pool in the community was small indeed. Bethany would have to look for a marriage partner farther afield if Jesse or Jedidiah didn't work out.

Michael couldn't seem to curb his curiosity about her and her family. "What's the story with her brother?"

Jesse was silent for a long moment. "I'm not one to speak ill of another."

"I'm sorry. I wasn't looking for gossip. I can form my own opinion of the family. You don't have to say anything."

"It's not that. We are newcomers to this area. Bethany and her family have been here the longest. Two years now. I came sixteen months ago. Jedidiah and the other families came after I did. We get along with the *Englisch* and for the most part they get along with us. There are a few exceptions. People who would like to see us leave. When something goes wrong, those few are quick to point to the Amish and say it must be our fault. Ivan has been a mischief maker for as long as I've known him, but I don't believe all that is said against him these days."

"You think he is getting blamed for what someone else is doing?"

Jesse stared into the distance for a long minute, and then he looked Michael in the eye. "I think he makes an easy target."

Michael considered Jesse's carefully worded reply. "What does the bishop think?"

"He hasn't confided in me. I should get back to work. I don't want him to think I slack off when he's gone. Oh, and I meant to tell you I've got some extra nylon webbing if you want to fashion a collar for your mutt. What did Bethany want, anyway?"

Michael followed Jesse to the skeleton of the shed he was putting up. "She discovered her grandfather did rent a cabin to me. She found my rent check last night. She came to give me a choice of getting my money back or staying on the property."

"So, am I losing you as a roommate already?"

"You are. I'll leave tomorrow."

"*Goot.* That makes you the best kind of houseguest."

Michael glanced his way. "What kind is that?"

"One who leaves before he has worn out his welcome." Jesse grinned and clapped Michael on the back then pulled his hammer from his tool belt and went to work.

Michael relaxed. He laid down the boards he'd cut and walked back to the workshop. He thought getting a few answers about Bethany would appease his curiosity but he had been mistaken. It seemed it wasn't so easy to put her out of his mind.

Maybe he'd made a mistake telling her he still wanted to rent the cabin. How was he going to stop thinking about her if he lived fifty yards from her home? If he took the job she was going to be his boss.

He would have to discourage her from visiting the

workshop. He worked best alone and he liked it that way. That was the reason he had come to Maine. She would just have to learn to accept it.

Bethany opened the oven to check her peach pie and decided it was done. The crust was golden brown and the juices were bubbling up between the lattice strips. She pulled it out and placed it on the cooling rack at the end of the counter. She then lifted the lid on the pot of chili and sniffed the mouthwatering aroma. Using a spoon, she scooped up a sample and blew on it before tasting it. The deep, rich, spicy flavor was delicious but it needed a touch more salt. After adding two shakes, she stirred the pot and replaced the lid. All she needed now was the rest of her company.

Would Michael come? She hoped he would.

"It smells *wunderbar*," Gemma said as she set the plates on the table.

"Let's hope it tastes as good as it smells." Bethany walked to the window that overlooked the path up to the cabin. She had invited Gemma to join them as a defense against her attraction to Michael. Gemma's lighthearted and flirty ways were sure to liven the evening and keep Michael entertained.

"Any sign of him?"

Bethany dropped the window shade. "Any sign of who?"

"The person you're hoping to see. You realize you've been to that window ten times in the last thirty minutes. I can't imagine that you are this anxious to catch sight of Pastor Frank. Therefore, it must be someone else. I'm going to take a wild guess and say it is a man. A newcomer. Someone who walks with a cane." She raised one eyebrow at Bethany. "Am I close?"

"If you must know, I did invite Michael Shetler. He plays chess and I know that Pastor Frank misses the games he used to have with Elijah."

"That was very thoughtful of you. Why am I here? I don't play chess."

"You're here because I didn't want it to look like I had invited Michael for personal reasons. You know what I mean."

"You didn't want him to think you were angling for a return date? Or were you hoping I would catch his interest?"

"Both. When he sees I invited a single woman from our community to join us, he won't think I have designs on him myself."

A sly grin curved Gemma's lips. "What if this backfires and he *does* like me better?"

"Then I will be happy for both of you and you can name your first daughter after me."

Gemma laughed and returned to setting the table. Bethany resisted the urge to look out the window again. It was possible Michael had made his way to the cabin without her seeing him, but she hoped he would at least stop by and let her know he had taken possession.

The rumble of a car announced the arrival of Pastor Frank. Bethany went to the front door to greet him and saw Michael turning in from the highway in a small cart pulled by a black-and-white pony. To her chagrin, he simply waved and went past the house on the track that led to the cabin. She tried not to let her disappointment show. She stepped aside to allow Frank to enter the house and closed the door against the chilly afternoon. It was clear Michael wasn't eager to see her again.

After seeing Bethany's smile fade when he drove past her home, Michael almost changed his mind and went back. Almost. His best course of action was to see as little of her as possible. Out of sight, out of mind. He hoped. While he found her attractive, he couldn't offer her anything but a business partnership. To encourage anything else would be grossly unfair.

The cabin he had rented was set back in a small grove of trees up the hillside behind her place. As she had promised, the road up to it was well marked and had been plowed recently.

A small weathered barn came with the cabin and he stopped Jesse's pony beside it. A quick tour proved it would be enough for his two buggy horses and his buggy when he got one. The only drawback to the property was the steep hillside behind the barn. With his bum leg he'd never be able to get down to the bottom and lead his horses back up when he turned them out to pasture in the summer. He unharnessed the pony and led him inside to a roomy stall. Jesse had supplied Michael with enough hay and horse chow to last him a week.

He moved the horse feed inside and left the hay

in the back of the small wagon. He was thankful to see a water pump stood near the barn. It would make keeping the animals watered easier even in the winter.

As he was heading to the cabin with his duffel bag over his shoulder, he saw the dog come trotting up the road. She had followed him from town as he'd hoped she would. He had tried to coax her into the cart, but she'd refused to have anything to do with it even after he lifted her into the bed. "You're a good girl. I'm glad to see you made it."

She ignored him and went to explore in the barn. Michael put his bag down on the porch and tried to open the door. It was locked. He was sure Bethany had told him it would be unlocked. He tried again to make sure the door wasn't just stuck but it wasn't.

He made his way to the back door with difficulty. The snow was deep enough in places to leave him unsure of his footing. If not for his cane and the wall of the cabin, he would have fallen several times. After all his struggles he found the back door was locked, as well. He could see that it had been opened recently by the arch of snow that had been pushed aside. A trail of footprints led from the stoop up the hill into woods. They were small footprints, those of a woman or a child.

Making his way back to the front porch was easier. The dog was sitting by the door waiting for him. He looked at the house below him on the hillside. It seemed he would have to face Bethany after all to get the key. He made his way down the road and knocked on her front door.

Chapter Five

The moment Bethany opened her door Michael knew he was in trouble. Her bright smile and the eagerness in her eyes pushed at the mental wall he had erected to keep people from getting too close.

He didn't want to shut her out. He wanted to be worthy of the friendliness she seemed so willing to share.

"You have decided to join us, after all. Come in, Michael. Please have a seat." She stepped aside and gestured for him to enter.

He shook his head. "I'm not here to eat."

Disappointment replaced the eagerness in her eyes. "Oh? What can I do for you, then?"

She moved back and he stepped inside. The dog squeezed in to stay at his side. Bethany frowned slightly but didn't say anything.

The house was typical of the Amish houses he'd seen all his life. From the entryway a door to his right led directly into the kitchen. Beautiful pine cabinets lined the walls. The floor was covered with a checkerboard pattern of black-and-white linoleum. The windows had simple white pull-down shades instead of curtains. The delicious aromas of Bethany's home-cooked meal filled the air. His stomach growled.

He resisted the urge to stay and make her smile again. "The cabin is locked. I can't get in."

Bethany cocked her head slightly. "Are you sure? Maybe the door is just stuck."

"I'm sure. The back door is locked, too."

"Why does he need in the cabin?" Ivan demanded, scowling at Michael.

Bethany gave her brother a sharp look. "Michael is going to be living there. Daadi rented the place to him. Do you know anything about the cabin being locked?"

"I don't know why you're asking me," Ivan snapped. "Every time something goes wrong I get blamed." He pushed to his feet and rushed out of the room.

Color blossomed in Bethany's cheeks as she glanced at her guests. "I apologize for Ivan's behavior. I thought he was doing better. Jenny, did you lock the cabin?"

Jenny shook her head, making the ribbons of her *kapp* dance on her shoulders. "I play there sometimes with Ivan and Jeffrey, but I didn't lock the door."

Bethany met Michael's gaze but quickly looked away. "I believe there is a spare key in Grandfather's bedroom. If you'll excuse me, I'll go find it. It may take me a moment or two. I'm not sure where Daadi kept it."

The dog suddenly left Michael's side. He made a grab for her and missed. "Mutt, get back here."

She ignored him and went to investigate the new

people in the room. She gave the young Amish woman and the *Englisch* fellow at the table a brief sniff, then rounded the far end. Jenny had her hands out. The dog settled her head in Jenny's lap and looked up with soulful adoring eyes as the girl scratched her behind her ears.

"What a beautiful dog." Jenny stroked her soft fur. "I think she likes me."

Michael walked over and took hold of a length of black nylon webbing Jesse had fashioned into a makeshift collar. "I'm afraid she hasn't learned any manners."

"What's her name?" Jenny asked.

"Mutt." He still wasn't sure he would keep her, although she seemed to have attached herself to him. Maybe she would like Jenny better and stay here.

The slender man in *Englisch* clothing rose to his feet. "Mutt is not much of a name but it's better than Cat. I'm Pastor Frank Pearson. You can call me Frank." He swept a hand toward the young Amish woman seated across from him. "This is Bethany's friend Gemma Lapp and you must be Michael Shetler."

The pastor held out his hand. Meeting new people made Michael uneasy. He rubbed his sweaty palm on his pant leg before taking the man's hand in a firm grip. "I take it you are the chess player."

Frank's expression brightened. "I am. Do you play?"

"Now and again."

"We'll have to arrange a match someday. I'm sorry you didn't get to meet Elijah. He was a true master of the game. He told me quite a bit about you."

Michael grew cold. "Is that so? I don't know what he could have told you. We never met."

The pastor's expression didn't change. "He said you came highly recommended by an old friend of his. I believe it was George Meyers and that you grew up near Sugarcreek in Ohio. My grandmother was from the Sugarcreek area, but she left many years ago. Please, have a seat."

It had been a long day and Michael just wanted to get settled in a place of his own. He accepted the invitation mainly because his leg was aching.

"Would you like some *kaffi*?" Gemma asked.

He nodded. She rose and brought him a cup and saucer with three pale yellow cookies on the plate. "These are lemon crinkles. My specialty. I hope you like them."

"Danki." The coffee was black and bracing. The cookies were light, tart and delicious.

"You can't call her Mutt," Jenny said from the other end of the table.

"Why don't you name her?" Gemma suggested.

Jenny peered into the dog's eyes. "I'm going to call you Sadie Sue. Do you like that name?"

The dog barked once and everyone laughed.

"That settles it," Michael said. "She is now and forever Sadie Sue."

"How are the cookies?" Gemma gave Michael a smile every bit as sweet as the pastry.

"They're delicious. They remind me of the ones my grandmother used to make." He prayed Bethany would hurry up before he was subjected to more questions. She came back in the room a few seconds later.

"Found it." She held the key aloft.

Michael grimaced as he stood and leaned heavily on the table. He had been sitting just long enough for his leg to stiffen. When the sharp pain subsided he picked up his cane.

"Are you all right?" Bethany asked, reaching a hand toward him.

Her sympathy irritated him. He hated when people treated him as if they expected him to topple over at any second. "I'm fine."

"How were you injured?" Gemma asked softly.

His throat tightened. He couldn't draw a full breath. The walls of the house started to close in. He needed to get outside. "I've got to get going."

He saw the confusion in Bethany's eyes, but nothing mattered except getting enough air. He pushed past her and went out the door. On the porch he stopped to scan the yard and outbuildings for signs of danger. Was someone lurking in the woods beyond the road? He took a step to the side and backed up to the wall of the house so that no one could get behind him. Sadie followed him out and sat at his side, nuzzling his hand. He stroked her head.

After a few deep breaths of the cold air, Michael's panic receded. It was okay. There wasn't any danger. He took one step away from the safety of Bethany's house and then another, glad to escape without having her watch him fall apart.

* * *

Gemma propped her elbow on the table with her chin in her hand. "Did that seem odd to anyone else?"

Bethany had to admit Gemma was right. "He acted like he couldn't get out of here fast enough."

"I hope it wasn't my cookies." Gemma sat back and folded her arms across her chest.

Pastor Frank took a sip of his coffee. "I don't think it was anything we said or did. Michael has been through a rough time."

Bethany turned to Frank. "What do you know about him?"

"Only a few things that your grandfather shared with me. I don't feel it's my place to repeat what was said."

Gemma arched one eyebrow. "Okay, now you've made me curious."

Frank smiled but he shook his head. "Many people tell me things in confidence. I take that responsibility seriously. I think it's enough to say that Michael came to New Covenant seeking privacy and a chance to heal in body and mind."

"Is there anything we can do for him?" Bethany asked.

"We can invite him to our Thanksgiving dinner," Gemma suggested. "He shouldn't spend the holiday alone."

Pastor Frank nodded. "Good idea. Treat him like you would anyone else. Be friendly, be kind, be compassionate, don't pry. I suspect he will discover soon enough if he truly belongs here."

Gemma rolled her eyes. "One winter was enough to convince me I didn't belong here. I don't mind snow, but when it gets so deep you can't see the cows standing out in it, that's too much snow."

Bethany chuckled. "And yet here you are facing another winter in northern Maine."

"I can't. What would you do without me?"

"I honestly don't know," Bethany admitted. Gemma was a dear friend and she would miss her terribly if she ever left New Covenant.

"Gemma, will you serve the peach pie and ice cream for me? I must speak with Ivan. His behavior tonight was not acceptable." Bethany braced herself for a verbal battle with Ivan as she climbed the stairs to his bedroom. She knocked softly. He didn't answer.

She opened the door and discovered he wasn't in his room. Her conversation with him would have to wait but it would take place. He wasn't getting out of it this easily. She checked the other rooms and the attic, knowing he sometimes liked to hide in those places, but she didn't find him.

When Bethany came downstairs she joined the others and enjoyed a slice of pie and ice cream. When everyone was finished, Gemma began clearing the table.

Pastor Frank patted his stomach. "That was a very good meal. Invite me more often, Bethany."

She summoned a smile. "Come anytime. I'll feed you."

He laughed as he rose and got ready to leave. She handed him his gloves after he finished buttoning his coat. "I'm glad you came tonight, Frank. We have missed your company."

"I'm glad I came, too. What did Ivan have to say for himself?"

She clasped her hands together. "He wasn't in his room. He must have slipped out the back door. What am I going to do with him?"

"He's a troubled boy. All you can do is show him you care about him, give him the opportunity to confide in you and pray he finds the courage to tell you what's bothering him."

"I know he doesn't want to be sent to live with our uncle. I had hoped learning that he only has until Christmas to mend his ways would be incentive enough."

"Unfortunately, it may only add to the pressure he's under."

"Will you talk to him?"

"As a family friend or in my official capacity as a psychologist? Would your bishop approve of that?"

Bethany squeezed her fingers together tightly. She wasn't sure but she was willing to risk more of the bishop's disapproval. "I think he would allow it but I'm asking as a friend."

"Then I will be happy to see Ivan. Bring him by my home any day after school this week. If he'll come."

"I will do that."

He started out the door but stopped and looked back. "One more thing. Will you give a message to Michael Shetler for me?"

"Of course."

"Tell him my door is always open if he needs someone to talk to. That's all. Good night."

"I'll tell him. Good night, Frank." Bethany closed the door behind him. What did Frank know about Michael's past that he felt he couldn't share with her?

Michael unlocked the front door of the cabin and stepped inside. Instantly he knew someone had been there before him. The back door was open a crack. He was sure it had been locked earlier. He crossed the room and closed the door, uneasy at the thought of someone having access. His anxiety level climbed as he thought about trying to sleep in an unsecured place. He thanked God for the dog at his side. A dead bolt and new locks for the doors were a must first thing in the morning.

The dog stayed by his side as he searched the building. Her calm attitude reassured him that the visitor was long gone. The place was neat and cozy. The cabin was a single room with a tiny kitchen in one corner. A bump out beyond the kitchen contained a modern bathroom with a shower and a propane hot water heater. Two big windows on the south wall let in plenty of evening light. A metal bed frame in the far corner held a bare mattress with a sleeping bag on it. A glance around the room gave him the impression that someone visited often. There were empty food wrappers and several magazines beside the fireplace. Perhaps Ivan and Jenny played here. He walked back to pick up his bag near the front door.

Glass shattered, startling him. Michael saw two

boys through the broken window before his leg gave out and he hit the floor. Instantly, he was back in the jewelry store, in the middle of the robbery. He had to get out. He crawled toward the door and pulled it open, expecting another bullet. Someone was screaming. Sirens grew closer. Red lights flashed on the ceiling overhead. The smell of gunpowder choked him.

A dog started barking. There hadn't been a dog there that night. He tried to concentrate on the sound. The dog was real. The rest was a nightmare, so realistic he could hear the robbers' voices, he could see their mask-covered faces, he felt the impact of the bullet and the burning pain in his leg. He kept crawling to get away from them.

"Mister, are you okay?"

The new voice, like the barking dog, wasn't a part of the past. Michael struggled to focus on it. Bethany's brother was kneeling beside him. He didn't want anybody to see him like this. "Go away."

"I'm going to go get help." The boy jumped to his feet and ran toward the house down the hill. Michael crawled after Ivan but couldn't stop him.

Not Bethany. Don't bring Bethany.

It was his last thought before the nightmare sucked him back into the past and made him relive the unbearable. He screamed in pain as a bullet shattered his thigh. He wept as his coworkers were murdered one by one. The wail of sirens grew louder. He knew he was next.

"Michael, can you hear me?"

Another voice not from the past.

"Don't shoot," Michael begged, but the gunshots came again and again. He jerked each time.

"Can you tell me what's wrong? Are you hurt?" The different voice was insistent. Michael tried to hold on to it. He reached out his hand. Someone took hold of it.

"It's Pastor Frank Pearson. We just met. What's wrong, Michael?"

"He's killing them. He's killing them all. Don't shoot."

"Michael, I want you to listen to me. You're safe. No one is shooting. You're in Bethany's cabin in Maine. No one can hurt you here. You're safe. Michael, you're safe."

"I'm in Maine." Harsh panting filled his ears. He knew he was making that sound but he couldn't stop.

"I want you to listen to my voice. No one is hurting you."

Michael turned his head and tried to focus on the man kneeling beside him. He wanted out of this nightmare, but he didn't know how. "Help."

"I'm here to help you. I think you are having a flashback to something bad that happened before. It's not happening now. It's all in the past. Do you understand? You are safe. No one will hurt you."

Michael had no idea how long he lay on the snowy ground listening to Pastor Frank's voice, but slowly the cold air began penetrating the nightmare. The cold was now. The cold was the present. He took a deep breath and then another. He was looking up at darkening sky. There was a single white cloud drifting overhead. It looked like a catcher's mitt. He heard soft whining. Turning his head slowly, he focused on Sadie Sue. She lay beside him with her head on his thigh.

Michael's pounding heart began to slow. He laid a hand on her head. *"Goot hund."*

"Are you feeling better?" Pastor Frank was still kneeling at Michael's side.

Embarrassed that anyone had seen him like this, Michael struggled to sit up. "I'm fine."

"I'm glad to hear that. If you would like to tell me about what happened, I will be happy to listen."

"I don't want to talk about it." Michael struggled to get up. Pastor Frank gave him a hand and helped him to his feet.

"That's perfectly understandable."

Michael looked around. "Where is my cane?"

Sadie sat at his side, her wagging tail sweeping the snow from his doorstep. She leaned against him as he patted her head.

Pastor Frank located Michael's cane inside the door and handed it to him. He smiled at the dog. "The Lord provides comfort for us in many amazing ways."

Michael wanted nothing more than to retreat inside the cabin and lock the door. "Thanks for the help. I was fortunate I fell at your feet."

"Actually, you didn't. You fell at Ivan's feet. I had just finished having supper with Gemma and Bethany. I was getting in my van when Ivan raced up and said you needed help."

Ivan was standing a few yards away from them.

His pale face and wide eyes revealed how frightened he was. Michael rubbed his hands together to warm them. "I'm sorry I scared you, Ivan."

"You may have done more good than harm," Frank said softly and beckoned Ivan closer. "He insists he was the one who threw a rock through your window, but I have my doubts."

"I saw two figures," Michael said.

Ivan approached slowly. "I thought you had been hit in the head or something. I thought you were dying."

Michael managed a half smile. "As you can see, I'm not."

"Why did you break the window?" Frank asked.

Ivan stared at the ground and shifted from one foot to the other. "I don't know."

"I think you do," Frank said.

"Jeffrey and I like to hang out here. We were mad that we couldn't use it as a meeting place anymore. I guess we thought you might not stay if the window was broken. We didn't mean to hurt you."

"Actions have consequences," Frank said sternly. "Your wrath served no good purpose. Before you act in anger again, you must think about this day."

"I will. Are you going to tell Bethany about this?"

"No," Michael said emphatically.

Frank placed a hand on Ivan's shoulder. "You'd better go home. Your sister was looking for you."

"To scold me again, right?"

"To talk to you about what's really bothering you. Your sister loves you. You know that."

"Sure, that's why she's sending me away." The boy turned and walked toward the house with lagging steps.

"He's got a chip on his shoulder," Michael said.

"He does, but right now I'm more concerned about you."

Michael grew uncomfortable under Frank's intense scrutiny. "I told you I'm fine."

"How often do you have these flashbacks?"

"I don't know what you're talking about."

"Yes, you do. Why deny it? What's important is that I know exactly what you are going through. I used to be in your shoes. I dealt with PTSD for three years before my symptoms improved. I haven't had a flashback for five years now."

"How?"

"How did I get better? Time and therapy. Why don't we step inside out of the cold?"

Michael limped into the cabin. The dog followed him in and went to lie in front of the fireplace.

"I don't have much in the way of furniture yet. I'm having some stuff shipped from home." There was an overstuffed green leather chair by the fireplace and two straight-backed chairs that came with the cabin. Michael lowered himself into the upholstered chair and glanced at Frank. "What caused your PTSD?"

Frank turned one of the wooden chairs around and straddled it. "I served in the military right out of high school. I saw some brutal fighting and horrible situations at a very young age. I married while I was in the service. I thought I was tough. I thought I was okay but a few months after I got home I started having episodes where I relived the most frightening events I went through. I started having nightmares, panic attacks. I became moody, bitter and depressed. My wife didn't know how to deal with me, and we divorced. Thankfully a fellow veteran recognized what was wrong with me and got me help."

"You stopped having them?" Michael wanted desperately to believe it was possible.

"In time they went away. I found God and He changed my life. I wanted to do His work, but I also wanted to use modern medicine to help people suffering with mental health issues. I went back to school to become a psychologist and counselor, and then I became a minister. Michael, what triggered your episode today? Do you know?"

Michael shook his head. "It just came out of the blue."

"It may seem that way but there is often a trigger associated with an episode. It can be a sensation that recalls the trauma, such as pain. Strong emotions, feeling helpless, trapped or out of control can bring on a flashback or panic attack. A trigger can be as simple as a smell, a phrase, a sound."

Michael turned to look at the window. "The glass breaking. That's what triggered it today." One of the thieves had broken the glass jewelry case and triggered the alarm.

Michael gazed at Frank. "You said I can get over this."

"Recovery is a process. It takes time and there are often setbacks. It's important to stay positive, but yes, the majority of people with PTSD recover in time. For a few it is a lifelong battle. Therapy can help enormously. Talking about your trauma in a safe environment is a way to lessen the hold it has on you. How often do you have these flashbacks?"

"Three or four times a week. Sometimes every day. This is the first one since I arrived here. That was three days ago."

"And how long do they last?"

"It feels like an eternity but maybe ten minutes." Michael rubbed his thigh. It always ached worse after an episode.

Frank nodded. "And how long does it take for you to recover from one?"

"Twenty minutes or so. Will you have to tell someone about what happened today?"

"I don't but I wish you would let me help. I have a survivors' support group that meets every other week at my church. I invite you to check it out. You aren't the only one dealing with a traumatic past."

Michael shook his head. "I'd rather no one knows about this."

Especially Bethany. It shouldn't matter so much what she thought but it did matter.

Pastor Frank didn't argue. "As you wish. Please let me know if I can be of help in any way. Don't get up. I'll see myself out. I've got some plywood to cover the window. I'll be back with it in half an hour."

"I appreciate that. And for all your help earlier."

After Frank left, Michael set about building a fire in the fireplace. He was surprised that the ashes were still warm. Ivan or his friend had recently had a blaze going here. When Michael had a decent fire burning to drive off the chill, he sat down to wait for Pastor Frank's return. It wasn't long before there was a knock at the door. He got up to answer it.

Ivan stood on his doorstep looking dejected. Bethany stood behind him with her hand clamped on his shoulder.

Michael tried to disguise his rising panic. What had the boy told her?

Chapter Six

Michael didn't look happy to see her. Why should he be?

Bethany kept her chin up in spite of the mortification that weighted her down. Her brother was bent on making it harder for him to remain with her. He should be improving his behavior but he wasn't. Instead he had shown that she couldn't keep him in line. Once again she was forced to apologize for his actions.

She took a deep breath. "Good evening, Michael. I understand that Ivan broke one of the windows here. I'm truly sorry. I will have it replaced as soon as possible. In the meantime, my brother has something he wants to say to you."

"I'm sorry," Ivan mumbled.

It wasn't much of an apology, but she let it pass. "He also told me you were hurt."

"I was startled. I tripped and fell but I wasn't hurt. As you can see."

She couldn't read Michael's reaction. His face was

blank. How upset was he? She wanted this awkward episode over as quickly as possible.

"I'm sure that you and I can find a way for Ivan to make amends and decide on a punishment."

"That won't be necessary."

Her brother wasn't getting off the hook so easily this time. "I insist. He needs to take responsibility for what he has done."

"I agree, but Ivan and I will work out the details. He is old enough to decide what's appropriate."

She pressed a hand to her chest. "As the adult in the family, I feel I should have a say in this." Surely he wasn't going to disregard her position as head of the family?

"Ivan and I can reach an agreement that's fair."

Her brother peered up at her. "I am old enough."

Michael nodded and stepped back. "Come in, Ivan, and we will discuss this. I'll send him home after we get the window boarded up. The pastor has gone to get some plywood."

Ivan went inside the cabin and Michael closed the door, leaving Bethany standing on the porch feeling foolish as well as incompetent.

She stomped back to the house but she couldn't stop thinking about Michael's high-handed attitude. *She* was responsible for Ivan. *She* should be a part of any discussion that involved her brother, not dismissed by some stranger as if she were a child.

Inside the house she went to the linen closet and pulled out sheets, pillows and several quilts, knowing there weren't any in the cabin. With her excuse for returning in hand, she headed out of the house. Michael Shetler had a thing or two to learn about dealing with her.

Ivan looked nervous but ready to accept his punishment. Michael walked over to the chair and sat down. The dog moved to sit beside his knee and leaned against his leg. He waited for the boy to speak first.

Ivan stuffed his hands in his pant pockets. "I'm sorry about the broken window."

"It can be fixed. What sort of punishment do you think you deserve?"

A flash of bitterness crossed Ivan's features. It was gone before Michael could be certain of what he'd seen. He leaned forward. "Why didn't Jeffrey stick around? Why didn't he stay to make sure I was okay? He has been staying here, hasn't he?"

"His dad gets mad real easy. Jeffrey sometimes hangs out here when he does. He took off tonight because he was afraid of getting in trouble at home."

Ivan took a seat beside the dog. "What happened to your leg?"

Michael wasn't prepared to have the tables turned on him but something told him that Ivan could be trusted with at least part of the truth. It might be what the boy needed to hear. "I will tell you on one condition. I don't want this mentioned to your sisters. Okay?"

The boy nodded.

"I was shot during a robbery."

"Are you joking?" Ivan's eyes grew wide.

"No joke."

"Wow. That's—I mean—you are the only person I know who has been shot."

"I would rather you didn't share the story with your sisters or your friends. It's not a pretty memory for me and I don't like pity."

"Sure. I can see you wouldn't want people talking about it. Does it still hurt?"

"All day every day but I was blessed. Other people died."

"People you knew?"

"They were my friends." Michael could feel his anxiety level rising as it did every time he thought about that night. Sadie Sue tried to climb in his lap and lick his face. He stroked her head and grew calmer.

Ivan shook his head in disbelief. "That's awful."

"The man who shot me, what kind of fellow do you think he was?"

"Evil."

"You would think so, but he wasn't much more than a scared boy pretending to be tough. Do you know what his first crime was?"

"What?"

"The first time he was arrested it was for stealing money from a neighbor. He was fourteen."

Ivan pinned his gaze to the floor. "Maybe he didn't have a choice."

Michael pushed Sadie Sue off his lap. She sat quietly beside his chair and watched him intently.

"We all have a choice. Your sister is mighty worried about you, Ivan."

The boy reached out and stroked the dog's head. "What's her name?"

Michael let him skirt around the issue of his sister's concern, knowing the boy would come back to it sooner or later. "I called her Mutt. Your sister, Jenny, named her Sadie Sue."

Ivan chuckled. "Sadie Sue. Only Jenny would think a dog needed a middle name."

"I like your little sister."

"Me, too."

"Bethany has treated me with kindness. She strikes me as a good woman."

"She treats me like I'm a little kid."

"Stop acting like one."

Ivan shot him a sour glare. "I don't. She should treat me like the man of the family."

Michael shrugged. "Being the man of the house isn't about how people treat you. The man of the family takes care of the people in his family. What have you done to take care of Bethany or Jenny lately? Think about it."

Ivan was silent for a few minutes. Finally, he looked up. "I don't have the money to pay for a new window, but I'll split wood for your fireplace for two weeks."

"A month."

"Okay, a month."

"And you are not going to skip school again, not even if Jeffrey asks you to do it."

Ivan tipped his head to the side. "How did you know Jeffrey asked me to skip with him?"

"Because Jeffrey took off tonight and left you to

face the consequences alone. Something tells me he is at the bottom of some of your troubles."

Ivan scrambled to his feet. "He's my friend. You don't know anything about him."

"You're right. I don't and I'm sorry. I was wrong to say that."

Ivan relaxed his stance. "My grandfather used to say a wise man is the one who can admit when he is wrong."

"I wish I'd had the chance to meet your grandfather. I owe him a lot."

"You would have liked him."

"I'm sure of it. Ivan, you value your friend Jeffrey and rightly so, but don't value your sisters less because of that friendship. Do you understand what I'm saying?"

"I think so."

"Catch up on your schoolwork and don't skip."

"Okay."

"You should get on home now. Remember, take care of your sisters. Don't expect them to treat you like you're the man of the family. Be that man. The same way your grandfather was. They will respect you for that."

"I'll try."

Sadie Sue rushed to the door and barked once. Michael got up and went to open it, expecting Frank. Bethany stood on his doorstep, her arms loaded with linens. "I knew you would need sheets and blankets."

"Come in." He glanced at Ivan. Would the boy

keep his secret? He hoped his trust wasn't misplaced. "Ivan and I have come to an agreement."

Turning to Ivan, Michael held out his hand. "We have a deal, right?"

"Right." Ivan shook on it. "I have some homework to finish. See ya." The boy went out the door, leaving Michael and Bethany alone.

Suddenly alone with Michael, Bethany stepped past him, determined to show him she wasn't intimidated by his presence. "Where would you like these?"

"On the bed will be fine."

How silly of her. Of course he would want sheets and pillows there. She crossed the room and tossed her burden on the foot of the bed. "I see you have a sleeping bag. You came prepared to rough it."

"It's not mine. I think it belongs to Ivan's friend Jeffrey. Apparently he stays here sometimes when his father is upset with him."

"I wasn't aware of that. Was that the reason the doors were locked?"

"It would be a good guess. What do you know about the boy?"

"Not much. He's been friends with Ivan since we arrived. His family lives over the ridge about a half mile as the crow flies but farther by road. His father drives a delivery truck. I don't think the mother works." She crossed her arms as she faced him. "But I'm not here to talk about Jeffrey."

"You want me to know you are in charge of Ivan, and you don't want me to interfere."

He had practically taken the words out of her mouth. Some of her bluster ebbed away. "That's true. I'm the head of the household."

"I understand and I respect that," he said softly.

His intense gaze left her feeling exposed and vulnerable. Could he tell she doubted her ability to keep her family together? That she felt backed into a corner by the bishop's words? There was no way he could know what was in her mind yet she was sure that he did. She started for the door. "I hope you will be comfortable here."

"I hope so, too. Good night, Bethany."

The gentle way he said her name with such longing brought goose bumps to her arms. She hurried out the door before she could change her mind and stay to learn more about her unusual new neighbor.

Early the next morning the sound of someone chopping wood woke Bethany from a restless sleep. Knowing it would be useless to stay in bed, she got up and dressed for the day. Downstairs she put on a pot of coffee and enjoyed one cup in solitude. As she watched the eastern sky grow lighter, her thoughts turned to Michael. Her annoyance had vanished in the night.

Was he right to exclude her from his talk with Ivan? Last night she didn't think so, but now she was able to look at the situation without embarrassment clouding her thinking. She had been prepared to be a buffer between Ivan and Michael. She wanted her brother to make amends, but she didn't want his punishment to be unjust. Perhaps it was better that she stayed out of it and let Ivan face the consequences of his actions alone.

She glanced at the clock on the wall. Once the children were off to school she still intended to have a talk with Michael. Rising to her feet, she started on breakfast. When the eggs and oatmeal were ready, she called up the stairs. "Ivan, Jenny, time to get ready for school."

She returned to the kitchen and set plates and bowls on the table. It wasn't long before Jenny came down still in her nightgown. She made a beeline to the stove, where she warmed her hands. The upstairs bedrooms weren't heated. Hot flannel-wrapped bricks helped stave off some of the chill, but they didn't last all night. The heavy quilts only helped as long as a person stayed in bed.

When Ivan didn't appear, Bethany went to the staircase again. "Ivan. Time to get ready for school. Did you hear me?"

As she was waiting for a reply, the back door opened and he came in bundled from head to toe in his work clothes. He bent to pull off his boots. "We got four more inches of snow last night. The snowplow just went by on the road and left a huge pile of snow on our side."

She stared at him in amazement. "What were you doing outside?"

"I was chopping wood for Michael, and I shoveled the path to his house. I fed and watered our animals, too, but I didn't gather the eggs. Jenny should do that for you. I'm really hungry. What's for breakfast?"

"Scrambled eggs and oatmeal. It is nice of you to make sure Michael had wood for his fireplace."

"I have to do it for a month." He didn't sound resentful at all. He was actually smiling as he sat down at the table and pulled off his stocking cap.

"How long is he making you do my chores?" Bethany asked.

"He isn't making me do them, and they are my chores now."

Somewhat taken aback, Bethany filled their plates and took her place at the foot of the table. She looked at Ivan. "Would you like to sit at the head of the table and lead the prayers from now on?"

Both his eyebrows rose. "Really?"

It was the responsibility of the male head of an Amish household to signal the beginning and the end of the silent blessing before meals. Their grandfather had always been the one to lead prayers. After his death Bethany took over the task, never once considering that it should have fallen to Ivan. To her, he was still a child, but he wasn't little anymore.

She realized her brother was waiting for her reply. "Of course you may."

He moved his plate and sat down opposite her. Bowing his head, he clasped his hands together. Bethany did the same and silently repeated the blessing. When she was finished she waited with her head bowed for Ivan's signal. He unfolded his hands and picked up his fork. Jenny had her eyes closed. Ivan cleared his throat.

Jenny peeked at him with one eye. "Are you done?"

He nodded once. "I am."

"Goot." She reached for her glass of milk.

Ivan poured honey and milk on his oatmeal. "Jenny, I want you to gather the eggs for Bethany every day."

Jenny looked puzzled. "I do it when she asks me to."

"It will be your chore every morning before school, starting tomorrow. Bethany has enough to do."

Jenny shrugged. "Okay. Pass me a piece of toast, Ivan."

Bethany couldn't understand this sudden change in Ivan. What had Michael said to him? She wanted to ask but she didn't want to discuss it in front of her little sister. Jenny had a habit of blurting out things she had overheard.

Later, when the children were ready to go meet the bus, Bethany brought out their lunch boxes. "Ivan, did you complete the homework your teacher gave you?"

"Not all of it, but I'll stay in at recess and get the rest of it done."

"I'm pleased to hear you say that." But could she trust that he meant what he said?

"And you won't skip school again. Is that clear?" she said firmly.

"Michael and I talked about it last night. I won't skip." Ivan took his lunch box from her. "He's a *goot* fellow."

"I like him and his dog." Jenny grabbed her lunch box and headed out the door. Ivan followed close behind her, leaving Bethany more curious than ever about what Michael had said to inspire her brother.

After dressing warmly, she hiked up the hill to the cabin and knocked. She waited and knocked again but he didn't answer. She checked the barn and found his pony and cart were gone. Disappointed, she went back down the hill. Her talk with him would just have to wait.

For most of the next day and a half Michael wrestled with the notion of leaving New Covenant. He came here because he hoped the remoteness of the settlement and a change of scenery would put a stop to his anxiety attacks and flashbacks. To have such a profound episode occur within a week of his arrival was deeply disappointing. In the end he decided he had to stay. There was nowhere else to hide. He didn't want his decision to be emotional. As much as he tried to dismiss one important factor, he couldn't. Bethany was here.

If he was going to stay, he needed to work. He had a choice between building sheds with Jesse and the bishop or doing what he loved. The only drawback with repairing timepieces was that he'd be working for Bethany. He liked her. A lot. But there was no future there as long as he could fall apart at any second. His episode Sunday night had driven that fact home.

He would go back to his original plan. Bury himself in his work and remain apart from people as much as possible. He walked down the hill and found Bethany hanging wash on the line at the side of the house. Her clothesline stretched from the back porch to a nearby pine tree. A pulley system allowed her to pin her clothes on the line and move them out without stepping off the porch into the snow.

He nodded to her. "*Guder mariye*, Bethany. May I see your grandfather's workshop?"

She hesitated a fraction of a second then nodded. "Of course. It's this way."

She walked through the house into the kitchen and opened a door. "This was my grandfather's workroom."

His disappointment must have shown on his face. She tipped her head slightly. "Is something wrong?"

He didn't want a workshop attached to the house where family members could come and go as they pleased. He wanted a space all to himself. "I thought the workshop was one of the other buildings on the farm."

She shook her head. "Grandfather liked being close to us. He usually kept the door open, but if you're thinking that we will disturb you, you can keep it closed."

"I don't like interruptions while I'm working."

Her smile was forced. "That's understandable. We will make it a point to not interrupt you. You may add a bolt to the door or a lock if you prefer."

"That will not be necessary. As long as everyone's aware that I'm not to be bothered while I'm working, that should suffice." He stepped through the doorway into a tidy room with a long workbench in front of a large window. The workbench itself was made of oak. It had four shallow drawers across the front.

He opened the first drawer. Numerous screwdrivers

were lined up by size in a wooden holder that had obviously been custom-made. The next drawer held a jeweler's loupe and several magnifying lenses all nestled into cotton batting. The third drawer held an assortment of gears and springs.Elijah must have scavenged from clocks of all types. The fourth drawer held ledgers, receipt books, stationery and padded envelopes.

Michael looked around the room at the dozen or so clocks hanging on the walls, some in various stages of repair. The running ones ticked softly. "Your grandfather was obviously a man who took great care with his tools." He ran his finger along the top of the workbench. It was satin smooth.

"Daadi believed in a place for everything and everything in its place. He liked to use authentic old tools. He said they simply do the job better than the new ones."

"I have to agree." Along the back of the workbench were several dozen books stacked on top of each other. Michael picked up one and read the title. *"Clocks of the 1800s."*

She picked a book up and ran her fingers over the colorful cover. "Daadi would spend his free time reading about the history of clocks. I would often find him in here late at night poring over antique books on the ancient practice of clock making. I could never understand how he knew what all those little gears and wheels did."

"Repairing a clock can be complicated work, but it can also be simple when the pieces speak for themselves."

"How so?"

"Everything inside of a clock's mechanisms has a purpose. Everything is there for a reason. If you work backward, if you understand what part connects to another part and then another, the clock will tell you what each part does."

She swept her hand through the air, indicating all the timepieces on the walls. "I think you love the art of this the way he did."

"There is something fascinating and beautiful inside each clock I open. I'm happy when I can return it to someone who has treasured it. Often I see them smile when they hear a clock chime again because it brings back good memories."

She smiled softly and swiveled the old leather chair around to face her. "Good memories are important."

She looked at him. "Now that you have had a chance to see the workshop, what do you think? Are you interested in a partnership?"

"I can work in here."

She held out her hand. "Do we have a deal?"

He hesitated a second but then accepted her handshake. "We have a deal."

He held on to her fingers a few seconds longer than he needed to. She blushed as she pulled her hand away.

Bethany couldn't ignore the attraction she felt for Michael. The amazing thing was she had only known him a few days. Maybe letting him work here wasn't a good idea. For some reason she felt off balance when he looked at her with that penetrating gaze of his.

She gave herself a hard mental shake. She was being ridiculous. He needed the work and she needed the income. It wasn't like antique watch repairmen grew on trees. She would have to make sure she kept the relationship strictly business.

"Are you comfortable in the cabin?"

"It's snug. Or it will be when the new window gets in. Pastor Frank took the measurements last night. He's going to order a replacement for me."

She slipped her hands in the pockets of her apron. "Make sure the bill is sent to me. Ivan mentioned that you encouraged him to remain in school. I don't know what else you said to him but he is a changed boy. He's doing chores without being told. He's catching up on his schoolwork. Is he still splitting wood for you?"

"Without fail."

"Good. However, I still think I should have been included in the conversation."

Michael faced her. "Ivan said you treat him like a little child and not like the man of the house. I doubt he would have spoken so plainly about it if you had been in the room. I told him if he'd act like a man he would be treated as such."

"I don't agree with his assessment."

Michael grinned. "I didn't think you would. You have to admit that you don't treat him like a grown fellow."

Of all the nerve. "You haven't been around this family long enough to make an assumption like that."

"It wasn't my assumption. It was Ivan's." He smiled

broadly as if inviting her to share the joke. She didn't find it funny.

"And if Ivan's change of heart wears off in a week or two, I imagine I'll be the one to blame." What possessed her to imagine she was attracted to this man? She knew from the first time they met that he was laughing at her. He was still laughing at her.

His smile faded as he seemed to realize she was upset. "I'm sure he will backslide a time or two. That's only natural. No one is looking to assign blame to you."

"That's just it. Men are assigning blame to me. The bishop, my uncle, they assume I can't control a boy Ivan's age. They want to take the problem off my hands. He isn't a problem. He's my brother. I don't know what we will do if the bishop insists on separating us, but I can tell you I won't stand still for it."

"Defying the bishop could get you shunned."

"There are other Amish communities in Maine. As much as I loved my grandfather and shared his vision for New Covenant, I will move lock, stock and barrel before I give up my brother. You don't need to worry about putting a lock on this door. I will not set foot in this room while you are here."

She walked out and slammed the door behind her.

Chapter Seven

"**Y**ou should invite Michael to eat with us," Ivan said at the dinner table three days after Michael had moved into the cabin.

Bethany had spent much of the time regretting her outburst. She owed him an apology. Michael wasn't the cause of her problem. She shouldn't have taken her ill temper out on him. He had been trying to help.

Michael *had* helped although the bishop might not be able to see the improvement in Ivan's attitude. She was also certain he wouldn't simply take her word for it.

"Why can't Sadie Sue eat with us, too?" Jenny asked.

Bethany leveled a don't-be-ridiculous look at Jenny. "Because I won't allow a dog in the house at mealtime. I don't care how much you like her. As for Michael, I haven't asked him because he specifically said that he likes working alone and he likes his privacy. Now that he is going to be working in Grandfather's shop, I want you both to understand that when that door is closed you are not to go in there."

"But what if I need something?" Jenny asked.

Bethany put down her fork to stare at her sister. "What could you possibly need from Grandfather's workshop?"

"I don't know. I might need to play with Sadie Sue. She likes to fetch sticks."

Bethany tried not to smile at her sister's cajoling tone. "I'm sure there will be plenty of times that you can play with her. Just not while Michael is working."

Ivan helped himself to another dollop of potatoes. "Michael might like to work alone but that doesn't mean he likes to eat alone. You should ask him."

"I'll consider it." That was all she was going to say on the subject. "Are you excited about having Thanksgiving dinner tomorrow at the Lapp farm?"

Jenny held her hand high in the air. "I am. No school for four days."

Bethany looked at her brother. "What about you, Ivan?"

"Jeffrey won't be there. I won't have anyone to hang out with."

"I'm sure that the Miller boys will include you in any games they start." The trio of cousins were in their late teens but they normally included Ivan in their group sports during church get-togethers. There were so few people in New Covenant yet. She wasn't sure that all of those would stay after enduring a Maine winter.

"Is Michael going to be there?" Ivan looked at her hopefully.

Bethany thought back over the times she and Michael had spent together. "I don't believe I mentioned it to him. Jesse may have told him about it."

Ivan pushed back his chair. "I'll go invite him."

"After you finish your supper." Although Bethany hadn't liked hearing that she treated Ivan as a child, she had to admit there were some things their grandfather had done that Ivan could take over.

"I thought perhaps you could read some passages from the Bible for us tonight. I have to work on Jenny's Christmas program costume."

"You really want me to?" He looked amazed.

"Absolutely."

"Sure. I'd be happy to do that. When I'm finished eating can I invite Michael to the Thanksgiving dinner?"

She glanced at the door and then back to her brother. "You'll have to go outside and check if there is a light in the workshop windows. If there is, wait until he is finished working. If there isn't a light, go ahead and go up to the cabin. But first, how was your day at school?"

"I'm caught up on my work." His comment lacked enthusiasm. He wouldn't meet her gaze.

"I'm happy to hear that. What else happened today?"

"Somebody said I stole money from their locker. I didn't but I'm not sure the teacher believed me. She looked through my desk and didn't find anything."

"Oh, Ivan, I'm sorry."

"It's okay."

It wasn't okay but Bethany didn't know how to deal with it. Her brother had built himself a bad reputation. Repairing it would take time. Time he might not have. The bishop would be at the dinner tomorrow. Could she convince him that Ivan had seen the error of his ways after the bishop had heard Jedidiah's tale?

Michael's input might sway the bishop if he could be convinced to attend the dinner. He knew Ivan was chopping wood each day and doing his chores and doing better in school.

She pushed the chicken casserole around on her plate as her appetite vanished. The bishop wouldn't hear Michael's observations if Michael didn't speak to him. She was going to have to apologize to Michael and then ask him to speak on Ivan's behalf as a favor.

Her chicken casserole might as well have been crow. That was what was on the menu for later.

"Ivan, I'll invite Michael to the Thanksgiving dinner at the Lapps' tomorrow. I want you to help your sister practice her lines for the Christmas program."

He looked ready to object but nodded instead. "Okay. I will."

She rose from her chair. "*Danki*. The two of you clear the table. I'm going to speak with Michael."

"Invite Sadie Sue, too," Jenny said.

"*Nee*, I will not invite the dog. If you wish to do something special for her you will have to do it here."

"Can I bake her some cookies?"

"Learn your lines for the Christmas program first."

"All right," Jenny said, but she didn't look happy about it.

Bethany checked the workshop first. The light was off. He must've gone home. She trudged up the hill, bemoaning how quickly it got dark this time of year. As she drew near the cabin she saw Michael was filling a pair of pails at the pump in the yard. His dog sat by his side. She woofed several times, causing him to look around. He caught sight of Bethany and stopped. He watched her with a hint of uncertainty in his eyes. She couldn't blame him.

She forged ahead. "It seems like I am apologizing every time I see you."

He just stared at her.

He wasn't making it easy.

"I wanted to say that I'm sorry for the way I behaved the other day. Although it isn't really an excuse, I am very concerned about my brother. I do not want to send him to live with our uncle. Onkel Harvey is a good man, don't get me wrong. He has a fine family. My reason for wanting to keep Ivan with me is a selfish one. I love my brother. I promised my mother as she lay dying that I would take care of Ivan and Jenny. I don't want to break that promise."

"That's understandable. You are forgiven. There was no need for you to come and apologize."

She pressed a hand to her chest. "I *needed* to apologize."

He picked up one bucket of water and started toward the barn. Bethany picked up the second bucket and followed him. He frowned as he glanced at her. "I can manage this."

"Many hands make light work. Did you find everything you need in my grandfather's workshop today?"

"I did, plus I have many of my own tools."

"I guess that makes sense." In the barn she put the bucket down as he poured the first one into a small tank in the pony's stall. He handed her the empty pail, picked up the full one and poured it into the tank, as well.

He walked out of the barn and Bethany followed him. It appeared that he wasn't in the mood to talk. She followed him anyway.

"I don't know if Jesse mentioned it but our church community is having a Thanksgiving dinner tomorrow. I wanted to make sure you knew you were invited."

"I'll be working."

"It will be a great opportunity to get to know the other Amish families here."

"I'll meet them in time."

"Why wait?" She tried to sound cheerful not desperate.

"Because I'm working tomorrow."

She had hoped she wouldn't have to beg but he left her no choice. "All right, I have a favor to ask of you."

A slight smile curved his lips. "Really? I can't wait to hear this. Has Clarabelle given you the name of a new marriage prospect that you want me to check out?"

"I wish you would forget about the cow."

"I've tried but I can't. It's stuck in my brain."

"Oh, never mind." She turned to go. She'd only taken a few steps when he spoke again.

"Wait. What is it that you need?"

She stayed where she was with her hands pushed deep into the pockets of her coat, so he couldn't see how tightly clenched her fingers were. "The bishop will be there. I need your help convincing him that Ivan has had a change of heart. That he's doing better." She stared at the ground, afraid to see him refuse. "Will you do that? Please?"

Michael groaned inwardly. She had no idea what she was asking. A dinner with dozens of strangers in an unfamiliar house. A crowd. The noise. He grew tense just thinking about it.

Why did she have to look so dejected? So vulnerable? Why was she pinning her hopes on him? It would be amazing if he didn't end the dinner as a babbling ball of fear hiding under the table. He couldn't do it.

She glanced at him from beneath lowered lashes. How could he not do it?

She wanted to keep her family together. He prayed for strength for the first time in months. Sadie Sue whined as she gazed up at him. "I know, I know. It's a bad idea."

He crossed the few steps between them and stopped inches from Bethany. He lifted her chin so she would look at him. "Okay, I'll do it, but you must understand that my words may not carry much weight. I'm new here. I'm not even a member of your congregation yet."

He would speak to the man and then leave. He didn't have to stay for the meal. He would come home and work in peace.

The joy on Bethany's face was almost worth the discomfort he knew he was going to endure. Beneath his fingers her skin was soft as the silk cloths he used to polish his work. Her beautiful eyes were damp with unshed tears. Her lips were red because she had been biting them. He wanted to soothe them with a kiss.

As sure as the sun would rise again tomorrow, he knew one kiss would not be enough.

He stepped away from her. She blinked rapidly and swiped at her unshed tears with both hands. *"Danki."*

"Please tell me I don't have to cook something and take it to eat."

Her laugh was shaky. "I'll make enough for both of us."

"Where is this party taking place?"

"At the Lapp farm. It's about a half mile from here. You met Gemma the other night. The farm belongs to her parents. We might as well ride together, don't you think? I have to take some tables and chairs for them to use. I'll pick you up at noon. That should give you plenty of time to meet people before they start serving at two o'clock."

A half mile wasn't too far. He could walk that distance home alone.

Bethany grabbed his hand. "Bless you. I mean that from the bottom of my heart. Bless you and the good you are doing for my family."

"I'm doing it for Ivan. The kid deserves a break."

She let go of him and pushed her hands deep into her coat pockets. "Of course. He may not realize it yet, but you are a true friend."

As she hurried away he shook his head. Thanksgiving Day would end in disaster for him. He looked down at Sadie Sue. "I am an idiot. Did you know that? You've adopted an idiot for a master."

Michael waited on the porch with his back against the side of the cabin as Bethany drove up in a large wagon the next morning. The children were sitting beside her. His nerves had been on edge since he woke well before dawn. Sadie Sue was shut inside the cabin. He wished he could take her with him.

"Happy Thanksgiving," Bethany called out. The children echoed her greeting. They were staring at him.

All he had to do was walk down the steps and get in her wagon. His palms were damp; his heart was racing. He counted to three and pushed away from the wall. Bethany had Ivan and Jenny get in the back, giving him more room. Getting up onto the seat was easier said than done. The wagon seat was much higher than a buggy. It wasn't graceful but he finally hauled himself up and onto the padded wooden bench.

"All set," he muttered between his clenched teeth.

"Thank you again for doing this."

"Sure, no problem." He hoped.

"I don't see Sadie," Jenny said.

"I locked her in the house." He couldn't believe how much he'd come to rely on the dog. She alerted him when someone was near. When she was at ease, he was at ease.

Bethany spoke to the team and the wagon lurched forward, jarring his leg. Out on the roadway the going was smoother. He let go of his death grip on the side of the seat.

Bethany glanced his way. "Is your leg paining you?"

"Some. I think there's a change in weather coming."

"The newspaper this morning said we could expect a significant snowstorm over the next three days."

"What is 'significant' to the people of Maine?"

"Two, maybe three, in places."

"Inches?"

"Feet," she said with a smile. "Don't worry. Jesse plows our lanes open with his big team but you should invest in some snowshoes before long."

Snowshoes and a cane. How was that going to work? Maybe moving here had been a mistake.

It didn't take long to reach the Lapp farm. Bethany drew the horse to a stop by the front door. The children jumped off the back of the wagon and ran inside. Bethany turned to him. "Can I help you get down?"

He shook his head. "I don't need help. Besides, if I fall I only want one person to get hurt."

She ignored him, jumped down and came around to his side. "I won't let you fall."

"I should believe a woman who talks to cows? Stand aside." He grimaced as he swung his bad leg over the side.

"Nope. Keep one hand on the seat and put your other hand on my shoulder and lower your weight slowly."

"I'm not getting down until you're out of the way."

"You will get very cold sitting here when the sun goes down."

"Stubborn woman."

"I've been called that before."

"Why am I not surprised." He searched for a way to get down without help. It was a long drop. "Okay, I hate to admit it, but your idea looks like my best option."

He gave her his cane and she leaned it against the wagon wheel. Placing his hand on her shoulder, he scooted over the edge of the seat and started to lower himself to the ground.

One horse took a step forward. The cane fell, clattering against the wheel spokes. The other horse tossed her head and took a step, jerking the wagon. Michael lost his grip on the seat and pulled Bethany off balance.

The second he started to fall Bethany wrapped her arms around him and threw herself over backward, trying to take the brunt of his weight. Her head struck the ground with a painful-sounding thump. She didn't make a sound.

"Are you okay? Bethany, are you okay? Speak to me." Michael was holding himself above her on his forearms. His face was inches from hers. Her lids fluttered up. She looked at him and blinked twice.

"You have pretty eyes." Her voice was a bare whisper.

"What?"

She closed her eyes. "Nothing. I'm okay. Are you hurt?"

At least she was talking. "My pride has a big dent in it, but I don't think anything is broken."

"Then could you get off me? You're very heavy." She winced in pain.

"What is going on here?"

Michael looked up to see an older Amish man with a graying beard glaring at him. Jesse stood at his side.

"Hi, Jesse." Michael rolled off Bethany and lay sprawled beside her. His bad leg was on fire, his shoulders ached, and he had skinned both hands trying to keep his full weight from crashing down on her.

"Michael?" Jesse's eyebrows rose until they touched the brim of his black hat.

"It's me. Happy Thanksgiving."

"What are you doing on the ground?"

Michael laughed even though it hurt. "I put my trust in a woman who has conversations with her cow. Big mistake." He turned his head to gaze at Bethany. "Are you sure you aren't hurt?"

"I'm still checking." She pressed a hand to the back of her head.

Her friend Gemma came out of the house. "What has happened? Bethany, is that you?"

Bethany pushed herself into a sitting position. "Hello, Gemma. Happy Thanksgiving."

Jesse was still frowning at Michael. "I don't understand what you are doing on the ground."

"Bethany kindly gave me a ride here, and when I was trying to get out of her wagon, I fell on her. It was an accident. I think she hit her head pretty hard."

Gemma helped Bethany to her feet. "You poor thing. Are you injured?"

Bethany managed a half-hearted smile. "Only bumps and bruises. I'm afraid Michael is the one who is hurt."

Michael struggled to his feet with Jesse's assistance

and leaned against the wagon. "I'm fine. Where's my cane?"

The elderly Amish man beside Jesse picked it up and handed it to Michael with a scowl on his face. "I am Bishop Schultz."

"Just the man I wanted to see. I'm Michael Shetler. I'm a newcomer to the area."

The bishop stroked his beard as he stared at Michael. "Jesse has told me about you."

"I need to unpack the tables and chairs," Bethany said.

"Someone else can take care of that. You need a few minutes' rest to regain your wits," Michael told her in a stern tone.

She scowled at him. "My wits are not scattered."

"That's open to debate. You hit your head pretty hard. You could have a concussion. Gemma, make her go inside and rest."

Michael caught the sidelong glare Bethany shot at him. She wasn't happy to have him telling her what to do. Too bad. In his opinion, she was too pale. He didn't want her keeling over and spoiling the party. That was his job.

Gemma smiled kindly at Michael as she took Bethany's arm. "He is right. Come in. I have some fresh brewed sweet tea and my special lemon cookies, and I'm going to fix an ice pack for your head."

"I would speak with you, Bethany, when you are recovered," Bishop Schultz said. Bethany grew a shade paler.

Inside the house the mouthwatering smells of roasting turkey, fresh baked breads and pumpkin pies filled the air. Michael saw Ivan seated beside two teenage boys looking through a hunting magazine. He beckoned to the boy. "Ivan, can I see you a minute?"

Ivan came over. "What's up?"

"Ask your friends to help you bring in the tables and chairs from the back of the wagon and take care of the horses."

"Sure." He went back to the boys and they all walked outside. A few minutes later they came in carrying the extra seating. Gemma's mother directed them where to set up. Another family arrived with baskets of food, and a festive air began to fill the room as happy chatter and laughter grew in volume.

Michael stayed beside Bethany, who was seated in a wingback chair near the fireplace. She soon had a plate of cookies on her lap and a glass of tea in her hand. Her color was already better when Gemma brought her the ice pack. Michael knew Bethany had taken the brunt of the fall trying to protect him. It should have been the other way around.

His gaze was constantly drawn to her. Her color returned to normal, but the longer he watched her the more flushed she became. Every time he caught her eye she looked away.

After ten minutes, Bethany set her empty glass aside. "I should be helping in the kitchen."

Bethany couldn't take Michael staring at her another minute. Didn't he realize everyone was noticing his attention? She blushed at being the recipient of so many speculative looks. She was about to get up when the bishop approached her with Jedidiah a few steps behind him.

The bishop settled himself in a nearby chair. "Are you feeling recovered, Bethany?"

"I have a headache that I'm sure will get better quickly. Jedidiah, did you get my letter and the check?"

"I did. It was a fair price, though the cost was not the issue. I trust Ivan will repay you?"

She clasped her hands together. "I want you both to know that my brother has improved his attitude one hundred percent since that incident."

"Even if that is true, it is too little too late." The bishop's stern look chilled her.

She gestured to Michael. "This is Michael Shetler. He has taken over Grandfather's watch repair business. He can attest to Ivan's improvements. He has seen it firsthand."

"In what way?" Jedidiah asked.

"The boy broke a window in the cabin I rented from Bethany. I had a talk with him. We settled on his punishment. He has split wood for me every morning, has taken over many of Bethany's outdoor chores, and he has improved his grades at school. I believe his friend has been the instigator of much of the trouble Ivan has been in."

The bishop folded his arms over his chest. "If that is true, the boy has shown bad judgment in his choice of friends."

Jedidiah shifted his weight from one foot to the

other. "I spoke with his teacher yesterday evening. We happened to be in the grocery store at the same time. She tells me some of the *Englisch* children have accused Ivan of stealing money."

"One child did. She searched his desk and didn't find anything. It wasn't Ivan," Bethany insisted.

The bishop's face grew somber. "I wish I could give him the benefit of the doubt, but there have been too many instances where he has been involved. Jedidiah has offered to take the boy until his uncle arrives. He feels he can give Ivan the supervision he needs. I have agreed to this."

"*Nee*, you can't take him from me. You can't."

"What if I were to take responsibility for the boy?" Michael offered.

Chapter Eight

Michael was certain that he had lost his mind. The look on Bethany's face told him she thought he was her hero.

The bishop regarded him intently. "Are you sure you understand what this means?"

"I do. I will oversee the boy's discipline. I will stand as substitute for his father. Any person who has difficulties or accusations against the boy can address them with me. If you will allow me, then the boy does not have to leave Bethany's care or his home. Should he go to live with Jedidiah now, he will be unable to complete the bargain he has with me."

The bishop nodded slowly. "I appreciate what Jedidiah has offered. I didn't feel right taking the boy from his sister's care, but I saw no other choice after Jedidiah told me about the theft of his goods. You have given me one. You are new to us but Jesse has vouched for your character, Michael, otherwise I would not agree to this, but I trust his judgment. This arrangement will be only until the boy's uncle arrives at Christmas," the bishop added. "I want to be clear that this isn't a permanent situation, and that you are accepting financial responsibility as well as a moral responsibility to see that Ivan behaves himself."

"I understand that."

Bethany's hopeful gaze was pinned on Michael. "You don't have to do this."

He considered retracting his offer but he wasn't prepared to see the Martin family split up. "I understand that. I want to do it. I'll speak to Ivan about it when we get home today."

"Agreed." The bishop smiled broadly. Even Jedidiah looked relieved. The two men walked away.

"I can't thank you enough," Bethany said with tears in her eyes.

"Let's hope Ivan feels the same way." He was already regretting his rash gesture. His intention was to spend less time with Bethany and her family, not more.

Bethany heard the hesitancy in Michael's voice. "You won't be sorry you did this. It proves that you believe in my brother and that is priceless to me."

Michael rubbed his hands on his pants. "I think I need some fresh air."

He left the room. Once he was out of sight, Gemma hurried over to sit beside Bethany. "What was that all about?"

"Ivan."

"I was afraid that's what the bishop had on his mind

when he cornered you. Is he still sending the boy away at Christmas?"

"He wanted to send him to live with Jedidiah until then, but Michael volunteered to be responsible for him."

"How did you manage that?"

"It was his own idea."

Gemma leaned forward eagerly. "Tell me all about your mystery man."

"There isn't much to tell. Apparently, he corresponded with Daadi about working for him. He had already paid the first and last months' rent on the cabin. He likes to keep to himself. And he's from Sugarcreek, Ohio."

"I don't mean the dry details. Does he have a girlfriend back in Ohio? Is he looking to marry? Does he have money?"

"How would I know that?"

Gemma chuckled. "You don't know how to snoop. I could find all that out in ten minutes."

"I'm not so sure. He doesn't like to talk about himself."

"Then he is hiding something. I wonder what it is. How did he know your grandfather?"

"He didn't really. A jeweler by the name of George Meyers recommended Michael to my grandfather and that's all I know. He and Ivan get along. I'm grateful for that."

"You like him, don't you?"

Bethany was wary of the eager look in her friend's eyes. "He's nice enough."

"I'd say he's a lot better than Jesse Crump or Jedidiah. I can't believe he fell into your lap and all you can say is that he's nice enough. He is the answer to your prayers."

"What are you talking about?"

"You need a husband by Christmas and Michael Shetler appears out of the blue. God moves in mysterious ways."

"You're being ridiculous. There is nothing between us."

"I wouldn't say that. I noticed the way he looked at you when he was sitting beside you. We all noticed. He's interested. The man has potential. With a little effort on your part, you could have him eating out of your hand. I've got to go help Mamm. Can I get you anything else?"

Bethany shook her head and winced. She pressed a hand to the back of her aching head. "I'm gonna sit here with my ice pack for a little longer."

Gemma patted Bethany's knee. "Let me know if you need anything."

Jenny came running to Bethany's side along with Sadie Sue. "Look, sister. I didn't invite her. She came all by herself."

"I wonder how she got out." Bethany stared at the dog. She was sure Michael had locked her in.

Sadie's attention turned to the tables where the food was being set out. She licked her chops. Bethany foresaw a disaster. "*Nee*, Jenny, take her outside."

"But why?"

"Because I asked you to."

"Okay. Come on, Sadie Sue." Jenny headed toward the back door, taking Sadie within a few feet of the table and a steaming plate of sausages. The dog stopped and eyed the dish as Jenny went out the door. No one else was near the dog.

Bethany rose from her chair. "*Nee*, Sadie Sue. Don't do it."

Jenny opened the back door and looked in. "Sadie, come on."

The dog gave the sausages a forlorn glance and trotted out the door. Bethany sank back in her chair with a sigh of relief.

"Was that my dog?" Michael asked as he came in from outside.

"*Ja*, it was Sadie Sue." Remembering Gemma's comments, Bethany found herself tongue-tied. Did he find her attractive? Or was his attentiveness just part of his makeup that had nothing to do with her? Bethany wished she could tell what he was thinking.

He scratched the back of his head. "I wonder how she got out of the house."

Bethany shrugged.

"How are you feeling?" he asked.

"Better." She kept her demeanor cool. Were people watching them and speculating? She caught sight of Gemma smiling widely. Her friend winked.

"I'm glad to hear you are better. I'm going to go take Sadie home and see how she escaped. I hope we don't have to replace another windowpane."

"Will you be coming back?"

"*Nee*, you stay and enjoy your friends. I have work to do."

She didn't want him to go. She was torn by her conflicting feelings. "Don't you even want something to eat?"

"I have plenty back at the cabin. Get someone to drive you home if you aren't feeling better."

"Ivan can drive the wagon."

Michael nodded and walked away. When he opened the door he glanced back at her with such a look of longing that it startled her. Was there something between them and she had been too blind to see it?

Bethany decided the family would walk to the church service on Sunday instead of taking the buggy. The preaching was being held at the home of Nigel and Becca Miller. Their farm was little more than a quarter of a mile beyond the Lapp place. Nigel was a carpenter who made furniture in the off-season.

An unexpectedly warm southern wind was melting the snow, making the sunshine feel even brighter. Rivulets of water trickled along the ditches and flowed out of the snow-covered fields. Amish families—some on foot, most in buggies—were all headed in the same direction. Cheerful greetings and pleasant exchanges filled the crisp air. Everyone was glad to see a break in the weather.

Bethany declined numerous offers of a ride, content to stretch her legs on such a fine morning. The icy grip of winter would return all too soon. Jenny and Ivan trudged along beside her, enjoying the sunshine.

She turned in at the farm lane where a dozen buggies were lined up on the hillside just south of the barn. The horses, still wearing their harnesses, were tied up along a split-rail fence, content to munch on the hay spread in front of them or doze in the sunshine.

The early morning activity was focused around the barn. Men were busy unloading backless seats from the large gray boxlike bench wagon that was used to transport the benches from home to home for the services held every other Sunday. Bishop Schultz was supervising the unloading. When the wagon was empty, he conferred with his minister.

Bethany entered the house. Inside, it was a flurry of activity as the women arranged food on counters and tables. Several small children were being watched over by the Millers' niece. She beckoned Jenny to come help her. The Miller boys were outside playing a game of tag and Ivan went to join them.

Catching sight of Gemma unpacking baskets of food, Bethany crossed the room toward them and handed over her basket of food for the lunch that would be served after the service. "*Guder mariye,* Gemma."

"Good morning, Bethany. Isn't the weather wonderful?"

"It is." Turning to Becca Miller, Bethany grinned at the baby she held. Little Daniel was six months old with a wide toothless grin and a head of white-blond curls. "Wow, how this little boy is growing. May I hold him?"

"Of course. I hate to admit it but he gets heavy quickly these days." Becca handed the baby over with a timid smile.

Bethany took Daniel and held him to her shoulder, enjoying the feel of a baby in her arms and his wonderful smell. "You're not so heavy."

"He should be. He eats like a little piglet." There was nothing but love in Becca's eyes as she gazed at her son.

Gemma said, "I see the bishop and minister coming. We'd best hurry and join the others in the barn."

As she spoke, Bishop Schultz and Samuel Yoder entered the house and went upstairs, where they would discuss the preaching that was to be done that morning. The three-to-four-hours-long service would be preached without the use of notes. Each man had to speak as God moved him.

Bethany handed the baby back to Becca. The women quickly finished their tasks and left the house.

The barn was already filled with people sitting quietly on rows of backless wooden benches with the women on one side of the aisle and men on the other side. Tarps had been hung over ropes stretched between upright timbers to cordon off an area for the service. Behind them, the sounds of cattle, horses and pigs could be heard. The south-facing doors were open to catch what warmth the sunshine and wind could provide.

Bethany took her place among the unmarried women. Gemma and Jenny sat beside her. In front of them sat the married women, several holding infants. Becca slipped a string of beads and buttons from her pocket. She handed them to her little one. He was then content and played quietly with his toy. Her older boys sat beside their father.

From the men's side of the aisle, the song leader announced the hymn. There was a wave of rustling and activity as people opened their thick black song-books. The *Ausbund* contained the words of all the hymns but no musical scores. The songs, sung from memory, had been passed down through countless generations. They were sung slowly and in unison by people opening their hearts to receive God's pres-ence without the distraction of musical instruments. The slow cadence allowed everyone to focus on the meaning of each word.

At the end of the first hymn, Bethany took a mo-ment to glance toward the men's side. She spotted Michael sitting behind the married men with Ivan. Her brother squirmed in his seat, looking restless. Michael, on the other hand, held his songbook with a look of intense devotion on his face.

He glanced in her direction and she smiled at him. He immediately looked away and she felt the pinch of his rejection. She hadn't spoken to him since Thanks-giving. Was something wrong? Was he regretting his decision to mentor Ivan? Her brother was thrilled. He didn't object to Michael standing in his father's role.

The song leader announced the second hymn, "O Gott Vater, wir Loben dich" ("Oh God the Father, We Praise You"). It was always the second hymn of an Amish service. Bethany forgot about Michael and her brother as she joined the entire congregation in singing God's praise, asking that the people present would receive His words and take them into their hearts.

At the end of the second hymn, the minister and Bishop Schultz came in and hung their hats on pegs set in the wall. That was the signal that the preaching would now begin. Bethany tried to listen closely to what was being said, but she found her mind wandering to the subject of Michael. What might he be looking for in a wife?

Michael sat up straight and unobtrusively stretched his bad leg. He was still stiff after his fall on Thursday. The wooden benches were not made for comfort. At least he hadn't fallen asleep the way their host Nigel Miller was doing. A few minutes after the preaching started, the farmer started nodding off in front of Michael. When Nigel began to tip sideways, Michael reached up and caught his arm before he tumbled off his seat.

Nigel jerked awake. *"Danki,"* he whispered as he gave Michael a sheepish grin.

Michael ventured a guess. "Working late?"

Nigel shook his head. "Colicky baby."

He leaned forward to look over at the women. Following his gaze, Michael saw Nigel's wife sitting across the aisle. Becca Miller held the baby sleeping sweetly in her arms. Her face held an expression of pure happiness when she caught her husband's glance. Bethany sat behind her.

What Michael wouldn't give to see Bethany look at him with a similar light in her eyes.

He quickly focused on his hymnal. Such day-dreaming was foolishness. He wasn't husband material. He might never be. He tried to push thoughts of Bethany aside but they came back to him at odd times and more often than he cared to admit. He hadn't had another flashback or panic episode since the previous Sunday, but that didn't mean he was well.

Three hours into the service, the bishop stopped speaking and the song leader called out the number of the final hymn. Michael ventured a look in Bethany's direction. She held her songbook open for Jenny seated beside her. She pointed out the words as she sang them.

Bethany should have children of her own. She would make a good mother. He couldn't imagine why God had chosen not to bless her with a husband and children of her own. It didn't seem right.

The song drew to a close. Ivan was up and out the doors the second it ended. Teenage boys were expected to sit at the very back. Michael always assumed it was so their late arrivals and quick getaways didn't disrupt others. He followed more slowly. His eyes were drawn to Bethany as she walked toward the farmhouse with the other women.

How much of his life would he spend like this, watching her from afar, wishing for something that could never happen? Months? Years? What if he never got well?

* * *

On Monday afternoon just before the children came home from school, Bethany got out her crafting supplies and spread them on the table. She made a batch of oatmeal cookies and a pot of peppermint hot chocolate and left it simmering on the back of the stove.

She was cutting and folding card stock paper when Ivan and Jenny came in the door. Jenny's eyes lit up. "Is it time to make our Christmas cards?"

"*Ja*, it is time. Do you have your lists of the people you want to send them to?"

Both children were well prepared and provided a list of more than a dozen people each that they would handcraft a greeting card for. Bethany had her own list that included every family in the New Covenant congregation as well as Pastor Frank, the children's teachers, bus driver and many of the merchants in town that she did business with.

After two mugs each of the hot chocolate and a plate of cookies, they were laughing and sharing ideas for cards. Jenny loved to draw a snow-covered tree branch with a cardinal sitting on it. She added silver glitter to the snow and red glitter to the birds. Ivan liked making construction paper cutouts of a horse and sleigh and gluing them to the card stock. He covered the snowy foreground with glitter. Bethany enjoyed making snowmen out of cotton balls glued together inside the card.

Before long there was glitter on the table, glitter on the floor and glitter on the children, but Bethany didn't care. She had to make this Christmas a special one in case they weren't together next year. "Ivan, you didn't tell me what song you'll be singing at the community Christmas program." Since religious-themed programs could no longer be held in the public schools, the community had decided to keep the Christmas pageant alive and well in the community center. The children and their teachers who wished to participate were eagerly welcomed.

Ivan didn't look up from crafting his card. "I'm going to sing 'O Come, O Come, Emmanuel.'"

"That's one of my favorites. Will you sing it for me now?" she asked with a catch in her throat.

He did and there were tears in her eyes by the time he finished. "That was fine. God has blessed you with a wonderful singing voice."

Jenny laid down her scissors. "I want to sing a song."

Bethany blinked away her tears and smiled. "What song would you like to perform?"

"'Go Tell It on the Mountain.'"

"That's a fine song. Let's all sing it together." Bethany hummed the first note and they all joined in singing at the top of their lungs to the very last verse.

"I don't know how you expect me to get any work done with all the noise and the delicious smell of hot chocolate coming from this room."

Bethany looked up to see Michael standing in the doorway with an indulgent smile lighting his face. Sadie Sue ambled over to Jenny. She got a hug and a pat before settling to the floor beside Jenny's chair with a sprinkling of red glitter across her head.

Bethany pointed at Michael. "That door is to remain closed while you are working."

He held his hands wide. "I'm done for the evening."

"In that case, pull up a chair and start making your Christmas cards. They have to go in the mail by the end of this week if you want them to arrive on time."

"I haven't sent many cards in the last few years, but I will definitely take some of that hot chocolate. Is that peppermint I smell?"

"Help yourself. I will make a list of people for you. Let's start with your mother and father. They will get a card, right?"

He nodded as he filled a white mug from the pot. "I have three brothers and two sisters."

She wrote down the names and addresses that he gave her. She sat poised with a pen. "Grandparents?"

"Gone, I'm afraid."

"Mr. Meyers at the jewelry store where you used to work? Grandfather always sent him one. How about some of the people you worked with? Are you still friends with them?"

He paused with the mug halfway to his mouth. He slowly lowered it. "I don't have friends there anymore."

He put the mug down, walked back into the workroom and closed the door.

Bethany didn't know what to make of his abrupt retreat. She looked at Ivan. "Did I say something wrong?"

Ivan shrugged. "He was shot during a robbery there. He doesn't like to talk about it."

Bethany stared at her brother, unsure she'd heard him correctly. "Michael was shot?"

Ivan nodded. "That's why he limps. I wasn't supposed to tell you. You won't tell him I mentioned it, will you?"

Bethany shook her head. "I won't say anything."

No wonder Michael didn't like to talk about his injury. Someone had robbed him at gunpoint and shot him. Was he the only one? Or were there others, too? She thought back to something her grandfather had mentioned. He told her the man who sent him watches to fix had a store robbed. Somewhere she had her grandfather's correspondences. He kept everything in case he had to prove the work had been done and the timepieces had been returned.

Some things about Michael began to make sense. The way he was always vigilant. He didn't like crowds. He often stood with his back to the wall. She assumed he was leaning against the wall to rest his leg, but he might just as easily have been doing it to assure himself there was no one behind him.

She looked at Ivan and Jenny. "Let's make Christmas cards for Michael's family. It can be our Christmas gift to him. What do you think?" They both agreed and got to work.

Later that evening, Bethany carried a lantern into her grandfather's room. She put it down on his bedside table and pulled a large box from under his bed. She opened it and began to search for letters from George Meyers. She found the one she was looking for. Holding it in her hand, Bethany was torn by the feeling that she was invading Michael's privacy by snooping into his past. Would it tell her what she needed to know about Michael and what troubled him? Like her brother, she didn't know how to help Michael if she didn't know what was wrong.

She opened the letter and began reading.

Chapter Nine

Michael peered through his jeweler's loupe at a tiny screw he was attempting to insert into the mechanism of an antique gold pocket watch. His concentration was broken by the thump-thump-thump of Sadie Sue's tail against the floor. It was her signal that he wasn't alone but the visitor was someone she knew.

He couldn't believe what a difference having the dog had made on his anxiety level. He was confident in her ability to alert him to strangers. He didn't feel the need to constantly scan his surroundings for danger as often. When he did get agitated, she would distract him by nuzzling him for affection or bringing him the red ball she loved to fetch and dropping it in his lap.

"What are you doing?" Jenny asked as she came up beside him. His workbench was just high enough to allow her to rest her hands and chin on it.

"I'm working. Are you supposed to be in here?"

"I can't come in when the door is closed."

"Is the door closed, Jenny?" He turned the loupe up so that he could see her face. She was the perfect picture of boredom.

"It was closed but then it opened, so I came in."

He tipped his head to the side. "Did it open because you turned the doorknob?"

"Maybe. Are you mad?"

He sighed heavily. "What do you need, Jenny?"

"I want someone to play hide-and-seek with me. Will you, please?"

"I'm working. Ask your sister to play with you."

"She's doing the laundry."

"Then perhaps your brother would enjoy playing with you."

"He says I'm too little and that I'm just a pest. I'm not a pest, am I?"

Michael put down his screwdriver. The tiny screw popped off the magnetized end and went rolling off the workbench onto the floor. He pressed his lips into a hard line. "You are not a pest, but I don't have time to play, Jenny. I have work to do."

Her hopeful expression dissolved into a serious pout.

He got off his stool and awkwardly dropped to one knee to see under the bench. Jenny picked the screw up and handed it to him. "No one wants to play with me."

He paused and thought for a minute. "Why aren't you in school?"

"'Cause the teachers have to go to meetings for two days."

He got back on his work stool. "Play with Sadie."

"Sadie Sue can't play hide-and-seek. She can't count."

He put his loupe back on. "I'm sure Sadie can learn to play hide-and-seek with a little help from you. You go hide, and I will send her to find you." If he was fortunate, he could have ten or twenty minutes of uninterrupted work time before she came looking for the dog.

Bethany opened the door. "Jenny, I thought I told you to stay out of the workroom while Michael is in here."

"He wants me to play with Sadie Sue."

Bethany folded her arms across her chest. "Then bring the dog with you and leave Michael alone."

"We're playing hide-and-seek. I'm going to go hide. Michael, you count for her." Jenny took off at a run.

He waited a long moment, then looked at his dog. "Ten." She wagged her tail.

Bethany grinned at him. She had the most contagious smile. It boosted his spirits every time he saw it. "I'm sorry Jenny bothered you. She has been out of school for the past two days because of teachers' meetings. I think she has a touch of cabin fever."

"I'm ready," Jenny called from somewhere in the house.

Michael looked down at the dog. "Go find Jenny."

Sadie Sue didn't move. He patted her head. *"Goot hund."*

Bethany arched one eyebrow. "I see your plan. Jenny stays hidden and you get some work done?"

"It was the dog's idea." He put his tools down. "What are you baking that smells so good?"

"It's a turkey-and-rice casserole for supper. Is your compliment a sly way of asking if you can join us for supper?"

"You read me like a book."

She tipped her head to study him. "I wish that was true."

He looked away first. He would be in deep trouble if she actually could read his mind. At the moment he was wondering what it would be like to kiss her.

"You are always welcome to eat with us, Michael. You never need an invitation." She paused, looking as if she wanted to say something else. Her indecision vanished. She smiled softly. "If you'll excuse me, I have to go find Jenny."

She clapped her hands together. "Come on, Sadie. Let's leave Michael to finish his work." Sadie rose and followed Bethany out of the room.

Michael picked up his screwdriver but working had lost its appeal. He laid his equipment aside and went out to the kitchen.

Bethany was diligently checking hiding places for her sister. He was the one who happened to notice that the door to the cellar was open a crack.

He clicked his fingers and Sadie trotted to him. He whispered in her ear and then gave her a small push toward the door. She trotted right past her quarry without seeing her. Jenny would've been safe if she hadn't giggled. Sadie spun around and pushed her nose in behind the door.

"Aw, you found me." Jenny patted the dog's head

and looked to Michael. "Keep her here while I go hide again."

"Wait a minute." He turned to the refrigerator and opened it. There were several links of cooked sausage left over from breakfast. He picked up the plate and looked at Bethany. "Is it okay if I give this to the dog?"

"Feed *goot* food to a dog? Are you serious?"

"Please?" he cajoled. He used the same tone on Bethany that Jenny had used on him. To his surprise, it worked.

"Very well, but I don't see why the dog needs sausages. She's filled out fine on dog chow."

He motioned to Jenny. "Come here. We are going to teach Sadie Sue to find you so you two can play hide-and-seek and leave me alone."

Bethany's eyes brightened. "That might work. Good thinking. Where did you learn how to train dogs?"

"I've never owned a dog before. This will be trial and error." He crumbled the links into pieces and gave them to Jenny. "Put these in your pocket. When I say 'find Jenny,' I want you to hold out a piece in your hand. Got it?"

"Sure."

"Sadie, find Jenny." Sadie cocked her head to the side as she stared at him.

Jenny fished a piece of sausage out of her pocket and held it out to the dog. "Here, girl."

Sadie never needed a second invitation where food was concerned. She ambled over to Jenny and gently took the piece of meat from her hand.

"That was fine," Michael said. "Now I will take her

a little farther away. This time, Jenny, don't say anything. Just hold out your hand."

He took Sadie by the collar and led her to the other side of the room but her eyes were still on the little girl. He turned the dog so she was facing the other way. "Sadie, find Jenny."

Sadie spun around and made a beeline for Jenny, gulped down the piece of meat and barked.

Jenny laughed. "I think that means she wants some more."

"She will have to earn another piece." He took the dog by the collar and led her to the other side of the room.

Bethany regarded him with an amused expression. "You have taught a dog to eat sausage. Everyone will be amazed."

"Don't be a doubting Thomas." This time he took Sadie out into the workroom. "Sadie, find Jenny." The dog galloped from the room straight to Jenny and claimed her tidbit.

He was pleased with his experiment so far. "Now comes the real test. Jenny, I want you to go into the other room where Sadie can't see you. I want you to be quiet. Don't call her. Let's see if she will go look for you."

Jenny hurried out of the room. Bethany smothered a giggle. "I think the command should be 'go find sausage.' If I ever lose my breakfast meat I'll know who to call on. Michael and his amazing Sadie Sue."

"Scoff all you want. This is going to work." He looked down at the dog. "Sadie, find Jenny."

Sadie remained at his side watching him intently

with her whole back end wagging. Bethany started laughing. She swung her arm out, pointed toward the doorway and yelled, "Find sausage!" Sadie started barking at her.

As much as he enjoyed the sound of Bethany's laughter, he didn't appreciate her lack of confidence. "She is going to get this. Jenny, come back here."

Jenny walked in the room looking confused. "Did I do it wrong?"

He shook his head. "You did fine. It is Sadie who needs a little more work. Why don't you go put on your coat and boots and we will take this outside, where there aren't so many confusing smells for Sadie and fewer people who want to make fun of her."

Jenny put her arms around Sadie's neck. "You'll get it. I know you will. You're the smartest dog in the whole wide world." Sadie licked her face, making her giggle. Jenny headed for the coatrack. Sadie Sue followed with her nose pressed to Jenny's pocket.

Michael met Bethany's gaze and saw her affection for him in the depths of her eyes. His heart tripped over itself. She cared for him. He knew it as surely as if she spoke the words out loud.

He was falling for this amazing, beautiful, caring woman and he had no idea how to change course.

He had little to offer. He was a broken man. Nothing more than a jumble of pieces like some of the watches that came to him. Sometimes a boxful of gears and a dial couldn't be assembled to work properly no matter how much the owner wanted it repaired.

Bethany tipped her head slightly. "What?"

He shook his head and looked away. "Nothing. I was thinking about a broken watch I received the other day."

"Why does that make you sad?"

"Who said I was sad?"

She leaned closer. "I read you like a book, remember?"

Then she should be able to see how much he had grown to care for her. "It's sad because the watch can't be fixed."

"Why not?"

He turned away, afraid she could see what he was thinking. "An important part is broken. It can't be mended." He was the broken timepiece and could never forget it.

"Do you think another watch repair business might have the part you need?"

"It's not likely."

"If you really want to restore it, you should ask if someone else can help you. What about asking Mr. Meyers for help?"

Michael heard something in her voice he didn't understand. He looked at her sharply. "What do you know about George Meyers?"

She rubbed her hands together. "He supplied my grandfather with the majority of his work. He also suggested my grandfather write to you and offer you a job here."

Michael tensed. "I told you that."

"I was going through some of Grandfather's things last night and I found the letter George Meyers sent to Grandpa."

Michael swallowed hard. What else was in the letter? "Was it informative?"

"He said you were injured during a robbery at the store."

He shouldn't be surprised. It was newsworthy. "What else did the letter say?"

"That three of his employees were killed by the robbers," she said gently.

He closed his eyes. "That's true."

"I'm so sorry. It must have been terrible for you."

He couldn't speak. Did she pity him now? He couldn't look at her. "What else did George tell your grandfather?"

"Mr. Meyers wanted you to have a chance to start over. I'm glad he asked Grandfather to contact you."

Michael glanced up at her. She meant it. If George had mentioned that Michael was off in the head, Bethany didn't share it. Michael relaxed. George Meyers had given him more than a chance to continue his work. He'd given him a chance at a new life. It had been nearly two weeks since his last PTSD episode. Perhaps he truly was getting better here.

Was his new life one that could include Bethany and the children?

The thought was almost unimaginable. His skin grew clammy. The idea that Bethany might one day love him was terrifyingly wonderful. Was it possible? Did he deserve such a gift? If only he could be sure he would get well.

"I'm ready," Jenny called from the front hall.

"I'll meet you on the back lawn." He was glad of

the distraction. He needed to forget about a relationship with Bethany that was anything other than professional. He went out to the workroom, grabbed his coat, pulled on his overshoes and went out the side door with Sadie at his heels. He didn't want Bethany drawn into the darkness that hid inside him, waiting to spring out.

Jenny, dressed in her dark blue coat and bright red mittens, was waiting for him on the snow-covered lawn. She had a red-and-blue knit cap pulled over her white prayer *kapp*. Scooping up some snow, she formed a snowball and tossed it from hand to hand.

"Fetch it, Sadie." Jenny threw the ball, and the dog made a dive for it into a drift, leaving only her back legs and tail visible. She pulled out of the snowbank and shook vigorously, pelting Jenny with clumps of snow. Jenny stumbled and fell. Sadie started licking her face, making Jenny giggle as she tried to fend off the determined pooch. "Stop it, Sadie, stop it."

"She must think you're a sausage," Bethany called from the doorway. She had her arms crossed over her chest and her shoulders hunched against the cold.

Michael packed a snowball and threw it. It smacked against the side of the house above Bethany's head, sending a shower of snow her way. She ducked and brushed the crystals from her clothes. "Hey, that's not fair. I'm not dressed for a snowball fight."

"Then go back inside. Sadie needs to concentrate. You're distracting her." In truth, he was the one distracted by her presence.

"Well, don't expect to get any more sausage from me." She was smiling as she shut the door. A few seconds later he saw her draw the shade aside at the window so she could watch them.

For the next hour he and Jenny worked at teaching Sadie to find the girl. By the time they were both too cold to continue, Sadie was getting it right about half the time. She was still more interested in hunting among the trees than she was in finding Jenny even for a piece of sausage.

"I say we call it quits," Michael said as he sat down on the back porch steps and rubbed his aching thigh.

"She's almost got it." Jenny sat beside him.

"If we work with her a few more days I think she will find you most times, as long as a rabbit doesn't run in front of her."

Jenny tipped her head to smile at him. "Maybe if I had a rabbit in my pocket instead of sausage she would do better."

"You may be onto something. Where can we get a bunch of pocket-size rabbits?"

"You're funny, Michael."

"You are, too, Jenny."

"Are you going to stay with us a long time?"

He shrugged. "That's a hard question to answer."

"Don't you like it here?"

"Truthfully, I don't like the cold."

"Wait till summer. Then you'll really love it here."

He brushed snow from the top of her hat. "I will be here that long, anyway."

"Why don't you have a wife?"

He leaned back to stare at her. "That's kind of a personal question."

"Well? Why don't you?"

"I guess because I've never met someone that I wanted to marry."

"Gemma says my sister needs to be married so Ivan can stay here and not have to go live with our *onkel* Harvey."

"I know your sister loves Ivan just like she loves you. But when people get married it has to be because they love each other and not for any other reason."

"You don't have a wife. You could marry Bethany and you'd sort of be my *daed*."

"It's not that simple.

"All the kids in my class have *daeds*. Sometimes they feel sorry for me. There is going to be a father-daughter program in the spring. It would be nice if you could come as my *daed*."

"Jenny, Bethany and I are not going to get married, but I will take you to the father-daughter program anyway. How's that?"

She smiled brightly. "You will?"

"I promise."

"That makes me happy. Can we go in now? My toes are cold."

"Excellent idea. My everything is cold."

She got up and took hold of his hand to pull him to his feet. To his surprise, she hung on to his hand as they walked into the house.

Bethany was sitting beside the window, mending one of Ivan's shirts, when Jenny and Michael came in. "How goes the training?"

"We've decided that to be one hundred percent effective Jenny must have a rabbit in her pocket when she gets lost. Sadie Sue likes hunting rabbits a little bit more than she likes tracking down Jenny even for a bite of sausage."

The dog, who had been sitting quietly beside Michael, suddenly took off toward the front door. She barked several times when someone knocked.

Bethany got up and went to answer the door. Her *Englisch* neighbor, Greg Janson, tipped his hat. "Good evening, Ms. Martin. I would like a few minutes of your time to discuss something that happened on my farm last night."

A sense of foreboding filled Bethany. "Does this have anything to do with Ivan?"

"In fact it does. I've come to you first. But I'm not opposed to going to the sheriff."

Bethany invited him in. Michael stood in the hallway. Bethany indicated him with one hand. "Michael, this is Greg Janson. He has the farm south of here. Mr. Janson, this is Michael Shetler. He is a business partner."

Mr. Janson nodded. Bethany led the way into the kitchen. "Would you like some coffee, Mr. Janson?"

"No, thank you, ma'am. I'll get right to the point. Last night someone broke into my henhouse and stole three laying hens. The commotion woke my son. He looked out and saw Ivan running down the road with a gunnysack slung over his back."

"If it was nighttime, how was your son able to recognize Ivan?" Michael asked.

"My boy is in the same class as Ivan. He knows him pretty well. They've even been in a scuffle or two together. Plus, the boy was dressed Amish with those flattop black hats you folks prefer."

"I appreciate you coming to me first," Bethany said quietly.

"We have heard a lot of good things about having the Amish for neighbors and for the most part you folks have lived up to your reputation. I don't want to bring the sheriff into this if I don't have to. Things like this can get blown out of proportion. Anybody who has a pig or goat come up missing, they can point a finger at the Amish without any proof. You folks just accept that and forgive the accusers. Nothing gets solved and folks keep on thinking you're guilty. I don't want to see that get started here."

"We appreciate your attitude, Mr. Janson. Would you like to speak to Ivan?" Michael asked.

"I'll leave that up to you."

"I will pay you what the hens are worth." Bethany got up to find her checkbook.

Michael stalled her with a hand to her shoulder. "I'm responsible for Ivan now. I will take care of this."

Mr. Janson held up one hand and shook his head. "I could just as easily have lost them to a lynx or coyote. I don't want to be paid for them. I came here because I want your boy to know that he was seen and that next time he comes on the place I will call the sheriff."

The outside door opened and Ivan came in. He stopped and his eyes grew wide when he saw Mr. Janson. Bethany beckoned to him. "We were just talking about you."

"About me? Why?"

"Because my boy Max saw you stealing our chickens last night," Janson said.

Ivan shook his head. "It wasn't me."

"Max knows you. He was certain."

Ivan looked at Michael. "Honest, I didn't go out last night. Why would I take chickens?"

Michael laid a hand on Ivan's shoulder. "Do you know who might have done it?"

Ivan stared down at his feet. "I only know it wasn't me."

Bethany turned to Mr. Janson. "Thank you for bringing this to our attention."

"Like I said, I don't want it to get out of hand." He tipped his hat to her and left.

Bethany waited until the door closed and then she turned to Ivan. "How could you do something so foolish?"

"I knew you wouldn't believe me."

Michael kept his hand on Ivan's shoulder. "I believe you. Why would someone want to make it look like you are the one who took them?"

"I don't know."

"But you do have an idea who it was, don't you?"

Ivan turned his pleading eyes to Michael. "I can't tell. I promised I wouldn't tell."

Chapter Ten

Bethany was shocked that Michael believed Ivan. Even she doubted her brother's innocence. Yet the crime didn't make any sense. Why would Ivan steal three chickens?

Why would anyone? The vast majority of farms in the area had their own chickens as she did.

"Go on and get ready for supper, Ivan." When her brother left the room, Bethany looked at Michael. "What are we going to do with him?"

"The next time there is a report about something Ivan is suspected of doing, I think it would be best to involve the police."

"The bishop would not agree to that. Our community has taken great pains to avoid any involvement by the *Englisch* law."

"The police can easily rule out Ivan as a suspect by fingerprints or by DNA. Their findings will carry weight with the *Englisch* community."

"You really think someone is deliberately blaming Ivan?"

"I do."

She wished she could be so positive. This setback was crushing. "I'm not sure I can simply wait for another incident to occur."

"It's the only choice we have unless Ivan can be convinced to break his promise and tells us what he knows."

"Do you know who he's protecting?"

"I think I do but I have no proof. I think you know, too."

"Jeffrey?"

He nodded. She shook her head in bewilderment. "But why? Do you think we should tell the bishop about this?"

Michael took his time answering her. "I'd rather not, but if you feel you should, then I'm okay with it."

"What do we do?"

"We keep to a normal pattern of activity. And we keep a good eye on Ivan. What are your plans for this week?"

"I have a lot of things that need to be done. Christmas is getting closer by the minute. I have a ton of baking to get finished. On Saturday I plan to send the children out to collect fir branches and winterberries for the house and for wreaths. I was hoping that you would go with them."

"I can."

"On Sunday Pastor Frank is coming to supper."

"Why?" He looked at her suspiciously.

"Because he's a friend. We enjoyed his company. He frequently drives us and other Amish people in his van at no charge."

"I see."

She walked to the window and stared out at the low gray clouds scuttling across the sky. A few snowflakes floated down from them. She wound the ribbon of her *kapp* around one finger. "I had asked Frank to speak with Ivan about his behavior but I never took Ivan to see him. He's been doing so much better lately. You have been a good influence on him. But now this."

Michael walked up to stand behind her. She could see their reflection together in the window. She was becoming dependent on him for advice and for comfort. She longed to rest her head against his shoulder and feel she wasn't facing this problem alone.

"I know you're worried," he said quietly.

If she leaned back, would he take her in his arms? It was a foolish thought. "To worry is to doubt God's mercy. I try not to, but it seems to be my best talent."

He chuckled. "I thought speaking Cow was your best talent."

She smiled. "Don't tell Frank I get my advice from Clarabelle. He went to many years of school to become a psychologist and counselor so he could advise folks."

"Jenny thinks you should marry. That way Ivan won't be sent away."

Bethany looked down as her face grew hot. "She's been listening to Gemma. Husbands don't exactly grow on trees in New Covenant."

"Anyone you chose would be getting a fine wife."

She looked up to study his reflection in the glass but it wasn't clear enough to let her see what he was thinking. "Are you making me an offer?"

"You would be getting a very poor bargain if I was."

She turned around so she could look into his eyes. "Why do you say that?"

"Because it's the truth."

There was so much pain in his voice and deep in his eyes that she wanted to hold him and promise to make everything better. She couldn't. She knew that, but it didn't lessen her desire to help him.

The letter from Mr. Meyers hadn't told her why Michael didn't return to work in his store or why he left his family in Ohio to come to Maine. He could have easily fixed watches for Mr. Meyers there the same way he was doing here. "What's wrong, Michael?"

He laid a hand against her cheek. "Nothing that you can fix."

"How do I know that if you can't tell me what troubles you?"

"Trust me. You don't want to know." He turned and walked down the hall and out the back door.

He was so wrong. She wanted to know everything about Michael Shetler. Her mother's voice echoed from the past. *If you don't know a man inside and out, don't marry him. He'll bring you nothing but pain.*

Michael was up early on Saturday because he knew Ivan and Jenny would be over as soon as they could. He hoped that Bethany would accompany them on their trek into the woods to gather winterberries and fir boughs for wreath making but he wasn't sure that she would. It was hard for him to believe that he had only been in New Covenant a little over two weeks. So much had happened. So much had changed. He hadn't had a flashback for thirteen days and not a single panic attack. Maybe his PTSD episodes were behind him for good. He prayed it was true.

Sadie alerted him that the children had arrived by scratching at the door and woofing softly. He opened the door and she shot outside, barking and bounding around Jenny. The girl was pulling a red toboggan. She dropped to her knees and threw her arms around Sadie's neck. The dog responded by licking her face. Jenny's giggle was so much like Bethany's that anyone could tell they were related. Ivan stopped to pet the dog, too.

Bethany came up the hill behind the children. Her bright welcoming smile was like the sun breaking through on a dreary day. He was happy to see her smiling again after the depressing visit with Mr. Janson.

Michael's refusal to talk about his past troubled her, too. He knew that, but his decision would never change.

Bethany pulled a blue toboggan with a bushel basket on it. Like the children, she was bundled for the outdoors with a heavy coat, mittens and snow boots. The red-and-white-striped knit scarf around her neck was identical to the one Jenny was wearing.

Ivan patted Sadie and then hurried to Michael's door.

He was pulling a yellow disk sled. "*Guder mariye*, Michael."

"Morning, Ivan. So where are we going?"

The boy pointed up the ridge. "I know the perfect place to get pine boughs. It isn't far."

Michael looked at the pine-covered forest stretching up into the mountains. "I hope that's true. I'm not sure my leg will hold up in all this snow. Besides, don't we have about a million trees to choose from close to home?"

"It has to be balsam fir and we will pull you on the sled if you get tired." Bethany stopped beside Ivan.

"I give up. Why balsam?" Michael returned her smile. The darkness of his past was etched deep in his soul, but just being with her gave him hope that he could be healed. He prayed that God would show him mercy.

Michael couldn't plan any kind of family life until he was sure, but he could dream of the day when he had the right to tell Bethany how he felt about her.

"I want balsam fir because of its wonderful, spicy scent, its lovely color and its short dense needles."

Michael looked at both of their sleds. "Are we planning to bring back a lot of branches? I was thinking we'd have an armful or two."

Bethany began counting on her fingers. "Gemma and her mother want some. We need enough for our house and for your cabin. Plus, I will make some for friends and I also plan to sell a few at the grocer's. Mr. Meriwether lets us set up a display in front of his store. Last year I sold thirty-eight of them and made almost a thousand dollars."

"I didn't know you operated a seasonal business."

"We have to make ends meet any way we can. Are you ready?"

He nodded even though he wasn't looking forward to the hike. Sadie Sue took off after a rabbit.

Ivan put Jenny on her sled and pulled her along as he walked beside Michael. Ivan met Michael's gaze. "The snow might get too deep for her. A man takes care of his family, right?"

Michael smiled. "Right."

When Sadie Sue returned without a bunny, Jenny coaxed her to sit on the sled with her. She and Ivan took turns pulling the dog along. Sadie wasn't sure she liked the ride and kept jumping off and then back on. Their antics had Michael and Bethany laughing as they made their way up into the forest.

Ivan was true to his word. He led them to a small grove of the fir trees less than three hundred yards beyond Michael's cabin. The trees were almost all the same size at about eight feet tall and evenly spaced.

Michael glanced at Bethany. "Someone planted this grove. Do we have permission to harvest these?"

She gave him a reassuring grin. "We do. This land belongs to Pastor Frank. We are free to use what we like. If we take a whole tree, he asks that we replant one to replace it."

"He's a generous man." Michael hadn't seen him since the night of his flashback. Although he had been tempted to attend the survivors' group meeting, he wasn't ready to have others know about his problem.

Bethany distributed clippers to everyone and they set about filling the sleds with piles of the wonderfully pungent branches. When the children had finished cutting, they went exploring while the adults cinched down the loads with lengths of rope.

Michael tied off the last knot, dusted the snow from a nearby fallen log and sat down to rest. Bethany came over to join him. The view spread out before them was breathtaking. They could see the winding course of the river down below, the silver ribbon of highway that paralleled the river's course and the houses of Fort Craig. In the distance the Appalachian mountain range provided a beautiful backdrop. It was a lovely spot and he had a beautiful woman beside him.

She rubbed her hands up and down on her arms. "It's getting colder."

He slipped his arm around her and she moved closer, making his heart beat faster. Not with fear but with joy.

"How long have you been taking care of your brother and sister?" Michael asked gently. He leaned forward to see her face.

Bethany smiled. "A long time."

"What happened to your parents? Does it bother you to talk about it?"

She shook her head. "My mother passed away shortly after Jenny was born. The doctor had a medical reason but I think she died of a broken heart. My father had left us about a month before that."

"I don't understand."

"Neither did I. If you are thinking that my father died, you are mistaken. My father packed up and moved away. He didn't want to be Amish anymore. It was the third time he had come back into our lives, begged for forgiveness, and was welcomed by our Amish community. I would like to give him credit for trying to shoulder his responsibilities, but I'm not sure he tried very hard."

"He left your mother twice before that? Left her and his children?" Michael could barely believe what he was hearing.

"The first time he went away I was six. I woke up on my sixth birthday to find my mother crying and my father gone. Just gone. He didn't bother to tell me goodbye."

"I'm sorry. That was cruel."

"He came back two years later, said he was sorry and begged Mother to give him another chance. She did. I was overjoyed. Mother was, too, but only for a while. He stayed for three years but even as a child I could see they weren't happy together. He left again. The next time he came back he only stayed a year."

"Did he ever tell you why he couldn't stay or what he did when he was away?"

"Not to me. He refused to talk about his other life. He did come to Mother's funeral. I thought he would take care of us but he said he couldn't. I was sixteen. He left me with a brokenhearted little boy and a newborn babe. We haven't seen or heard from him since."

"It's hard to believe a man could cast aside his responsibilities that way." No wonder she was so committed to keeping the children with her.

"Fortunately, our mother's father, Elijah, stepped up to take us in. My father's brother, Onkel Harvey, was willing to accept us but I wanted to stay with Grandpa. That's how I ended up helping Elijah look for a place to start his new Amish community. Each fall after the farm work was done, we would travel to different locations, looking for a place to settle. When we received a letter from Pastor Frank telling us about New Covenant, we decided to visit during the winter to see just how bad it was going to be. The road leading to our farm was merely a tunnel plowed through four feet of snow."

"I'm sorry about your father."

"Our faith requires a strength of character that he didn't possess. My mother could have gone with him, but she refused to abandon her faith and break her vows to God."

"She must've been a strong woman."

"She was, but each time my father came back and then left again, it was like he took pieces of her strength with him until there was nothing left."

"You have inherited your strength from her."

"I hope so. She wanted Father to come back so badly. She prayed for it. When she knew she was dying, she made me promise I would keep the family together. She didn't say she wanted it for him in case he came back, but I think that's exactly what she hoped for."

"It was a big burden to place on a young girl." He bent and kissed her lips gently.

He felt her sharp intake of breath and he drew back. "Maybe I shouldn't have done that."

"I didn't mind."

He looked away from the comfort she offered. "Did you ever consider leaving the Amish?"

"I think we all question at one time or another if this path to God is the right one for us. I never seriously considered leaving. What about you?"

"I did more than question. I left the Amish life behind and lived in the outside world for five years."

She gave him a funny look. "You did? What made you come back?"

"That is not something I care to talk about." His answer seemed to take her by surprise.

"I'm sorry. I'm just trying to understand. You say you want to live alone but you spend almost as much time with my family as I do."

"Ivan and Jenny can be hard to resist." As was their big sister. He rose to his feet and held out his hand to her. "We should head back."

"Will you remain Amish?"

He could tell it was important to her to know the answer. "I will."

Bethany allowed him to help her up but she pulled her hand away from his quickly. She had shared the most painful part of her life but he was unwilling to speak of his past. Until this moment she considered him someone she could count on. Someone dependable, but was he? He'd left the Amish once. What if he decided to leave again? A seed of doubt had been sown in her mind.

She shouldn't have let him kiss her. There was no promise between them. No plan for the future. That knowledge alone should help keep her emotions from carrying her away where he was concerned.

Ivan came through the trees with a big bundle of winterberry branches in his arms, leaving a thin trail of red berries on the snow behind him. Sadie Sue walked beside him. He laid the branches on top of the blue sled. Bethany looked around. "Where is Jenny?"

"She said she wanted to play hide-and-seek with Sadie Sue. She's gone to hide."

Michael patted the dog's head. "Let's hope she has a bunny in her pocket."

Bethany didn't look amused. "Let's pray we can find her if the dog can't."

"That will be easy. We'll just follow her footsteps in the snow," Ivan said.

Michael took Sadie Sue's head between his hands. "Find Jenny."

Sadie took off into the trees. He looked at Bethany. "Do we follow the dog or just hope she finds Jenny before it gets dark?"

"I'm going to follow the dog." She pointed to the log they had been sitting on. "You don't need to do more hiking than you have already. Rest."

Ivan sat on the log. "I'm going to wait here."

They heard Sadie barking in the distance. Bethany started toward the sound. She hadn't gone far when she saw Jenny and the dog coming toward her. Jenny was covered with snow but she was smiling from ear to ear. "She found me. I buried myself under the snow and she found me. She's the smartest dog in the whole wide world."

Bethany smiled at her sister. "Well, for that she deserves a whole sausage. Are you ready to go home?"

Jenny nodded and they began to walk side by side. She glanced up at Bethany. "Can I ask you something?"

"Sure."

"I've been thinking that you should marry Michael."

Bethany arched one eyebrow. "You've been thinking that, have you?"

Jenny cocked her head to the side as a serious expression settled over her face. "I like him. Ivan wouldn't have to go away and you could have babies."

"I see you have this all figured out. How many babies do you think I should have?"

"Three or four. Mostly girls but you could have one boy if you wanted to."

It hurt Bethany's heart to know her little sister was worrying about Ivan, too. She managed a reassuring smile. "I don't believe the bishop is going to send Ivan away, so I'm not going to marry Michael or anyone else until you and Ivan are grown up. You are my family. I don't need anyone else."

Jenny kicked at the snow. "Ivan said you would say that."

Bethany patted her sister on the head. "Then Ivan is smarter than I gave him credit for."

* * *

On Sunday evening Michael was reading Elijah's book on the history of clocks when Sadie perked up and thumped her tail on the floor. She kept her eyes on the front door. A knock followed. Michael knew who was there before he opened the door.

"Good evening, Frank."

"Evening, Michael. I thought I would stop by and see if I could interest you in a game of chess." He had a case under his arm.

"I have a strong suspicion that I'll be outclassed, but sure, come in."

Frank looked at Sadie. "Is this the same dog you had before?"

"It is."

He bent to pat her head. "Living with you certainly agrees with her. I don't see a single rib sticking out anymore. Her coat is gorgeous. Such a pretty golden color." He glanced at Michael. "How have you been?"

Michael led the way to a small table and two chairs set in the corner. He clicked on the floor lamp and took a seat. "Sadie is not the only one improving. I've come a long way."

"Really?" Frank opened his case and lifted out a chessboard and pieces. "Tell me about it."

"I haven't had a flashback or a panic attack since the last time we spoke. I've never gone so long without an episode."

Frank glanced at Michael. "I'm glad to hear it. I've been expecting you to show up at one of my support groups but you keep disappointing me."

"I don't see the need for therapy if I'm getting better on my own. You said some people get over it by themselves."

"I did say that. What do you think has made the difference?"

"Sadie Sue, for one thing. She always alerts me if someone is near. I depend on her sharp nose and ears. If I start getting edgy, she will come over and distract me. She's amazing."

"So instead of being hypervigilant, you rely on the dog to do that for you. I don't want to belittle your progress, but isn't that substituting one kind of crutch for another?"

"Maybe it is but it makes life bearable."

"Bethany tells me Ivan has been in trouble again but that you are sticking up for the boy." Frank began to place the chess pieces on the board.

"I think the saying is 'innocent until proven guilty.'"

"Sadly that is sometimes forgotten in today's society. Have you thought more about your flashback triggers?"

Michael shifted uncomfortably in his chair. "Like I told you, I haven't had one since the night we met."

"I'm glad to see you are improving but I hope you understand that recovery is a slow process. There will be setbacks. They may not be as severe as what you've had in the past but you should be prepared for them. Being prepared ahead of time makes it easier for you and for anyone with you to get through an episode. Black or white?" He held out two chess pieces.

"White. How can I be prepared for one if I never

know when they will occur?" Michael positioned his men on the board.

"That's a good question. Since you are working and living close to Bethany, she might benefit from learning about this, too."

Michael glanced up sharply. "I don't want her involved."

"Is that wise? She has a good head on her shoulders. She won't panic."

"No!"

"Okay, but I think you're making a mistake."

"It's mine to make." He was aware of Bethany's withdrawal at the pine branch gathering. Was it because of his kiss or something else? It had been hard for her to relate the story of how her father bounced in and out of her life and then abandoned them. When Michael admitted that he had left the Amish once before, it touched a nerve for her.

Maybe her coolness was for the best. He was better. He knew he was better, but he wasn't sure if it would last.

After beginning the game in silence and playing for a while, Michael realized he wasn't outclassed by Pastor Frank. They were evenly matched and he began to enjoy the game.

"Do you have plans for next Saturday evening?" Frank asked.

"Nope. Why?"

"The city of Presque Isle puts on a holiday parade every year that's worth going to see. I'm getting together a vanload of Amish folks and driving them up to enjoy it. Would you like to join us?"

A big outing, crowds—he wasn't sure he was up to it. "Is it something Ivan and Jenny would enjoy?"

"Absolutely. It's fun for all ages and it's free. I've already asked Bethany and she said she would come."

"I'll consider it. I believe this is checkmate." Michael moved his queen to trap Frank's king.

Frank studied the board and sighed heavily. "I concede. Nice game."

"Another?" Michael asked.

Frank shook his head. "I should get going. I'll save you a seat in the van if you decide to go with us. Think about what I've said. Being prepared to endure a flashback or panic attack can make it easier on everyone involved."

"I'll keep it in mind."

But he wouldn't involve Bethany. Not ever.

Chapter Eleven

Bethany lifted Jenny to stand on a chair. The girl was wearing her Christmas costume and Bethany wanted to make sure the hem was straight. "Hold your arms out," she mumbled around the three straight pins she held between her lips. Two dozen more were stuck into the pincushion shaped like a tomato that she wore on her wrist.

The house smelled of pine and cinnamon. Green boughs graced the window ledges and the fireplace mantel. Christmas cards from faraway friends had started arriving. They were displayed nestled in the pine branches or hung from red yarn stretched across the windows. Christmas was fast approaching, and in spite of her assurance to Jenny, Bethany's last hope of keeping Ivan had crumbled. Her uncle had included a letter in his Christmas card. He strongly believed the bishop was right and Ivan should return with him. It was a bitter blow. It seemed to be God's will to separate her family.

She folded the material of the white gown under and pinned it across the top of Jenny's feet. "Is this how long you want it?"

"I don't know," Jenny said quietly.

"Did the play director tell you if you had to have wings?"

"I can't be an angel without wings."

"But you are the narrator. Should your costume be different than the other angels or the same?"

Jenny put her arms down. "I don't know." Her lower lip trembled.

Bethany took a hold of her sister's hand. "Don't cry. This is for your Christmas pageant. This should be fun. I'll make it long enough to touch the floor and if the director says it should be shorter then I will shorten it. You don't have dress rehearsal for a few days, so I have plenty of time to change it."

"Good thinking." Michael stood in the open doorway to his workroom. "If you cut it too short you won't be able to lengthen it."

She rolled her eyes at him. "Have you had a lot of experience as a seamstress?"

Michael had been joining the conversations more often in the past few days. The workroom door hadn't been closed all week. She welcomed his interactions with her family but she couldn't forget the all-too-brief kiss they'd shared. What did it mean? Did it mean anything to him? During his time in the outside world, had he kissed lots of women?

"As a matter of fact, I have had some sewing experience," he declared. "My brother and I made a camel costume for our Christmas pageant when I was in the sixth grade. We were told it was very lifelike."

Bethany looked around for her fabric marker and realized she had left it in the sewing room. "I'll be right back, Jenny."

She left the room, grabbed the marker from the sewing machine and started back into the kitchen. She was in the hall when she heard Michael say, "Of course you can ask me anything, Jenny. What's wrong?"

Bethany waited in the hall to hear what Jenny had to say. Why was her sister confiding in Michael instead of in her?

"I don't want to be the narrator," Jenny said.

"You don't? Why not? I think you will make a fine narrator."

"Mrs. Whipple says my voice is too small. I didn't know I had a small voice. How do I get a bigger one?"

"I don't think there's anything wrong with your voice, Jenny. Who is Mrs. Whipple?"

"She's one of the ladies helping our director, Miss Carson. I heard her tell Miss Carson that someone else should be the narrator because she couldn't hear me in the back row."

"That made you feel bad, didn't it?"

Bethany didn't hear anything. She assumed Jenny was nodding.

"Jenny, I will be happy to help you make your voice bigger."

"You will?" Jenny sounded thrilled.

"Absolutely. We will practice once your sister is

finished with your costume. Just come into the work-room when the two of you are done."

"I'm not supposed to bother you in the workroom."

He chuckled. "That's only when the door is closed. When the door is open you can come in whenever you like."

Bethany walked into the kitchen and saw Jenny had her arms around Michael's neck. He pulled her arms away as a fierce blush stained his cheeks.

"I have to get back to work," he mumbled.

He was so good with children. He should have a dozen of his own.

When she realized where her thoughts were taking her, she pushed them aside. He wasn't the one for her. How could she consider a relationship with someone whose past was so full of secrets, with a man who didn't feel he could confide in her?

Michael closed the cover of a grandmother clock after setting the time. He waited as it ticked its way to the top of the hour. The chimes rang out in clear pure tones. He wiped his fingerprints from the glass. Tomorrow he would pack it up and mail it back to George Meyers. His former boss had been sending a steady stream of work his way, and Michael was grateful.

Jenny appeared in the doorway. "Can I come in?"

"Sure."

She came in and climbed up on his work stool. She opened the drawer and lifted out one of the tools. "Will one of these tools make my voice bigger?"

He smiled and took the pliers from her. "We will

save those as a last resort. You stand on a stage, don't you?"

She nodded. He lifted her onto the workbench. "There are a few things you have to do to get a bigger voice. Right now, I want you to close your eyes. And I want you to whisper your first two lines."

Movement caught his eye and he glanced over to see Bethany watching him. He beckoned her to come in. She did but she stayed by the door.

"How was that?" Jenny asked.

"Fine. I want you to keep your eyes closed and pretend you need Ivan to come in from the other room. He's pretty far away but you can't yell. Want to try it? Talk loud. Say your lines."

"Ivan, a long time ago, in a land far away, there were shepherds tending their flocks in the hills near the little town of Bethlehem. Can you hear me?"

"That's pretty good. Now I want you to try telling him again but this time he is upstairs."

She shook her head. "I don't think he can hear me upstairs."

"Bethany, will you go to the stairwell and see if you can hear Jenny?"

"Of course." She turned and walked out of the room.

Jenny repeated her lines in a loud voice. A few moments later Bethany returned.

"Well?" Michael looked at Bethany for confirmation.

"I heard her, but just barely."

"Hmm. I wonder what will help. Bethany, do you have any suggestions?"

They conferred and with some practice they were able to get Jenny to be heard by someone standing on the stairwell. Jenny was excited that she wouldn't have to give up being the narrator and promised to speak loud enough to be heard on the roof. As she went to change out of her costume, Bethany stayed in the workroom.

She opened one of the drawers. "I've often wondered what all these things are for."

He sensed that she wanted to talk about something else. He would let her work up her courage. "It looks like a lot of stuff but there are just different sizes of the same items. Gears and pins. Pliers and screwdrivers. Tweezers and little magnets to retrieve dropped pieces of metal."

She picked up his jeweler's loupe. "And this is to let you see things more clearly, isn't it?" She held it to her eye and turned so she was looking at him.

"Is it working?" he asked gently.

"I'm not sure." She pulled it away from her face. "Every time I look I see something different." He knew she was talking about him.

"That is one of the drawbacks of looking too closely."

"I think the problem is I didn't have my subject in focus. What can I do about that?"

"Not much, I'm afraid, if your subject is unwilling to cooperate." He wasn't ready to risk her knowing the whole truth.

"So the loupe is for seeing small pieces in great detail. How do I see the whole picture in greater detail?"

"The trick is to take a step back," he said bluntly.

Their relationship had progressed so quickly he wasn't sure of his own feelings or of hers.

She laid the lens down. "I think that's what I need to do."

"I think it would be best if we both did that."

A wry smile curved her lips. "I agree."

She started to walk past him but he caught her arm. "Can we still be friends?"

"I don't see why not," she replied, but he couldn't tell if she meant it.

Bethany expected her next meeting with Michael would be awkward. To prolong the inevitable, she went to visit her friend Gemma after the kids were off to school the following morning.

Gemma welcomed her with a hug and then intense scrutiny. "Okay, out with it. What's troubling you?"

Bethany turned away from her friend's sharp eyes. "The same thing. Ivan." It was true but it wasn't the whole truth.

"I know you are worried about your brother but something else is on your mind or you wouldn't be here."

Bethany began to remove her bonnet and coat. "You make it sound like I never come to see you unless I'm in some kind of crisis."

Gemma poured two cups of coffee and sat down at the table with them. She pushed one across to Bethany when she sat down. "You visit me without a crisis often, but I know you well enough to see you are deeply troubled. What is it? I'm here to help."

Bethany prided herself on being in control. She didn't believe women were weaker than men, but when she looked up and saw the sympathy in Gemma's eyes, Bethany's pride flew out the window. Tears welled up and spilled down her cheeks. "I'm so confused."

"Oh, you poor dear." Gemma was around the table in a moment and gathered Bethany into her arms. "It's okay. Go ahead and cry."

"I can't abide women who act like watering cans." She sniffled and continued to cry.

Gemma patted Bethany's back. "No one could accuse you of being a watering can. You are one of the strongest women I have ever had the privilege to know."

"Then why do I feel like such a fool?" Bethany wailed.

"Because love makes glorious fools of us all."

"I'm not in love. I can't be in love."

"And yet here you are crying on my shoulder because your mystery man has stolen your heart."

Bethany drew back to stare at Gemma in amazement. "How can you know that?"

"Because I have been in love myself."

"You have? With who?"

"A fellow who is denser than a post. But never mind about me. This is about you. First I have to know how bad it is. Has he kissed you?"

Bethany buried her face in her hands and nodded, unable to speak.

"Did you kiss him back?"

"Maybe just a little," she whispered.

"Do Ivan and Jenny like him?"

"Jenny adores him. Ivan looks up to him and tries to emulate him."

"All right. Has he told you that he loves you?"

"*Nee*, we've not spoken of our feelings."

"So you haven't professed your love. Okay. Things aren't as bad as you are making them out to be."

"How can you say that? I spend my days and nights thinking about him, wondering if he's thinking about me."

"That's normal in any new relationship. I know that you are a wonderful catch for any man. I don't see the problem on this end. Why is he all wrong for you?"

Bethany wiped her face with both hands and drew a ragged breath. "Because I don't know anything about him."

"You know a lot of things about him."

"You don't understand. Something bad happened to him. He has told me in general terms what happened but I know there is something else. Something he won't talk about. He's so secretive. I'm worried that I really may not want to know what he did."

"Bethany, you have to ask yourself what is the one sin that you can't forgive."

She frowned slightly as she looked at Gemma. "There is no sin that cannot be forgiven."

"You believe that with all your heart, don't you?"

"Of course I do. Jesus died on the cross for all men's sins. We are instructed by God to forgive those that have trespassed against us."

"What is the one thing in Michael's past that you could not forgive?"

That made her pause. "I would forgive anything."

"Then why do you have to know what he has done?"

Bethany pulled her coffee mug close and took a sip. It was lukewarm. "It's not that I can't forgive his sins great or small. It's that I believe you can't love someone that you don't trust. How can he love me if he doesn't trust me enough to share his burdens?"

"Has he said that he loves you?"

"*Nee*, he has not."

"But you are in love with him?"

Bethany gave her friend a beseeching glance. "Maybe. I don't know. What would you do in my place?"

"Sell the farm and move to someplace warm."

Bethany managed a half-hearted smile. "You know I'm being serious."

"I do. I trust your judgment, Bethany. Therefore, you should trust your own judgment. You have so many things vying for your attention and that keeps you from thinking straight. You and I both know that you won't marry anyone before Christmas, even if it is the only way to keep Ivan with you. You're much too smart for that. An Amish marriage is forever. Ivan will return to us when he is older. It will be a hard separation, but it won't be forever. If you like Michael Shetler, even if you think you love him, you still need time to get to know one another."

"He asked me if we could be friends."

"Did he mean it?"

Bethany thought back to that moment. "I believe he did."

"That's a good sign. It means he cares about you and he values the relationship the two of you have. What did you say?"

"I said I didn't see why not."

"Well, that should give him some hope. Can you be his friend even if he never confides in you?"

Bethany pondered the question. She liked Michael. More than that, she cared deeply about him. He made her laugh. He understood Ivan better than she ever could. Jenny adored him and looked up to him. Bethany realized her life would be poorer if Michael Shetler wasn't in it. If his friendship was all that she could have, she would gladly hold on to it.

She nodded. "I can be his friend. You, Gemma, are such a wise friend. You give much better advice than Clarabelle."

Gemma looked appalled. "I should hope so. Isn't that your milk cow?"

Bethany chuckled. "Someday I will tell you the story. I will take your advice. I won't rush into anything. I still believe that Ivan is better off with me. I'm not letting him go without a fight."

Gemma took a sip of her coffee and made a bitter face. "That sounds like the Bethany I know and love. How about a fresh cup of hot coffee?"

"And a lemon cookie?"

"Absolutely. They come free with all my advice.

How would you like to stay and help me bake cookies for the holidays? I need eight dozen."

"I would be delighted to repay even a small portion of your kindness."

Bethany spent the entire day with Gemma, enjoying her friendship, sampling new cookie recipes and making several dozen of each type to take home. Chocolate chip cookies, oatmeal cookies, gingerbread men, moose munch, sugar cookies and lemon crisps because she knew Michael would enjoy them. With several large plastic containers in her arms, she paused outside Gemma's front door.

"Thank you again."

Gemma waved aside Bethany's gratitude. "Someday I will need your shoulder to cry on."

"It will be available day or night. Are you going with Pastor Frank to see the Christmas parade in town?"

"I am. So are my folks. What about you?"

"The children and I are going for sure. I don't know about Michael."

"We will enjoy it with him or without him, right?"

"Right."

Bethany waved goodbye and headed home. As she approached her lane, she saw the school bus pull away. Four of the local schoolchildren went swarming up the mounds of snow left by the snowplows on her side of the road. She noticed Jeffrey was one of them but she didn't see Ivan.

She stopped to watch them playing king of the mountain. The one who obtained the summit then had to keep others from claiming his throne. There was more pushing and shoving than she liked to see, but all she did was caution them. "Make sure you don't push anyone toward the road. Stay on the outside of those piles."

"We know, Ms. Martin," one of the younger boys replied.

She left them to their fun and walked up her drive. Pastor Frank's van sat parked in front of the house. The sound of laughter and the smell of pizza greeted her as she entered. She stepped into the kitchen to see Pastor Frank, Michael, Ivan and Jenny seated around the table, making Christmas wreaths. All of them wore pine branch crowns around their heads. Michael's held two long branches upright like antlers. Jenny had two small upright branches near the front of her head. Ivan had two bushy branches hanging down. The pastor had red winterberries woven into his.

Bethany shook her head. "What is going on in here?"

"We're making Christmas wreaths to sell at the market," Jenny said.

Bethany set down her containers of cookies. "I see. Who are you supposed to be?" she asked, looking askew at all of them.

"I'm a bunny," Jenny said with a giggle. She got down from the table and hopped around the room.

Ivan slid off his chair. "I'm a hound dog." He started barking and chasing Jenny. Sadie Sue immediately got up from her place under the table and started barking at them as they ran up the stairs with her close on their heels.

Bethany looked at Michael and tried not to laugh. "I assume you are a Christmas reindeer?"

He shook his head, making one of his antlers fall off. He picked it up and tucked it in again. "I am a Maine moose."

"Of course you are. Pastor Frank?"

"I'm a pastor with a limited imagination wearing a pine branch wreath on my head decorated by Jenny." He gave her a big smile.

She looked at the number of wreaths stacked against the wall. "You have been busy. I know the children just got home a little while ago, so, Michael, did you make these by yourself or did Frank help you?"

"Those were all done by Michael," the pastor said. "I just brought the pizza. It's baking now. You are always feeding me. I thought I'd return the favor."

Michael stretched his neck one way and then the other. "I was tired of fixing clocks and decided to try my hand at wreath making. What do you think?"

She picked up several and checked the construction. "Not bad at all. I'm sure these will sell well with a little more decoration added."

"Did you have a good day?" he asked with a shade of uncertainty in his eyes.

She smiled. "I did. I went to visit Gemma and we baked cookies all day."

"Are there samples?" Pastor Frank's gaze slid to the counter and her plastic containers.

"There are. Pastor Frank, I know you enjoy oatmeal cookies. I have two dozen set aside just for you." She handed him a full plastic baggie.

"These are going straight out to my van so I don't forget them later." He removed his crown before heading out the door.

Bethany held out a container. "I actually made some moose munch if you want to try that, Michael the Moose."

He got up from his chair. "You don't have to ask me twice."

Opening one of the containers, he took a handful of the mix and turned to face her with his hip leaning against the counter. "How are you today?" he asked.

She cocked her head slightly. "I'm better. I had a wonderful time with Gemma and I've come to realize how truly valuable a great friendship can be."

"Present company excluded?" he asked.

"Present company included," she assured him. His smile warmed her all the way through.

Pastor Frank returned a few minutes later. The children thundered down the stairs when he called out that the pizza was ready. Bethany smiled as they crowded around him eagerly. This was the way it had been before her grandfather died. Friends stopping by. Storytelling, good food and good company. It was comforting to know it didn't have to change.

After supper Bethany and Jenny rehearsed her lines as the men decided to teach Ivan the game of chess. The boy had an aptitude for it and was soon intent on learning more moves. It was almost ten thirty when Bethany called a stop to the game.

"It's a school night and it is way past Ivan's bedtime." She had tucked Jenny in hours ago.

Pastor Frank pulled on his coat. "I apologize for keeping you all up so late. It was like old times and I guess I got carried away. Good night, all."

Bethany and Michael watched him leave from the doorway. When he drove out of sight, she closed the door.

"I'd better leave, too," Michael said. "I had a fine time tonight, Bethany. I've forgotten how satisfying an ordinary night with friends can be."

"I'm glad you enjoyed yourself. We'll do it again soon."

He put on his hat and coat, but instead of leaving he seemed to come to some decision. "The weather isn't bad and I've been sitting too long. Would you care to take a walk with me?"

"That would be nice." She put on her coat and gloves and walked out the door to stand beside him. "Which way?"

"You have lived here longer than I have. You choose the direction."

"There is a path that leads to an overlook. It's not too steep."

"I'll keep up. Don't worry about me."

She took him at his word. They walked in silence for a time with Sadie Sue ambling alongside Michael. The crunch of their boots in the snow was the only sound. It was cold, but Bethany was warmly dressed and exercise kept her from getting chilled. "What do you think of New Covenant?" It was a safe subject and she was interested in his opinion.

"It's a long way from being a self-supportive community."

"What do you think we need here?"

"You don't have a blacksmith or wheelwright."

"We have a blacksmith coming in the spring. A man with three boys."

"You don't have an Amish school."

"Once we reach ten school-age children in the community, the bishop will allow us to hire a teacher and open a school of our own."

"You need a grocer. Mr. Meriwether's prices are too high."

She chuckled. "Tell me something I don't know. I shop there every week."

"And where is the nearest pizza parlor? What is an Amish settlement without a pizza parlor?"

"There is one in Fort Craig. They even deliver."

"I'll have to get their number. What about you, Bethany? What do you want out of New Covenant?"

"I want to see a happy, healthy, thriving community. We are so few and far between right now. I pray the community survives."

"And if that doesn't happen? What if there is a split in the church? It happens all the time. You won't be immune because of your remoteness."

She shrugged. "I guess we'll just have to face that issue when it comes, if it comes. I like to expect the best that life has to offer."

"Isn't it better to expect the worst and then be pleased when it doesn't show up?"

"I reckon you and I simply look at life differently. Here is the overlook I mentioned. I don't see anyone around now, but it's a popular place with young lovers in the spring and summer."

They came out onto a rock ledge that jutted out between two old pine trees. Below was a stunning view of the Aroostook River. It was a silver ribbon winding its way through the countryside illuminated by a full moon just rising. She pointed east. "See where the farmland stops and the forest starts?"

"I do."

"That is Canada."

"Good to know in case I ever want to leave the country in a hurry."

"It is farther than it looks. Shall we go back?"

"Are you getting cold?"

"A little," she admitted.

They walked back to the house in silence. Bethany was overwhelmed by the smell of pine boughs when she entered the front door. The scent would always remind her of Michael in the future. She turned to face him. "Good night, Michael."

"You take care," he said as he went out into the night with Sadie Sue at his heels. Bethany sighed as she watched him walk up the hill. Being friends was truly the best path for them. Wasn't it?

Only the ache in her heart said it might not be enough.

Chapter Twelve

Bethany rose from bed feeling more rested than she had in weeks. Her first thought was to wonder if Michael shared the same feeling of relief that they were remaining friends, or did he hope for more one day?

She was fixing herself coffee when she heard a truck pull up in front of the house. She looked out the window. Mr. Meriwether got out of his delivery van and started for the house. The sheriff's SUV pulled up behind him. The look on their faces said it wasn't a social visit.

Bethany clutched her chest. "Oh, Ivan, what have you done now?"

Since he wasn't out of bed yet, he couldn't very well answer her question. She opened the door before Mr. Meriwether knocked. He inclined his head. "Good morning, Ms. Martin."

"Good day to you, Mr. Meriwether, Sheriff Lundeen. What can I do for you gentlemen?"

"I'm afraid we are here on an unpleasant errand," the sheriff said.

Mr. Meriwether nodded. "It sure is. Last night a little after midnight someone broke into one of my warehouses. They took several thousand dollars' worth of mechanic's tools, and brand-new toolboxes."

"What does that have to do with me?" she asked, fearing she knew the answer.

The sheriff removed his hat. "Is your brother, Ivan, at home?"

"*Ja*, he is here, though he is still abed."

The sheriff came in, forcing Bethany to step out of his way. "We're going to need to talk to him. The perpetrator was caught on a surveillance camera. It appears to be your brother arriving on foot and then he begins loading the stolen merchandise into a white panel van that pulled up just outside the fence. We didn't get a good look at the driver or the plates."

"It was an Amish boy fitting your brother's description," Mr. Meriwether added as he followed the sheriff inside.

Bethany led them into the living room with her heart pounding so hard she thought they must be able to hear it. This was serious. Thousands of dollars' worth of tools? This wasn't three chickens. She grew sick at heart. "I will go upstairs and get my brother. I'm sure he had nothing to do with this. Please have a seat."

"Thank you for your cooperation, ma'am." The sheriff sat on the edge of her sofa.

She hustled Ivan out of bed with only the briefest of explanations. She went into Jenny's room. "Jenny, get up and go get Michael. Tell him I need him right away."

"But I haven't had any breakfast."

"You can eat later. Now go."

The shock on Ivan's face when he saw the sheriff waiting for him told her he knew nothing about what was going on.

She stood beside Ivan. The sheriff began questioning him. Michael arrived twenty minutes later. "Can you fill me in?" he asked the law officer.

The sheriff looked him up and down. "Are you the boy's parent?"

"I'm not. I'm a friend."

"Then I don't see how this concerns you."

"I gave my word to our bishop that I would assume responsibility for Ivan's action. Anything that concerns him concerns me. If not, we must ask you to leave until the bishop and church elders can join us."

Bethany could see the wheels turning in the sheriff's mind. Did he want one Amish man or a whole roomful of them present for his questioning? Reluctantly he agreed to have Michael present and filled him in on what was known.

Michael was the one who picked up on a discrepancy. "You say the robbery took place a few minutes before eleven. We were here with Pastor Frank Pearson until ten thirty. We all saw Ivan go upstairs."

"But you admit that he could have left the premises after you did," the sheriff pointed out.

"You say a boy arrived on foot and a second perpetrator in a white panel van pulled up a few minutes later. Even if Ivan left here at 10:31, he would have been hard-pressed to run three miles in very cold temperatures and then calmly walk into Mr. Meriwether's warehouse and carry out the tools you claim were stolen."

Bethany could see the sheriff wavering. He said, "It's not outside the realm of possibility. He could have gotten a ride with the person in the van."

"But it is reasonable doubt," Michael insisted. "Were there fingerprints? Do you have a full view of his face on tape?"

Bethany was grateful for Michael's presence. He seemed to know exactly what to say.

The sheriff leaned forward on the couch and stared at Ivan. "We can't make a positive ID but it appears to be a boy wearing gloves, a dark coat and a black Amish hat."

Michael turned to Ivan. "Did you do it?"

Ivan shook his head. "*Nee.* I did not."

The sheriff sighed as he rose to his feet. "I don't have enough to hold the boy at this point. I have to wait for my forensics team to process the scene. Ivan, you can't leave town. Do you understand?"

Ivan nodded. Michael said, "Believe me, we want you to find this guy as much as you want to find him."

After the sheriff and Meriwether left, Bethany knelt in front of her brother and took his hand. "What do you know about this?"

"I think I can get the tools back, but I'm not going to turn anyone in."

"You can't protect Jeffrey forever," Michael said softly.

"You don't understand. I have to help him."

"Do you know who was driving the van?" Michael asked.

He shook his head. "I'm not sure."

Ivan left the room and Bethany didn't think twice about throwing herself into Michael's arms. She needed him. And he was there for her. "What should I do? I thought sending him to live with my uncle was terrible, but sending him to jail is unthinkable."

"It won't come to that. He's a juvenile. Besides, the evidence they have is circumstantial."

She leaned back to look at his face. "How do you know so much about police proceedings?"

"You know the store where I worked last year was robbed. I answered questions from the police for weeks on end. I can't believe I was able to listen to his interrogation without breaking down. I guess I really am doing better," he mumbled more to himself than to her.

She gazed at his dear face. "Thank you for everything."

He held her away and took a step back. "That's what friends do."

Early the following morning, Bethany heard a car turn into her drive. It was the sheriff again. Had he come to arrest Ivan? He stopped a few feet from her walkway and got out. She opened the door as he reached the porch with her heart in her throat. "Good morning, Sheriff."

"Good morning. Is Ivan here?"

"I hope so. I haven't seen him yet. Has there been another robbery?" She braced herself to hear the answer.

"No. In fact, just the opposite has occurred. Sometime during the night all the tools and equipment stolen from Mr. Meriwether's property were left outside his gate. There doesn't appear to be any damage. Nothing is missing. Mr. Meriwether is dropping all the charges."

Relief made her knees weak. "That's wonderful news." It wouldn't keep Ivan from being sent to live with Uncle Harvey, but it was so much better than having him go to jail that it didn't seem horrible anymore. She couldn't wait to tell Michael.

After the sheriff left, Bethany pulled on her coat and boots, intent on seeing Michael, but a knock on the door stopped her. She opened it and saw Mrs. Morgan, Jeffrey's mother, on the porch. The woman had a large bruise on her face and a split lip.

"Mrs. Morgan, what happened? Come in. Do you need to go to the hospital?" Bethany put her arm around the woman and helped her inside.

"Don't mind me. This is nothing. Is Jeffrey here? He didn't come home last night."

"He's not here. You must be out of your mind with worry. Let me get Ivan. Maybe he knows where Jeffrey is. Come in and sit down." The woman entered the kitchen and sat down as Bethany raced up the stairs to Ivan's room. She sagged with relief when she saw he was still in bed. She shook his shoulder. "Ivan, wake up. Mrs. Morgan is downstairs. She says Jeffrey is missing. Do you know where he is?"

Ivan sat up, rubbing his face. "I thought he was at home."

"When was the last time you saw him?"

"About midnight."

"Midnight? You went out last night?"

"Yeah. I'm sorry. I had to."

Bethany considered sending him to fetch Michael, but she realized there was nothing Michael could do. She went downstairs and found Mrs. Morgan with arms crossed and her head down on the kitchen table, weeping.

Bethany sat down beside her and put her arm around the woman's shoulders. "It's going to be all right. Ivan hasn't seen him since last night."

Michael appeared in the workshop doorway. "What's going on?"

Bethany quickly filled him in. He came and sat down across from Mrs. Morgan. "I think you should call the police."

Mrs. Morgan looked up and clutched Bethany's arm. "No. I can't do that."

Two nights later, Sadie's low growl brought Michael wide-awake. She left his bedside and trotted to the door. He sat up in bed. "What's wrong, girl?"

Sadie whined, looked back at him and whined again. Michael slipped out of bed, pulling the top quilt over himself against the cold night air. "I'm coming."

He made his way to the window beside the door. He used the corner of the quilt to wipe the frost from the center of the glass. He was expecting to see a lynx or coyote. Instead he watched a human figure approach the back door of Bethany's home and disappear into the shadows. His heart started pounding. Was she in danger?

He tossed the quilt aside, quickly pulling on his clothes and boots. He grabbed his coat from the hook by the door and pulled it on as he stepped outside. Sadie stood by his side but she wasn't growling. She looked at him. He nodded. "Go find him."

She started toward Bethany's house with Michael close behind her. The beam of a flashlight shone from the open back door. Michael couldn't see who was holding it, but he did see the person the light settled on. It was Jeffrey Morgan. The boy entered the house and the light went out. When the kitchen light came on, Michael decided to investigate further. Sadie was already at the back door, scratching and whining to be let in. Michael stood in the shadow of the pine tree off to the side and waited. When the door opened it was Ivan. "Sadie, stop it. You'll wake everybody. Go home."

Michael stepped out of the shadows. "Good evening, Ivan."

The boy's eyes widened in shock. "Michael. What are you doing here?"

"Sadie alerted me to a prowler. You've got some explaining to do."

"I reckon I do. Come into the kitchen." He turned and walked down the hall. Michael followed him.

Jeffrey was at the kitchen table, eating baked beans straight out of the can. As Michael watched Jeffrey tear into his food, it reminded him of the first time he saw Sadie gulp a sandwich down in one bite. Michael looked at Ivan. "What's going on?"

Jeffrey stopped eating to glance at Ivan and shook his head no.

Ivan spread his hands wide. "We can't do it by ourselves. Michael will help."

"He'll make me go back."

Michael took a seat across the table from Jeffrey. Ivan sat beside his friend. "Jeffrey can't go home. He isn't safe there."

Jeffrey had stopped eating and was staring down at the table. "I won't go back."

Michael reached across the table and put two fingers under the boy's chin. Jeffrey flinched but didn't pull away. Michael lifted the child's face until Jeffrey looked at him. "I know a lot about being afraid. I won't make you do anything that you don't want to do. Why don't you tell me about it?"

Jeffrey compressed his lips into a thin line. It was Ivan who spoke. "His dad beats him."

"He hits my mom, too," Jeffrey added in a small voice.

Michael sat back. He had suspected as much after Mrs. Morgan refused to call the police or go to the hospital, but this was beyond his ability to help. He wished Bethany was here.

Jeffrey stuck his fork in the empty can. "That's why I got so mad when I learned you were going to be staying in the cabin. I used to stay there when things are bad at home. I'm sorry I broke your window."

"I thought Ivan threw the rock." Michael glanced between the boys.

Jeffrey looked at Ivan. "He took the blame for me. He sticks up for me a lot."

"The stolen supplies from Jedidiah—was that your doing or Ivan's?"

The boys exchanged guilty glances. Ivan wrinkled his nose. "It was sort of my idea. The bishop preaches that we have to share with those in need. I figured Jedidiah would share if he knew, so I took what I thought he could spare. I didn't know he'd be so upset about it. I was going to leave him a note but I didn't have paper or a pen with me."

"He only did it to help my family. Sometimes my mom and my little brother and sister don't have enough to eat. I helped him carry the stuff," Jeffrey added. "We're sort of both to blame."

Michael sighed. "I see you are equal partners in crime, as it were."

The boys nodded.

Michael shook his head in disbelief. "It's always better to ask first. And the chickens?"

"Mom had to cook our laying hens a few weeks ago. The little ones missed having eggs in the morning. I only took what we needed to eat."

"How did you boys get the tools returned to Mr. Meriwether?"

Jeffrey looked pleased. "I sort of borrowed my dad's van. I know how to drive it. He hadn't sold the stuff yet." The boy's grin faded. "He got real mean when he found the stuff was missing. I had to get away."

Ivan locked his pleading gaze on Michael. "What are you going to do now? You can't make him go home."

Michael rubbed his aching leg, stalling for time. He didn't know what to do. If Jeffrey was a member of the Amish faith, he would take this to the bishop. This required someone with a level head and a compassionate heart. "Ivan, I think you should go wake your sister."

"I'm up." Bethany came into the room, pulling the belt of her pink robe tight. "I overheard most of this conversation. Jeffrey, do you know your mother is worried sick about you?"

He shrugged one shoulder. "I left her a note tonight. She'll know I'm okay when she reads it."

Michael exchanged a knowing look with Bethany. She sat down beside him. He was glad of her presence. She smiled softly at Jeffrey. "You're a thirteen-year-old boy and it's winter in Maine. How are you surviving? Where are you staying?"

Jeffrey wouldn't look at her. "Here and there."

"And how often in the past two days have you had a decent meal?"

He lifted the empty can. "Tonight."

Michael shared a speaking glance with Bethany.

"What should we do?" she asked, speaking Pennsylvania Dutch. "He isn't Amish. The *Englisch* have many rules about children."

"They do have complicated laws about child custody. I know that much from my time in the outside world. We could be in trouble for not telling the police he is here."

Jeffrey surged to his feet. "I don't know what you're saying but I won't go back."

Michael held up one hand to reassure him. "We are not suggesting that. I think going to Pastor Frank is our best option. He will listen to you, Jeffrey, and he will make the right decision. He will not put you in harm's way."

Jeffrey sank back onto his chair. Ivan laid a hand on his shoulder. "Pastor Frank is a good fellow. You can trust him."

Bethany leaned forward and took Jeffrey's hands in hers. "You have to trust us. We want what is best for both you and your mother. You can't stay out in this weather. You could die."

"That would be better than going back to him."

Michael stood up. "You and I are going to go see Pastor Frank and tell him the situation. I know he will do the right thing. You can try running away again, Jeffrey, but you will be easy to track in the snow. I don't think you'll get far."

Jeffrey put his head down on his folded arms and began to cry.

Bethany waited for Michael to return. She left a lamp on so he would know she was up. It was almost four thirty when he stepped through the door. He looked tired and he was limping heavily. She wanted to throw her arms around him and help him to the sofa but she wasn't sure he would appreciate that gesture. "How did it go?"

He sat down on the sofa beside her with a deep

sigh. "Children are complicated creatures. I'm surprised parents choose to have more than one."

"That's a very cynical thing to say. Humans are indeed complicated creatures. Since the good Lord made more than one of us, I assume He sees something wonderful in each of us."

"Even Mr. Morgan?"

"Even him. He deserves forgiveness and our prayers as much if not more than anyone."

Michael sighed. "I know you're right. That is what our faith teaches us. That is what our Lord commands us to do, but sometimes it is hard living by those words. That boy was covered with bruises."

"Pastor Frank didn't make Jeffrey go back to his father, did he?"

"He knew exactly what to do. He notified the police and reported the child abuse. Jeffrey and his brother and sister were taken to a children's home where they will be well cared for until permanent placement can be found. Frank is sure they'll go back to their mother when she is ready. Jeffrey's mother chose to go to a women's shelter."

"And Jeffrey's father?"

"Mr. Morgan was arrested and taken to jail. He is wanted in another state for burglary and arson. Apparently he often made Jeffrey steal stuff for him. It was his idea to dress Jeffrey in Amish clothing in case he was seen. Jeffrey said it was his father who damaged Greg Janson's tractor and let Robert Morris's cattle loose. He felt both men owed him more money for work he'd done for them last summer. It seems they fired him and hired two Amish fellows instead."

"At least everyone will know now that Ivan wasn't to blame for those things. I hope the bishop will reconsider letting him stay with me now. I'll speak to him tomorrow."

"Ivan still made some poor decisions but his heart was in the right place."

She reached out and covered Michael's hand with her own. His fingers were cold. "I was truly glad that you were here to help tonight. I have no idea what I would have done without your guidance."

A small smile lifted one corner of his lips. "You would have figured it out."

She shook her head. "I don't think so. When that little boy started crying at the table, I just wanted to wrap him in a warm blanket and carry him up to a soft bed. He broke my heart."

Michael laced his fingers with hers. "I know just what you mean. It was like finding Sadie all over again. Speaking of which, where is she?"

"Jenny had a nightmare about an hour ago. Sadie is sleeping with her."

He drew back a little. "You let a dog sleep in Jenny's bed? This from a woman who says dogs don't belong in the house?"

"I can admit when I am wrong. Sadie will always be welcome in my house. Provided she has had a bath and that she doesn't have fleas."

"I knew I was forgetting something."

"What?"

"Flea powder for her. Did you notice her scratching a lot?" He began scratching the back of his head.

Bethany popped him on the shoulder. "You are not as funny as you think you are."

He winked. "I'm funny enough to get a smile out of you."

As he gazed at her, his grin slowly faded. She sensed a change come over him. Her heart began beating heavily. He moved closer and she didn't pull away. He cupped her cheek with one hand, sending her pulse pounding and stealing her breath. She waited for his kiss. He caressed her lips with his thumb. "I should go."

She couldn't think clearly, let alone come up with a single objection.

He rose abruptly and left the house.

Chapter Thirteen

Bethany spoke to the bishop the next afternoon at his business. Michael wasn't with her. She relayed her brother's involvement and stressed his innocence. "He believed he was protecting Jeffrey from his father's foul temper. You have to respect him for trying to do good."

"I'm sympathetic to your position, Bethany, but I haven't changed my mind. Ivan followed too eagerly after this *Englisch* boy and he had made poor decisions. You can't deny that. I still feel the boy will benefit from a full-time male role model."

"Michael is providing Ivan with guidance. The two of them get along well and Ivan has improved so much." She held her breath, praying the bishop would see things her way.

"My mind is made up on this. The boy will benefit from his uncle's counsel evermore."

She pressed her hands together. "Please reconsider—"

He cut her off. "Bethany, go home and raise your

sister. Your brother will return to you in time if it is God's will."

She had lost. Bethany left the bishop's workplace devoid of hope. If she wanted to keep her family together, the only thing left for her to do was to move away from New Covenant and start over somewhere else, but she had no idea where to go and no money to start over with.

The evening of the community Christmas play was chilly with overcast skies that promised more snow. Ivan insisted they use the sleigh to travel to the community building. He said it was more Amish and it felt more Christmas-like. Both children were excited because there would be a small gift exchange after the program that the bishop had agreed they could participate in.

Michael brought the sleigh to Bethany's front door and spread a thick lap robe over her when she got in. "I don't want you to catch cold."

"Ivan! Come on," Jenny shouted from the back seat, causing the patient horse to toss his head and snort. Ivan came out the door, letting it slam shut behind him. He had been trying to act as if the program was no big deal, but Michael could see he was excited, too. The teenager piled in the back seat with his sister.

After a second or two of getting settled, Ivan said, "Scoot over, Jenny, and give me some room."

"I'm cold and you have more of the blanket."

"I do not."

"You do so."

"Enough," Bethany said, putting an end to the rising family squabble.

Michael lifted his arm and laid it along the back of the seat to give Bethany more room. She moved closer. As much as he wanted to slip his arm around her shoulders, he knew it would be a bad idea. He was already having far too much trouble remembering to treat her as a friend.

"Ready, everyone?" Michael asked. Three confirmations rang out. He slapped the lines and the big horse took off down the snow-covered lane.

Sleigh bells jingled merrily in time to the horse's footfalls. The runners hissed along over the snow as big flakes began to float down. They stuck to Michael's and Ivan's hats, turning their brims white. Jenny tried to catch snowflakes on her tongue between giggles.

Michael leaned down to see Bethany's face. "Are you warm enough?" She nodded, but her cheeks looked rosy and cold. Michael took off his woolen scarf and wrapped it around her head to cover her mouth and nose.

"*Danki,*" she murmured. "Won't you be cold?"

"Nope. It's a perfect evening, isn't it?" The snow obscured the mountains. The fields lay hidden beneath a thick blanket of white. Pine tree branches drooped beneath their icy loads. A hushed stillness filled the air, broken only by the jingle of the harness bells. It was a picture-perfect moment in time and Michael wished it could go on forever.

The community building was only a few miles from the farm in a converted brick factory not far from the city center. For Michael, they reached their destination much too quickly. As they drew closer they saw a dozen buggies and sleighs parked along the south side of the building out of the wind while the parking lot in front of it was full of cars and trucks.

As the kids scrambled out of the sleigh, Michael offered Bethany his hand to help her out. When she took it, he gave her an affectionate squeeze. She graced him with a shy smile in return.

Inside the building, the place was already crowded with people. What had once been the factory floor held rows of folding chairs facing a small stage at the front. Swags of fragrant cedar boughs graced the sills of the tall multipaned windows. A Christmas tree stood in one corner, decorated with colorful paper chains, popcorn and cranberry strands, and handmade ornaments made by the children. A table on the opposite wall bore trays of cookies and candies and a large punch bowl. An atmosphere of joy, goodwill and anticipation permeated the air.

Several *Englisch* people Michael didn't know approached Bethany to tell her how happy they were to learn Ivan had been cleared and how glad they were to have Amish neighbors. Everywhere Michael looked there were welcoming smiles. He had been prepared to feel uneasy in the crowd but he didn't. The Martin children hurried to join their classmates behind the stage. Michael and Bethany found seats out front a few minutes before the curtain rose.

The children performed their assigned roles, singing songs and reciting poetry. Then it came time for

Jenny to narrate the Christmas story. She walked out on stage in her white robe with her long hair in two golden braids. Michael glanced at Bethany. Her eyes brimmed with maternal pride. He squeezed her hand and together they watched the community's children bring the story of the first Christmas to life.

When the play was over, Jenny held one hand high. *"Frehlicher Grischtdaag*, everyone. Merry Christmas!"

The curtain fell and Michael clapped until his hands hurt. The last song of the evening was Ivan's solo. To Michael's surprise, the boy had a beautiful voice. His a cappella rendition of "O Come, O Come, Emmanuel" brought tears to a few eyes, including Bethany's.

Later, when everyone had a plate of treats, Jenny squeezed in between Bethany and Michael. He said, "You did well, Jenny. Your narration was very good."

"Danki."

Bethany slipped her arm around the child and gave her a hug.

Michael rubbed Ivan's head. "Who knew you could sing so well?"

The boy blushed with happiness. Everyone seemed happy, only Bethany's joy appeared forced.

It was full dark by the time the festivities wound down and families began leaving. Michael brushed the accumulated snow from the sleigh's seats and lit the lanterns on the sides. The horse stood quietly, one hip cocked and a dusting of snow across his back. Michael stepped back inside to tell Bethany they were ready.

Scanning the room, he saw her with a group of

young Amish women. Two of them held babies on their hips. Bethany raised a hand to smooth the blond curls of a little boy. As she did, her gaze met Michael's across the room.

In that moment, he knew exactly what he wanted. He wanted Bethany to have the life she was meant to live and he wanted to be a part of it. He wanted to spend every Christmas with her for the rest of his life. If only he could be certain his PTSD wouldn't return.

"Is it time to go home? I'm tired." Jenny, sitting on the bottom bleachers, could barely keep her eyes open.

"Yes, it's time to go home." He picked her up and she draped herself over his shoulder. Bethany joined them a minute later. In the sleigh, Michael let Ivan take the reins while he settled in with Jenny across his lap and Bethany seated beside him. The snow had stopped. A bright three-quarter moon slipped in and out of the clouds as they made their way home.

Snuggled beneath a blanket with Bethany at his side, Michael marveled at the beauty of the winter night in the far north and at the beauty of the woman next to him. When they pulled up in front of her house, Michael carried Jenny inside and up to bed while Ivan took the horse to the barn.

Michael stepped back as Bethany tucked her sister in. "I had a wonderful time. Thank you for inviting me."

"I'm glad." She closed the door to Jenny's room and faced him in the hall.

He stepped closer. She didn't move away. Reaching out, he cupped her cheek. "Good night, Bethany."

"Good night, Michael." Her voice was a soft whisper. Slowly, he lowered his lips to hers and kissed her.

Bethany melted into Michael's embrace. His kiss was gentle and so very sweet. Their mutual decision to take a step back and simply remain friends vanished from her thoughts as she slipped her arms around his neck. He briefly pulled her closer, and then he let her go and took a step away. "I'll see you tomorrow."

She pressed a hand to her lips to hold on to that wondrous moment. Ivan came walking up the stairs and passed them on the way to his room. Embarrassed, Bethany wondered if he had seen her in Michael's arms. He muttered a polite good-night and went in his room. Maybe he hadn't seen anything.

She mumbled a quick goodbye to Michael and fled into her room. She closed the door and leaned against it. There was no way they could go back to being just friends now.

Could she accept him without knowing the secret part of his past he wouldn't share? His kiss seemed to indicate he wanted to be a part of her life, but he hadn't said anything about what kind of future he saw and if she had a place in it.

Christmas was less than two weeks away, and she was going to lose her brother if she failed to convince the bishop to change his mind. Was Gemma right? Was Michael the answer to her prayers?

Chapter Fourteen

Sadie rose from her spot beside the fireplace the next morning and trotted to the front door, wagging her tail. She looked back at Michael and whined. A second later he heard a timid knock. He sprang out of his chair, hoping it was Bethany, and twisted his bad leg in the process. There was so much he wanted to say to her.

He pulled open the door. Jenny, not Bethany, stood on his stoop. She was dressed in a dark blue snowsuit and coat with bright red mittens on her hands. The ribbons of her *kapp* dangled out from beneath her hood. Behind her stood four other bundled-up children. Two boys wore flat-topped black hats, so he knew they were Amish *kinder*. They were all pulling colorful plastic toboggans.

Jenny grinned eagerly. "Can Sadie come out and play with us?"

He glanced down at the dog standing beside him. She wiggled with excitement but she didn't dash out the door. She looked to him for instructions. "I reckon."

He held the door wider and tipped his head toward the outside. "Go on. Have some fun."

Sadie bounded out of the house, jumping in circles around the children and barking.

"*Danki*, Michael," Jenny shouted as they headed toward his barn. He noticed that she was pulling two sleds, one red and one yellow. Why two? Every other child had one. Perhaps they were meeting someone else. They'd only gone a few more feet when he saw Jenny give the rope of one sled to Sadie. She held it in her mouth and trotted along with the group.

They disappeared behind the barn where the ground dropped away sharply, making a perfect hill for sledding. Although he couldn't see them, he could hear them calling encouragement to Sadie. The day was warmer than the past two weeks had been. He glanced back at the business paperwork waiting for him and decided it was time for a break.

He grabbed his hat and coat, put them on and closed the cabin door behind him. A walk in the fresh air was exactly what he needed. Maybe he would walk down and see Bethany. He smiled at the memory of their kiss last night. He was head over heels for her and he believed she felt the same but they hadn't discussed their feelings.

Maybe he was reading more into a kiss than he should. Bethany didn't know about his PTSD. Would that change her feelings toward him? He was better, it had been almost a month since he'd had a flashback, but was he well enough to consider a future with her? How would he know when he was healed?

A freshly shoveled path led from his cabin to Bethany's house. Ivan kept it open for him when he came to chop wood. That was the direction Michael wanted to go but he didn't have an excuse to see Bethany. He didn't want to appear too eager or pushy. The tracks of the children and dog led the other way.

He followed along, trying not to slip and fall in the new snow. When he reached the edge of the barn, he had an excellent view of the children sledding down the hill. Sadie was at the bottom with Jenny. They began to trudge back up, taking care to avoid the others flying down the hill toward them. Jenny was pulling her sled while Sadie pulled the other up the incline. He had never seen a dog do that.

At the top of the hill Jenny positioned her sled, sat down and pushed off with her hands. To his amazement, Sadie jumped on her own sled and went flying down the hill with her ears fluttering backward.

"Michael?"

He turned at the sound of Bethany's voice and saw her walking toward him. She held a package under her arm. He beckoned her closer. "You have to see this."

She smiled as she approached him. "This came for you in the mail. I thought it might be important and you weren't in your workshop."

"I was catching up on some paperwork. You need to see what the children are up to. Jenny stopped by to ask if Sadie could come out and play."

Bethany giggled. He would never tire of hearing

her mirth. It always made him smile. He stepped to the side so that she could have his vantage point. He stumbled and would have fallen if she hadn't grabbed his coat to steady him. It was a good reminder that he wasn't fit. Sometimes he forgot how damaged he was when she was around.

She didn't say anything but set his package on a stone by the barn door. She stepped to where he had been standing and looked at the children. "Your dog is sledding all by herself. Did you teach her to do that?"

The wonder and amusement in her voice eased the embarrassment he felt. "*Nee*, this is the first time."

"Oh, she's pulling it back up the hill. I don't believe it. It's like she's one of the children. That is a remarkable animal."

And you are a remarkable woman. For a second he was afraid he had spoken aloud.

"What are you two looking at?" Ivan asked as he walked up beside them. Jeffrey was with him. The boy, his younger siblings and his mother had returned to their home a few days after his father's arrest.

"We are watching Sadie use a sled," Bethany said.

"Are you fooling me?" Ivan walked to the edge of the slope and Jeffrey followed him. They began packing the snow into a ball and rolling it around to make it bigger. When they had one about a foot in diameter they pushed it down the hill toward the group of children.

"Not a good idea." Michael shouted, "Look out below!"

The snowball quickly gained size and speed. Both

boys sprinted after it as did Bethany. Michael watched helplessly, knowing he wouldn't be of any use.

Sadie barked and raced up the hill to meet the ball. She leaped to the side and tried to bite it as it rolled past. Her actions changed the direction just enough to let it roll harmlessly past the little girl who fell trying to scramble out of the way.

The snowball came to rest a few feet away from the trees that separated the field from the road. Michael heard Ivan apologizing. "I didn't think it would get so big. I thought it would break apart."

Bethany eyed him sternly.

"Honest, sister. I wasn't trying to hurt anyone. I thought we could make a snowman faster by rolling the balls down the hill to make them bigger."

She looked up at Michael as if seeking his opinion. He didn't think the boys meant any harm, either. He nodded slightly. She turned back to her brother. "Okay. It was almost a good idea. It just shows that you have to consider all parts of a problem before you decide on a solution. The easy way is not often the best way."

The younger children eagerly began creating snowmen of their own.

Jenny beckoned to Michael. "Help me make a tall snowman, Michael."

He wanted to join them. How many happy memories would it take to make him forget the horrible ones? Even if he wanted to, there was no way he could get down the hill without falling and arriving at the bottom inside a massive snowball. He shook his head and held up his cane.

Jenny pulled her sled over to Sadie and whispered something in her ear. Then she gave her the rope. Sadie came charging up the hill, pulling the empty sled. She skidded to a stop in front of Michael, dropped the rope and began barking furiously.

He looked at his dog. "You can't be serious. You want me to sled down the hill." He took another look at the terrain. It actually wasn't a bad idea. He looked at all the people beckoning him to come down. Getting down was the easy part. Getting up the slope would be the real challenge.

Sadie jumped up and put her paws on his chest. He ruffled her ears. "What kind of Amish man gives in to the whims of children and dogs?"

She barked once and looked downhill.

He followed her gaze and saw Bethany watching him. "Good point. She is down there. I was looking for an excuse to spend some time with her. When an opportunity falls into my lap I shouldn't waste it."

He awkwardly lowered himself into the red plastic sled and used his cane to pull himself to the edge of the incline. He looked at Sadie. "If I break my other leg I'm going to blame you." He pushed off and went flying down the slope.

He remembered how much fun it was to go sledding down a hill when he was a child. As an adult, he was a little more concerned about arriving at his destination in one piece.

* * *

Bethany held her breath as Michael shot down the hill with more speed than any of the children had obtained. To her relief, he used his cane as a drag to slow down when he neared the bottom. He came to rest a few feet in front of her. All the children applauded. Ivan jumped forward to help him to his feet. Michael was laughing like one of the *kinder.*

She had never seen him so lighthearted. It seemed that whatever had plagued him when he first came to New Covenant was giving way to a happier man.

She turned around with a snowball in her hand. "I've been wanting to do this for quite some time." She threw the ball and it hit him in the chest.

He brushed at his coat. "I refuse to get in a snowball fight with you. It's not dignified."

"You're right." She scooped up another handful of snow and packed it together. "I wouldn't want you to do something undignified." She let fly and this one struck him on his shoulder.

He brushed the loose snow away with one hand. "You are asking for trouble."

"I don't think so. I'm pretty sure I can outrun you."

"That was a low blow."

She tossed a newly formed snowball from one hand to the other. "You said you didn't like being treated differently because you need to use a cane."

"I think I will have to make you pay for that remark." He advanced menacingly.

She scuttled backward. "Forgiveness is the foundation of our religion. You don't want me to tell the bishop that you threatened me, do you?"

He kept coming and she kept backing up. "I think he would understand," he growled.

She took another step and tripped over the snowball Jenny had left unfinished. Michael scooped up a handful of snow. Standing over her, he dumped it on her face. She shrieked and rolled away. Surging to her feet, she shook her head to get rid of the snow and then glared at him. "That was just plain mean."

She was adorable. Her cheeks were bright red from the cold. Snow sparkled on her hair and eyelashes. The joy that filled his heart caught him off guard. Meeting her was the best thing that ever happened to him. How had she managed to worm her way so firmly into his heart in such a short amount of time?

"I apologize. I promise no more snow in the face, but I must remind you that you started it."

She looked as if she wanted to argue but gave in. "Okay, that is true. Now I have had my comeuppance and we are even, right?"

"I'd say so."

The boys had managed a haphazard snowman with a ragged straw hat, but they decided to go on to other adventures, leaving the slightly crooked fellow leaning into the wind.

"He looks lonely," Bethany said.

Michael put his hands on his hips. "I think he just looks homely."

Bethany moved several paces back. "I've been told I need to look at the whole picture."

"And what do you see?"

"A homely, lonely snowman. Let's fancy him up."

They found some winterberry and holly to decorate his straw hat. Bethany used a handful of red berries pressed into the snow to form his mouth. Michael supplied the branches for his arms and he sent one of the children to get a carrot for his nose.

Bethany withdrew a pace to look at him when he was finished. "There's still something missing."

"What?"

"I know." She pulled the red-and-white-striped scarf off and wrapped it around the snowman's neck. "There. He looks great."

Michael chuckled. "He looks like a mighty fancy Amish fellow. Is he one of your suitors?"

"He is and I will accept his offer." It was now or never. She smoothed the snowman's rough cheeks with her mittens, knowing Michael was listening. She'd never been so bold in her life, but she had to try. "The bishop understands why Ivan acted as he did when I explained things to him the other day, but he is still convinced a firmer hand could have prevented much of the trouble Ivan became embroiled in. He won't reconsider sending my brother away. I need an Amish husband before Christmas and the Lord has provided. That is, unless another suitor speaks up and asks me for my hand in marriage." She couldn't look at Michael.

He stepped close to her. "I don't think you should marry this fellow."

She looked into Michael's troubled eyes. "Do you think I'll get a better offer?"

He shook his head and walked away from her. "I wish I could be the man you need, but I'm not, Bethany."

"I think you are."

"You make it so hard to say no."

She moved to stand in front of him. "If it's hard to say no, then maybe you should say yes. I won't make any demands on you. Your time will be your own. You can have one hundred percent of the business. I need your help, Michael."

"I'm sorry."

Jenny came walking back to see what they were up to. She clapped her hands when she saw the snowman. "He's beautiful. He can be Bishop Schultz come to marry Michael and Bethany." Jenny looked at her sister.

Bethany gave Michael a sidelong glance. His face could have been carved from stone. She leaned over and forced a smile for her little sister. "There isn't going to be a wedding. I told you that."

Jenny's face fell. "Okay. I'm going to help Jeffrey and Ivan build a snow cave."

Michael glanced at Bethany and then quickly looked down at his boots. "Are you going to the Christmas parade in the city with Pastor Frank?"

"Yes, we are. What about you?" She avoided meeting his gaze.

"I think I will go." Maybe during the Christmas parade would be a good time to gauge how she felt about them.

Bethany retreated a pace. "I'd better get started on lunch. They're going to be a hungry bunch when they come in."

"I've got some work to do, too."

She regained some of her composure. "That's right. A box came for you. I left it at your barn."

He looked up the slope. "I might work on something that's already in the workshop."

"I'll get the box." She grabbed the empty toboggan that Jenny had left by her snowman's head and trudged up the hill. She picked up his box, got in the sled and pushed off.

When she came to a stop two feet in front of him, he arched one eyebrow. "Show-off."

"I'm just using the gifts God gave me." She handed him the box and walked beside him all the way to his workshop, but the awkwardness between them persisted. Had she ruined their friendship with her desperate attempt to keep Ivan?

A half hour later Bethany was at the kitchen sink, peeling potatoes for French fries, when Jeffrey came in. "I'm hungry. Can I have a sandwich?" Sadie Sue followed him in and plopped down in front of the fireplace with her tongue hanging out.

His cheeks were rosy red from the cold but his lips were tinged with blue. "I think you should stay in for a while. Take off your boots and let me check your feet."

She had learned her first winter here that frostbite was nothing to be trifled with. He did as she instructed. His toes were bright pink but there was a patch of white skin on the back of his left heel. "You are definitely not going back outside. I'm going to get a pan of cool water and I want you to keep your foot in it until I tell you otherwise."

"But we just finished a great snow cave. Ivan is expecting me to come back."

"I'll explain to him why you have to stay in."

Michael had been working in his shop but apparently he had overheard her conversation. "I'll go tell Ivan what's going on."

"Danki," Bethany said and smiled at him. He was always willing to lend a helping hand. In many ways he reminded her of her grandfather. He had the same kind of gentle soul. She fixed a pan of water and had Jeffrey soak his foot.

Michael put on his coat and hat. "Where is your snow cave?"

"Out by the highway. The snowplows have made huge piles there." The snow the previous night had left four more inches on the roadways.

Michael stepped out onto the porch. "I see the piles, but I don't see the kids."

Bethany came out and stood beside him. She shaded her eyes with one hand against the glare of the sun off the white snow. "I don't see them, either."

Mike took a pair of snowshoes off their hooks on the porch. As he did, Bethany heard the grading rumble of the snowplow coming down from the ridge. The truck with a large blade on the front blasted through the new snow, easily making bigger drifts along the side of the road. It was headed down to the intersection where Jeffrey said Ivan and Jenny were playing.

The snowplow driver couldn't see the children for they were on the far side of the high snowbank away from him. She saw a flash of red in the snow and thought it must be Jenny's glove. The snowplow hit the side of the big pile and pushed it farther off the edge of the highway, adding a huge new supply of snow on top of what was already there. The place where she had seen Jenny's glove was completely covered. She started screaming and ran toward her sister.

Michael saw the whole thing happen and was helpless to stop it. How much time did they have? A few minutes? Maybe more if the children were in any kind of air pocket. He turned around and hurried to the house. "Jeffrey, get your shoes back on and run to the neighbors. Jenny and Ivan have been buried by the snowplow. We need everybody who can get here to dig. Go."

Jeffrey rushed to do as he was told. Michael ran to the tower of snow. Bethany was on her knees, digging with her bare hands. Michael grabbed a snow shovel from the porch and rushed to her side. He gave it to her and began using his cane as a probe into the snow, hoping to come in contact with a body. Each time his cane sank all the way in, he prayed harder.

It seemed like hours but it could've only been minutes when he heard the sounds of shouting from up the road. A dozen Amish men came rushing toward them with shovels and rakes. They spread out on either side of Bethany and Michael and began digging.

Jeffrey was digging frantically with them. Bethany was crying. She kept saying "no, no, no."

He kept probing inch by inch, knowing Jenny and Ivan were under there somewhere and running out of time. He had never been so scared in his life. Not even when he knew the gunman was going to kill him. Suddenly Sadie Sue was beside him, whining. Bethany stopped digging and looked at the dog and then at Michael.

"It's a long shot," he said. He knelt beside Sadie and said, "Find Jenny." She whined and didn't move. Bethany came to stand beside Michael. "Find Jenny, please."

The dog trotted away from where they were digging and Michael's hopes crashed. He went back to probing and Bethany returned to digging.

Twenty feet away, Sadie Sue started barking and digging at the snow.

Bethany looked at Michael. "I saw her glove here. I know I did." She kept digging and uncovered a red plastic candy wrapper.

Jeffrey had returned. He took Bethany's shovel away and raced over to the dog. He began frantically scooping the snow aside as she dug her way in. Suddenly the dog disappeared completely.

Bethany heard crying and knew at least one of them was alive. Praying as she had never prayed before, she stumbled to where Jeffrey was kneeling. The rest of their neighbors gathered around the hole and began widening it. Sadie came backing out, but she was dragging something. With two strong tugs she emerged from the hole, pulling Jenny out by her coat. Ivan crawled out on his own.

Cheering broke out from everyone. Bethany grabbed up her sister and held her tight and threw her other arm around Ivan. "Thank you, merciful Lord."

She looked at Michael and held out her hand. He came and embraced them all. He never wanted to let them go. As his frantically beating heart slowed, he added Sadie Sue to the group hug. She started licking Jenny's face, making the child giggle.

Ivan looked at Michael. "I knew you'd find us."

Not once during the emergency had Michael thought about the robbery or its aftermath. He had faced a life-and-death challenge without triggering a flashback or a panic attack. He had worked side by side with Bethany to save her family. A family he wanted to be a part of forever.

He caught Bethany's eye. "If you haven't said yes to the snowman, I'd like to reconsider your offer."

"You would?" Hope brightened her face.

"I would."

"Is that a yes?" A grin spread across her face.

"If you'll have me."

"I will." She hugged Ivan and Jenny harder. "I most certainly will."

Chapter Fifteen

On the Saturday evening before Christmas, Bethany, Michael and the children climbed into Pastor Frank's twenty-passenger van with sixteen other members of their Amish community, including the bishop, Jesse, Gemma and her parents.

Bethany kept Jenny close to her. The child had been subdued since the accident and wanted to constantly claim Bethany's attention. Michael didn't seem to mind. Bethany loved him for that. Ivan seemed far less affected.

As the van rolled down the highway Ivan began leading them in song. Michael joined in with his pleasant baritone voice. Christmas hymns new and old filled Bethany's heart with the joy of this most holy season. She knew how blessed she was to have Jenny and Ivan with her and how easily it could have turned out differently. Every time she caught Michael's eye he smiled at her. She hoped it was just a matter of time before he declared his love.

When they reached the city Pastor Frank parked the van on a side street and everyone made their way to the parade route. The streets were lined four deep with bundled-up people all sharing the holiday spirit on a frosty evening. Lavish holiday lights decorated the buildings along Main Street, blinking red and green and ice blue. Lit displays filled every business window.

Jenny, standing at Bethany's side, tugged on her coat. "I can't see."

Jesse leaned down to her. "Would you like to sit on my shoulders? I can see everything and you'll be even taller."

Jenny glanced at Bethany and then took Jesse's hand. "Okay."

He hoisted her to sit piggyback on his shoulders and she laughed. "Ivan, look at me."

"Hey, that's not fair," her brother shot back, but he was smiling.

Bethany reached for Michael's hand and gave it a squeeze. "She's feeling better."

"Kids are resilient and there is nothing like seeing a parade from the back of a giant to perk someone up."

Bethany chuckled and leaned against him. "You can always make me laugh."

Michael knew a depth of joy he never thought he would experience. His PTSD had improved enough for him to believe he was finally over it. The stress of searching for Jenny and Ivan hadn't triggered a flashback. He hadn't even had a nightmare afterward. That horrible part of his life was well and truly over.

He smiled at Bethany and took her hand. Although she hadn't said that she loved him, he was sure that love would blossom in time to match his. And he did love her. With all his heart.

A PA system announced the parade was about to start and the crowd pressed forward. The canon across the park boomed and fireworks lit up the sky. The red streaks in the darkness held his attention. A shiver crawled down his spine. He couldn't shake the sight of red streaks on the floor and red flashes lighting up the night beyond his window.

Sirens sounded. People cheered as the local police and firefighters led the parade in their new machines with lights and sirens. The crowd behind him pressed closer. Michael couldn't breathe. He started hearing a scream and knew it was coming from him. He couldn't shut out the screams. Someone was talking to him, asking him what was wrong. A hand grabbed him and he swatted it. He had to get away.

He felt the impact of the bullet hitting his leg. He fell to the ground and started moaning.

Bethany had no idea what was wrong with Michael. She cried out for help as she knelt beside him. People gathered round, pressing closer, staring, uncertain how to help. Michael gazed wide-eyed into the space, hitting at her when she touched him. Bethany didn't think he knew she was there. Suddenly Pastor Frank was beside her.

"It's okay, Michael. It's Pastor Frank. You're having a flashback. It isn't real. You aren't in any danger.

You're safe. Can you hear me? Bethany is here beside me. Is it all right if Bethany holds your hand?"

Michael's hand opened and closed on the sidewalk. Bethany took hold of it. "It's all right, darling. I'm here. I'm with you."

Pastor Frank patted her shoulder. "Keep talking to him. He needs to know that what he is seeing and hearing isn't real. I think we're going to need to get him away from this noise and commotion. I'm going to bring the van up."

Pastor Frank summoned a police officer who went with him.

Bethany held Michael's hand but he kept moaning and muttering people's names. She had no idea how to help him. She'd never felt more useless in her life. She didn't understand what was wrong. Was this what he was afraid of? Jenny was on her knees beside Bethany, crying. "What's the matter with Michael?"

Ivan took his little sister by the shoulders. "He's going to be okay. He'll get over this soon."

Bethany prayed Ivan's words were true.

Michael refused to come out of his cabin the next day. He didn't want to see anyone. He didn't answer the door although he knew both Frank and Bethany were outside. What was the point? Everyone knew now that he was just a shell of a man who looked normal but wasn't. Pastor Frank had been right. He wasn't going to be able to heal himself. He needed help. If he had tried to get help earlier maybe he could've salvaged something of his relationship with Bethany.

When the sun started to set, he went out and harnessed the pony. Pastor Frank's survivors' support group was tonight. Michael wasn't sure he was a survivor, but he definitely needed support.

At the church, he left his horse and cart and walked around the back of the building. A set of steps led to the basement. The door of the room where support group meetings were held stood open. A hand-lettered sign on the wall said Welcome to a Safe Place.

He wasn't sure what a safe place felt like anymore but if he was ever going to find one he had to start somewhere. He stepped inside and stopped in surprise. There were eight *Englisch* men and women seated at a round table with the pastor, but there were a dozen chairs lined up across the back of the room filled with the men and women of his Amish community. Jesse and the bishop. The carpenter Nigel Miller and his wife, Becca. Gemma Lapp and her parents, plus a dozen other Amish people he didn't know by name.

Bethany rose from her seat and came toward him. She held out her hand but he didn't take it. "What are you doing here?"

"I'm here to learn about PTSD and how to help the man I love cope with and overcome this disorder. We all want to be able to help you when you need us."

"The man you love? How can you still say that after what you saw? I was on the pavement, sobbing like a frightened child. I wasn't even aware that you were beside me. How can you love someone who is so damaged? 'The man that you pity' is what you really mean to say. You pity me."

"How can I not love you? In all the world you are the man who opened my heart so that I could clearly see God has chosen you to be my beloved. Are you a perfect man? *Nee*, for only God is perfect. Are you a good man? I believe, I know that you are."

Michael tried to swallow the lump in his throat as tears stung his eyes. "I don't deserve your love."

She smiled at him softly. "I have news for you. God and I believe you do."

Pastor Frank came to stand beside Bethany. "I am delighted that you came tonight, Michael. I wasn't sure that you would, but all of your friends have expressed a sincere interest in learning about PTSD and about how to deal with someone who suffers from it."

Michael started backing away. "I can't do this. Not yet. Not here. I'm sorry, Bethany."

"Michael, please." She held out her hand.

"*Nee*, whatever you thought was between us is over. I'm no good to you." He turned and walked out the door.

Bethany watched helplessly as Michael turned his back on her and left. She didn't understand why he wouldn't even try to accept their help. She looked to Pastor Frank. "What do I do?"

"That's why you're here. To learn about what you can do."

"Should I go after him?"

"No. I'm going to ask everyone to have a seat and I'm going to talk a little about PTSD and what it means to a person suffering from that disorder."

Bethany returned to her seat. Gemma grasped her hand.

Frank smiled at the crowd. "Some of you know exactly what I'm talking about. Others are just learning about the existence of this cruel disorder. Someone with PTSD will experience horrible events over and over again in a way that is so real they believe they are back in that situation."

Bethany listened and tried to learn all she could, but the magnitude of the problem was daunting. After the meeting was over she stayed to talk to Frank alone.

"Tell me how I can help Michael. Why did he push me away? I believe he loves me. I know he does."

"Michael considers himself weak. He is fearful that others, that you, will see him that way, too. Yet he can't hide from what has happened to him. He has tried to run away from it by moving to this remote settlement, but the change of scenery hasn't changed the disorder. But there is help and there is hope. I believe that shining God's light into the dark recesses of our pain will take away the power the trauma has over us."

"What do I do now?"

"When someone you love suffers from post-traumatic stress disorder, it can be overwhelming. You may feel hurt by your loved one's distance and moodiness. However, it's important to know that you're not a helpless bystander. Your love and support can make all the difference in Michael's recovery. Don't try to pressure him into talking. It may make things worse. Just let him know you're willing to listen when he wants to talk."

"I'm frightened. I'm not sure what I'm walking into but I love him. I have to help."

Michael had to leave. He couldn't stay and see the woman he loved look at him with pity for the rest of his life. He couldn't do it. He didn't own much. Just a few tools, some clothes and a big yellow dog. It should be easy to pick up and go, except it wasn't easy.

He was in the workshop, carefully packing up his tools, when the door opened. He knew who it was without looking. His eyes filled with tears but he refused to let them fall.

She spoke softly. "Please don't leave us."

"You must be out of your mind to want me to stay."

She stepped closer. "I don't think so. I think you're the man I need. You also happen to be the man I love."

His gaze flew to hers. "You don't know what you're saying."

"I know exactly what I'm saying. I am in love with you, Michael Shetler. My heart tells me you are the man I have been waiting for all my life."

He turned away and continued packing his tools. "You want a man who can fall apart in the blink of an eye because some sound or smell triggers a flashback? Is that your idea of an ideal mate? What if I'm driving a team and the children are with me and I don't see the train coming when I cross the tracks?"

"Michael, I know your problem looms large to you, but for me it is only one part of who you are. You are a kind, loving man. You are hardworking. You try to live your faith by caring for those around you. You are great with children and with dogs. You walk with a cane and you have PTSD. I won't pretend to understand what that is like for you. But do you really want to give up a woman who loves you, two children who adore you, and a mangy mutt that thinks you hung the moon?"

He put down his screwdrivers. "Sadie Sue isn't a mangy mutt."

"You're right. She is a very special gift sent by God to help us. She saved Ivan's and Jenny's lives, but I would trade places with that dog in a heartbeat. Do you know why? Because you accept that she loves you regardless of the difficulties you face. I wish you had half that much faith in my love. If you don't, then maybe I am wasting my breath."

Michael wanted to deny his love for Bethany but he couldn't. He knew it took a great deal of courage for her to come to him this way. She was the most remarkable woman he'd ever met.

"Bethany, I don't want to burden you with my weakness. You deserve a strong and stable man."

"I do." She gave him a sly smile. "Unfortunately, Jesse won't have me. That leaves you."

He grinned in spite of himself. "Jesse wouldn't stand a chance against your wit."

"You once told me that you would help me with

anything I needed if it was within your power. Did you mean that?"

"I did."

"Then here is what I want. I want to be the person beside you the next time you have a flashback if you ever have one again. I want to know and understand what you are going through, what you are seeing and hearing so I can lead you to a safe place. Tell me what happened to you. Make me understand."

Michael shook his head. "I will never do that to you."

Her eyes filled with disappointment. "Why won't you let me help you?"

"You don't understand."

"Make me."

He stepped close and took her hands in his. "Bethany, if I share with you the pain and guilt and the horrible events that I lived through, then they can become your nightmare, too. You will be haunted by the things I tell you because you love me. I don't want you to know even a small part of the horror I endured."

"I'm a strong woman."

"I know you are."

"Frank told me he suffered with PTSD for many years after he came back from his military service. It destroyed his marriage and almost took his life. He found a way to deal with it by helping others. He also told me that talking about what happened to you is a way to decrease the power it has over your mind."

"He may be right. I will share my story with him but not with you."

"Don't you trust me?"

"I trust you with my life and all that I have. You must trust me when I say there are some things you are better off not knowing."

"I guess you are asking me for a leap of faith. Okay. I will not ask about it again. Are you going to marry me?"

He shook his head in bewilderment. "You are too bold to be a *goot* Amish maiden."

"I'm an Amish maiden who knows what she wants. You think that marrying me will ruin my life. I'm going to tell you that the only way you can ruin my life is to not marry me. Don't break my heart."

She stepped closer and slid her arms around his neck. "Please, Michael, say that you love me or don't say it—because it doesn't matter. I already know you do. I see it in your eyes. I feel it in your touch. I know it by the way your heart calls to mine."

He groaned and wrapped his arms around her to pull her close. "I can't believe I'm about to give you the opportunity to tell me what to do for the rest of my life."

Michael leaned close. Bethany knew he was going to kiss her. She had never wanted anything more. His lips touched hers with incredible gentleness, a featherlight touch. It wasn't enough.

She cupped his face with her hands. To her delight, he deepened the kiss. Joy clutched her heart and stole her breath. She'd been waiting a lifetime for this moment and never knew it.

He pulled her closer. The sweet softness of his lips

moved away from her mouth. He kissed her cheek, her eyelids and her forehead, and then he drew away. Bethany wasn't ready to let him go. She would never be ready to let him go.

"I love you, Bethany," he murmured softly against her temple. "You make me whole. I am broken but you believe I can be mended. You make me believe it. I have lived in despair, ashamed of what I don't understand. I thought I was beyond help. And then you came into my life and I saw hope."

"I love you, too, darling, but it is God that has made us both whole. Will you marry me?"

"To keep Ivan with you?" he asked.

She rose on tiptoe and kissed him. "To keep you by my side always. Will you?"

"Can't you hear my heart shouting the answer?" He kissed her temple and held her close.

Bethany had never felt so cherished. The wonder of his love was almost impossible to comprehend. Emotion choked her. She couldn't speak.

"Did he say yes?" Jenny's whispered question was hushed by Ivan.

Michael choked on a laugh as he realized they weren't alone. He looked up at the ceiling to compose himself. Bethany shook silently in his arms. He knew she was trying not to laugh out loud.

He mustered his most authoritative voice. "Eavesdroppers are likely to be sent to bed without their supper for a week."

Jenny popped up from behind the desk. "I wasn't

eavesdropping. I just came in to ask my sister a question."

Michael kept his arm around Bethany as she turned to face her sister. "Ivan, what is your excuse?" she asked.

Ivan rose more reluctantly. "I came in to keep Jenny from interrupting the two of you."

"And what is the reason the two of you were hiding behind my desk?" he asked.

"I wasn't hiding. I was scratching Sadie's tummy," Jenny announced with a smile at her brilliant excuse. "But I did happen to hear my sister ask you to marry her, Michael. I thought men were supposed to ask first. Did she do it backward?"

Ivan took her hand and started to lead her from the room. "You have a lot to learn, sis. Women like to let men think it was their idea."

Jenny tried to get her hand loose. "Wait. We didn't hear his answer." Ivan didn't let go of her. She grabbed the doorjamb and held on as she looked over her shoulder. "Please, Michael, say you want to marry us."

A tug from her brother propelled her out of the room. He shut the door with a resounding bang.

Bethany turned and leaned against Michael's chest as she shook with laughter. "I'm the one who should tell you to run and get as far away from us as fast as you can."

"I'm afraid that no matter how far I went I wouldn't survive long."

She leaned back to look at his face. "Why is that?"

"Because my heart would remain here in your keeping and a man can't live long without a heart."

"Then you will marry me?" she asked hopefully.

"On one condition."

A faint frown appeared on her face. "What condition?"

"That I also get to ask the question. Bethany Martin, will you do me the honor of becoming my wife?"

"I will."

"Then I promise to love and cherish you all the days of my life," he said and bent to kiss her once more.

The door flew open and Jenny charged in with Sadie at her side. "He said yes and she said yes. We're getting married!" Sadie started barking wildly as she bounced around Jenny. Ivan stood in the doorway with a bright smile on his face.

Bethany gazed up at Michael with all the love in her heart. "Are you sure you want to marry all of us?"

He kissed the tip of her nose. "I want an Amish wife for Christmas, two fine Amish children, a fine house with a workshop and a *goot hund*. What more could a man need?"

"Maybe another kiss from his Amish wife?"

"My darling Bethany, you read me like a book." He leaned in and kissed her again, knowing no matter what trials he faced, he would never face them alone. God and Bethany would be with him always.

Chapter Sixteen

The morning of Second Christmas, December 26, dawned clear and bright in New Covenant, Maine. Bethany and Michael stood in the entryway of her house and greeted their wedding guests. Bethany's aunt and uncle had arrived on Christmas Eve and had helped take over the preparations for the wedding. Ivan and Jesse showed the guests to their seats.

Bethany glanced at her soon-to-be husband. He looked very handsome in his black suit and black string tie. He smiled back at her. "It's not too late to call it off."

She shook her head. "I think it was too late the day I met you."

He snapped his fingers. "That's who we forgot to invite."

"Who?"

"Clarabelle."

Gemma entered with her parents. "A blessed Christmas to you and may you have a blessed life together."

"Thank you for agreeing to be my sidesitter," Bethany said.

"I am honored to be your attendant at your wedding. Michael, who is going to stand up with you?"

"Jesse has agreed to do me the favor."

Gemma made a sour face. "That man is as dense as a post." She went in to take her place on the front bench where Bethany would sit during the ceremony.

"What does she have against Jesse?" Michael asked.

"Nothing, except he hasn't noticed her in all the time she has been trying to catch his attention."

"She likes Jesse? Are you sure?"

"Very sure. Do you think this is everyone?" She glanced into the full living room, where the church benches had been set out in two rows for the men and the women.

"I think so."

"Where are the children?" Bethany looked around. "I hope Jenny is not getting her new dress dirty."

"I think she's trying to figure out some way to smuggle Sadie Sue in."

"As much as I like your dog, I'm not going to have her at my wedding."

He laughed and pointed up the stairwell. "I wouldn't be too sure about that."

Jenny was kneeling at the top of the steps with Sadie Sue lying beside her. The two of them scurried back down the hall when they realized they had been spotted.

"Do you want me to speak to her?" he asked.

"*Nee*, she knows better. She will behave. I hope."

The bishop came up to them. "Are you ready?"

They smiled at each other and nodded. "We're ready," they said in unison.

While the preparations had been rushed, the ceremony itself went off without a hitch. The bishop was short-winded for a change and the preaching lasted only three hours. As Bethany stood beside Michael in front of the bishop, she couldn't help but realize how very blessed she was to have found the perfect man. She couldn't stop smiling.

Afterward, Bethany went upstairs to change her black *kapp* for a white one. In the corner of the room facing the front door, the Eck, or the "corner table," was quickly set up for the wedding party.

When it was ready, Michael took his place with Jesse and Ivan seated to his right. Bethany was ushered back in and took her seat at his left-hand side. It symbolized the place she would occupy in his buggy and in his life. Her cheeks were rosy red and her eyes sparkled with happiness. They clasped hands underneath the table. Michael squeezed her fingers. "You are everything I could have asked for and so much more."

"I promise to try and be a *goot* wife to you," she said with a meekness he distrusted.

"Just be yourself. That will be good enough."

"You realize you get to choose the seating arrangements for the single people this evening, don't you?" Gemma asked.

Michael shrugged. "I haven't given it much thought."

"This might be the first wedding in New Covenant

but I'm going to make sure it isn't the last," Bethany said with a wink at her friend.

Jenny sat on the other side of Gemma. "Are you going to pick a husband for me?"

"I may just do that." She smiled at her sister.

Michael leaned back in his seat. "Are you taking up matchmaking now?"

She chuckled. "Clarabelle is my only local competition. I think I can do better than her."

He leaned close to her. "The old cow did right by me."

"I beg to differ. She never once mentioned your name."

"Do you know what?"

"What?" she asked, intrigued by the light in his eyes.

"I can't wait to kiss you again."

Bethany felt the heat rush to her face. "I can't wait for that myself, my husband."

* * * * *

HER SURPRISE
CHRISTMAS COURTSHIP

Emma Miller

Cast not away therefore your confidence,
which hath great recompence of reward.
—*Hebrews* 10:35

Chapter One

Honeycomb, Delaware

"Penny is feeling so much better since the visit from the vet," Millie said as she used a pitchfork to toss fresh straw into the goat's stall. It had been her twin sister's turn to clean the stalls, but Willa wasn't much for outdoor chores. Willa thought the barn smelled and she was afraid of mice, so Millie was doing it for her. Millie wasn't scared of anything she could think of. Certainly not a little mouse.

"You remember John Hartman, don't you?" Millie murmured as she pushed the straw around on the packed dirt floor. "From Seven Poplars? He grew up Mennonite but went Amish to marry the widow Hannah Yoder?"

Her mother's favorite goat was getting on in years and Millie wanted to be sure it was comfortable. Past the age of bearing young or even providing milk, the goat had been put to pasture. And Millie figured that having provided for the family for so many years, Penny deserved as good a care as anyone on the farm.

"I'm glad Penny is on the mend. Aren't you, *Mam*?"

Her mother didn't respond.

Tearing up, Millie leaned on the pitchfork. Of course her mother didn't say anything.

Her mother was gone.

The Lord had taken her home more than a year ago.

Unlike her father, Millie never forgot that *Mam* had passed, but she still liked to talk to her sometimes. It comforted her. And maybe she *was* listening. Who knew?

Satisfied that the area was clean, Millie rested the pitchfork against the wall and walked out into the freshly swept aisle that ran between the stalls of the barn. "Come on with you." She took Penny by her leather collar and tugged, but the goat didn't budge. Penny was too busy eating her oats from a bucket. "Going to be stubborn this morning, are you?" Millie asked patiently.

The brown-and-white Nubian bleated and stuck her head back into the bucket.

Millie laughed. "Fine." She stroked Penny's warm, soft back. "You've nothing but scraps left, but you can take them with you." Leading the goat with one hand and enticing her with the bucket with the other, she returned Penny to her stall and closed the door.

According to her sister Henrietta—whom they called Henry—Penny's stall was the last of the three that needed to be mucked. Because her parents had been cursed—or blessed, depending on the situation—with seven daughters and no sons, Millie and her sisters had always done barn chores at their father's side. Now that their *dat* wasn't dependable when it came to such matters, the girls worked on a rotating schedule, with Henry overseeing them.

With the task done, now all Millie had to do was dump the wheelbarrow of dirty bedding and she could return to the house to see if there were any apple pancakes left over from breakfast. The manual labor had made her hungry again. And maybe she'd have a hot chocolate, too. As she hung the pitchfork on the wall, she wondered if there were any marshmallows left. She'd bought two big bags at Byler's store, but her father loved marshmallows and often sneaked them from the pantry. If Millie's eldest sister, Eleanor, found out he was eating handfuls of marshmallows, she'd be cross with him because, according to his doctor, he was supposed to be watching the amount of sugar he ate.

Millie adjusted the blue wool scarf she wore over her head and tied under her chin, and grabbed the wheelbarrow handles. There were a lot of things she didn't like about being a big girl—as her father called her—but one of the good things was that she was strong. As strong as any man. Stronger than some. She could easily roll a whole wheelbarrow to the manure pile without a problem. Whereas Willa, a thin wisp of a girl, had to make two trips.

As Millie rolled the wheelbarrow out of the double doors into the barnyard, she raised her face to catch a few warm rays of the sun. It was early October, and they had woken to the welcome relief of a cool breeze. It had been a long, hot summer and she was thankful for the change of seasons. Plus, fall brought all kinds of delicious foods to the table: sweet yams, apple turnovers and savory cabbage stews. And then there was Christmas to look forward to.

As Millie pushed the wheelbarrow toward the manure pile, she spotted Willa under the clothesline in the backyard. Millie had dressed for barn work in an ugly, stained brown dress and her father's oldest denim barn coat. Willa, however, was dressed for chores in a new peach-colored dress and knit sweater that was more suited for Sunday visiting than housework. Covering her blond hair, Willa wore a white organza prayer *kapp* rather than a sensible headscarf like Millie.

As Willa clipped a pillowcase to the line, she leaned forward, looking at something in the distance, her pretty face in a scowl. Suddenly she drew back, her eyes going wide, and, spotting Millie, began to wave her arms, shouting something at her. However, between the sound of the howling wind and the creaking of their metal windmill as it spun, Millie couldn't hear her sister. Then their flock of sheep caught sight of her and must have thought she intended to feed them, because they all came running to the fence, bleating and hitting their front hooves on the rails.

Millie let go of the wheelbarrow handles. "What?" she hollered to Willa, cupping her hand to her ear.

Willa began jumping up and down, pointing. It

sounded like she was hollering "Wow!" or maybe "Pal!" *Pals?*

"I can't hear you!" Millie called.

Willa ran toward her, flapping her arms. "The wows are out!"

The wows? Millie thought. What on earth was her sister talking about? She turned in the direction Willa was pointing. Then she saw them. Beyond the barn, through several small, fenced corrals and across the pasture was their herd of a dozen cows.

On the far side of the fence.

Millie brought her hands to her cheeks. *The cows had broken out of their pasture!* "The cows are out!" she cried to her sister.

"I know!" Willa shouted, running toward her. "That's what I was trying to tell you! We have to get Henry! She'll know what to do!"

Millie rolled her eyes as Willa came to a halt beside the wheelbarrow. "We don't need Henry. They're our cows, too. Come on," she said, hurrying toward the gate. It would be quicker to cut across the field to the cows than to go around the barn and down their long lane to the road.

"Millie, we can't herd cows," Willa fretted, following her. "That's Henry's job. You know how she is. Henry's not going to like it."

Millie flipped the latch on the gate. "*Ach*, but Henry's not here, is she?"

"She's not?"

"*Nay.*" Millie started across the pasture. "She took *Dat* visiting. Remember?"

"Wait! You're going too fast. Wait for me," Willa called, closing the gate behind her.

"We have to get them before one of them gets hurt," Millie said, refusing to slow down. If Willa weighed half what Millie weighed, she ought to be able to go twice as fast, shouldn't she?

"Oh! Oh my," Willa cried as they crossed the field.

Millie looked over her shoulder to see her sister hopping in one direction and then another, as if moving from one lily pad to another on their pond. "What are you doing?" she asked.

"Cow pies."

Millie had to cover her mouth to keep from laughing aloud. She loved her sister. Adored her. But Willa was what their mother had called *fussy*. Their mother had always said Willa was too persnickety for a farm girl. She didn't like to get dirty or sweaty or touch anything she thought was icky—which was a lot of things.

"I could go back to the house and tell Eleanor the cows are out. She could send Jane or Beth to help you." Willa backtracked, to dart around a patch of high grass.

Millie slowed from a trot to a fast walk, keeping an eye on the cows on the far side of the fence. They were moving along the road, sampling the fresh, uncut grass. She tried not to think about what could happen if one of the cows ventured into the road. The year before, a family in a neighboring church district had lost their only milk cow when it broke through their fence and was hit by a big truck.

Reaching the fence that ran along the road, Millie halted, looking one direction and then the other. Where was the hole in the fence? She'd assumed their two dairy Holsteins and the beef cows had broken through an opening along the road. She had intended to go through the break in the fence and herd the cows back in the way they'd gone out, but there was no break there.

Willa stopped beside Millie, panting. Petunia, the older of their milk cows, lifted her head, chewing a mouthful of clover while she stared at them as if wondering how they had gotten inside the pasture.

"Where did they go through?" Willa asked.

"I don't know." Millie looked in the direction of their driveway to the north, squinting in the hope of seeing the break, but she didn't.

Just then, Petunia began moving toward the road.

"*Nay*," Millie murmured, snatching a handful of green grass and waving it at the cow. "Come this way. Look what I have. It looks so good. Mmm," she said, trying to entice Petunia.

The cow lifted her head but didn't move toward the bouquet of grass Millie held out.

"We have to climb over the fence," Millie told her sister, afraid to look away from Petunia for fear she would take off for the road.

"Climb the fence?" Willa protested. "I'm not climbing a fence. This is my new dress. We'll have to walk back to the gate."

Millie watched the black-and-white Holstein out of the corner of her eye, while continuing to look for the break in the stockade fence. Her father had built it twenty years ago from heavy-gauge wire fencing strung between posts and lengths of lumber across the top of each section. Still seeing no break in the fence, she glanced at the herd again. The other cows seemed content, at least for the moment, to eat along the far side of the fence, but Petunia kept turning away from Millie to look at a patch of thick clover across the road in their neighbor's ditch.

"I'm cold. I should go back to the house and get help." Willa hugged herself for warmth. "Or...or maybe we could get Elden to help." She pointed in the direction of the Yoder farm across the street.

They'd grown up with Elden Yoder and attended school together. He had been a year ahead of them and the best-looking, most popular boy in their one-room schoolhouse. Millie had always liked him; in fact, she liked him so much that she avoided him whenever possible. Even as an adult she felt tongue-tied around him. He'd become engaged earlier in the year, but the wedding had been called off. It had been a bit of a scandal because no one in the town of Honeycomb knew why the betrothal had ended, but there was a lot of speculation. Willa and their youngest sister, Jane, had talked about nothing else for weeks after it happened.

"I don't need Elden Yoder's help to catch my own cows," Millie argued. She looked the stockade fence up and down. "I guess we're going to have to go over it." She dropped the grass she'd been trying to tempt the milk cow with and placed her foot gingerly in one of the squares of the metal fence, testing to be sure it would hold her weight.

"But Elden's right there," Willa said.

"He's right *where*?"

Petunia turned away from Millie and started for the road just as a pickup truck whizzed by.

"Nay!" Millie cried, scrambling up the fence. At the top, she pressed both hands on the board and awkwardly threw her leg over. If she could just hoist herself over—

Millie didn't know what happened next. Maybe her sneaker slipped, or maybe the old wire fencing broke, but suddenly she was falling. It seemed like such a long way down. She cried out as she went over, spooking the cows, who all took off in opposite directions, bellowing and mooing loudly.

"Millie!" Willa screamed.

Millie hit the ground, arms flailing, and rolled down the slight incline, coming to a rest with her face planted in the drainage ditch.

"Oh!" her sister cried from the other side of the fence.

Millie wondered if she had blacked out for a moment because the next thing she knew, someone was leaning over her. And then a deep, masculine voice asked, "Mildred? Mildred, are you okay?"

Elden had spotted the twin Koffman sisters hurrying across their pasture and had wondered what they were up to. He'd lowered the blade of his scythe to the ground to rest his aching shoulders as he watched. He'd been working on clearing his meadow since breakfast and was thankful for the respite. Then he saw that their cows were on the wrong side of their fence and had dropped the scythe to run to their aid. He was crossing the road when Mildred, head down, not seeing him, had started to climb the fence.

Elden had shouted for her to wait, that he was coming, but he guessed she hadn't heard him in the wind. He was halfway across the road when Mildred tumbled head-over-teacup, as his mother liked to say. And then the girl hit the ground. Hard.

Elden had sprinted the last few feet.

He now crouched beside her as she lay facedown in the ditch, not moving, and he feared she'd been severely injured. He hesitated, not sure if it was okay to touch her, but then gingerly laid his hand on the small of her back.

"Oh my!" Mildred's twin, Willa, fussed from the other side of the fence. "She's broken her neck, hasn't she? She's dead."

"She's not dead," he told Willa. With his hand on Mildred's back, he could feel her breathing. He leaned down, bringing his face close to hers. "Mildred, can you hear me?"

"Millie," Mildred said softly, still not moving.

Elden leaned closer. "What's that?"

Mildred moved her head ever so slightly and opened the eye he could see. He had always thought she had pretty eyes—they were big, and the color of nutmeg with little flecks of cinnamon.

"Millie," she repeated. "No one calls me Mildred. Not since my school days."

Elden couldn't resist a smile of relief. If she was correcting him, she had to be okay, didn't she?

He and Mildred—*Millie*—Koffman had never been friends, even though their families had lived across the street from each other since they were kids. But he had always liked her. Over the years, he'd heard derogatory remarks from others about her being chubby. Some even called her fat, but he had always thought she was pretty. The way he figured, God had made them all in His image and everyone was beautiful in their own way. Millie had beautiful eyes, beautiful golden hair and a beautiful personality. And most importantly, she was a woman of deep faith. Even though they weren't exactly friends, he often saw her at social events. She was always optimistic, never gossiping like her twin, and she had a way of looking at the world that made those around her more positive. "Are you okay, Millie?"

"Fine," she mumbled. "You can go. I'm fine."

He glanced up at the cows that had scattered when she had fallen. Thankfully, none of them had bolted across the road. "You don't seem fine. Can you...can you move?" he asked, worrying that she had broken something when she hit the ground. Why else would she still be lying there?

"I can," she said.

"Then why aren't you? Do you...do you need a hand to get up?"

She looked up at him with her one visible eye. "I'm not moving because I'm too embarrassed."

Again, he smiled. Lots of people got embarrassed, but few ever admitted it. Certainly not to others.

"I'm thinking that if I lie here and pray harder than I've ever prayed in my life," Millie told him, "maybe I'll just die and my mother will come for me."

It was all he could do not to laugh. But he knew better than to do so because then she'd be even more embarrassed. "What? You're embarrassed because you fell going over a fence?" He snorted. "That's nothing. Last Sunday at church, I was carrying a bench, tripped and landed at our bishop's feet in front of the whole congregation."

Millie rolled over onto her side and looked up at him, smiling. There were bits of dead grass and leaves stuck to her face. "It's too bad we're not in the same church district. I'd like to have seen that."

"It was quite a sight, I'm sure." Elden stood and offered his hand to her. "You think you can stand now?"

"Sure." She gazed up at him, her cheeks rosy, the scarf tied over her hair askew. "Just got the wind knocked out of me. You didn't have to come over. My sister and I can round up our cows."

He still held his hand out to her. "If it was my cows loose, would you help me?"

She scrunched up her nose, which made him want to smile again. Goodness, she was pretty. And there was a sparkle in her eyes that made him feel good. Better than he had in months.

"Of course I would help," she told him.

"Then get up, Millie, and let's get these cows back in the pasture." He thrust his hand out to her again and this time, she grabbed it. And when she did, he felt a spark leap from her hand to his. The kind he had feared he would never feel again.

Chapter Two

The next morning, Millie's sixteen-year-old sister, Jane, stood frowning in their bedroom doorway, one hand on her hip. "Eleanor sent me up to see what's taking you so long." She walked in and plopped down on Millie's bed.

"Sorry," Millie, still in her flannel nightgown, said as she gathered clean underclothes from a chest of drawers.

"Eleanor isn't going to be happy if breakfast is late getting on the table," Jane said. "Then dinner will be late." She rocked her head left then right. "Which means supper will be late and she'll be in a bad mood all day fretting over it. You know she likes us to stay on schedule."

Millie sighed but made no comment on their eldest sister's constant need to mother them. With six younger sisters in the house, she supposed it was to be expected that after their *mam* died, Eleanor, as the eldest, felt she was responsible for taking her place. But Eleanor took the role too far. She fussed over the family more than their mother ever had.

"I didn't mean to lie abed so late." Millie glanced at the battery-powered alarm clock on the nightstand between her and Willa's beds. It was 7:15 already. "I couldn't sleep last night. I don't think I really fell asleep until after three."

Millie didn't tell her little sister that what had kept her awake was reliving over and over again her tumble over the fence. She'd obsessed about the accident that had landed her in the ditch and finding Elden Yoder looking down at her. She'd been beyond embarrassed. She'd been mortified. She'd hoped he'd just walk away and leave her there, but he hadn't. Instead, he'd helped her up and assisted her in finding the break in the fence. Then, after Willa had gone back to the house to report on the situation, he'd helped Millie herd the cows back to the barn.

Millie had gone over in her mind that part of her encounter with him repeatedly, too. His smile. The twinkle in his blue-gray eyes. The jut of his square chin when he'd smiled and the span of his broad shoulders as he walked away.

Somewhere between the ditch she landed in and the barn where he'd helped her give the cows hay, Millie had fallen in love with Elden. She had known at that moment that she'd never love another man. Not that she thought anything would ever come of it. She knew very well it wouldn't. Handsome, kind, hardworking men who owned their own two-hundred-acre farm didn't fall for fat girls like her. They fell in love with and married skinny girls like Willa. In fact, she was certain Elden was already in love with Willa. Why else would he have asked her where Willa had gone after she returned to the house?

"Well?" Jane asked, bringing Millie back to the moment. She gestured with both hands. "Are you coming or not?"

"I'm coming. I didn't expect anyone to wait breakfast on me." Millie went to the corner where her dresses hung on a pegboard on the wall and took down her blue dress. It was her Friday dress, one that made her feel good every time she wore it. And today was going to be an extra good day. She could feel it in her bones.

"*Ach.* Eleanor said to tell you not to wear that," Jane said.

"But it's Friday." Millie clutched the dress to her chest. "I always wear the blue on Friday."

Jane pursed her lips. She was a pretty girl with hair redder than blond that peeked from beneath her starched, white prayer *kapp*. Their *mam* had called the color strawberry blond and hers had been the same shade. Eleanor and Henry had it, too. "Eleanor says it's too short on you and she's expecting a visit from Aunt Judy today. Judy sees you in it, you know she'll go right home to her husband and tell him the Koffman girls are running wild with their short skirts."

Millie wrinkled her nose, thinking about her mother's older sister. "Would Judy do that? I wouldn't think that would be one of the duties of a bishop's wife—tattling on the congregation."

Jane shrugged and got up to start making Millie's bed for her. Willa's and Jane's were already neatly made. "I'm just telling you what Eleanor said. Wear the new beige one she made for you. It's plenty long enough."

"It's long enough, all right," Millie said. "It's so long I'll trip on the hem. You'd think she was making it for herself, it's so long." Eleanor was the tallest of the sisters, taller than their father. She had an imposing way about her and her height made her even more so. "And one sleeve is longer than the other. I wish she'd leave the sewing to Willa. Willa's much better at it."

Jane tucked the handmade log cabin quilt neatly at the end of the bed and began to fluff Millie's pillow. "I'm only telling you what Eleanor said. And she's already in a bad mood because Willa went out to get eggs from the henhouse and only came back with two."

Millie's mouth puckered in indecision as she held up the blue dress with its neat tailoring, looking at it and then the beige one hanging on the pegboard, then back at the blue. She liked the blue one. It went well with her eyes and her blond hair, but she was particularly fond of it because she and her mother had cut and stitched it together. Maybe the blue *was* a little shorter than her other dresses, but it covered her knees and the neckline and sleeves were modest enough to satisfy any bishop in Honeycomb. Especially one new to the roost. Bishop Cyrus had only just been elected to the position in early summer.

Millie made a face. "Why did she only bring back two eggs?"

Jane popped up off the bed. "Because it's Willa," she said as if that was enough. "Whoever heard of an Amish girl who's afraid of chickens?"

Millie headed out the bedroom door on her way to the upstairs washroom, the blue dress still in her arms. "Tell Ellie I'll be right down."

"You better not call her that this morning," Jane called after Millie. "She's not in the mood!"

Ten minutes later, Millie was dressed and ready for the day, whatever it might bring. As she came down the steep steps of their farmhouse, she heard the comforting sounds of mornings with a big family and it made her smile.

Lately, she'd begun worrying about whether she'd ever marry. With so many pretty sisters, so many pretty, thin, unmarried girls in their community, it was only logical that she would be last in line to ever have a beau.

If she was ever actually in line.

But hearing Beth's laughter and the chatter of her sisters, smelling the fresh scrapple and bacon cooking, she decided that maybe it wouldn't be such a bad thing not to marry. If she didn't marry, she could stay home and take care of their *dat*, freeing her sisters, including Eleanor, to marry.

Eleanor had it in her head that no one would ever marry her because as a baby she'd been diagnosed with a congenital disorder. Before she was old enough to walk, she'd had her leg amputated below the knee and now wore a prosthetic. She moved as fast as any of the sisters—certainly faster than Willa on her best day. And no one would even know Eleanor had a prosthetic leg unless she told them. She was as graceful as the ballet dancers Millie had once seen on Dover's Green at a festival. Eleanor wore regular shoes and the prosthetic looked no different than her other leg beneath the skirt of her dress. But that was Eleanor. She was stubborn the way their mother had been, and once she decided something, she stuck to it, even when all evidence suggested she was wrong.

"*Goot* morning," Millie greeted everyone in the kitchen.

"Cold," *Dat* told Millie, setting down his coffee mug as she walked into the room. He was seated at the head of the long trestle table in their country kitchen. "Don't like my coffee cold."

Millie took a piece of scrapple from a serving platter on the counter, and Eleanor, who was frying bacon, swatted at her with the pair of tongs she was using to flip the bacon.

"You're late," her eldest sister said. "Of course, I don't know what we're having for breakfast now because we've only two eggs to feed the eight of us."

"Two eggs?" Millie asked, savoring the crispy scrapple. Some folks didn't like scrapple because it was made from the scraps left over after butchering a pig. Plus cornmeal and spices. But she thought those people were just plain silly. God made the scraps the same as He made the pork chops, didn't He? What made one piece of a pig good and another bad?

"We have some leftover potatoes from last night," Cora suggested from her seat at the table where she was reading a book. She was a year older than Millie and Willa and was always reading. Unless she was writing. She was the smallest of the sisters, just five feet tall and wore wire-frame spectacles, which seemed like such a stereotype to Millie—that the big reader in the family wore glasses. She was the only one of them besides their *dat* who had prescription glasses. Their *mam* had never been able to decide if the books had caused Cora's poor eyesight, or if it was poor eyesight that made people readers.

"Is there something wrong with the hens?" Millie asked, not directing her question to anyone in particular.

"Who drinks coffee cold?" their father grumbled. He shook his head in displeasure and tried to pull a page of the *Budget* newspaper out from under Henry, who had a doorknob in pieces on it. "How's a person supposed to read with stuff all over their paper?" he grumbled.

"There's your paper, *Dat*. You already read this one cover to cover." Henry pointed to the latest edition of the nationwide newspaper, still rolled up in front of him. Amish and Mennonite households all over the world received the *Budget* every week. For many, especially the Amish who didn't have phones in their homes, it was a way to keep up with other Amish communities, and family and friends who lived far away. "I'm using an old one to keep the table clean."

Still nibbling on the scrapple, Millie glanced down

at Henry's pile of doorknob parts. "He take it off the door again?" One of their father's odd new habits was to try to fix things that weren't broken, often rendering them so afterward.

"*Ya.* Said it was squeaking. Only now there's a part missing. I'll probably have to run to the hardware store."

"Can I go with you?" Cora asked. "And stop at Spence's Bazaar on the way home. I need more writing paper."

"You need paper or you just want to flirt with JJ Byler?" Jane teased. As she spoke, she set a plate down in front of Cora. JJ's family owned a deli at the bargain flea market and auction that featured Amish food shops, and if he wasn't working construction, he helped out on Fridays and Saturdays.

"JJ Byler?" Cora scowled. "Not interested." She cut her eyes at Willa, who was standing in the doorway between the kitchen and the mudroom, the egg basket in the crook of her arm. "Willa's the one who's sweet on JJ."

"Am not!" Willa argued, but it was only half-hearted, because everyone in the kitchen knew she liked him. Willa had had her eye on him since he'd stopped seeing another girl.

"Well, I hope everyone is fine with scrapple, bacon and toast," Eleanor announced. "Because apparently we're not having eggs this morning."

Millie looked to Willa and mouthed, "Why didn't you get the eggs?"

"Because those chickens are mean," Willa whispered. "They bite."

"Oh, they do not—"

"What does a man have to do to get a hot cup of coffee around here?" their father bellowed. Which was unusual for him because he rarely raised his voice. At least he hadn't before the dementia had taken hold.

"*Dat*," Eleanor said gently, walking over to him. "It's orange juice, not coffee. Remember? You asked for orange juice this morning."

"It's in a coffee cup," he argued.

"Yes, *Dat*, but look. It's orange juice." She pointed into his mug. "You asked for it in your mug."

"I like my coffee hot," he answered, pushing his round wire-frame glasses up on his nose.

Millie glanced at Eleanor. "I'll take care of *Dat*'s coffee and the eggs." She cut her eyes at Willa.

Eleanor went back to the stove and began to take the bacon from the cast-iron frying pan to lay it on paper towels to drain. "You can't do everything for her all the time, Millie. She's got to learn how to do these things for herself. How's she going to collect eggs at her own house once she's married if she doesn't learn now?"

Millie scooped up her father's coffee mug of orange juice. "That is cold, isn't it, *Dat*?" Then to Eleanor she whispered, "Sometimes I think when he complains it's just that he wants to feel like he has control over something." She picked up the old percolator coffee-pot that was being kept warm on the back of the eight-burner propane stove, and gestured as if to pour coffee into the mug. Only of course she didn't. "Hot coffee freshened right up, *Dat*!"

"Who took my old apron, the one with the hole in the pocket?" Beth demanded, walking into the kitchen.

Cora looked up from her book to point at Jane while Jane pointed at her. "She did," they said in unison. It was a family joke, always blaming someone else for borrowing each other's things.

"Here you go, *Dat*," Millie set the coffee mug of orange juice in front of her father.

He picked it up, took a loud slurp and said, "Now, that's what I call a cup of coffee."

Millie smiled and brushed her hand across his shoulders. He'd always been a big man, not tall but muscular, but he was beginning to look thinner. Some of the hardiness she associated with him had withered. "Willa and I will get the eggs," she said to the room. "Be right back."

Eleanor started in again about it being high time her sisters got serious about their housekeeping skills, as Henry dropped something on the floor and got down on her hands and knees to crawl under the table. At the same time, Cora, who was now setting the table, dropped a plate, startling everyone, including Jane's big, fluffy gray cat, who shot out of the kitchen.

It was a normal morning in the Koffman kitchen and it made Millie smile as she linked her arm through her twin's. "Come on. Let's go get the eggs before Eleanor fries one of us up for breakfast."

"But I don't like chickens," Willa whined under her breath.

"You make them nervous. You have to be calm around them if you want them to stay calm," Millie explained at the back door as she looked around for her barn boots. "*Ach*. Where are my boots?" she wondered aloud, scanning the mudroom that clearly needed *retting* up. "Beth! Did you borrow my barn boots again?" she called out. Beth was the only one who wore the same size shoe as Millie. They both had big feet, size ten if the shoe was generous. Of course that didn't always stop another sister from *borrowing* her boots.

"Just put on *Dat*'s," Willa suggested.

"But they're too big."

"We're just going out to the henhouse." Willa opened the door that led to the open back porch. "Come on, let's go. Otherwise, Eleanor will pick on me all day."

Millie stared at her father's big, ugly rubber boots that were a good two sizes too big for her. Worse, he had used a permanent marker to write a shopping list on the toes of both boots. Even with the mud caked on the left shoe, she could make out the word *Cookies*, spelled with a *K* instead of a *C*.

Millie hesitated.

"Just put on the boots," Willa repeated impatiently, handing her a barn coat. "And this."

"That's *Dat*'s, too." Millie stepped into her father's boots. "I don't see you wearing our *vadder*'s old clothes."

Willa continued to hold out the jacket, saying nothing.

With a sigh, Millie gave in and accepted the jacket.

As she slipped her arms into it, she told herself that Willa had a point. What did it matter what she wore outside? No one was going to see her. Aunt Judy wasn't expected until late morning. "You owe me," she told her sister.

"I owe you what?" Willa asked, stepping out onto the porch.

"I don't know. I'll think of something." Millie closed the back door behind her and gazed out at the barnyard. It was a gorgeous fall morning with the smell of freshly cut corn on the air, and the breeze was cool and refreshing.

As they crossed the yard toward the cluster of outbuildings, she tried to walk without tripping, her feet sliding around in her father's boots. "Did Henry say when she could have a look at the fence where the cows broke through? I hate to see them all cooped up in the small pasture."

"I dunno. I heard her and Eleanor talking about it this morning." Willa swung the egg basket on her arm. Henry already had a whole list of things she wanted to do today, and repairing the fence wasn't on it. "Thanks for going to the henhouse with me, *schweschter*. I know you think I'm just being silly, but chickens really do scare me." She shuddered.

Millie smiled, feeling bad for her sister. She couldn't imagine what it was like to be afraid of things. She had never been afraid of anything, not of snakes or bugs or even trying one of Jane's strange recipes. Jane liked to take an ordinary recipe and add "a twist" as she called it, which might mean bacon in apple crumb muffins or bananas in split pea soup. Some of her recipes were better than others.

"You're welcome, Willa," Millie said. "I just hope that—" She caught movement out of the corner of her eye and came to such an abrupt halt in the middle of the driveway that she almost tripped in her father's enormous boots. There was Elden Yoder, coming right toward them.

And Millie was dressed in a man's barn coat that was dirty and oversize rubber boots with writing all over them.

She glanced at the house. It didn't usually feel like a long walk to the chicken coop from the back porch, but suddenly it seemed like miles. She didn't want Elden to see her dressed like this, but there was no way, even if she ran, she could get inside before he reached them.

"Willa!" he called, waving to them. He had his little bulldog with him. "Millie," he added. As an afterthought, Millie was sure. Because he was a nice young man. He was too polite to ignore her.

"*Guder mariye.* I was just headed up to your house." He pointed in that direction of the two-story clapboard farmhouse. "Wanted to let you know I patched the hole in the fence. A bit of wire had rusted and the top rail had rotted. The cows must have just pushed their way through. Good as new now. You can let them back out into the pasture."

"*Danki*, Elden." Willa smiled prettily.

Willa had a peachy complexion, unlike Millie's,

which tended toward red and blotchy, especially when she was nervous or embarrassed. Like now.

Millie could feel her face growing warm. Elden was so handsome, though he looked as if he could have used a few pounds on him. That morning he was wearing denim pants, work boots, leather suspenders and what appeared to be a brand-new work shirt that was a charcoal color, a shade that made his blue eyes look even grayer. Like any Amish man, he wore a wide-brimmed straw hat with a leather band, but there was a tiny blue jay feather tucked into the band. For some reason, the whimsical feather tickled Millie. Maybe because it was very unlike an Amish man. A feather in a hat wasn't against the *Ordnung* their Old Order community followed, but it was unusual.

As Millie tried to think of something to say, Willa, thankfully, kept talking. Willa was like that. She could talk to anyone, even *Englishers*, and always seemed to know what to say. She never got tongue-tied like Millie did.

"We'll tell Henry," Willa continued. "I imagine she'll be relieved. She was fussing this morning about having too many things to do today. And something about not having something she needed to stretch something?" She looked up at him quizzically.

"Right. A fence stretcher. It's a metal bar used to tighten the metal fencing to make it taut. I brought mine along. Made the whole job go easier. And faster." He looked at Millie. "So…you feeling okay today? After your tumble?"

"You mean my dive over the fence?"

The moment the words came out of Millie's mouth, she wished she could catch them and stuff them into the pocket of her father's coat. Her father's coat that she now realized smelled of cow dung.

Why, oh why, hadn't she taken the extra minute to find her own coat? Millie fretted. Elden must think she looked ridiculous. And the huge rubber barn boots with the writing on them? There was no way he could miss them. But men weren't always that observant. Maybe—

"Going grocery shopping later, Millie?" Elden asked, interrupting her thoughts.

"What?" she asked in an exhalation of breath.

He pointed at her feet, the corner of his mouth turning up in a grin. "Your grocery list."

Millie closed her eyes for a moment. She was beyond embarrassed now. Beyond mortified. Again. What word was there to describe beyond mortified? "I… My…" She didn't know what to say.

"They're our *dat*'s boots," Willa explained. "We were headed out to the henhouse to gather eggs. Millie is helping me because the hens are mean to me." She held out her finger. "Look. The red one with the speckled wings bit me when I tried to get the egg out from under her."

"Daisy," Millie muttered.

Willa looked quizzically at her sister. "What?"

"Daisy." Millie stared at the gravel driveway between her and Elden. "The hen with the speckled wings, she's Daisy."

Elden laughed, his voice a rich tenor. "You name your chickens?"

Again Millie was embarrassed. It wasn't a very Amish thing to do, to name your chickens. "I know. Our aunt doesn't approve." She held up a finger, imitating her aunt Judy with a high-pitched voice. "And God said, 'Let us make man in our image, after our likeness. And let them have dominion over the fish of the sea, and over the fowl of the air, and over the cattle, and over all the earth, and over every creeping thing that creepeth upon the earth.'"

"I know that verse but not word for word," Elden said. "You have a good memory."

Millie lifted her gaze to meet his and she felt an unfamiliar surge of warmth tickle her empty tummy and radiate outward. It felt something like embarrassment, but different. It also felt exciting. He was looking at her in a way that few people outside her family did. Folks tended to avoid eye contact with big girls like her. But not Elden. At this moment he seemed to…to *see* her.

"I do have a good memory," Millie admitted. "Our *mam* used to say it was a handy thing, except when she didn't want me to remember something she'd said or done that she shouldn't have. Or if she'd tried to hide the cookies. I always remembered her hiding places."

Again, he smiled. "I gave two of our chickens names. My *mam* refuses to call them by their names, though. She's like your aunt. She doesn't like the idea of naming animals. Says God didn't intend us to give them names. Same with the dog." He indicated the bulldog that had dropped to a seated position patiently at his master's feet. "His name is Samson but *Mam* refuses to call him that. She just calls him Dog."

Millie dared a half smile. "Like Willa said, these are my *dat*'s boots. He wrote on them, not me."

Elden pushed back his hat and laughed. "I didn't think they were yours. They look a little big. But then I thought—" he shrugged "—maybe they are hers. Maybe Millie is a girl who likes plenty of room in her barn boots."

Millie found herself chuckling with him.

"The boots are my fault," Willa piped up. "I made her put them on. Eleanor wanted to make fried eggs to go with our breakfast this morning and I didn't bring in the eggs," she explained. Then she looked at Millie. "We should get the eggs, *schweschter*, before someone comes looking for us."

"*Ya*. And I should go, too," Elden said. "I started clearing the meadow along the road." He gestured toward his property. "I've got a lot of work ahead of me. Hoping to plant it next spring. That's why I was out there yesterday when your cows got out."

It seemed like he was stalling, not ready to go yet. Millie glanced at her sister, whose cheeks were turning pink in the morning coolness. It was no wonder he didn't want to go. Who wouldn't want to gaze at Willa's beautiful face? Did he want to court her? Was that why he'd fixed their fence? Neighbors did things to help each other, but repairing a neighbor's fence when they could fix it themselves—that was being more than neighborly.

"It was nice of you to fix our fence, Elden," Millie heard herself say. "Would…would you like to come to supper tomorrow night? I know Henry will want to thank you. And Eleanor, too, and our other sisters." Now that Millie had started talking, it seemed like she couldn't stop. "Eleanor so appreciates anything anyone does to help us. You know…now that *Dat* isn't well."

Elden lifted his brows. "Supper, huh?"

"*Ya*," Millie murmured, now feeling less sure of herself. Maybe it was a silly thing to do, to invite him. "To thank you."

And let you get to know Willa better, she thought. Because it was pretty much a given that Elden was still standing there because of Willa. It wouldn't surprise her if they were betrothed by Epiphany. She knew a man like him would never be interested in a woman like her, but the idea of having Elden sit at their kitchen table, even if he was there for Willa, made her heart flutter. Just sitting across the table from him, looking at his handsome face, would be more than enough for her.

"All right if I bring my *mutter*?"

"*Ya, ya*, of course," Millie stumbled, not quite able to believe that he had accepted. *Was* accepting. She couldn't remember the families ever eating together before. Not even when their *mam* was alive.

"What can we bring?"

"N-nothing," Millie stammered, unable to believe he'd agreed to join them. "Six o'clock."

"We'll be here." He smiled at Millie, then nodded to Willa.

When he turned and walked back down the gravel lane, Millie felt her knees go weak.

Elden Yoder was coming to supper!

Chapter Three

The sun hung low in the sky as Elden walked down his gravel driveway, wearing the denim pants and green shirt his mother had recently stitched for him and his going-to-town suspenders. To ward off the chill, he'd pulled on his new barn coat and a black wool beanie his mother had knitted. In one hand he carried a flashlight for the walk home; in the other, the basket his mother had handed him in their kitchen. There was a refreshing breeze coming out of the west and the air smelled of freshly cut field corn, soybeans and, oddly enough, hope.

He glanced at his mother walking at his side in her long black wool cloak and black bonnet. When he'd told her about the invitation the morning before, he'd half hoped she'd suggest he go to the Koffmans' without her. She'd been talking for weeks, months, about how he ought to start getting out again, going to singings and bonfires and mingling with young folks. She insisted his period of mourning what could have been had passed and it was high time he started seriously looking for a wife. One better suited to him than *her*, meaning the woman he almost married. His mother rarely spoke Mary's name. She hadn't since the day he and his betrothed had talked on his porch and Mary had walked away and he'd never seen her again.

Elden pushed the memories of the heartbreak into the recesses of his mind where they belonged. He was in too good a mood to let them ruin his evening. He was excited about having supper with the Koffman family and pleased to be excited about something. About anything. Since Mary had broken their engagement, he'd had a hard time being enthusiastic about anything. He didn't think he'd been depressed so much as...disheartened. He'd had his whole life planned out with Mary, and then it had been taken from him in a split second. With a single brief and confusing explanation from her, all his hopes and dreams had crumbled and fallen at his feet. Elden had known for months now that it was time to pull himself out of the hole he felt like he was in. However, knowing you needed to do something and being able to do it were entirely different things.

It was Millie who was putting a lightness in his step this evening. He was still shaking his head over it. Over her. He'd known Millie since he was ten, when he and his *mam* and *dat* and big sisters had moved to Honeycomb to be closer to his *vadder*'s brother Gabriel. At first, they had rented property nearby, but a year before his father's death when Elden was thirteen, they'd bought the farm directly across the street from the Koffman family. Being a year older and a boy, Elden and Millie had never really been friends, but he had always admired her from afar. She had been a girl of faith, of smiles and laughter. And at some point, when he had glanced away, she had become a woman with the same virtues.

And now he was having supper with her. With her family, he reminded himself. No need to get too excited; this was merely a thank-you supper. She wasn't interested in him. Millie had only invited him to be polite and to show the family's appreciation for his help with the cows and the fence, which of course wasn't necessary. But when she had invited him, he'd said yes without so much as a second thought. It was the first invitation like this he'd accepted since Mary had walked out of his life.

"Couldn't you make that dog stay home?" Elden's mother asked, pulling Elden from his thoughts. She was glancing over her shoulder, her nose in the air in disapproval.

Elden looked back at the little brown-and-white mixed-breed bulldog trotting behind them. He'd found the dog that spring wandering the road, starving and flea-bitten, and on an impulse, he'd brought him home. "*Nay*. Samson goes everywhere with me. You know that."

His mother frowned disapprovingly. "I suppose you'll expect Felty Koffman to invite it in for supper? Maybe sit in a chair at the dinner table?"

Elden chuckled, swinging the basket with dessert his mother had made. He'd told her there was no need to bring anything, but she'd insisted it would be rude not to. When she said she was making dessert, he'd been concerned. Lavinia Yoder wasn't much of a cook. She never had been and her repertoire of what she could bake that was edible was rather small. He had prayed she wouldn't make anything that was unpalatable, and his prayers had been answered because she'd made her usual, rice cereal bars, which were actually good.

"I doubt Felty will invite Samson to his table, but even if he does, Samson will have the good manners to say no, thank-you," Elden teased, knowing she hated it when he gave human qualities to animals. As a child he'd never been allowed to even read books with talking animals. He remembered vividly when she'd taken the book *Charlotte's Web* away from him and returned it to his teacher with strict instructions that he never ever be allowed to read another such book again. He hadn't checked the book or any like it from the school's little library after that, but he had managed to get friends to do so for him and he'd read *Charlotte's Web* from cover to cover three times in the fourth grade.

Elden pushed a small rock with the toe of his boot, making a mental note that it was time to level out the lane again. "Samson doesn't care to dine with folks. He'll wait on the porch, same as he does whenever we go to Gabriel and Elsie's." His father's brother had become more like a father to Elden after *Dat* had passed, and Gabriel and his wife and their adult children were the only folks Elden had socialized with since Mary left him.

His mother harrumphed loudly. She was a formidable woman, nearly as tall as Elden, and what his father had always called pleasingly plump. Her size and how she carried herself made her intimidating to some. He hoped not to Millie. She didn't seem like a woman who could be easily unsettled, but in their culture where a young, unmarried woman was expected not just to respect her elders, but sometimes submit to them, he wasn't sure.

"I've been thinking on the matter, praying, and I've come to believe it was wise of you to accept this supper invitation," his mother said, changing the subject abruptly. She did that anytime she didn't like the direction of a conversation.

He raised his eyebrows. They were nearing the end of their long driveway and he could see the glimmer of lamplight in the windows of the Koffman farmhouse in the distance. "You do? Just yesterday you thought it was a terrible idea."

She pursed her lips, jutting out her chin. "It was only that I was wondering what kind of meal a gaggle of motherless girls could possibly throw together."

"The youngest is the only Koffman sister you could call a girl," he pointed out.

She eyed him severely. "A girl is a girl until she's wed. Only then is she a woman." She went on without giving him a chance to comment. "I always liked Aggie Koffman, you know. God rest her soul. She had a kind heart. But the truth of the matter is that she let those girls run too free. I've heard some call them wild."

Elden pressed his lips together to keep from laughing out loud. His definition of wild was obviously different than his mother's. Anytime he had ever seen any of the Koffman sisters, whether it was at Byler's store, or in their yard, they were always dressed appropriately Plain, their hair and bodies properly covered. As for wild behavior, none to his knowledge ever drank alcohol or smoked like some of the other young women he knew who were out sowing their oats before they settled into the life of a baptized congregant. The closest to *wild* behavior he'd witnessed came from the nineteen-year-old middle sister, Henry, who wore her father's pants under her dress in the winter. He'd caught a glimpse of a pant leg when she was shoveling snow in their driveway the previous winter. But what sensible woman wouldn't wear pants under their skirts in below-freezing weather?

"How could they possibly know how to prepare a proper meal for guests?" his mother asked. "It wouldn't surprise me a bit if we had lunch meat sandwiches and soda pop."

Elden shrugged. "I like sandwiches and soda pop. Especially if it's root beer," he teased.

She looked at him, narrowing her gaze. "A new wife should come to her husband well schooled in household skills. Food preservation, cleaning, sewing, cooking. If a woman can't cook, how does she ever expect to marry?"

"Who says the Koffman sisters can't cook?" he

asked, refusing to be annoyed. He was too happy this evening to allow himself to be pulled into his mother's fretting that could easily be interpreted, by those who didn't know her, as negativity. She didn't mean to be critical of others. It was just the way she thought things through. Elden had learned long ago that getting upset with his mother or, worse, confronting her about things she said, only made matters worse. Mostly for him. "If I remember correctly, you bought one of Jane's rhubarb-strawberry pies at that auction a few months ago and said a finer one you'd never tasted."

She clasped her hands together, drawing herself up. They had reached their mailbox and were waiting for a car to pass before crossing the road. The bulldog stood obediently at Elden's side, watching the car intently.

"A husband can't live on his wife's rhubarb-strawberry pie!" his mother exclaimed.

Elden chuckled. "Good thing I won't be marrying Jane Koffman, then, *ya*?"

"I can't believe you invited Elden Yoder to supper, Millie!" Jane exclaimed excitedly, as she turned chicken over in a frying pan with a pair of tongs. "He is *so* handsome. And so single." She giggled.

Millie smiled to herself and continued to set the table. She placed the eating utensils just the way her mother had taught her: fork to the left of the plate, knife on the right and a spoon beside it. The table looked so nice. Beth had picked some wheat still standing in the west field and placed it in a blue canning jar, making a beautiful arrangement for the center of the table. And the meal was going to be outstanding. Millie was sure of it.

Eleanor had decided on serving fried chicken, smashed potatoes, roasted carrots, cinnamon cranberry applesauce and buttermilk biscuits. The kitchen was filled with the scent of the frying chicken and the first batch of biscuits that had just come out of the oven. It all smelled so delicious that Millie's mouth was watering. But she was nervous. She glanced at the big wall clock over the pie safe to see that it was nearly six. Elden would be there any moment and she was beginning to question if she had made a mistake inviting him. Now that he was about to arrive, she wondered what she had been thinking when she had blurted out the invitation.

The idea that his mother was coming as well was scarier. Lavinia was a woman with many opinions and criticisms and she had no trouble expressing them. Because they attended different church districts, even though they lived across the street, Millie didn't cross paths often with her, but when she did, she always tried to get away from Lavinia as quickly as possible.

"Oh dear, look at the time," Eleanor remarked, grabbing hot mitts off the counter. "I knew this was too soon for visitors. And us barely out of mourning."

"It's going to be fine, Ellie," Beth said, opening a jar of the previous year's applesauce. "Your fried chicken is good. Almost as good as mine."

"*Ya.* I love your fried chicken," Millie piped up, wanting to be encouraging. She understood this was a difficult event for Eleanor. "It's that little bit of cayenne pepper you add. And the buttermilk you soak it in overnight, of course."

Eleanor hadn't been thrilled by the idea of Elden and his mother coming for supper and had fussed about having to go to the grocery store to put a decent meal on the table. Her eldest sister preferred to stick to their routine, and it did not include guests on Saturday nights. In fact, Millie couldn't recall having dinner guests since their mother had passed. Before their mother died, they'd had family, friends and neighbors over for supper more than once a week. Anyone who came to the door near a mealtime was invited in and somehow their mother always found enough food to put on a nice spread. There was always enough to go around and then some—like the fishes and loaves of bread story in the Bible.

Eleanor didn't have the same gift of hostessing that their mother had. She fretted about the quality of the food she served, the dishes she served it on and the cost of the meal that would set their budget off-kilter for the rest of the month. But none of that surprised Millie. It was just how Eleanor was. What *had* surprised Millie was the lack of interest on Willa's part in Elden coming over.

Didn't Willa realize that Jane was right? Elden was the best-looking unmarried man in Honeycomb? More importantly, he'd proved he was the kindest man in Honeycomb the day their cows had gotten loose.

Maybe Willa hadn't cared all that much because all the good-looking, eligible men were already interested in her.

Jane was still chattering. "Susie told me—"

"Which Susie?" Willa interrupted. She stood in front of their father in the hallway, combing his hair for him.

Millie noticed that their *dat* had put on clean pants, his good suspenders and a blue shirt that Willa had stitched for him. She was glad he'd smartened himself up for their dinner guests. Like their mother, he'd always been a social person and Millie worried about him. He seemed lonely, even in a houseful of daughters who loved him. What she didn't know was whether his loneliness was born of the loss of his beloved wife of twenty-six years, or the loss of his memory.

"Susie Beiler," Jane said, cutting her eyes at Willa, annoyed that she'd been interrupted. "Susie said that her sister—the one who lives in Hickory Grove—said that Elden's mother was the one who drove a wedge between him and Mary."

Shocked, Millie turned to look at her little sister. She'd heard whispers about Lavinia and how she might have come between her son and the woman he had intended to marry, but she hadn't considered they might be true.

"Susie said," Jane continued, going on faster than before, "that Lavinia thinks no one is good enough for her son, and that included Mary Yost. Susie says her mother said she doubts he'll ever marry. Him being responsible for caring for Lavinia, what with her daughters living so far away."

"I heard Lavinia never liked her because she was from Kentucky," Willa offered, walking her father to his chair at the head of the table. At Eleanor's insistence, Willa had replaced the mauve scarf that had covered her head with a proper organza prayer *kapp*. They were all wearing *kapps*, even Henry. "Sit right here, *Dat*. You're going to lead us in silent prayer, right? Once everyone sits down. You remember how to do it?"

Their father eased into his chair looking a bit confused, but he nodded.

"And no matter what Mary did," Jane said excitedly, "Lavinia wasn't satisfied. Nothing was right, how Mary dressed, what she cooked, how she drove her uncle's buggy. Mary was living with her aunt and uncle in Hickory Grove, you know. And Lavinia was so mean to her that Susie said—"

"Jane," Eleanor interrupted. "Haven't you and I, *and* Willa," she added, eyeing Millie's twin, "talked about this?" She didn't speak unkindly, but her tone was firm. "Gossiping is a terrible habit. *And withal they learn to be idle, wandering about from house to house; and not only idle, but tattlers also and busybodies, speaking things which they ought not*," she quoted from the Bible.

"First Timothy," Beth announced. She had the best memory of any of them.

A knock on the back door startled Millie and she

looked from the table, where she'd just set down a basket of paper napkins.

"Oh my," Eleanor said in a breathy exhalation." She wiped her hands on her apron, looking quite nervous now. "They're here." She looked at the clock on the wall. It was one minute after six. "Prompt, aren't they?" She gave a half-hearted chuckle. "Someone call Henry. I think she's still in the cellar working on the shelving. Millie, could you answer the door?"

Millie froze, her eyes wide. *No, no, no, not me. Anyone but me*, she thought. "You want *me* to answer it?" she asked Eleanor, her voice sounding squeaky.

A timer went off and Eleanor grabbed the hot mitts again. "*Ya*, you. What's gotten into you, Millie? You invited the Yoders'. Don't you think it would be nice if you greeted them at the door?"

Millie's mouth was suddenly dry. After Elden had repaired their fence, it had seemed like a good idea to invite him to supper, but now she regretted it. She hadn't thought that she'd have to *speak* to him. She didn't want to speak to him. All she wanted was to sit across the table from him and steal glances at his handsome face when no one was looking.

"I:.. Willa, you should let them in." Millie whipped around to her twin, who was licking chocolate brownie dough off her finger, having sampled Jane's new recipe for double chocolate chip brownies with caramel sauce on top.

"Me?" Willa asked. "I didn't invite them. You did."

A knock came again at the door. This one louder.

"Millie!" Eleanor begged, pulling the second pan

of biscuits out of the oven. She shot Millie a look, pleading with her eyes.

Millie took a deep breath, grabbed Willa's hand, and dragged her through the kitchen and into the mudroom. Through the parted curtain on the window in the back door, Millie saw Elden trying to peer in and she ducked behind Willa and pushed her toward the door.

"Really?" Willa chastised. Then she opened the door, smiling her pretty smile. "Elden, Lavinia. We're glad you could come. Supper's almost ready."

"Good of you to have us." Elden came in, pulling off his beanie and stuffing it into the pocket of his jacket. He looked past Willa and made eye contact with Millie.

She held her breath, wishing the moment would last forever.

Chapter Four

After everyone greeted their guests, Eleanor announced that supper was ready. That prevented Millie from having to figure out where to stand in the kitchen, what to do with her hands and what to say if Elden tried to make conversation with her. As her sisters began to pull out the ladder-back chairs around the large, oak-hewn kitchen table, Millie scooted into a chair two seats to her father's left. It was a plan she had landed on after fretting for hours over where she ought to sit. She had made that decision based on the assumption that Elden, being the only other male there, would be seated to Felty's right. That chair would put Elden in Millie's view, but they wouldn't be directly across from each other, so it wouldn't be obvious she was admiring him. However, when Eleanor suggested Elden sit to the right of their *dat*, Lavinia plopped down in Elden's chair, leaving Elden to sit next to Willa.

And directly across from Millie, which immediately sent her heart racing.

After their father led the families in a silent prayer of thanks, everyone began passing the heaping platters around, the sisters all talking at once, like any ordinary Saturday night supper. But it was far from ordinary because Elden was sitting right in front of Millie with only a lazy Susan full of condiments between them. When she'd invited him, she'd had in mind that she'd be able to watch him and listen to him talk. But she hadn't meant for him to sit right in front of her! When she opened her eyes following grace and saw him there, she'd feared she wouldn't be able to eat a thing. But once the food came around, she somehow found her appetite.

She was eating a biscuit, listening to Eleanor tell Lavinia about a new quilting circle being organized, when she realized Elden was looking at her. Looking *right* at her. Millie swallowed hard and patted her napkin to her mouth, fearing the honey from her biscuit was in the corners of her mouth. Why was he looking at her, she wondered, feeling heat spread across her face. And then she wished she'd worn her favorite blue dress, even if it wasn't blue dress day.

Elden made eye contact with her, smiled and took a big bite of his biscuit, which had more honey on it than hers. It dribbled off his biscuit onto his third piece of fried chicken on his plate. She smiled bashfully and looked down, scooping up mashed potatoes with her fork. Why did he keep looking at her?

He was seated next to Willa, the prettiest girl at the table, maybe the prettiest in Honeycomb.

"My friend Sara is organizing a quilting circle," Eleanor explained to Lavinia, sounding more at ease now that everyone was enjoying the meal. "You should join us. She had the idea to start making quilts before we're asked to donate for one fundraiser or another. She's just had her first baby and she's realizing how much harder it will be to do her chores with a little one on her hip"

"One baby," Lavinia said, scooping more applesauce onto her plate. "That's nothing. It's the second one that upsets the apple cart. Salt," she said to Elden, pointing to the lazy Susan, without so much as a please.

Elden passed her the salt, catching Millie's eye. Millie could tell by the look on his face that he'd noticed as well that his mother had forgotten to ask nicely, but instead of being embarrassed, he looked amused.

"Will you be joining the quilting circle, Willa?" Lavinia leaned in front of her son. "Willa!" she said louder when Millie's sister didn't reply at once.

Willa had been busy talking to Jane and swung around to look at their guest. "I'm sorry, Lavinia. I didn't hear you. What was that?"

"Quilting!" Lavinia said so loudly that she startled their father. "I said I know you must be an excellent quilter."

Jane giggled. "Willa hates quilting."

Willa wrinkled her pert little nose. "I'm not very

good at quilting. Our *mam* always said my hand stitching was too higgledy-piggledy."

Lavinia drew back. "I thought you could sew. The new bishop's wife told me you were an excellent seamstress."

"Aunt Judy?" Jane gave a wave. "She must have meant Willa's better at quilting than she is. Which isn't saying much."

Lavinia looked down her long nose at Jane as if the teenager were a fly on the biscuits, and Jane lowered her gaze to her plate.

"Willa's good with a sewing machine. And flirting with boys," Beth piped up.

Lavinia turned her attention to their father. "Willa's a modest girl, isn't she, Felty?"

"What's that?" He tucked the cloth dish towel Eleanor had draped over his chest more tightly into his shirt collar.

"Your daughter." Lavinia raised her voice again. "Willa. The pretty one. I hear she's quite a seamstress."

"I wouldn't know anything about that." Felty looked to Eleanor. "Where are the brownies? I smell brownies."

"After supper, *Dat*." Eleanor patted his arm.

"I like my brownies before supper. Don't you, *sohn*?" He pointed at Elden.

"I do. I like brownies before supper and then again after supper." Elden looked at Millie again, his mouth turned up ever so slightly in a smile.

She felt herself blush again and looked down at her plate.

"Speaking of fundraisers," Lavinia said, looking past Elden to Willa again. "I suspect you heard about the apple social coming up next Saturday at the Masts' orchard."

Before Willa could respond, Lavinia went on. "Here's how it's going to work. All the single ladies will bring a dessert." She held up one finger. "But no one is to know which dessert belongs to which girl, then the single men will bid on the desserts and have the privilege of sharing with the baker. A pretty girl like you, I know you're going." She smiled at Willa. "You can ride with us."

Willa stared at Lavinia and then cut her eyes at Millie, the look on her face obvious to anyone who knew her. Willa was saying, *Help me,* without the words coming out of her mouth.

"What do you say?" Lavinia pressed, leaning so far in front of her son that her nose was practically in his plate. "Elden can drive us." She smiled again, but this time her smile was different. It was…sly. "And I imagine he'll be able to figure out what you've made because it will be in our buggy." She sounded pleased with herself.

Looking embarrassed, Elden studied a spot on the far wall, and Millie couldn't decide whom she felt worse for, Willa or Elden.

"Shall we pick you up, Willa?" Lavinia asked. "Or do you want to walk over? Not to worry, Felty," she threw over her shoulder. "I'll chaperone."

Everyone at the table had gone quiet except for the girls' father, who was singing an old hymn to himself as he sawed on a biscuit with his knife, cutting it into bite-size pieces.

Eleanor leaned over to speak softly to their father. "Pick the biscuit up with your hand, *Dat*. No need to cut it."

"Well, Willa?" Lavinia asked, her tone changing in pitch.

"I… I…" Willa stumbled.

Then Eleanor came to the rescue. "So nice of you to invite Willa," she said, looking directly at Lavinia. "But we'll be attending as a family. *Dat* will expect her to go with us." Her gaze flicked to Willa and then back to their guest, her smile matching Lavinia's.

To Millie's knowledge, there had been no talk of attending the social. Since their mother's death they hadn't attended anything as a family except church. It had been too hard for them without their mother.

"I'm sure we'll see you there," Eleanor went on diplomatically. "I think it sounds like a nice day. The Masts' orchard is such a pretty place to have a gathering. I understand they'll be closed for business the whole afternoon to host us."

Lavinia sat back in her chair. "I don't see why—"

"Sounds like it's settled," Elden interrupted, finishing the last bite from his plate. "Delicious meal, Eleanor. Thank you. You're every bit as good a hostess as your mother."

Millie looked at her eldest sister and saw tears in her eyes. Eleanor had done a good job with the meal, but the fact that Elden had made a point of saying so made Millie's heart swell. Eleanor deserved the praise, but coming from their neighbor, it would mean so much to her. Elden seemed to have sensed that. There weren't many men who could stop for a moment and consider a woman's feelings.

And Eleanor had handled Lavinia's pushiness quite well, Millie thought. But why didn't Willa want to go with them to the apple social? That would make it almost a date with Elden, and he would make such a good husband to her sister. Millie was going to tell her so just as soon as they had a moment alone. It was time Willa thought about marrying. A man like Elden, living across the street from them? Not only would he make a good husband to her sister, but he would be a good son-in-law for their father, and a good brother-in-law for a gaggle of sisters.

"Just a little something we threw on the table, but *danki*," Eleanor said to Elden, her face reddening with pride. "We'll have to do this again. It's been too long since we had friends in our home." She glanced at their father. "*Dat* likes it, I think."

"You're a blessed man, Felty," Elden said. Then he looked around the table at the sea of white *kapps*. "Now, what's this I heard about freshly baked brownies?"

Millie met the following Saturday with a mixture of excitement and anxiety. Eleanor had been true to her word and the entire family had packed baskets of homemade apple desserts to be auctioned off at the Masts' frolic. They'd also brought sandwiches and fruit in case anyone got hungry. After the auction there would be softball and volleyball games and those who stayed through supper or returned after feeding their animals would be able to enjoy a bonfire. The annual event benefited all three of the Amish schools in Honeycomb and would be an afternoon of eating, playing games, laughter and friendship.

Millie loved social gatherings and was thrilled to be attending one after their long year of mourning. And it felt good to not be so sad. But she was also nervous about a whole handful of things, none of which she had any control over. Would her father have a good day? This was the first time many people in their community would see him at a social event since the death of his wife, and his health had suffered greatly in those long months. Before Millie's mother died, there had been subtle signs that her father was struggling with his memory, but they had hidden it well and only those closest to him had seen it. But then, after he lost his beloved wife, his mind began to slip quicker. He still had good days when it seemed as if the illness had been Millie and her sisters' imagination. But then there were days when he couldn't remember how to use a toothbrush or called Eleanor by their dead mother's name.

Next on Millie's worry list was Willa. Millie wanted so badly for the day to go well for her—for her and Elden because he would certainly bid on her apple crumb cake cookies. Willa just needed to forget about JJ, who courted a different girl every month, and give Elden a chance. Millie imagined Willa and Elden spending time together on a blanket under an apple tree and love blossoming. The thing was, Willa didn't seem all that interested in spending time with Elden. Millie couldn't figure out if Willa was nervous or what, and when she'd asked her, Willa had dodged the subject, not really giving an answer.

Millie also worried who would bid on her salted caramel apple galette. She knew the dessert tasted as delicious as it looked. She'd made it twice that week to practice and barely gotten a sliver of it herself each time before it was inhaled by her family. But would the young man who bid on it be sorely disappointed when he realized whom he would have to spend time with?

It had happened the spring before her mother died. Millie had attended a lunch basket auction in Seven Poplars with her sisters, and Harry Renno had bid on it. Then, when Millie identified the basket as hers, she'd seen the look of disappointment cross his face. He'd ended up inviting all nine of his younger siblings to join them for the picnic and Millie had spent the hour trying to keep the children from falling in the pond while Harry ate. He hadn't been mean to her exactly, but it had still hurt when he admitted he'd thought the basket belonged to the "pretty Koffman girl"—meaning Willa.

"Millie!"

Her friend Annie Lapp tugged on the sleeve of her dress, bringing Millie back to the moment. Millie was wearing her blue dress—even though it wasn't Friday. They were standing in the sun beside the Masts' back porch where they could observe the activity. Buggies were still coming up the driveway and the yard was full of women of all ages in colored dresses and white *kapps*, dropping desserts off. Men, young and old, clustered in groups talking horses and crops and the previous Sunday's sermons. Dozens of children, boys and girls, raced between the adults chasing each other, laughing and enjoying the perfect fall day.

Jim Mast, who owned the orchard, and several of his sons were putting the desserts they would auction off on plastic folding tables they had lined up under a big sugar maple that was shedding its red and oranges leaves, sending them fluttering across the yard. Jim's wife, Edna, was directing the setup and fussing at her son Freeman, who had stuck his finger under plastic wrap to taste a bit of frosting on a cake.

"Did you hear *anything* I just said?" Annie asked indignantly.

"Sorry." Millie smiled sheepishly. She and Annie always stuck together at social events. They'd been friends since they were children and had always gotten along well. They understood each other. Annie was a pretty girl with dark hair and dancing green eyes, and she was big like Millie. In fact, she was bigger. Hanging out together, they had learned, made it sting less when no one asked to drive them home from a frolic.

Annie sucked on a piece of butterscotch candy. She'd offered Millie one from her apron pocket, but Millie had declined. "I said you were right. Look who's talking to your sister."

Annie pointed and Millie followed her line of vision.

Beyond the tables of desserts, she spotted Willa and Elden standing next to each other. Deep in conversation, Willa was smiling up at him, which made Millie smile. Her chest tightened a bit, though, seeing them getting along so well. He would make a good husband for her sister. And it would be so wonderful to have her twin living across the street after she was married. Millie always worried that Willa might meet someone visiting from another state. It happened all the time. If that happened, once Willa was wed, she might move away as far as Wisconsin or Kentucky and they would rarely see each other.

Annie sucked loudly on her candy. "You think Elden's asking her which dessert is hers so he can bid on it? You're not supposed to do that, but boys sometimes do."

"If he's smart, he's asking her." Millie continued to watch them, and while she was happy for her sister, she was sad for herself. Even though she knew it would never happen, she realized she wanted to be the one smiling up at Elden Yoder.

For a split second, Millie imagined spending the afternoon with Elden and him asking if he could court her. She imagined them riding home together from frolics in a courting buggy, maybe even holding hands when no one was watching. She imagined planning a life together with Elden, a life of happiness and joy in a marriage like her parents had shared.

Of course that would never happen. But it was fun to daydream.

"Look at the way she's smiling at him," Annie said, rummaging around in her pocket for more candy.

Millie watched as Willa said something to Elden and he nodded. Then Willa walked away, her *kapp* strings fluttering at the nape of her neck as she said something over her shoulder to him. A moment later, JJ walked over to Elden and the two men put their heads together.

"Oh, dear. What am I going to do if Junior Yoder bids on my apple pear pie?" Annie fretted. "The last time I had to eat with him, he started telling me how he liked a woman with meat on her bones. Right before he took his false teeth out and set them on his knee so he could gum his supper."

Millie pressed her lips together so as not to giggle. Twice Annie's age, Junior was widowed and had had his eye on Annie for months. He owned a huge farm and still had three children at home, and had made no bones about wanting to make Annie his wife. He'd even gone so far as to speak to Annie's father, Jeb, but nothing had come of it because Jeb didn't want his only daughter married to the hog farmer, either.

Just then, Jim Mast rapped one of the plastic tables with a rubber builder's mallet he was using as a gavel. "Just about ready to get started here," he bellowed. Jim was a small man with a ruddy face and a big Adam's apple, always cheerful, always ready to help someone in need in their community. With eleven children, ages three to twenty-five, he was busy sunup to sundown, but the smile on his face seemed glued there.

"Come on closer, men," Jim coaxed. "Don't be shy! We've got plenty of good eats here. You know how it's done. Bid on a dessert that looks tasty to you and enjoy some time with the girl who made it." He held up one finger. "Of course it's supposed to be a secret who made what."

"What if I want to bid on my girl's pie?" his son Jon called.

Jim winked at the gathering crowd of *kapps* and straw hats. "Then you best bid high because I think your brother Freeman has his eye on the same girl."

Everyone burst into laughter, except for Mary John Beiler, who covered her face with her hands in embarrassment. They all knew she and Jon Mast had been walking out together for weeks. And everyone *also* knew that Freeman Mast liked nothing better than to get under his brother's skin.

"Should have brought two pies, Mary!" shouted a boy from Seven Poplars who was known to be courting one of Jim Mast's girls. "Then you could sit with the both of them."

More laughter followed, then the auction began in earnest. Jon did outbid his brother for Mary's pie. And one after another, the rest of the desserts were auctioned off. Millie's sister Cora's apple muffins were bought by Andy Kertz, Annie's cousin, and Beth and her platonic friend Johnny joined them on a blanket with Beth's apple raisin cookies and a big jug of homemade cider the Masts sold in their shop.

Millie watched apprehensively as Jim auctioned dessert after dessert off to husbands, beaus and single men hoping to meet a girl who might become their wife one day. As the event wound down, Millie kept eyeing Willa's cookies, which would, because of the order of the desserts on the tables, be auctioned off ahead of Millie's galette. But then, Jim started grabbing random plates, and the next thing she knew, he was holding up her galette.

"My, my, my," Jim said tipping the square wooden tray Millie had put it on. "Have you seen anything so beautiful?" He leaned down and took a deep, exaggerated sniff. "And the smell of it!" He shook his head in amazement and Millie felt herself blush.

"I wish you could smell this because you're all going to wish you had a slice of it," Jim went on. "In fact, I might just snitch a piece before I turn it over to the man blessed to win the bid." He looked up at the crowd that had dwindled as couples and families had taken their sweets and settled on the grass or in lawn chairs on the edge of the apple orchard. "Let's say we open the bid at five...no, no, this is too fancy a dessert for five. Eight dollars. Eight is the opening bid."

"Eight," a male voice called. "I'll pay eight." The bidder looked in Millie's direction.

It was Ronny, Annie's brother, who was as wide as he was tall. Ronny wouldn't be awful to spend an hour with, though Millie had kept her distance from him since Epiphany. At a holiday gathering at Matt and Ellen Beachy's place, he'd tried to kiss her behind a buggy when they were out of sight of others. When Millie had pushed Ronny away, he'd fallen into the snow so hard that she'd felt bad and given him a hand getting up before telling him that if he ever tried that again, he'd get worse.

"Good start, good start," Jim encouraged. "But come on, boys. You don't bid higher than that, I'll be winning the bid and Edna and I will be digging into it with the person who made this fine dessert."

"Ten dollars," Junior Yoder shouted.

Annie giggled and squeezed Millie's arm.

Millie groaned. *Come on, Ronny*, she thought. *Outbid him. Please outbid him. I'm not in the mood to look at Junior's false teeth for an hour.*

"Twelve dollars!" Ronny shouted, moving closer to the front of the crowd. Then he glanced over his shoulder and made eye contact and Millie realized he knew she had made it. Annie must have told her brother. Millie couldn't decide if she was angry or happy, because the truth of the matter was that at the end of the day, it was nice to be appreciated, even if it was by Ronny Lapp.

"Fourteen," Junior declared with a raise of his hand.

Millie groaned again.

"I've got fourteen," Jim called. "Fourteen is generous, but who out here is feeling even more generous than that? Remember, this is for a good cause. Money goes to all three schools. We've got books to buy and the school over on Clover Road needs a new floor in the coat room after that leak this spring."

Murmurs of agreement rippled through the crowd. The auction *was* for a good cause, and if that meant Millie had to look at Junior's teeth for an hour, she could somehow do it for the benefit of Honeycomb's schoolchildren, couldn't she?

"Last chance, Ronny. You sure you don't want to part with a couple more dollars for this—what did you say it was called, Edna?" Jim asked his wife, his wide forehead crinkling.

"A galette," she told him, rolling her eyes. "How's a man get to be fifty-some years old and not know an apple galette when he sees it?"

Again, there was more laughter from the friends and neighbors, but the warm kind that was obviously meant only in jest.

"Guess I can go sixteen," Junior said kicking at a clump of grass as his feet.

"Sixteen." Jim pointed. "Going…going—"

"Thirty," a male voice shouted.

Everyone's eyes got big and they began to murmur under their breath as they looked around to see who had spoken.

"Thirty?" Jim asked, looking past Millie to someone in the back. "Are you bidding thirty dollars or thirty apples, *sohn*?"

Everyone laughed and the elderly John Mast, Jim's father, gave a hoot from a lawn chair near the tables, slapping his thigh as if it was the funniest thing he had ever heard.

Then came the voice again. "Thirty dollars, Jim. Cash money."

Millie recognized the male voice now, except that she had to be mistaken. It couldn't be…

"Not going to give it to me all in quarters, are you?" Jim shouted back good-naturedly.

As Millie turned to look over her shoulder, she heard Elden say, "Nope. Nice clean, crisp bills, fresh from the bank."

Millie stared at him thinking, *Oh my, he's somehow gotten mixed up.*

Had Willa told Elden about Millie's galette when they were talking? When Willa told him she'd made the cookies, had he somehow gotten confused and thought Millie had made the cookies and Willa had made the galette? At any other moment, that might have made Millie laugh. A galette was beyond Willa's baking skills. Willa had burned two sheets of cookies, then underbaked one and had to make another batch of them that morning. Jane had helped her with the baking this time, which was the only reason Willa had a dessert to donate at all.

"Junior?" Jim asked. "Got another bid in you?"

Junior shook his head.

"Ronny?"

"Nay." Annie's brother scowled, obviously disappointed.

"Good enough," Jim announced. "Then this fine apple—" he looked at his wife "—*ga-lette* goes to Elden Yoder. Congratulations. I'm jealous. I just hope the special girl who made this will be willing to share the recipe with my Edna." He gazed at the cluster of people. "Who's the fine lady who baked this?"

For a moment, Millie just stood there wishing she

could close her eyes and disappear. Or get down on her hands and knees and crawl away.

"Don't be shy. Someone made this dessert," Jim called out.

Annie nudged Millie. "Speak up," she whispered. "Elden Yoder just bought your dessert."

"It's mine," Millie croaked, raising her hand in the air. "I... I baked it," she said loudly.

A woman gasped and harrumphed. Lavinia.

Suddenly feeling as if she couldn't quite catch her breath, Millie searched for Willa in the crowd with her eyes. She was standing with two of her friends near the table with only a few desserts left on.

I'm sorry, Millie mouthed silently.

Her sister knitted her brows questioningly.

Meanwhile, Elden had made his way to the front, handed Edna his cash, which the older woman tucked into a sewing box. The next thing Millie knew, Elden was standing there in front of her, the galette on the wooden platter in his hands.

Annie giggled, squeezed Millie's arm and excused herself with a shy mumble to Elden.

"Where do you want to sit?" Elden asked Millie.

Millie stared at him, not sure what to say. "Did you make a mistake?" she whispered.

"Mistake? What do you mean? *Nay*, I didn't make a mistake. I love an apple...apple..." He seemed to be squinting, though she couldn't be sure, since he was wearing dark Ray-Ban sunglasses. "What's it called again?"

Realizing this had to be some kind of cruel joke,

Millie thrust out her jaw. "What? Do you think you're funny, making fun of me?" she demanded. A lump rose in her throat, and she fought the tears she could feel all scratchy behind her eyelids. On impulse, she grabbed the platter from Elden's hands and strode away, leaving him to stand there and watch her go.

Chapter Five

Pushing up on the brim of his straw hat, Elden watched, perplexed, as Millie walked away. *What had just happened?*

Women were so hard to understand.

After the mention of the apple frolic at the Koffmans' the weekend before, he had mulled over the idea of bidding on Millie's dessert so he could spend time with her. Eleanor's dodge of his mother's invitation to Willa had been clever and had left the door open for Elden if he chose to walk through it. But was he ready?

All week he'd vacillated, going between telling himself he wasn't yet fit to court another woman and thinking about Millie. It kept going through his mind how pretty and intelligent she was and how kind she was to her sisters and father. She'd been through such a tragic loss and yet she had found a way to smile, to laugh, and he envied that. He envied her.

Elden eventually landed on the idea that there was nothing wrong with spending an hour or two with

Millie at the orchard. It was for a good cause; he had to bid on someone's dessert. Why not Millie's? Getting to know her didn't mean he had to walk out with her. For all he knew, she wasn't interested. Though he had a sneaking suspicion she was because of the way she had looked at him across the supper table Saturday night when she thought he wouldn't notice. Elden's heart still ached over the loss of Mary, but since the incidence with the cows—with Millie—the ache hadn't been so overwhelming. Now his loss felt more like a blister that was still sore but healing at last.

Once Elden decided that he wanted to bid on Millie's dessert, the trick had been to find out what she would bring to the auction. He hadn't been bold enough to ask her directly but had decided to ask Willa once he arrived. When he told Willa what he wanted to know, she had seemed pleased and given up the secret. In return, he'd offered to let JJ, the boy she was sweet on, know what *she* had made. And it had all seemed to be working out; Elden had been thrilled when he'd won Millie's apple galette. He thought she'd be happy that it was him and not Junior or Ronny, but somehow it had gone all wrong. Did Millie dislike him so much that she didn't want to spend a single hour with him?

Elden watched Millie striding away with determination. She was almost to the barnyard and headed straight for her family's wagon. His impulse was to go after her but then he had second thoughts. What if she really didn't want to sit with him in the orchard? After all, Mary had made it clear that not only did she not want to share any desserts with him, but she also didn't want to live in the same state. Was this another rebuke? Should he abandon the idea before he embarrassed himself even further? The town had been gossiping for months about his breakup with Mary. Would this just throw wood on the fire?

As he watched Millie in her pretty blue dress walking away, he knew he had to go after her. He had to try to find out what was wrong.

Elden felt a tap on his shoulder. "What do you think you're doing, *sohn*?"

His mother's voice startled him and he whipped around. "What?"

She threw her hands up in the air. "You bid on the wrong dessert. I *told* you which one was Willa's. *Ach*, you certainly don't give the impression of a man as smart as I know you are."

Two girls in matching brown dresses walked past them with blatant interest in their conversation.

His mother ignored them. "But don't worry. I can fix this." She glanced over her shoulder toward Jim who was still auctioning desserts. "You're going to have to hurry. Willa's cookies are about to come up. They're in the square basket." She laid her hand on his arm. "*Square basket*," she repeated. "I'll tell Millie that you bid on her apple whatever-it-is for me. So I could visit with her." She beamed at him. "See. All's well that ends well."

He glanced at Millie again. She had stopped before she reached her family's wagon and was now standing in the lane, the plate in her hand, her head hung low. He looked back at his mother. *"Nay."*

She frowned. *"Nay* what?"

"I am *not* bidding on Willa's cookies. I told you that this morning. And yesterday. And the day before. I'm not interested in Willa Koffman."

"A pretty girl like her? Of course you're interested in her. It would be so convenient for you to marry her. Then she'd be right across the street from her poor father. But she's not going to marry you unless you court her and you can't court her if you don't speak with her." She nudged him. "Go bid on her cookies."

"Mam, I don't want Willa's cookies," he said, his tone firm. "I want Millie's apple galette. That's why I bid on it."

"Elden Yoder, surely you're not interested in a—"

"Let it go, *Mam,*" he interrupted, not sure exactly what she was going to say but sensing he wasn't going to like it. "We've discussed this. I'm not your little boy anymore and you can't keep trying to make decisions for me."

"But Elden!" she cried after him as he walked away. "This is not the plan!"

He kept walking, his gaze fixed on Millie's back.

Millie heard Elden's footsteps in the gravel behind her. Hot tears threatened to spill and she wiped her eyes with her sleeve. She didn't know what to do. Did she throw the fragrant galette in the field and walk home?

"Millie?" Elden called, fast approaching. "Millie, what's wrong?"

Her lower lip trembled. As she saw it, she had two choices. She could run or she could confront him. In a split second, she spun around, hugging the wooden platter to her chest. "Was this supposed to be a joke?" she demanded.

He halted two feet from her, drawing his head back. "What? What are you talking about?"

"Why did you bid on my dessert? Why did you bid all that money? It was to make fun of me, wasn't it? A joke between you and…and JJ? Your friends?"

Elden stared at her blankly. "Millie, I have no idea what you're talking about." He pushed his hands deep into his pockets. "I bid on your dessert because I—" He swallowed, seeming to struggle to get the words out. "Because I wanted to. Because I wanted to sit with you."

"You wanted to sit with *me*?" she asked suspiciously.

He nodded. "And have some of that. It looks delicious. It was the prettiest dessert on the tables. Everyone said so. Like it came from a fancy bakery." He pointed at the galette Millie was still holding against her chest as if it could somehow protect her feelings. "None of us could figure out what that icing was."

She bit down on her lower lip, studying his face. He looked sincere and maybe a little scared. Had he *really* paid thirty whole dollars for some sliced apples arranged on a piecrust because she had made it?

Because he liked her? "It's caramel. And bits of salt to bring out the taste of the brown sugar and butter."

"Ah. That's why Willa called it a *salted* apple caramel galette," he said. "I didn't even know what a galette was. Willa had to explain it to me."

She lowered the tray a bit. "You and Willa were talking about my galette?"

"I asked her what you brought so I could bid on it."

Her eyes widened. "You did?" She thought for a moment. "But wait, why didn't you ask *me* what I made?"

"Because..." He hesitated. "I guess I was afraid you wouldn't tell me."

She narrowed her gaze. "And you didn't want Willa's cookies? *Willa*," she added.

"Willa's a nice girl, but—" He hesitated and then went on. "But I wanted to visit with you."

Her gaze flicked in the direction of the auction. Every dessert was gone from the table and the remainder of the crowd had wandered off. She saw Willa and JJ walking, their heads together in private conversation. He was carrying her woven willow basket of cookies.

Millie looked back at Elden, studying his face. He had blue eyes that were so pale they looked gray. She didn't know many folks with gray eyes and she found them intriguing. His eyes were easy to read. And his eyes told her he was telling the truth. As hard as it was for her to believe. "You're sure you want to visit with me?" she asked again, just to be sure she had understood correctly. "Not Willa."

"*Not* Willa," he repeated.

"But your mother wanted you to bid on Willa's dessert. She invited Willa to come with you today. She has her eye on Willa for you to court."

He exhaled, pulling one hand out of his pocket to drag it across his face. "My mother has good intentions, but it's not up to her to say who I—" He halted again, seeming to choose his words carefully. "Whose dessert I choose to buy."

Millie giggled. Maybe she should have been embarrassed that she'd earlier misread his behavior and stomped off, but she wasn't. Now she was just happy, so happy that she was giddy. "I can't believe you paid thirty dollars for three dollars' worth of apples and flour. Are you always this thrifty with money?"

It took him a moment to realize she was teasing him. And then he began to laugh. "Three dollars? Come on. It must have cost you more than that. What about the caramel?"

"Elden, caramel is just sugar that's browned and then you add some butter and some cream. A little salt thrown in at the end makes it salted caramel." She cocked her head, looking at him. "But then I guess you wouldn't know that, would you? Because you probably don't make a lot of caramel."

"*Nay,* I do not." The tone of their conversation had changed entirely and now it was almost flirtatious. "I love caramel, but I buy it in a jar at Byler's."

"Your mother doesn't make it?"

He lowered his voice conspiratorially as he took a step closer to her. "You know my mother isn't much of a cook. Never learned. Everyone in the county knows. When my sisters married, their mothers-in-law had to teach them both."

Millie balanced the dessert platter with one hand and covered her mouth with the other, giggling behind it. He was right, everyone *did* know Lavinia Yoder was a terrible cook. Folks in Honeycomb were always on watch to see what she brought to a potluck so they could avoid it. Lavinia had once brought a cheese-cake pie to a barn raising and no one had touched it, so Millie had taken a slice so that she wouldn't feel bad. It was one of the worst things she had ever put in her mouth, and that included the beetle a boy at school had once dared her to take a bite of. Lavinia's cheesecake pie had somehow curdled, and it had taken two cups of cider for Millie to get the taste out of her mouth after she spit it into a napkin.

Millie lifted her gaze.

Elden smiled at her and her insides melted like the sweet caramel she'd poured all over her galette that morning.

He glanced over his shoulder and tipped his head. "You want to find a place to sit down and let me taste my three dollars' worth of apples that I paid thirty for?"

She pressed her lips together, knowing her cheeks had to be bright red. "*Ya*, I do. I have a blanket in our wagon we can use to sit on the grass. And I brought a knife and plates and a fork."

"Let's get them, then. I'm thinking over there on the edge of the lawn, near that big Red Delicious tree." He pointed at the tree that was laden with shiny apples, then took the galette from her. "Better let me carry that. I spent good money for it."

Millie grinned as she walked beside him toward her family's wagon. She was so happy that her heart was pounding. Elden Yoder had bought her dessert and he wanted to visit with *her*. Then suddenly, she stopped short. "What about your mother?"

He had to pull up fast to keep from running into Millie. "What about her?"

"Should we invite her to join us?" *Say no, say no*, a little voice shouted inside her. *But that wouldn't be charitable, would it?* "There's plenty," she said brightly. "And I brought some sandwiches in case anyone is hungry."

He frowned, looking unsure of himself again. "Do you *want* her to join us?"

Millie didn't know what to say. She was worried this was a test. Maybe she should say yes. Elden's mother was widowed, he was her only son and she was under his care. Perhaps he wanted to see if Millie would be willing to include her in an activity with them. Maybe the rumors were true and Lavinia had run his fiancée off and he knew Millie knew.

But what if it was a test of a different sort? What if he was trying to figure out if Millie liked him? If she said she wanted Lavinia to share the dessert with them, would he think she didn't want to be alone with him?

Elden waited for her reply.

"What do *you* want to do?" she asked haltingly.

He sighed. "I'm going to be in hot water over this for sure, but *nay*. I don't want to invite her. Her gaggle of friends are all together." He indicated a group of older women seated in folding chairs borrowed from one of the church wagons. "She can join them. None of the other single men are sitting with their mothers."

Millie met Elden's gaze, smiling. *"Oll recht,"* she whispered, thinking this might be the best day ever.

By the time Eleanor took up the reins and the family's wagon rolled toward home, the sun had set and there was a chill in the air that signaled that fall had, at last, come to Honeycomb to stay. Millie, Willa and Jane sat on the tailgate of the wagon, their legs dangling the way they had when they were children and their mother had still been here with them. Had it been any other day, Millie might have felt sad that her world had changed so drastically in the past year. But she was too happy to let herself be sad for things she couldn't change. *Gott* had His ways and, as her mother had reminded her often, questioning those ways only made a person discontent.

Millie's afternoon with Elden had been like a dream. She still wondered if she ought to pinch herself. After their misunderstanding, he had carried the picnic basket and the galette to the old Red Delicious apple tree. There, he'd spread out the blanket and in front of half of Honeycomb, he sat with her and ate slice after slice of her apple galette. And he'd eaten not one, but two of her egg salad sandwiches and drunk a full Mason jar of apple cider.

Millie had been so nervous when they sat down that she'd barely been able to eat, but as the minutes ticked by, she'd relaxed a bit. She found Elden so easy to talk to that she soon felt as if they had been friends their whole lives, rather than acquaintances. They hadn't talked about anything important. They'd recalled their school days together and covered numerous other topics: her mother's death, his dog, his plans for his east field that he was clearing and the fact that butter pecan was their favorite ice cream. Then, when the little groups had scattered, he'd helped her tuck the basket back in her wagon. There, she'd wrapped up the galette in aluminum foil and given what was left of it to him to take home for breakfast the following day.

Then, still talking, they wandered over to watch the softball game. When Elden's cousin Daniel had insisted he joined their team after their catcher injured his hand on a foul ball, Elden had at first said no. But then Millie had agreed he should play and she'd stood on the sidelines, clapping and cheering when Elden made a play at home plate and got JJ out, winning for his team.

Millie and Elden had later stood in the Masts' backyard talking as a long line of open wagons and black buggies went down the lane headed home for folks to prepare for church or visiting day the next morning. Millie had known it was almost time to go, but it had been such a wonderful day that she hadn't wanted it to end.

Then Lavinia had marched across the lawn toward them. She barely acknowledged Millie when she announced she was tired and wanted to go home. Elden had met Millie's gaze and murmured goodnight. Then they were gone and Millie had nothing but the memories. But they were good memories and she would hold them close to her for the rest of her days. Because she knew there were a hundred reasons why it would never happen again.

"Millie? *Hallo*?" Jane waved a hand in front of her face, a hand she couldn't miss, even in the darkness. "Did you hear anything I just said?"

Millie blinked, pulling her wool cloak closer, glad she had brought it. Because while it had been a beautiful day with temperatures rising to the mid-sixties, once the sun had set, the temperature had quickly dropped. "Sorry, Jane."

"I was telling you that Susie said that a bunch of girls were talking about how Elden must be looking for a wife again. They were talking about how he's now Honeycomb's most eligible bachelor and Susie said the girls were going to get their mothers to invite him and his mother to Visiting Sundays. They were making guesses as to who he'd ask out first now that he's gotten a little practice in with you."

"Jane!" Willa said sharply to their little sister sitting between them on the tailgate. "That isn't very nice!"

"What?" Jane looked at Willa. "I'm just telling you what Susie said the girls were—"

"We promised Eleanor no more gossiping, Jane. Remember? You know very well..."

As Willa chastised their little sister, their voices faded and Millie stared at the paved road as they rolled over it. She listened to the comforting sound of their horse's hooves as his metal shoes hit the blacktop, and the sound of their father, slumped between Eleanor and Beth, snoring.

Against her will, tears welled in Millie's eyes and she wiped them away impatiently, hoping her sisters were too busy quarreling with each other to notice. Jane wasn't saying anything Millie didn't already know. Of course, Elden would begin dating again. And when he did, he would choose one of those pretty girls, one of those slender girls.

One his mother would wholly approve.

Chapter Six

Elden's uncle Gabriel, stood beside him, watching as Elden set the new propane hot water heater squarely in the center of the overflow pan. "I appreciate you coming by to help me get this in," Gabriel said. "I probably could have installed it myself, but it would have taken me half the day." He chuckled. "And that broken one would have been a bear to get out of the house on my own. These old bones don't move as well as they once did." He tapped his temple. "I have to remind myself of that sometimes. I'm not the strapping young man I once was."

"I don't know." Elden glanced at him. "You're pretty fit for a man in his mid-sixties."

"Tell that to your aunt. If she had her way, I'd be sitting at her kitchen table all the day long so she could keep an eye on me. The woman gets herself worked up if I lift anything heavier than a carton of eggs."

Elden smiled and pointed to the toolbox he'd

brought along. "Could you grab that pipe wrench for me? Top tray." He could hear his mother chattering a mile a minute to his aunt Elsie in the connecting kitchen.

"I don't know what all he was thinking," Elden's mother said, slurping her coffee. "Just trying to be nice, I suppose. But it's high time he put this whole Mary business behind him and started looking seriously for a wife. Neither of us is getting any younger. I want grandbabies before I'm too old to enjoy them. Look at you, Elsie, with nine and two more on the way."

Aunt Elsie said something, but Elden didn't catch it. Aunt Elsie was a soft-spoken woman of few words—the complete opposite of his mother. And Elsie knew how to mind her own business when it came to her adult children, a trait he knew for a fact his cousins appreciated.

"But I suppose I should look at his behavior at the Masts' positively." Another slurp. "You have any more honey, dear? This coffee is bitter. You should buy the kind I buy. I'll write it down." *Slurp.* "Having practically half the county see my Elden showing such an act of charity will only make girls more interested in him."

Elden grunted as he realized he hadn't threaded the water connection on the top of the new heater correctly and unscrewed it to try it again. He pulled the roll of Teflon tape from his pocket and rewrapped the threads. Then, still not at the correct angle, he moved to the other side of the unit, closer to the kitchen.

"You know all the young women of marrying age at the apple frolic were talking about how handsome my Elden is. And how kind," his mother went on, making no attempt to prevent him from hearing her. As if she hadn't already made her opinion obvious. In the two days since the frolic at the Masts' orchard, she'd managed to bring up the subject nearly every time they exchanged words. Which was why he had jumped on the offer to come to his uncle's today rather than later in the week. What Elden hadn't considered was that his mother would insist on coming with him. "Surely you wouldn't keep an old lady from her sister-in-law, one of her dearest friends," his mother had proclaimed loudly in front of Gabriel when he stopped at their place to ask if Elden could help him with the water heater.

"Their parents think he's a good catch as well," his mother continued without seeming to take a breath. "I wouldn't be surprised if I didn't have mothers coming to me to arrange Sunday visits. You know, that's the way we did it in our day, Elsie. Mothers got together and matched their children. This whole idea that a young man knows what woman would make the best wife for him?" She laughed. "Nonsense. Pure nonsense. *Nay*, a mother knows best."

"Here you go. More honey." Elsie's voice.

"Thank you. And maybe another cookie or two? I do love your shortbread. I keep meaning to get the recipe."

As Elden tightened the water connection correctly this time, he heard what sounded like a jar being set down on the kitchen table. His mother always put so much honey in her coffee that it no longer tasted like coffee.

"I don't know, Lavinia," came Elsie's patient voice. "Millie Koffman is an awfully nice girl. She's a hard worker and she's always patient with her father, no matter what he gets into. You understand he's unwell, don't you?"

"A daughter's duty," Lavinia responded, her spoon clunking against the inside of her coffee mug rhythmically as she stirred. "He seemed well enough the night we had supper with him. Except that he likes his biscuits cut in bite-size pieces, but what man doesn't have odd habits, hmm? But I won't argue with you that one of the Koffman girls might be suitable. It would be so convenient. My Elden courting one of them. Willa is the prettiest of the lot and I'm sure she's kind to her father…but maybe Beth would be suitable," she added thoughtfully. "She has a pretty smile. Not as slender as Willa, but we can't all be so thin, can we?"

Elden gritted his teeth and checked the fitting again, verifying it was snug. Next, he tackled the heat trap fittings. As he worked, he noticed his uncle eyeing the open kitchen door.

"My worry is that Elden has given poor Millie the wrong idea," his mother said. "And then we'll have another mess on our—"

Gabriel slid the pocket door closed between the kitchen and the laundry room with a bang. "Women's chatter can give a man indigestion," he joked.

Elden set his jaw. "I think I'm ready for the pressure relief valve now." He put out his hand.

Gabriel walked over to his propane chest freezer, where Elden had laid out all the parts needed to connect the new hot water heater. "You know your *mutter* means well," he said quietly.

"I know she does."

Gabriel walked back with the valve in his hand, but he didn't pass it to Elden. "That doesn't mean she knows what's best for you."

Elden chewed on that for a moment.

"I can only imagine how hard losing Mary the way you did had to be," Gabriel said. "But I believe *Gott* had a different plan for you."

A moment of silence passed between the two men, but from behind the door, Elden could still hear his mother talking.

Gabriel cleared his throat as if considering whether to say something else and Elden glanced at him. He looked so much like Elden's father that sometimes seeing him brought a lump up in his throat. His uncle was the same height, white-haired with wire-frame glasses and a face wrinkled by sixty-five years of laughter. And some hardships, including the loss of a child, the death of the brother who was his best friend, and Elsie suffering a debilitating illness early in their marriage that had taken her some time to recover from. But like Millie, Gabriel always had a smile on his face and a sparkle of mischief in his eyes. Unless of course he was angry with something or someone, and then, like Millie, he could speak directly.

Remembering how Millie had snatched the galette from him and stomped off, Elden smiled. The girl had fire in her and she was strong-minded. Which wasn't a bad thing. At least a man knew where he stood with a woman like Millie. Which had obviously not been true with Mary. Otherwise maybe they could have talked things out and tried to work on their relationship rather than having it end so abruptly.

"I'm going to just ask you straight out." Gabriel met Elden's gaze. "You like her? The Koffman girl? Millie?"

Afraid the tone of his voice might suggest just how much he liked Millie, Elden only nodded.

Gabriel shrugged. "Then do something about it."

"But what?" Elden reached for the valve, but his uncle pulled it out of his reach.

Gabriel spoke softly so their conversation wouldn't be overheard. "One thing Lavinia is right about is that it's time you moved on. Mary broke your heart. We all know that. But the fact is, like it or not, she's gone, and she's not coming back. Those are the hard facts. Which means it's time you find someone better suited to you." He hesitated. "Ask Millie out."

Elden grimaced, the idea terrifying. He had given Mary everything he had and it hadn't been enough. Could he ever be enough for Millie? Did he even deserve a fine woman like her? Was he even meant to have a wife? "Like on a date?" he asked.

Gabriel shrugged. "If you're not ready for that, maybe start slow. Invite her for the Visiting Sunday coming up. Invite the whole family. I heard over at the mill that Felty did well at the apple frolic. Seemed more like himself. He might enjoy visiting as much as his girls would. It's time the whole family started getting on with life. It's been more than a year now since Aggie passed. She wouldn't want them to mourn any longer. Young women are meant to be out and about."

"Invite her for Visiting Sunday?" Elden echoed.

Gabriel nodded, stroking his white beard. "And Elsie and I can come, too, if you like. I'll ask Elsie to keep Lavinia busy. Give you and Millie time to talk."

"We don't usually have folks over on Visiting Sundays."

"Nope, you don't. Not since Mary left, at least. Which means it's high time you started up again. It will be good for your mother, too. Give her someone else to listen to her." Gabriel cracked a smile, still holding the valve just out of Elden's reach. "What do you say?"

"You really think I should invite Millie—all the Koffmans," he corrected, "over on Sunday?"

Gabriel smiled as he passed the valve to his nephew. "I do think you should invite her. Before some other young man catches her fancy. That dessert she made Saturday was the talk around town. Heard it from three different men at church yesterday. All talking about how they wished their wives could make one of those beauties. Ed Swartzentruber said his wife was thinking about getting their son Danny to take Millie home from the harvest frolic coming up. It's going to be a big to-do. I heard the matchmaker from Seven Poplars is bringing some young men from farther afield. You don't want someone from Ohio sweeping Millie off her feet before you've had a chance, do you?"

Elden thought back to the time he'd spent with Millie on Saturday and how good she had made him feel. How good it had felt to enjoy himself like that again. She'd been so much fun and she could talk about anything. She had seemed interested in most subjects, even boring stuff like what he was planning to sow in his east field once he had it cleared. "*Oll recht*. I think I will invite the Koffmans. I'll go over after we're done here and extend the invitation. Take Samson with me."

"Good idea." Gabriel pointed at his nephew. "But just the dog. Not Lavinia, if I was you."

They both laughed.

Millie was down on her hands and knees, trowel in hand, planting the last of the fall bulbs in the flower beds flanking the front stoop. Her mother had loved the way tulips, daffodils and crocuses popped up after a long winter. She had said that it was one of the comforting signs that spring had returned and with it, new life in *Gott*'s world. Their mother, an avid gardener, had painstakingly dug up every tulip bulb once it had bloomed. She stored them in their cellar, hanging from the rafters, sorted by color and type.

In the fall, their mother replanted them and Millie and her sisters had waited eagerly for spring to see the new beds their *mam* had created. Every year they looked different. Sometimes there were beds of a singular color—scarlet red, bright yellow, white or her favorite black. But she had also mixed colors: black and white, yellow and red.

Millie liked flowers well enough, but she didn't have the passion her mother had for gardening. She did, however, have a passion for keeping her *mam*'s memory alive, so when none of her sisters had the time or desire to fuss with the bulbs, Millie had dug them up. And now it was time to plant them again before they got a hard frost and the ground began to freeze. She knew the flower beds wouldn't look anything like the neat rows and intricate patterns her mother had planted, but she would do her best.

After putting the job off for a week, Millie had decided today was the day. However, she quickly realized it may not have been the best choice because it was also her day to spend time with her father. *Spending time* with him meant keeping him safe and out of trouble so that Eleanor wouldn't wind up giving them both a scolding over something. Millie had thought her father might enjoy helping her and had given him the task of cutting off the dried tops of the bulbs they had hung in bundles in the cellar. She showed him how to cut the tops off with gardening shears and explained that all he had to do was put them back in the same pile he had taken them from. She had patiently explained to him that it was important he do it that way so the colors wouldn't get mixed up. But either her father didn't understand, or he didn't care to do it the way she'd asked.

Millie glanced over her shoulder to watch her father pull a bulb from the red tulip bundle, cut off the top and toss it into the pile of yellow jonquil daffodils. "*Dat*," she said gently. "Put it back in the same bag, right?"

Without looking at her, he took a bulb from the pile of black beauties, topped it and added it to the giant whites. Millie sighed. She couldn't decide if she should give up for the day and wait until tomorrow to plant the bulbs, or push through. After all, her rows of bulbs were so wiggly, was it going to matter if the colors were mixed? They would still be pretty come spring, wouldn't they? And the following day, she and Willa and Beth were planning on going to the Masts' orchard to pick apples and she didn't want to miss the outing.

"*Dat*, would you like to try planting some of *Mam*'s bulbs? I could dig the hole and you could set them in. How does that sound?"

Her father, on the ground on his knees, pulled his handkerchief out of his pocket and wiped his nose. "Not much interested in planting. Aggie wouldn't want me interfering with her flowers. I think we best wait for her."

Millie sighed but didn't remind him that his wife was gone. There was no point, because when he was having this sort of day, when his mind was clouded, he'd only forget and have to be told again and again.

Her *dat* cocked his head. "Hear that?"

"Hear what?"

"A dog. We get a dog?" He glanced around curiously. "Blue died."

How could he remember that they'd lost their blu-etick hound that spring, but not that his wife was dead?

"I don't hear a dog, *Dat*."

He stuffed his handkerchief back in his pants pocket as he slowly got to his feet and turned to the lane that led to the road. "That looks like a dog to me."

Then Millie heard a bark. From her knees, she spotted Elden's bulldog. Shading her eyes from the sun, it took a second for her to see that someone was coming up the drive with the dog. It was Elden.

And here she was on the ground again. Her apron was covered in dirt and it had blueberry stains from the jam her father had spilled on her while trying to make his own peanut butter and jam sandwich. And she was wearing the ugliest dress she owned, complete with a torn hem she'd been meaning to repair.

"Afternoon, Felty," Elden called with a wave.

Felty tipped back his straw hat. "Afternoon, neighbor. That your dog?" He pointed at the bulldog trotting at Elden's feet.

"He is. Name's Samson."

"Good name for a pup." Felty whistled between his teeth to beckon the dog, tapping his thigh. "Come here, boy. Come on."

The dog panted, excited, but didn't move from his master's side. He kept looking up at Elden.

Elden raised his hand and the dog took off across the grass toward the older man.

Millie smiled as her father got down on one knee and greeted Samson with a pat and a laugh. "Nice boy. Good boy," Felty said, stroking the dog's back.

"*Dat* likes dogs," she said. She was still on her knees, debating whether or not to get up, because sometimes it was hard for her. Often she would grab onto something to heave herself up. She couldn't decide which would be more embarrassing—staying on the ground or having to haul herself up like a feed sack. "He misses our dog."

Elden nodded and walked over to her, leaving Samson to entertain her *dat*. "Whatcha doin'?"

"Planting my *mam*'s tulip and daffodil bulbs," she said, deciding she wanted to get to her feet. The question was, did she risk trying to do it without any help? To use the railing of the stoop, she'd have to crawl across the grass to get to it. "Trying," she murmured. Then she said a silent prayer, pressed her hands to the tops of her thighs, and was blessedly able to get to her feet without so much as a wobble.

Elden slid his hands into his pockets. He wore work pants and a barn coat, and his blue wool beanie pulled low on his brow. Today he wasn't wearing sunglasses, so she could see his blue-gray eyes.

"You like planting flower bulbs?" Elden asked.

Millie twisted her mouth one way and then the other. "I like seeing our *mam*'s flowers in the spring, so—" She shrugged. "I guess, in a way, I do like planting them."

Elden smiled nostalgically. "Her flowers were always so beautiful. I remember that spring a few years back when both sides of your lane at the road were a mass of red and yellow tulips. Don't know if I ever saw anything so stunning."

His kind words made her eyes scratchy. She didn't know many men who felt that way about flowers. Her father never had. It just wasn't in a man's makeup, she'd always thought.

But maybe she was wrong. At least about this man.

"You want to play?" Felty said.

Millie looked past Elden to see her father on his feet. He had a stick in his hand. "You know how to bring it back to me?" he asked the dog. "I throw it and you go get it and bring it back. Wanna try?"

Elden smiled. "Samson can fetch, all right. If he isn't being lazy," he told her father. He looked back at Millie. "Nice that your *dat*'s helping you. Good for him to get outside, I imagine."

Millie sighed. "*Ya*, he does like getting out of the house and out from under Eleanor's thumb. She fusses over him more than he cares for, but it's hard doing things with *Dat* sometimes. He doesn't understand—" She stopped, worrying she was saying too much. Talking too much.

Elden waited for her to finish her sentence.

Millie didn't know what came over her. Ordinarily she wouldn't share something like this, but she told Elden about the flowers being organized by color and what a mess her father was making of it. As she spoke, she heard her voice getting shaky and was afraid she might start to cry. Because deep down, she realized, she wasn't upset about the flowers but rather the fact that her father couldn't do what she'd asked. And it made no sense because he could still beat any of them at checkers.

If Elden heard frustration or sadness in her voice, it didn't seem to make him uncomfortable. He listened and then said, "Has to be hard, Millie, to watch him change. I saw the same in a great-uncle I had when I was a kid. Before we moved here." He met her gaze with unblinking eyes. "Felty's a blessed man to have a daughter like you. Daughters like you and your sisters."

She wiped at her eyes with the back of her dirty hand. "If you'd seen him throwing a fuss over how Jane had scrambled his eggs this morning, you might not think so."

She smiled tentatively and he smiled back.

"So…so I came by to ask you something." Elden hooked his thumbs in his pockets. "Um, if your family wants to come for Visiting Sunday, this Sunday coming up."

"You want us to come visiting?" she asked, unable to contain her excitement. "We haven't been visiting much since *Mam* got sick. I used to love Visiting Sundays."

He drew his hand across his mouth, smiling behind it. "We haven't been visiting much, either, nor had much in the way of visitors, not since—"

He went quiet and she knew what he was thinking. He hadn't been participating in the tradition of visiting with family, friends and neighbors on the off weeks when his church district didn't have services since his betrothal had ended. It was the first time he'd brought up the subject of his betrothal to Mary Yost and the breakup, even in a roundabout way.

When Millie realized he wasn't going to say any more, she nodded, touched that he would broach the subject of his betrothal, even if he hadn't been able to say the words. "I'd love to come. *We* would love to come," she corrected, not wanting him to think that she thought it was a date or anything. But wishing it was. "I'll check with Eleanor, but I'm sure we can come."

"Good." He nodded. "I'll tell *Mam*. And…and my uncle and his wife are coming, too. And maybe one of their sons and his family. We'll see."

His hands were back in his pockets and there was a slightly uncomfortable silence. Millie felt like she should say something but didn't know what. Thankfully, her father ended the awkward moment.

"Good dog you got here, *sohn*." Felty, now seeming light on his feet, walked over to Elden, the bulldog at his heels. "Good dogs like this are hard to come by. We had a hound dog, Blue. Best dog I ever had. But he passed. I like to think he's in heaven with my Aggie." He pointed at Elden. "But don't tell my bishop I said that. I don't think he thinks dogs go to heaven."

Elden and Millie both stood there for a moment, staring at her father. That was the most she had heard him say at one time in weeks, maybe months. And he sounded so clearheaded. Almost like the *dat* she had known her whole life. Elden picked up on it, too. She could tell by the look on his face.

Elden glanced back at Millie. "Guess I better keep my eye out, else your *dat* will steal my dog."

They both looked at Samson, who had dropped

to the dying grass at her father's feet, his muzzle between his paws.

"Well. Guess I best get on with the rest of my day," Elden said. "Got to walk out and check my deer stand."

"Be time for hunting soon, won't it?" Millie asked, hating to see him go. He was so nice and so easy to talk to. And he just made her…happy.

Elden worked his jaw. "I'm not much of a hunter. My *mam* would tell you I'm too soft. But my property can only support so many deer. They have to be culled every year so the rest will survive. My cousin hunts on our property and always gives us more venison than the two of us can eat."

"Mmm," Millie's father said, rubbing his belly. "I do love a good venison stew." He held up an arthritic finger to Elden. "But you've got to cook it low and slow in the oven all day to get it tender. That's how my Aggie always did it."

Elden nodded and then looked to Millie again. "So…see you Sunday? If not before."

He threw the last phrase in as if it was a second thought and she wondered what he meant. Was it just something impulsive he said, or was he *hoping* to see her again before Sunday?

Elden tapped his leg to call his dog and Samson came to his feet but didn't move away from Millie's father.

"You leaving already?" the older man asked. "Taking my dog?"

Millie couldn't tell if her father thought Samson was his dog or if he was just teasing.

"Sorry to say I am. I've got to take a walk through my woods." Elden hesitated and then met Millie's eyes and looked back at her father. "If you feel like taking a walk, Felty, you could join me and Samson. Not much more than a mile there and back."

Millie's gaze shifted to her father. She was immediately unsure of what to say. Sometimes her father didn't have the energy to move from one room to the next. Would he be able to walk so far? Would Eleanor want him leaving the property without one of his daughters? And was that too much responsibility to give a neighbor? What if her father became difficult?

"I—I don't know," Millie stammered. "Elden, you don't have to…"

Elden shrugged. "I'm thinking Felty and I and Samson would enjoy a walk together. Beautiful day for it. I don't know how many more we'll get. The woods are gorgeous right now with all the leaves changing. What do you say, Felty?"

Millie's father looked down at Samson. The bulldog looked up at his new friend.

"Think I would like to take a walk." Millie's father suddenly seemed to stand taller. "Just you and me, right?" he asked Elden.

"Just you and me," Elden repeated.

Her father nodded thoughtfully. "Be nice to get away from these women for a few minutes. Sometimes a man just needs some time away from skirts and bonnets."

Elden tried to suppress a smile as he met Millie's

gaze and she pressed her lips together to keep from giggling. *Danki*, she mouthed.

He broke into a wide grin. *Gern gschehne*, he mouthed back.

Chapter Seven

Sunday, just before one o'clock, Millie walked halfway down the porch steps, then turned and ran back up. In her rush to get out the door, she had forgotten the basket of ham-and-cheese sandwiches she and Willa had made to take to the Yoders'. "I'm coming!" she shouted. "Don't leave without me!"

Beth stood at the bottom of the steps, leaning on the banister, a look of boredom on her face. "No fear of that, I should think. This may take a while." She nodded in the direction of their other family members, all talking at once.

On the brick walk that led from the barnyard to the back porch, Eleanor, Jane, Willa and Cora had gathered around their father to try to convince him that there was no need to hitch up the wagon to go across the street. But for whatever reason, he wanted to take it and he wanted to drive. Each of the sisters there voiced their opinion on the matter while their father talked over them.

"*Dat*," Cora said, waving her hand. "It will take us longer to catch the horse out in the field and hitch him to the wagon than to just walk across the road."

"You don't drive anymore, *Dat*," Willa told him. "Remember? We've talked about this."

"I'm not going to be bossed around by women!" their father argued stubbornly.

Eleanor's voice could be heard above the din. "*Dat*, please be reasonable."

The only reason Henry and Jane weren't in on it was because Jane had one of her migraines and, even though she could certainly stay home alone, Henry had insisted she would remain behind with her. It was a perfect excuse for Henry, who didn't like social events where there was no work to be done. She was fine with a barn raising or a threshing party, but she was the one sister who'd been relieved when they'd stopped making social calls as a family when their mother had become seriously ill.

Henry didn't like social events involving Lavinia, a result of several encounters with the older woman before their bedridden mother had passed. Lavinia had come to the house with soup for the family but had insisted she see "her dear friend Aggie." Their mother and Lavinia had not been close, but more importantly, their mother had made it clear that she did not want anyone but her immediate family with her in her last days. While friends and neighbors may not have agreed with Aggie Koffman's choice, they had respected it.

Only Lavinia had come again and again, trying

to wear the girls down. Henry, for whatever reason, had made it her personal responsibility to keep Lavinia out of the house and she and Lavinia had gone at it several times. In the end, Henry had won, but only because she was more stubborn than Lavinia. Lavinia had been the first visitor after their mother had died and had made a point of telling anyone who would listen that "she had been the first to see her dear neighbor after her passing."

"I'll be right back," Millie repeated and hurried up the steps.

She was flustered because nothing seemed to be going right today, a day she'd been looking forward to all week. Maybe her whole life. It had all started that morning when they couldn't find their father. Everyone had thought he was still sleeping because he often slept until someone woke him. It turned out he had risen before dawn and was in the cellar rearranging the canning jars of summer vegetables.

Then, when they all sat down for a breakfast of oatmeal, Millie had jumped up to get maple syrup and bumped into the table, knocking a pitcher of fresh cream over, sending a river of white across the table and into Eleanor's lap.

After breakfast, Millie had gone to put on her blue dress, only to find it missing. After questioning one sister after the next, none of whom seemed interested in her clothing crisis, she had discovered that Jane was responsible for the lost dress. Trying to be helpful to Eleanor, who was always complaining about the mountains of laundry, Jane had taken the dress the day before, and washed it in a load of clothes, but forgotten to hang them out. Millie had found her favorite dress at the bottom of the washing machine wrinkled and still wet. Jane had apologized and insisted Millie's dark green dress was just as nice but Millie had nearly burst into tears. She looked best in her blue dress and she wanted to wear it; she *needed* to wear it to Elden's house the way a toddler needed her security blanket.

In the end Millie had hung it on the line and thankfully most of the wrinkles had come out and it had dried for the most part, though it was still a little damp at the arms. Which she realized now was making her chilly. Inside the house, she grabbed a sweater when she retrieved the basket of sandwiches, and when she came back outside, their father had relented and agreed to walk across the road rather than taking the horse and wagon.

By the time Millie came down the porch steps again, they were in the lane, headed toward Elden's. She scurried to catch up with Beth, who was carrying a jug of apple cider, bringing up the rear. "How did they convince him?" Millie asked, out of breath.

"Eleanor reminded him that it was Sunday and even animals needed a day of rest." Beth shrugged. "Then he just said *oll recht* and took off down the lane." She indicated their father out front and Eleanor and the others hurrying to catch up with him.

Millie smiled. "That was smart of her."

Beth shook her head as they followed their gravel lane toward the road. "Sometimes I think he argues with us just to argue. And to get Eleanor all worked up." She flashed a sly smile. "Because you know our big sister can get worked up."

Millie giggled, then realizing they were making fun of Eleanor, she sobered. It wasn't nice to make fun of people, especially on the Sabbath when their hearts were supposed to be turned toward *Gott*. "We shouldn't talk about Eleanor like this," she told her sister. "She does so much for us. She keeps the household running and worries about the money so we don't have to."

"Eleanor doesn't want us to know how worried she is about our finances," Beth said, keeping her voice low. "With *Dat* the way he is, he's not going to bring any income in anymore. His days of working as a mason are over. I overheard her telling Cora that we're going to have to figure out how to make money. Farming, even if we could do it ourselves, doesn't pay enough, not unless you're our neighbor." She indicated Elden's place. They were nearly to the county road now and once they crossed, they'd be in his lane. "I guess they owned two farms back wherever they came from."

"Wisconsin," Millie told her. They had caught up with their father and sisters but hung back to continue their conversation.

"Jane said she overheard Lavinia at the apple folic bragging about how well off her husband had left her and Elden. And Elden being the only boy, this farm is his to do with as he pleases. He's got plenty of irons in the fire. Apparently he's selling Christmas trees this year."

Millie hadn't really thought about Elden's financial situation, but, unlike most of the young men in Honeycomb who worked at a trade, he just worked his farm. She'd never really thought much about money because her parents had always provided for her. She felt bad that Eleanor was carrying that burden on her shoulders and hers alone.

At the end of the lane, Millie and Beth joined the others, and when it was safe, they crossed the road. As they walked toward the Yoders' house, Millie took in how neat Elden kept his two-hundred-acre farm. The land to their left where he had grown field corn for his stock had already been turned over, and winter wheat, a ground cover, had recently been planted. To the right was a pasture with a tidy, well-maintained fence and great patches of clover that had obviously been planted to give his horses a nice place to graze. The lane had just been leveled and he'd spread gravel to fill any holes that would prevent buggies and wagons from getting bogged down in wet weather. Their own lane had potholes in it and she wondered if she and Henrietta could *rett* it up before the fall rains came.

Halfway up the lane, Eleanor dropped back to speak to Millie and Beth. "I'll tell you the same thing I told the others," she said, looking a bit severe in her black church dress.

They weren't required to wear their black dress and white cape and apron on Visiting Sundays, and were free to wear what they *pleased* as long as it was neat and clean. At least Eleanor hadn't worn her white cape and apron, Millie thought. Eleanor was also wearing her black bonnet, which the rest of the girls had left home, opting for wool scarves tied over their organza *kapps* for warmth. Millie had chosen her dark blue scarf because she knew it looked nice with her dress.

"Each one of us will take a turn keeping an eye on *Dat*," Eleanor continued. "If it seems likes he's getting tired…"

As her sister went on, Millie's gaze strayed to the farmhouse coming into view. She'd been in the house over the years, but not in the last two or three. Unlike most Amish homes in Honeycomb, it wasn't an old-fashioned two-story farmhouse, but what her mother had said was called a Cape Cod. It looked sort of like a one-story house, only there were four big dormer windows and a sharply pitched roof. It had white vinyl siding and a huge front porch with two front doors, one in the center and one to the left in an addition. The center door led into a front hall and the other into a big mudroom and then the kitchen and pantry. When Elden's parents had bought the property, there'd been no house on it because the ramshackle farmhouse had burned down. Elden's father had built the Cape Cod with the help of neighbors he'd hired, including her father.

"Millie!" Eleanor grabbed Millie's arm, startling her. "Are you listening to me?"

She blinked. "*Ya*. I'm listening now."

"I *said* I don't know how long we'll be staying.

You know how *Dat* is with strangers nowadays. He might feel uncomfortable." She lowered her voice. "Even scared. So keep an eye on him and be sure he feels safe."

The sound of a barking dog, Elden's bulldog, caught Millie's attention.

"Samson!" their father called, patting his pant leg. The dog that had been sitting on the front porch steps leaped down and raced as fast as he could toward the new arrivals.

Eleanor rolled her eyes but didn't say anything. She hadn't been thrilled when Millie had let their father go with Elden earlier in the week, but after their father had talked nonstop about Samson for two days, she'd relented and admitted maybe it had been good for him to be in the company of other men sometimes.

"Afternoon!"

Millie heard Elden's voice and turned to look for him. He was coming from the opposite direction of the house, waving. Behind him were three men, one Millie recognized as his uncle Gabriel, but the other two, who were closer to Elden in age, she didn't. His cousins, maybe? He'd mentioned that one or two of Gabriel and Elsie's children and their families might be there. There were also four little boys, the youngest maybe three, the oldest six or seven, dressed just like the men in dark pants, homemade denim coats and either a knit beanie or a black Sunday hat. Gabriel and Elsie's grandchildren, Millie assumed.

As Elden approached them, Millie smiled at him, waiting for him to make eye contact.

But instead of looking and speaking to her first, he called, "Good to see you, Beth. Sorry the weather isn't better." He slid his hands into his pockets and looked up at the sky. "Supposed to be sunny all day. I don't know where these clouds have all come from. Makes it chilly, doesn't it?"

"*Ya*, no sun will make it chilly all right," Beth replied. "Take this into the kitchen?" She raised the jug of apple cider.

"*Ya*. I was hoping we could eat outside. But *Mam* thinks it's going to rain. She wouldn't even let me set up the folding tables outside. We'll be eating in the kitchen." His gaze shifted to Cora and he nodded. "Cora."

"Elden." Cora smiled and headed toward the house.

Next he greeted Willa. "Glad you could make it. I heard JJ enjoyed your cookies last weekend."

Elden smiled at Willa as if there was a private joke between them, which made Millie feel like a third wheel on a two-wheeled cart. Here she was, smiling foolishly at him and he hadn't even looked at her.

"Elden!" their father called, clapping his hands to get the bulldog to leap and bark. "Tell these women that Samson and I are friends."

Still not looking at Millie, Elden walked toward their father and Eleanor.

"*Dat*," Eleanor said. "Please keep your voice down. No need to make a fuss. I just thought you might want to come inside and sit. It was a long walk here."

"Oh, it was not," he retorted. "And I'm not coming inside with the women." He pointed at the fence where Gabriel Yoder and the two younger men were watching them with interest. "Men stand outside and we talk. Men stuff. Don't we, Elden?"

"Felty can certainly join us," Elden told Eleanor. "The women are inside putting together the meal."

Eleanor, looking severe in her black bonnet and three-quarter-length cloak, looked up at Elden, seeming none too pleased. "I thought *Dat* might want to rest."

"I'm not resting!" their father said, raising his voice again. The bulldog was standing at his feet, looking up at Eleanor as if pleading to let his friend stay out and play.

"*Dat*, it's cold, and—"

Their *vadder* gave a wave of dismissal and walked away, headed toward the other men. The dog followed.

Millie watched Elden as he chewed on the corner of his mouth and then, his voice low, said, "We're going to eat in twenty minutes or so, Eleanor. Then we'll all come inside." He met her gaze. "I'll keep an eye on Felty. He's fine."

Eleanor took a deep breath, her face tight with indecision.

"Let him go with the men, *schweschter*," Beth said impatiently as she walked past them. "How far can he go? Elden's with him."

Eleanor hesitated, then at last said, "Fine. But if it gets too cold out here before Lavinia calls you for dinner—"

"We'll all come inside," Elden promised.

Eleanor took another breath and nodded as if still

trying to convince herself it would be all right. "*Danki*, Elden." Then she followed the sisters toward the house.

Realizing she looked foolish standing there, Millie headed in the same direction. "*Goot nummadag*," she said as she walked past Elden, her head down.

"Hey, Millie." He looked away from her. "*Nay*, Samson." He strode back toward the men. "No jumping, Samson. Off! Off! Felty, tell him to behave himself."

Millie tried not to be upset that Elden had talked to Beth…and to Willa and Cora and Eleanor, and not to her. He was, after all, hosting. He didn't have time to talk to everyone. Not with his uncle and cousins standing there watching them.

Millie's feelings were hurt, though. The way he had spoken to her the day he invited them to come over, Millie had thought he was inviting the family because he wanted her to visit. Which, she realized, looking back, was ridiculous. He was just being a nice neighbor. And now that he was ready to start having folks over and making rounds on visiting days, it was only logical that he'd invite them first. A way of easing back into it.

It all made perfect sense. But Millie's eyes still felt scratchy as she hung up her jacket in the mudroom and walked into the kitchen, a smile plastered on her face. "*Goot nummadag*, Lavinia," she said brightly. "Everyone."

The room was bustling with her sisters and the other women going this way and that with three little girls, dressed like the younger woman chattering in *Deitsch* as they folded paper napkins on a bench. Some of the women were setting the large farm table and the three plastic ones, all covered in tablecloths while others were removing lids and foil from various dishes lined along the long butcher-block counter that ran between the eight-burner gas stove with its two separate ovens and the large farmhouse-style sink. Because it was Sunday, the food had been prepared the day before. They really weren't supposed to cook at all on the Sabbath, but heating soup on a burner or popping biscuits into the oven wasn't really considered cooking.

"*Goot nummadag,*" Lavinia said, barely looking at Millie. "Oh, Elsie! The corn bread. In the oven," she called from the far side of the kitchen.

Millie knew Elden's aunt, Elsie, though not well.

"Not to worry," Elsie, dressed as Lavinia and Eleanor both were, in black dresses, said. She grabbed a dish towel and opened one of the ovens.

"Not that one," Lavinia fussed, flapping her hands. "The other one."

Elsie said nothing, but obediently opened the other oven door and slid out a tray of corn muffins.

Millie stood in the doorway, her basket of sandwiches in her hand, not sure what to do. She'd be happy to help, of course, but was afraid to ask Lavinia what she needed because she was obviously already stressed. It was always better to make oneself busy and not pester their hostess, her mother had often said.

One of the two young women Millie didn't know walked past her, carrying a baby on her hip. The woman who looked to be around Millie's age stopped. "Hi, I'm Marybeth Kertz, Gabriel and Elsie's daughter." Petite with dark hair and rosy cheeks, she smiled up at Millie.

"Um, I'm Millie Koffman," Millie said, noticing that not only did Marybeth have a *boppli* in her arms, but she was expecting another. "I live...*we* live across the road."

"Ah, Elden's friend. I'm so glad you could—" She looked over her shoulder in the direction of the little girls. "Sarey, please don't tear up the napkins. Fold them nice. Your cousin Bernice will show you. *Danki,* Bernice." Marybeth looked back at Millie. "Do you want me to take those?" Holding the baby in one arm, she pointed at the basket hanging on Millie's elbow.

Millie looked down at the basket. "*Nay,* I can put them out. I just wasn't sure..."

Marybeth leaned closer so that only Millie could hear her. "So Aunt Lavinia doesn't fuss at you." She smiled conspiratorially. "I know. She can be scary. Best way to handle it is to put whatever you've brought out without asking her." She looked up with big brown eyes. "That's how my sisters and sisters-in-law do it."

Millie nodded, looking down at the baby in her arms. She was a sweet thing in a long white dress, a yellow pacifier in her mouth. She watched Millie with big brown eyes that looked like her mother's.

"And who is this *boppli*?" Millie asked, smiling at the baby.

"This?" Marybeth bounced the baby that was maybe six months old on her hip. "This is our Lizzy.

Aren't you?" she crooned to the baby. "And Sarey is ours, mine and Jakob's. And we have a little boy, Thomas. He's outside with his *dat*. Likely chasing Aunt Lavinia's chickens." She shook her head. "The boy loves to chase chickens. I don't know why." She looked at Millie's basket. "What did you bring?"

"Um…" Millie looked down, then at Marybeth and shook herself mentally. She was being silly about Elden not talking to her. Her expectations had been misguided by her own imagination. He hadn't said anything to her to suggest he was interested in her as a potential girlfriend. Men like Elden Yoder didn't date and certainly didn't marry big girls like her.

Millie decided then and there not to give Elden another thought. For months she'd been wanting to go visiting the way they had when their mother was alive and she was here and she was going to enjoy herself. "Ham sandwiches," she told Marybeth. "Little ones. On slider rolls. Have you seen them in the grocery store?"

Marybeth's eyes widened with excitement. "I love those little rolls. We use them for hamburgers when Jakob makes them on our grill. I thought the small burgers would be better for the little ones." She wrinkled her freckled nose. "But I like them, too. Just the right amount of bread to burger."

Marybeth's smile was infectious, and Millie's mood lightened. Elden had done nothing wrong. She had no right to be upset with him. He had been neighborly, and she had somehow misinterpreted his meaning. Yes, he had said he wanted to spend time with her, but he obviously hadn't meant it in the way she had hoped. And that was that.

Millie needed to enjoy the afternoon and not worry about Elden. *Don't fret over the things you can't control. Let them go,* her mother had always said. *Trust in Gott and His ways.*

And Millie decided to do just that.

Millie thoroughly enjoyed the communal meal, and was reminded again of how much she had missed Visiting Sundays. The Sundays where there was no worship was a time to relax and enjoy the friendship and fellowship of her Amish community. It was a reminder to be thankful for all *Gott* provided each day. As was often done in Amish households when there were multiple guests, the women sat separately from the men to eat. Lavinia presided over the two folding tables that had been set up for the women and children, while Elden, his uncle, the two younger men as well Millie's father sat together at the oak farm table.

Millie didn't mind not sitting with the men because if she had, she'd have spent the entire meal trying not to look at Elden. However, as she ate, talking to her sisters and her new friend Marybeth and Marybeth's sister-in-law, she decided that if she ever married and had a home of her own, she would insist men and women sit together at a meal. Segregation made sense to her when men wanted to stand at a fence and talk crops and hoof infections and women wanted to talk babies and quilting. But that type of segregation came naturally. In this case, Lavinia had been adamant about the seating, not wanting her son to sit with so many attractive young women of marrying age, Millie suspected. So the women talked among themselves, as did the men.

Once the delicious meal of soups, sandwiches, salads and such was done, the men took their leave, going back outside while the women cleaned up the kitchen. Eleanor had briefly tried to get their father to stay in, but he refused and had quite merrily joined the other men. As Elden left the kitchen, he told Eleanor not to worry about her father because he'd be with him.

Once the kitchen was *rett* up, Lavinia suggested the women all move into the parlor to chat while Elsie's daughter and daughter-in-law nursed their babies. As Millie sat, listening to the various conversations, she tried not to be disappointed in the day. Even though it hadn't turned out as she had hoped, it had still been wonderful. It had felt good to be out of the house and she had made a new friend. She and Marybeth had hit it off so well that Marybeth had asked her to stop by one day in the coming week. Only a year older than her, Marybeth had insisted it was lonely at home all day with her little ones while her husband, a framer who worked for a construction company, was gone all day. She said he worked five days a week, and sometimes even Saturday when the Mennonite contractor he worked for was busy.

After Marybeth had fed her little Lizzy, she asked Millie if she'd like to hold her while she took her three-year-old to the bathroom. Cuddling the baby on her shoulder as she drifted off to sleep, Millie was surprised by the emotions that welled up inside her. She had never thought much about having babies of her own. Maybe because she had told herself no one would ever marry her. But holding Marybeth's *boppli*, she felt almost a physical desire to have one of her own. Where had that come from, she wondered.

"Mildred?"

Millie looked up to see her father standing in the doorway to the parlor.

"Sorry to disturb," he told the other women, holding up his hand.

"What do you need, *Dat*?" Eleanor rose from a chair near the woodstove that was providing just enough heat in the room to make it cozy but not hot. "Are you tired? Are you ready to go home?"

He looked at Eleanor. "Not going home yet." He returned his gaze to Millie. "Walking down to the pond to see a dock. Elden built it. Want to come?"

Marybeth squeezed past him in the doorway, her daughter following behind. "I'll take her," she said to Millie, putting out her arms. "*Danki*. Oh my, she's sound asleep, isn't she?"

Millie carefully passed the baby back to its mother, wishing she could have held her a few minutes longer and breathe in her sweet, milky scent as Lizzy slept. But if she didn't deal with their father, Eleanor was likely to march them all home, and Millie wasn't ready to go yet.

"Come on, Mildred," her *fadder* said, hooking his thumb in the general direction of the pond. "Taking

Samson for a walk. Going to see the dock. I like a dock to fish on."

"*Dat*, maybe you should sit down and rest a while," Eleanor said.

Their father cut his eyes at his eldest daughter, giving her the look they had all known from their childhoods. *Dat* had always been easy to get along with. He'd been kind and set a good example in everything he said and did, but when he'd had enough of bad behavior or whatever earned his disapproval, he made his point with one look. The one he was directing toward Eleanor.

Eleanor sat back down.

"*Ya* or *nay*?" Felty asked Millie.

"Um…" Millie started across the parlor, glancing at Eleanor then back at their father. "Sure, *Dat*. I'll go see the pond."

"The *dock*," he corrected, then turned around and walked back through the house the way he'd come.

Millie heard the back door close before she entered the mudroom to collect her coat and wool scarf. As she turned the corner, she nearly walked right into Elden. She gave a cry of surprise, then pressed her hand to her heart that was suddenly pounding. "Sorry." Embarrassed, she kept her head down. "I didn't realize you were here. My father—" She pointed to the door that led onto the porch. "He…he wanted me to walk down to the pond with him."

"With us," Elden said. "Which one is yours?" He turned to the women's coats hanging on hooks.

"That one," she said, pointing, thinking it had to be obvious. Hers was twice as big as anyone else's.

Elden plucked it from the hook. "This your scarf?"

She nodded, not sure what was going on. Why was Elden here? Had he been waiting for her? It seemed like it.

Elden handed both to her and watched her slip on the coat, close it with the hook and eyes, and then tie her scarf carefully over her *kapp*. As Millie knotted the scarf under her chin she realized she should have been smart like Eleanor and worn her Sunday bonnet, which was made to fit over a starched prayer *kapp*.

"Temperature has dropped outside," Elden said, watching her. "You bring a neck scarf?"

She shook her head. "I was warm enough when we walked over."

"*Ya*, but days are getting shorter, aren't they?" He moved along the row of hooks on the wall, looking for something. He stopped and grabbed a dark blue knitted scarf. "Here, wear this. It will be chilly out near the pond."

He walked back to her and offered it.

"It's *oll recht*, I don't need—"

He lifted his brows and the look on his face made her fear he might try to tie it around her neck if she didn't take it. "*Danki*," she said softly, lowering her gaze as she accepted it. Then she quickly wrapped it around her neck. It was well made and the wool wasn't in the least bit itchy. "Nice scarf," she mumbled.

"*Mam* made it for me. She's good with knitting

needles." He opened the back door and looked down at her. "Ready?"

Still not quite sure what was going on, Millie followed him out onto the porch. None of the other men or boys seemed to be around, but her father was already halfway across the barnyard. He was headed north toward the pond, the bulldog trotting happily beside him.

Elden walked down the steps and she followed him. "Gabriel and his son and son-in-law are out in the shed checking out my new brush hog," he said.

She frowned. "I thought those kinds of big mowers were pulled behind a tractor. I don't know about your bishop, but my uncle would never approve of a tractor."

He smiled slyly at her. "Bishop Paul is a good man, but no, I can't own a tractor." He held up a finger. "I can drive one for an *Englisher* if it's required for work I get paid for, but I can't own one. Last spring when *Mam* and I went to Lancaster County to visit an elderly aunt, I saw a horse-drawn brush hog and decided I could use one here, what with all the land I still want to clear. Bought an old brush hog at auction and put a 15 horsepower engine on it. I hitch my cart to Clyde, my Clydesdale. I know, not an original name," he said with a smirk, "and I pull the brush hog behind the cart. I've still got a couple of adjustments to make, but I think it's going to work just fine."

She smiled at him. "That's clever. You figuring all that out."

He shrugged. "I like a challenge."

He looked at her when he said it, but then he kept eyeing her until she felt awkward and scanned ahead for her father. Her *dat* had stopped under an apple tree that was missing most of its leaves and he was making a little pile of sticks while the dog sat watching his every move. "What is he doing?" she wondered aloud.

Elden watched for a moment. "Ah, a jump."

"A jump?"

"My fault. I showed Felty how I was teaching Samson to jump over sticks and such." He shrugged. "Just for fun. And maybe to vex my mother." He pointed in her father's direction. "And now Felty's trying to get Samson to jump over all sorts of things. Don't worry. Samson won't jump anything higher than a woolly bear."

Millie laughed, trying to imagine the dog jumping over the thick, fuzzy black-and-orange caterpillars. "I can ask him to stop," she said.

"It's fine. Felty's enjoying himself." He looked at her again. "How about you? Having a good time?"

"Um, *ya*. I am. It's nice to get out. And to spend time with neighbors. Friends." It was on the tip of her tongue to ask what was going on. Why her father had come for her. Why Elden had been waiting, but she couldn't think how to phrase it, so she didn't say anything.

"Me, too," he said, sliding his hands into his pockets as they walked. "I'm having a good time. A surprisingly good day." He was quiet for a moment and then went on. "Sorry about sending your father in for you. I didn't know how it would look, me walking into my *mam*'s parlor and asking you if you wanted to go for a walk. I figured this way was safer. And your *dat* really did want to see the dock I built."

Millie felt her heart skip a beat. *He had sent her father in for her? So she could go for a walk with him?* This couldn't be real. It couldn't be happening. She felt a little out of breath, not because of the pace at which they were walking, but because the obvious conclusion was that…that Elden *did* like her. Why else would he want her to go for a walk with him?

Then she felt a sense of panic. *Unless maybe he was interested in Beth and he wanted to ask Millie about her.* Beth was the one he had spoken to first when they arrived.

"I wanted you to come walk with me—" Elden hesitated. "Because I wanted to ask you—"

Millie heard her father cry out and looked up to see him lying on the ground. *"Dat!"* She took off at a run.

Chapter Eight

"*Dat!*" Millie cried again, running toward him.

The way she took off surprised Elden. Typically, Amish women her age didn't run. For many, it was considered inappropriate. His mother certainly would have said so if she'd seen her. But Millie was not a typical young Amish woman, was she?

Elden had forgotten how fast she could run. In their school days he remembered that despite her size, she had always been picked for softball teams first, certainly before him. Everyone wanted her on their team because she could run fast and hit the ball over the fence into the Swartzentrubers' field where their schoolhouse was located. Millie had been so athletic that he'd been intimidated by her.

"*Dat*! Don't get up," Millie hollered, waving her arms at him.

Elden bolted toward Felty. Samson was barking as if to alert them that the older man had fallen. By the time Elden reached Millie and her father, the bulldog was standing over Felty, licking the older man's cheek. Her father's glasses were lying in a pile of dead leaves beside him.

"Samson, back up," Elden ordered.

Millie fell to her knees in the wet grass and picked up his glasses, which appeared unbroken. There had been a rain shower outside while they were having dinner and everything was wet. *"Dat?"* She reached out as if wanting to touch him, but not knowing where for fear he'd been seriously injured. He was lying face-down. *"Dat*, can you move?"

Elden went to his knees on the other side of Felty. "Catch your breath," he said calmly.

"Dat, can you hear me? I asked if you can—"

"Ya, dochter, I can *move*," Felty sputtered. He tried to push the bulldog off as he rolled onto his back.

"Samson, off!" Elden ordered sharply.

"Where are my glasses? Lost my glasses." Felty tried to sit up, bracing himself with his hands.

"Here they are." She slid them onto his face. *"Dat*, I think you should lie still," Millie fussed. "You might have broken your leg or arm. Maybe I should call an ambulance. I imagine someone here has a cell phone." While cell phones, like many other modern conveniences, were frowned upon in their Old Order community, the truth of the times they lived in was that families needed a cell phone, if not for work then to be able to place a call in an emergency.

Felty blew a raspberry at his daughter and sat up without assistance.

"Dat!" Millie cried, her tone reprimanding.

It was all Elden could do not to laugh. The older man couldn't have been hurt too badly to have that sort of sense of humor.

Millie brushed some dead grass off his face. "Can you move your legs?"

Felty kicked one leg out and then the other, demonstrating he could move just fine. "Stop your fussing, *dochter*. I tripped. I didn't fall off the top of a windmill!"

"How about your arms?" Millie ran her hand over her father's denim coat sleeves, one and then the other, brushing off bits of wet leaves and brown grass.

Felty flexed one arm and then the other. "Fine. See?" He reached out and stroked Samson's muzzle as the dog poked his nose at him. "Just a tumble, right, boy?"

"*Dat*, what were you doing? Did you fall walking?" She looked at Elden, the worry plain on her pretty face. "He's never been unstable on his feet before." She returned her attention to her father. "Did you get dizzy?"

Felty frowned and looked to Elden, extending his arm in silent request. Elden rose and took the older man's hand, helping him to his feet.

"Can you imagine what my life is like, Elden? It's this times seven." Felty pointed to Millie. "Yack, yack, yack." He was wearing fingerless cotton gloves, and he opened and closed his hand so that it looked like a bird's mouth.

"What happened, *Dat*?" Millie, still on her knees on the ground, asked again.

Elden picked up Felty's black, wide-brimmed Sunday hat, banged it on his knee to get the grass and leaves off and handed it to him.

"I didn't fall over like a *boppli*." Felty's tone was indignant. He pulled his hat down over his head. "I was showing Samson how to do it."

"Do what?" Millie asked.

Millie made to get to her feet, and before Elden thought better of it, he grabbed her hand to help her. As her hand touched his, he was surprised by a warm feeling that surged through him. Her touch, warm and soft, somehow made him feel…like everything was going to be all right for him. It felt so good that he hated to let go when she pulled her hand away.

Felty exhaled, getting more perturbed by the moment. "I was showing Samson how to jump over the little fence I made." He pointed at a small bundle of sticks in the grass that Elden hadn't noticed before. "I made a fence jump and he wouldn't go over it so I was showing him how."

Millie crossed her arms. "You thought you and that stumpy-legged dog were going to jump fences? What? Stick fences today, stockade fences tomorrow?"

"Maybe," Felty answered indignantly.

Elden had to press his lips together not to laugh.

But Millie didn't. She threw back her head and laughed hard, a big belly laugh that made her eyes water.

And Elden's heart melted. He wanted to ask her to the harvest frolic. He had nearly gotten up his nerve, but then Felty fell. He took a deep breath. What if she said no? Could he take the rejection now, when he was only just climbing out of the depths of disappointment and self-doubt?

"*Oll recht, Dat.*" Millie finally stopped laughing. "I think it's time we went home." She looped her arm through his and they started toward the yard.

The bulldog and Eden followed.

"What if I'm not ready to go home?" Felty asked, walking beside his daughter.

She tilted her head and gave a great, overblown sigh. "Then I'll have to tell Eleanor that you want to stay, even though you fell for no obvious reason."

Elden caught up to them and walked on Felty's other side. He wanted to ask Millie here and now about the frolic, but with her father there, that didn't seem wise. If she said no, he'd rather not have anyone else witness his embarrassment.

"I told you!" Felty blustered. "I was showing Samson how to take the jump."

Millie shook her head. "I don't know if Eleanor is going to accept that. She may not believe you. She may think you made it up to keep from getting into trouble with her."

"What would make her think that?"

"I don't know, *Dat.* Maybe because the other day when you were trying to make bird feeders with pine cones and peanut butter and seeds and you got peanut butter all over the counter and on the floor, you told her you were making a peanut butter sandwich. Even though there was bird feed on the counter and the floor."

"I like feeding the birds," he grumbled. "Birds have to eat, too, and I like watching them from my chair in the living room."

"I know you do." She stopped. "But I don't know how Eleanor's going to respond." She looked at him cheerfully. "So do you want me to go tell Eleanor we're ready to leave or should I tell her how you—"

"I think it's time we go home," Felty interrupted. He offered his hand to Elden and shook it warmly. "Thank you for having us. Hope we can return the favor, neighbor."

"I'll go round up the girls. It's time we got home to check on Jane, anyway." Millie's gaze met Elden's for a split second, and she smiled warmly. Then she walked away.

Elden watched her go and decided he was going to invite her to the frolic. If she said no, then she said no.

But he wouldn't ask her today. Maybe tomorrow. The following day at the latest.

But he would definitely ask her.

Wednesday morning after the breakfast dishes were cleared, Eleanor walked into the kitchen where Millie and her sisters were still tidying up, and clapped her hands together. "Applesauce day," she declared. "We've put it off long enough. It's a perfect day for it." She glanced out one of the big windows.

It was overcast and threatening to rain. When Millie had gone out to milk before breakfast, she'd been chilled by the time she brought the milk back into the house.

"*Ya*, I agree. A perfect day to make applesauce," Millie piped up when no one said anything. Since Sunday she'd been in a contemplative mood. She needed something to distract her from thoughts of Elden that swirled in her head.

She was so confused. Did he like her or not? She'd been upset when he barely spoke to her when they arrived at his house the other day. But then later, he'd sent her *dat* inside to ask her to go for a walk with them. With *him*. So maybe he did like her. Or maybe he only wanted to speak to her alone so he could ask about his prospects with Beth and had never gotten the chance before their father had taken his tumble.

Or perhaps he really *was* interested in Millie. Would that really be such a crazy idea? She was smart and resourceful, a good cook, decent at sewing and she was a woman of deep faith. So what if she was fat? She wasn't so fat that she couldn't do her chores or that she couldn't run when her *dat* had hurt himself. And *Gott* had made her this way, hadn't He? Which meant, she lectured herself, that she was good enough for any man, even Elden.

That was what she kept telling herself. On Monday she had hoped Elden might stop by to say hello. When he didn't, she thought he might come Tuesday. Today she'd woken up wondering if she had imagined the connection she'd felt to him on Sunday when they had taken a walk. With an inward sigh, she pushed those negative thoughts aside. There was no sense dwelling on them. *Gott* was good and He had a plan for her. Even if it wasn't the plan she was hoping for. And she had to make herself content with that.

"Love to help make applesauce," Henry said, stuffing the last piece of toast in her mouth as she headed out of the kitchen. "But I told Anna Mary I'd have a look at her stove. She says it's not working and with her being widowed and her boys living so far away, she doesn't know who to ask. She's been cooking on her old woodstove." Her last words were mumbled as she made a quick retreat.

"I'd help, but I promised Liz I would help her with her wedding chest," Willa announced, following Henry out of the kitchen. "Henry is going to drop me off. The wedding is only a month away," she threw over her shoulder. "I'll be home by supper."

"Wait!" Jane called, closing the refrigerator door. "Can I go with Willa? While she helps Liz, I can visit with Susie. Please, Ellie?" she begged, already starting to take off her dirty apron.

Eleanor, who had been busy wiping down the counter, turned around. "Who's going to help me make this applesauce?"

"Sigh so gude, schweschter? Plee-ase?" Jane, who they sometimes forgot was still a teenager, begged.

"Let her go. I'm here to help," Millie said. "I don't have anywhere to be. And Cora and Beth can help, too. That's four of us. Plenty of cooks in the kitchen." She placed her hands on her hips and glanced at the huge copper-bottomed pots that Henry had brought into the kitchen from the cellar. "It will be fun, just the four of us."

Eleanor hesitated and then with a sigh, said, "Fine, Jane. Go. See your friend."

"Danki!" Jane threw her arms around her eldest sister, gave her a hug, and raced out of the room.

"Do you two want to start carrying in the apples?" Cora, who had been reading a book at the kitchen table, asked. "We've got a lot of peeling and cutting to do before they're ready for the kettles."

"Sure," Eleanor agreed, seeming already frazzled although the day had barely begun.

"I'll help carry them in," Millie offered.

Bushels of Black Twig, Granny Smith, Winesap and Jonathan apples they had picked at the Masts' orchard the week before waited on the porch. Making applesauce with her family was something that Millie looked forward to all year. She loved picking apples. And she loved the heady smells of cooking apples and cinnamon and seeing the results—rows and rows of quart jars of applesauce lining the pantry and cellar shelves. There was something so satisfying about knowing that a few days' work provided good food that would last them until the next fall and the next crop of ripe fruit.

So the four remaining Koffman sisters began their task. The baskets were heavy, but Millie had done manual labor since she was young, and she didn't mind the lifting. Peeling was easy. Her fingers remembered what to do while she sat and chatted with her sisters. As the minutes, then hours, ticked away in the cozy kitchen, they laughed and jumped from one subject to the next. It was all great fun until Cora reminded Millie what she was struggling with.

"Sooo…" Cora drew out the word. "I saw you and Elden through the window on Sunday, Millie." She carried another big bowl of clean apples to the kitchen table. "How was it?"

Millie concentrated on the Black Twig apple she was peeling, keeping her gaze down. "Fine."

Cora glanced at Beth and the sisters exchanged looks. "What we were wondering is, does he like you?" she asked with a giggle.

Suddenly Millie felt anxious. Cora wasn't one for giggling. She was probably the most serious of all of them. Had she and Beth been talking about her and Elden? "I… I don't know if he likes me."

"Elden is a good-looking man," Beth declared, turning from the stove where she was stirring a pot of apples, water and sugar. "And single."

"*Very* single," Eleanor agreed, not looking up from her peeling. "He'd make a fine husband," she added.

"I have an idea. I think we should go to the harvest frolic," Beth said. "And then Elden can ask Millie to ride home with him." She looked to Eleanor. "Do you think we could go? Everyone is talking about it. There's going to be singing and games and a bonfire and they're going to roast marshmallows."

"Are they making s'mores?" Cora looked to Eleanor. "I'll go if there are going to be s'mores."

"I don't want to go to the harvest frolic," Millie said, continuing to peel an apple. "And Elden is not going to ask me to ride home with him."

"I think he is. Because he likes you." Beth sang her last words as she took a long-handled wooden spoon and scooped up a spoonful of cooked apples to taste.

"Well, I think he likes you, Beth," Millie blurted, startling them all, including herself. "He came right over to talk to you Sunday when we arrived." Flustered, she stood up and, in the process, dropped apples from her apron onto the floor.

Beth made a face. "He does not like me. You're the one he asked to go for a walk with him. I think he sent *Dat* in to ask you so his mother wouldn't know."

"Makes sense. Since she ruined his last betrothal," Cora pointed out.

"We don't know that to be true," Eleanor chimed in as she cut a peeled apple into chunks and dropped them into a bowl in her lap.

Millie pressed her lips together as she stooped to pick up the fruit she'd dropped. "Can we talk about something else?" One apple had rolled under the table and she had to get down on her hands and knees to retrieve it.

"No one would blame you if you set your *kapp* for him," Eleanor said. "Elden Yoder is a good catch. I think you two are well suited to each other."

"Is that what all of you are talking about behind my back?" Having captured the apple, Millie rose to her feet and set it on the table. "That I've set my *kapp* for Elden? Because that isn't true."

Beth and Cora exchanged meaningful looks.

"You never know," their oldest sister remarked, not

looking up. "Sometimes even a smart woman is the last to see what's plain as day to everyone around her."

"Plain as day," Millie muttered to herself a short time later as she came up the cellar steps, carrying two cases of quart-sized canning jars.

She knew Eleanor hadn't meant the comment unkindly, but it was upsetting. Maybe because Millie desperately wanted to think that Elden *was* interested in her. She wanted to believe that there was a chance that he could fall in love with her, because if she was honest with herself, she was already half in love with him. She knew it was ridiculous, but she'd felt that way since they were kids. Not all the boys had been kind to her at school. There had been the jokes about what she packed for lunch, comments about the shape of her body and the laughter directed at her, but Elden had always been kind.

At the top of the cellar steps, Millie set down the boxes and turned to lower the metal Bilco doors. It was cold and gray, and drops of icy rain were beginning to hit her as she eased the door down.

She remembered being in the third grade, sitting outside for lunch on a sunny day in May. Elden had been in the fourth grade. There had been picnic tables that one of the neighbors had built so the students could eat outside under the trees. She'd been sitting with Annie, whom she'd been friends with for as long as she could remember, along with some other girls. There had been a bunch of boys, including Elden, at the next table over. Millie had left her lunch on the table to fetch a cup of water for her and Annie from the well. When she came back, she'd unwrapped the peanut butter and honey sandwich her mother had made for her. She'd nearly taken a bite before she realized there was something sticking out of it that didn't belong. When she opened the sandwich, she found that someone had stuffed a bunch of grass and leaves inside it. Then one of the older boys, an eighth grader named Alvin, began to oink.

Millie had been so mad that she got up from the bench.

"I'm sorry," Annie had whimpered. "I didn't know how to stop him."

But Millie hadn't been angry at Annie; she was furious at Alvin. She'd marched over to the rude boy. "You think that's funny, ruining someone's lunch?" she'd asked him, hands on her hips.

Alvin had sniggered. Other boys at the table had joined him.

"That's just mean," Millie had told him.

Alvin had stood up and he was a lot bigger than she was, a lot taller. He'd leaned down and oinked right in her face.

That was when Millie had drawn back her fist with the intention of hitting him right in the nose. She didn't care if she was going to be in trouble with their teacher, or her parents, or the bishop, or even *Gott*. But just as she was about to throw the punch, Elden had appeared at her side and placed his hand on hers, lowering it gently.

"Not worth it," he'd whispered in her ear. "Here." He'd pushed a sandwich, still in a plastic baggie into her hand. "It's ham and cheese with mustard," he'd told her. "The spicy kind. A *goot* sandwich."

And then he had walked away, and Millie had gone back to sit with the girls. And she had never forgotten how good Elden's sandwich had tasted.

Millie dropped the second cellar door with a bang and picked up the cases of jars. She had almost reached the back porch when she heard a dog bark. A bark she was familiar with, now. She groaned. It was Samson, and if Samson was there, that meant Elden was there, too.

He'd probably stopped by to ask Beth if he could take her home from the harvest frolic.

"Millie," Elden called out.

She ignored him. She didn't know why. She'd almost reached the back door when she heard his footsteps on the porch steps.

"Millie!"

She spun around. "*Ya*, Elden." She held the jars against her. "What is it? I'm busy."

"H-hi." He slid his hands into his pockets but kept his gaze on her. "I... I see you're doing some canning."

"*Ya*." She looked down at the jars. "Applesauce."

"Mmm. I love applesauce."

She watched his dog trot up the steps so she didn't have to look at him.

"Uh...anyway. I... I was wondering if you—" He looked at his boots, then up at her. "If...if your family is going to the harvest frolic this weekend."

"I don't know," she said, wondering if she just

ought to ask him straight out if he wanted her to send Beth out to talk to him.

"It… It sounds like it's going to be nice. I… I'm going and I was wondering if you…if I could take you home after," he said all in a rush.

Millie's heart skipped a beat. *He wanted to take her home.* Which made it practically a date because that was how it worked in Honeycomb. Single men and women of marrying age met and got to know each other at singings and frolics and social gatherings, and if a boy was interested in a girl, it was tradition that he asked to take her home.

But did he really want to take her home or was this some sort of ploy to…what? She didn't know. Make Beth jealous? Or maybe he liked Willa and just was afraid to say so because she was so pretty.

"I don't think so, Elden." She turned away. "My sisters are waiting for the jars."

"Millie—I—" He took a breath. "Why not?"

She turned to look at him. "If you want to go out with Beth, you should just ask her. Or I can, if you want me to."

He frowned. Samson had moved between them and was now looking up at his master almost quizzically. "What are you talking about?" Elden made a face. "I… I don't want to take Beth home. I mean, she's nice and all but—"

"If you're not interested in her, then why did you talk to her instead of me when we arrived on Sunday?" she demanded.

"What?" He was still acting as if he had no idea what she was talking about.

Millie shifted the cases of jars in her arms. It was beginning to rain in earnest now. She could hear the pitter-patter on the tin roof of their porch. "Sunday. You walked right over and said hello to Beth and… and talked to her. And then you talked to Cora and you barely looked at me. You barely said hello to me and then off you went."

He shook his head slowly. "Millie, Beth was in front of me. It would have been rude not to speak to her. I didn't get a chance to talk to you because I knew your *dat* wanted to stay outside with the men and if I didn't get him—" He lowered his voice, she guessed in case any of her sisters could hear them from inside.

He took a step closer to her. "If I didn't walk your *dat* over to where the other men were, he'd have been stuck in my mother's kitchen with all the women. And I know that isn't what he wanted."

"Really?" she asked. "That's why you didn't talk to me?" She wanted to believe him.

"*Ya.* Why would I make something up like that? When you arrived, I wanted to ask you about the harvest frolic, but there was no chance to talk to you alone when we ate, not with my mother listening to every word I said. And then when you came outside, when we were walking, that's when I was going to ask you, but then Felty fell and…" He gestured with one hand and went silent.

The bulldog looked up at Millie.

Millie exhaled. "I have to go inside."

"Does that mean yes?" One side of his mouth rose in a half smile. "You'll ride home with me?"

"It means no such thing. I'll have to see if we're even going." She shrugged. "Who knows." She met his gaze. "Maybe someone else will ask me to ride home with them."

The look on his face told her he couldn't tell if she was joking or not. In truth, she didn't know, either.

"I suppose you better ask me again at the frolic." She turned to the door.

He reached around her and opened it. "Really? You're not going to just say yes now?"

"Nope," she said. "Have a good afternoon, Elden."

Then Millie walked into the house and closed the door behind her with her foot. She entered the kitchen carrying the jars and said with a big grin, "I'm going to the harvest frolic. Anyone else want to go?"

Chapter Nine

Elden set down his fork. He'd eaten only a few bites of scalloped potatoes floating in curdled cream and a half a corn muffin. He'd nibbled at the fried pork chop that was dry, even with all the canned gravy his mother had poured over it. After working himself into a headache, he didn't have much of an appetite. And he had more on his mind than eating.

He'd been surprised by Millie's response when he'd gone to her place to ask if she'd like to ride home with him from the harvest frolic. More than surprised. Maybe a little hurt. He thought she'd say yes. If he hadn't thought so, he wouldn't have had the courage to walk over and boldly ask her. He'd thought she liked him.

Maybe he wasn't meant to court. Maybe he wasn't meant to marry, he told himself.

But if *Gott* didn't mean for him to take a wife, why would He have put the desire in Elden? Elden had al-

ways wanted a wife and children. He thought he could
be a good husband and father. Was he wrong?

"*Sohn*, you barely ate a thing."

Elden pushed his plate away, giving up even the
pretense of eating. Usually he could eat whatever his
mother made. He was used to things being too salty
or a little burned, but tonight he didn't have it in him.

His mother's forehead wrinkled with concern.
"Are you feeling sick?"

Elden shifted back in his chair, wiping his mouth
with a paper towel. "*Nay*, I'm not sick. Just have a little bit of a headache."

"You got soaked this afternoon. You could be coming down with something."

"That's not how it works, *Mam*. The rain can't make
you sick."

"You sure it's just a headache? What if you've caught
the flu?" She rose, leaned over and pressed her palm to
his forehead. "You feel a little warm to me. You running a fever?"

"*Nay*, no fever." He leaned back, out of her reach.
He wasn't a child anymore and he didn't like it when
she acted as if he was.

She returned to her chair. "Earlier, you went across
the road to the Koffmans'. I saw you."

He looked at her. "You're spying on me?"

"It's not spying if I look out my own window and
see my own son walking down my own lane." She gestured with her fork. "Then back again. Why did you
go to the Koffmans'?"

He had half a mind not to tell her and, worse, to

lie. But he wasn't that person and he never wanted to become that person. "I'm thinking about going to the harvest frolic on Saturday."

"You are?" She smiled. "I think that's an excellent idea. It will be a good way to get your feet wet again. Start setting your intentions on a nice girl. I hear half the unmarried girls in the county will be there." Finished with her pork chop, she picked up her last bit of biscuit and started to sop up the gravy on her plate. Then suddenly her brow furrowed. "Wait. Why did you go to the Koffmans'? You wanted to tell them you were going to the frolic?"

He exhaled heavily. He didn't want to have this discussion with her. But here he was. "To ask Millie if I could take her home afterward." He met her gaze, almost daring her to make a comment. But after what had happened with Mary, he doubted she would. Since the breakup, she'd walked a fine line with her remarks concerning his situation as a single man.

His mother pursed her lips and dropped the leftover biscuit onto her plate as if she'd suddenly lost her appetite as well. She got up and began clearing away the dishes, but her silence and the pained expression on her face was an obvious sign of her disapproval.

Elden rose. "Can I help you clean up?"

She shook her head. "This is my job, *sohn*. It's the least I can do, being a widow and dependent on your charity."

Elden bit back the retort that this farm was hers as long as she lived, and that he loved her and would never consider her a burden. He'd said that many times before. Instead, he returned the buttermilk to the refrigerator.

There'd never been any doubt in Elden's mind that his mother loved him and wanted what was best for him. But this time around he was going to do this his way. If Millie *did* like him—which he wasn't even sure about now. But if she would be willing to walk out with him and get to know him, he was going to keep his mother out of it. Because he really liked Millie. Even when she was standing there on her porch, telling him she didn't want to ride with him, he still wanted to talk to her, to be with her.

It had crossed his mind when he walked home from the Koffmans' that maybe this was the same situation he'd had with Mary. He realized now that he had liked Mary far more than she had ever liked him. When he added his mother into the equation, he wondered if things with Millie would end the same way they had with Mary.

But Millie hadn't said she absolutely wouldn't ride home with him. So he still had a chance.

And as scary as it was, he liked Millie enough to think she was worth pursuing. Chewing that over, he headed for the mudroom.

"Where are you going?" His *mam* followed him, a dishrag in her hand.

"Out to my shop. I'm going to start making those frames for the wreaths. Another week and it will be November. I've got orders from both greenhouses in Hickory Grove and I imagine it won't be long before they're selling Christmas decorations. You know those

Englishers." He put on his hat. It was already dark outside, but he'd run a generator for light, and if it got chilly, he had a kerosene heater in his shop. A lot of evenings he sat in the living room with his mother and read or paid bills or something while she knitted. While she talked. But he wasn't in the mood for her chatter tonight. "By Thanksgiving weekend, they'll be wanting to buy wreaths to hang on their doors. It's too good an income making frames for the wreaths and such not to do it."

Like many Amish men, he did a variety of things to bring money into the household. He raised some crops, he sold firewood he cut himself, he sold extra vegetables they grew, and this year he was going to sell Christmas trees.

"*Ya*, Christmas will be here before we know it," his *mam* agreed.

Elden thought on that on the walk to his workshop in the dark, Samson trotting beside him. For most Amish, gift giving wasn't a big part of Christmas. The day was celebrated with devotions and a quiet meal with family and sometimes friends. But it had always been a tradition in their home to give each other something. When he was a boy, he'd wished for things: a new sled, a puppy, a baseball and bat.

He wondered if he could wish for Millie's hand in marriage.

As it turned out, the entire Koffman family went to the harvest frolic at the Beachys'. Even Henry, who avoided social events, especially ones intended for unmarried men and women to mingle with the ultimate intention of finding a spouse. Parents weren't specifically invited, but when their father heard there was going to be a bonfire, he'd been so excited that no one had had the heart to tell him he wasn't supposed to go. Rather than disappointing their father, Eleanor had talked to Alma Beachy, who had insisted that Felty and Eleanor were welcome at the frolic as they could use as many chaperones as they could get. They were expecting a big crowd.

Millie and her family took two buggies that evening, which had been Eleanor's idea. That way, she and their *dat* and Jane could go home when he got tired, leaving the second family buggy for the other sisters to take home. Should any of the older girls be asked to ride home with a boy, that would be just fine, too. Millie hadn't been sure if that comment had been directed toward her or Willa, but didn't ask for fear that simply by saying it aloud it wouldn't happen for Millie. She was already worried that she had ruined her chance with Elden by telling him no when he asked. She didn't know what had come over her, speaking to him that way. Maybe she'd just been scared.

She was certainly scared now as she crunched on a peppermint Annie had handed her as they stood in the ever-growing shadows, watching the Beachy boys—and there were nine in all—stack the wood for the bonfire that would soon be lit.

There must have been fifty or sixty people on the Beachys' property, most of them young and single. That included the matchmaker's gaggle of white-blond girls with black prayer *kapps* all coming from an Amish community in Wisconsin and staying with Sara Yoder in Seven Poplars, in the hopes of finding a husband. The matchmaker had brought several young men from out of town with her as well.

All around Millie and Annie there were girls walking around in groups of two and three, giggling and blushing. The boys tended to group together this early in the evening as well. Six or seven of them were throwing a football behind the chicken house and several had joined in to prep the bonfire. Alma and Fred Beachy, along with other chaperones, hung back, manning refreshment tables or sitting together among themselves, closer to the house. The idea of the chaperones was to keep behavior at a level acceptable to the bishops, while allowing the young folks to mingle and get to know each other. According to Alma Beachy, at least one marriage had come out of every annual harvest frolic they'd sponsored since they began having them six years ago.

"There's Elden again. See him over there?" Annie nudged Millie. "Near the fence. I think he's looking this way."

Millie turned to search for Elden and Annie pinched her. Millie yelped. "Ouch! What was that for?" Millie murmured under her breath. She rubbed her arm. "That hurt."

"You're not supposed to look at a boy who's looking at you," Annie admonished.

Millie had seen Elden twice already. The first time, he'd waved to her as he was tying up his buggy and she'd lifted her hand in greeting but kept walking. Then he'd started to approach her after the group singing, but she'd grabbed a tray of sandwiches and headed in the opposite direction toward the refreshment tables. She didn't know why. Maybe she wanted to be sure he really wanted to talk to her. If he did, he'd keep trying, wouldn't he?

"Don't you know anything?" Annie whispered.

"I don't know anything about dating," Millie said in exasperation. She was chilly. Beth had said to wear her cloak, but she'd chosen her navy blue going-to-town jacket because it went so nicely with her blue dress. Which she was wearing again even though it wasn't Friday. "How would I? I've never had a beau, same as you. I've never even been asked to ride home with someone before."

For a few minutes they stood side by side watching everyone. They spotted Willa with JJ, standing rather closely to each other. Then they'd giggled over Millie's sister Henry marching up to one of the older Beachy boys and telling him he'd never get the fire going stacking the wood like that. She'd then started bossing them all around, making them take the pile apart and rebuild it.

Millie was so happy to be at the harvest frolic. Things had been hard in the months leading up to their mother's death from kidney disease and then it had seemed as if they'd all been in a fog for a whole year. Now, at last, she felt more like herself again. She still missed her mother terribly, but just as so many people had told them, the pain wasn't so sharp anymore, though it was still there. Millie felt like she could breathe again and as if everything might be all right.

"Hey, do you know who that is?" Annie lifted her chin in the direction of a young man around their age walking toward the bonfire.

He had to have been a full head taller than any of the other boys there. Millie didn't think she'd ever seen such a tall Amish man before. He was wearing a hat that looked slightly different than the ones all the men wore in Kent County. His coat was different, too. It had buttons on it, whereas because they were a conservative community, their coats only had hooks and eyes. "Never seen him before," Millie said.

Grinning, Annie gave Millie a little push. "Cute, isn't he?" She nibbled on her lower lip. "Come on." She grabbed Millie's arm and dragged her toward the bonfire, which one of the Beachy boys was just getting ready to light. Under Henry's direction.

Annie walked right by the tall boy and then at the last moment *accidentally* bumped into him. Ten minutes later, Millie found herself still standing with Annie while she talked to the boy who they learned was Abe Kertz, a cousin to the Beachys, visiting from Ohio.

As Millie listened to them chat, she watched Elden move from the fence, where he'd been talking to a couple of young men, over to a picnic table where her father and Fred Beachy were standing. She smiled as she watched Elden interact with her father. Elden was so kind to him and her father lit up whenever he was around.

Millie returned her attention to her friend and the young man. They were talking about Abe's father's turkey farm and how many thousands of turkeys they sold to *Englishers* during the Thanksgiving and Christmas holidays. As the conversation continued, Annie seemed to be enjoying Abe's company so much that Millie wondered if she ought to excuse herself.

"I've got you trapped this time," a male voice said in Millie's ear, startling her.

She'd know that deep voice anywhere and she whipped around. There Elden was, dressed like all the other men in dark pants, clean work boots, a shirt and suspenders with a coat. But unlike most of the others, he wore a dark beanie pulled over his head. Hand-knit by his mother, she suspected. But he didn't look anything like the other young men milling around. Not to Millie. To her, he was by far the most handsome.

"I'm not going to let you dodge me again," he warned, his tone teasing.

"I'll talk to you later," Annie said, squeezing Millie's arm. "Good to see you, Elden." She and Abe walked away, living Millie alone with Elden.

"I was not—" Millie met his gaze as he lowered his chin, the look on his face telling her there was no denying it. "*Oll recht*, maybe I was avoiding you a little bit," she admitted.

"And why is that?" He looked around to be sure no one was close enough to hear their conversation. "Is it because you don't—you're not—you don't want to know me better?"

Millie was surprised by his forwardness. *Nay*, his

honesty. She hesitated. Did she give him another flip answer and walk off? Her response the other day seemed foolish now, especially because she desperately *did* want to ride home with him. She liked Elden. She *really* liked him.

But was there any sense in spending time with him, getting her hopes up? Because they would only be dashed. She knew that.

She met his gaze, not sure what to say.

"Just tell me the truth, Millie. If you really want me to go, I'll go. But—" He went quiet for a moment and then said, "But I don't think you want me to. I think you enjoy talking with me as much as I enjoy talking with you. I think you'd like to at least consider riding home with me tonight."

His blue-gray eyes held hers and she swallowed hard, her mouth so dry that she wished she had saved the peppermint Annie had given. Before she had a chance to speak, Annie walked back over.

Annie glanced at Elden, then at Millie, then at Elden again. "I'm going to borrow Millie for a second," she told him. "Don't move." She grabbed Millie's arm and pulled her away. "Did he ask you to ride home with him?" she whispered when they were a distance from him.

Millie nibbled on her lower lip. "He said he'd leave me alone if I wanted him to. But he said he thought I liked him and that he didn't really think I wanted him to leave me alone."

"Okay…" Annie drew out the word. "That's good, *recht*? A man who says what he thinks. How he feels."

She grabbed both of Millie's chubby hands between hers. "Millie, this is what you've been waiting for. He wants to get to know you better."

Millie groaned. "I know. Right in front of all these people," she said voicing her fears aloud. "Which means by tomorrow afternoon everyone in Honeycomb will know. Including his mother, and I already know she doesn't like me."

"I don't think that's true, but who cares about Lavinia?"

"I imagine Mary did when she sent her packing."

Annie frowned. "You need to work on your confidence, *fryn'd.*"

Millie ignored Annie's comment about self-confidence because she could only handle one problem at a time right now. "What about when he changes his mind? When he decides he doesn't like me?" Her lower lip trembled. "Or he finds someone skinnier or prettier or… *Ach*, I don't know," she fretted.

Annie sighed. "Nothing in this world is guaranteed but death and *Gott*'s love for us. And mice in your larder," she added with a wry smile. "That's what my *grossmammi* always used to say." She studied Millie for a moment, then laid both her hands on Millie's shoulders, looking into her eyes "What have you got to lose? He's not asking you to marry him. He wants to take you home in his buggy. He probably cleaned it all up and gave his horse a few extra brushes. You going to let that go to waste? And what about Elden? Maybe *he* needs this. Ever consider that? Can you imagine how terrible he must have felt when his mother ran his betrothed off?"

"So that is true?" Millie asked. "It's not just gossip."

Annie shrugged. "Knowing Lavinia, it's possible." She let go of Millie. "So spend the evening with him. Ride home with him. What's the worst thing that could happen? Nothing might come of it, but you'll have had a fun night with your handsome neighbor. I'd ride home with him in a second if he asked me."

Millie nodded. "You're right. I should just enjoy his company."

"*Ya.*"

"And...and if nothing comes of it," Millie said, thinking if she said the words aloud, she could convince herself. "Then at least I'll have ridden home with a boy for the first time."

"Exactly. So go on. And I'll talk to you tomorrow after church."

"*Danki*, Annie. You're a good friend," Millie said as Annie walked away.

Millie found Elden standing closer to the fire, his bare hands out for warmth.

"*Ya*," Millie announced to him, stretching out her own hands.

His forehead crinkled. "*Ya* what?"

"Yes, I'll let you take me home."

He broke into a grin. "You will?"

"Well," she said. "Probably. But first I'll have to see your marshmallow-roasting skills."

"Oh, I can roast a marshmallow," Elden told her, a

twinkle in his eyes. "And I can make the best s'more you've ever eaten. The marshmallow is toasted perfectly, so that the chocolate melts. Just thinking about it makes me want one."

Millie laughed and then realized he was still looking at her. Watching. "What?" she said.

He shrugged. "I was thinking how I like the sound of your voice when you laugh. It's so joyful. So genuine."

Millie didn't know what to say, because no one had ever said anything like that to her before. Certainly not a boy. But as it turned out, she didn't have to say anything because her father strode over to them with a big bag of marshmallows in one hand and saplings to use for roasting sticks in the other.

"You two look like you need some marshmallows," her father said, stopping in front of them. "What do you say, *sohn*? Going to make your girl a s'more?"

"*Dat*," Millie whispered, mortified. "I'm not his girl."

Elden didn't act as if he had heard the older man. If he did, he was too polite to say anything.

Her father ignored Millie's correction as he held out the bag to her. "Get a couple." He glanced around as if looking for someone, then said, "Don't tell your sister but I'm saving some for later." He patted his coat pocket, fat with marshmallows.

Millie made a face. "*Dat*, you can't carry marshmallows in your pocket." She fished two out of the bag for her and Elden while Elden grabbed two sticks. "They'll melt and get all sticky."

"Not if I eat 'em first, they won't," he countered, then he walked away leaving them both laughing.

It was after eleven when Elden steered his buggy up the Koffmans' driveway. A three-quarters moon hung low in the sky, so bright it lit their way. The temperature continued to drop outside and puffs of white frost rose from his gelding's mouth. But despite the cold, it was warm inside the buggy thanks to a space heater he ran off a car battery. As they made their way closer to Millie's house, he wished her driveway was longer. He wished she'd lived farther away from the Beachys'. He wished the night wouldn't come to an end.

It was time he got her home before her sisters or father began to worry about her, though. And they'd already taken the long way home. After they made s'mores at the frolic, they'd ended up sitting on a bale of straw near the bonfire and talking. And the more he talked to Millie, the more he liked her. She was so open. And funny. And smart. And she didn't just let him talk. She had plenty to say, and not once all evening was there an uncomfortable silence between them.

Riding home, as Millie chatted about her childhood and how wonderful her mother had been, it occurred to Elden that even though he had been sure six months ago he would never fall in love again, suddenly the possibility was there. It was right there beside him on the buggy seat. Millie was sitting so close that he could have reached out and touched her hand if he'd dared.

"I'm sorry," Millie said as the buggy rolled to a stop near her back door. "I've been talking your ear off."

"*Ya*," he teased, the moonlight coming through the windshield of the buggy so that it illuminated her face. "And I've enjoyed every word."

She looked at him and he noticed that a lock of blond hair had fallen from her *kapp* to curl at her temple. Her cheeks were rosy and her lips made him think of ripe strawberries in the summer sun. He wondered what it would feel like to touch that curl.

"Are you teasing me?" she asked. "Sometimes I can't tell when you're teasing or being serious."

"I'm serious." He couldn't stop smiling. "But in a teasing way."

"Well," she said, bringing her hands down soundly to her legs. "I should go. I'm sure Eleanor is waiting up for me. Likely watching us from the kitchen windows." She hesitated and when she spoke again, her voice softened. "Thank you for the ride home, Elden. I really had a good time."

"A good enough time to go out with me tomorrow night?" he asked before he lost his nerve.

"*Nay*," she said.

"*Nay*?" he asked in surprise. "Why not?"

Her eyes widened as if it was the silliest of questions. "Because tomorrow is a church Sunday and both of us will be busy all day. We'll be at the Masts' and you… I think Alma Beachy said they were having church tomorrow. She said with everything all *rett* up already, why not have another crowd tomorrow?"

He pressed his hand to his forehead. "You're right. Tomorrow is church. And Monday *Mam* has a doctor's appointment and I told her we could go shopping after. She doesn't like taking the buggy into Dover on her own. And Tuesday I promised my uncle Gabriel that I would— Wednesday," he said quickly. "How about if we do something together on Wednesday?" He tried to think fast. "I… I'm making wire frames for wreaths for some of the greenhouses nearby. I have to drop some off at the Millers'." He held his breath because tonight he'd had a better time than he could remember in a very long time. Maybe better even than when he was with Mary. "If Wednesday won't work—"

"*Nay*. Wednesday is good." She smiled at him as she reached for the door. "I have chores in the morning, but how about one thirty?"

"I'll be here to pick you up," he said.

"Sounds good." She slid her door open.

Elden watched as she landed gracefully on her feet.

"Good night, Elden," she said, looking up at him.

He sat there until she went into the house and then he drove the short distance home, smiling all the way.

Chapter Ten

A month flew by so quickly that Millie barely had time to catch her breath. One day she was riding home from the harvest frolic with Elden, then the next they were officially walking out together.

A week after they started seeing each other, Elden had taken her father for a ride into town to buy some lumber and had asked him if he might court his daughter. When they returned, Millie had been waiting nervously at the window, unsure of how her father might respond. She never knew how he would react to anything these days. Sometimes he woke up his old self, his mind clear, and sometimes he woke confused, and there seemed to be no rhyme nor reason to it. To her relief that day, when the men came up the lane, she couldn't tell who was grinning harder, her father or her new beau.

After that, she and Elden saw each other nearly every day, not just attending social events, but sometimes they would go for a walk, or he would ride into town with her and her father to get groceries or go to an appointment. It was the kind of courting she had imagined since she was old enough to dream of meeting and marrying a man and having a family of her own. Elden was sweet and attentive, and they talked a lot, sometimes about trivial things, sometimes important things. They talked about their favorite ice cream, about what it meant to them to be Amish. They discussed the sermons they heard on Sunday and wondered if the Almanac was going to be reliable that year. Were they really going to get a lot of snow?

One thing Millie and Elden hadn't done was have supper with his mother at their place. Elden and Lavinia occasionally came to the Koffman home to share a meal, but usually at Millie's father's insistence. Millie got the distinct impression Elden was keeping his mother and her apart, and while she kept thinking she should bring it up, somehow she couldn't do so. The same went for the subject of his betrothal to Mary. While he mentioned the girl in passing a couple of times, Millie got the idea he didn't want to talk about her. She'd always let the subject drop even though she wanted to know the details, because what if he was still in love with her? She didn't know if she'd be able to bear it if he was.

Midmorning on the day after Thanksgiving, Elden pulled onto the Koffman lane, wooden crates of wire frames to make wreaths, garland and table sprays from greenery stacked above his vehicle's wagon wheels. Millie was going with him to deliver them to Miller's greenhouse in Hickory Grove, five miles from Honeycomb.

By the time Elden pulled up near the back porch, Millie wore her cloak and a wool scarf tied over her head. Eleanor didn't approve of Millie being seen with Elden without a proper head cover, but Millie feared her prayer *kapp* might blow away and her black wool church bonnet was too much for such a casual outing. Beneath her cloak, she wore a blue dress, one of three she now owned because Willa, after saying she was tired of seeing her in the same dress every day, made her two more from fabric they'd discovered in their mother's sewing room.

"There you are," Elden said. He started to get down from the wagon to come to the door but settled back on the bench seat when he saw her.

Millie smiled. Her heart sang every time she saw his handsome face. How had she been so blessed to have him as her beau? "Here I am." She grasped an iron handhold and stepped up into the wagon. When they'd first started dating, he'd kept trying to help her in and out of his buggy, but she'd reminded him that it wasn't really the Amish way and they didn't need folks talking any more than they already were.

Willa and Jane kept Millie up-to-date on what people were saying in Honeycomb about her and Elden. Words like *mismatched* and *odd couple* were thrown around their community, but Millie tried not to pay any attention to it, although a part of her was still waiting for the romance to fall apart. Sometimes she had nightmares that he broke up with her to court Willa,

Beth or even her friend Annie. But by day, she enjoyed what she had with him and tried not to worry about the future.

Millie settled down on the bench seat beside Elden.

He lifted a wool lap blanket and covered her with it. "Hot brick at your feet. *Mam* said it might snow today. It's been years since we had snow this early in the season."

"*Ya*, the sky does have that color to it, doesn't it?" Millie said, looking up. She breathed deeply. "I think it smells like snow, too."

"I hope the ride isn't too cold for you. Sorry we couldn't do this in the buggy, but there was no way all of this would fit inside and I want to bring some greenery home to decorate the house. I thought you might like some, too. Maybe some pine boughs in the windowsills inside because they smell so good."

"I'd love that. We always used to decorate the windowsills with pine boughs. They make the house smell so good."

Elden slid his hand across the wagon seat and took hers, and even through their knit gloves, she could feel his warmth and tenderness. When they held hands, it was all she could do not to think about what it would be like to wake up each day to see his smiling face.

"Ready?" he asked.

"*Ya.*"

Elden took up the reins, murmured gently to the giant workhorse and off they went down the driveway.

"How was Thanksgiving at Gabriel's?" she asked as they waited at the end of the lane for cars to pass.

"It was nice. Quiet."

She nodded because it had been a quiet affair at their house as well. They'd fasted, as was the family's tradition, until supper when they'd a simple meal of white bean soup and fresh bread. They'd spent the day together talking, reading and knitting or mending with several breaks when their father had led them through devotions.

When Millie and Elden pulled into the gravel parking lot of Miller's greenhouse, which it shared with Miller's harness shop, the place was packed. There had to be at least a dozen parked cars, trucks and minivans as well as a horse and buggy and a wagon full of fresh greenery tied to a hitching post. *Englishers* crisscrossed the parking area, carrying armfuls of red and white potted poinsettias and big, beautiful wreaths made from pine boughs, holly leaves and mistletoe, all constructed on Elden's frames.

"My goodness," Millie said, her breath coming in puffs of white. "Look at all the people."

"*Ya*, Joshua Miller and his sister Bay's business has really taken off." He eased the Clydesdale in beside the other wagon and jumped out to tie it up. "Bay married a Mennonite, David Jansen, and they live down the road a piece."

Millie climbed down from the wagon seat, lowering her voice. "She left the order and her parents allow her to their home?"

He shrugged, walking around the horse to Millie. "They do. I know many don't allow *lost* children to come home, but I'd like to think that my *mam* wouldn't shun me if I chose to leave the church."

"*Ya*," Millie said, unable to imagine leaving her Amish life behind. "But that's not something you ever considered, is it?" He never suggested he was unhappy in the life he had been born into, but this wasn't something a couple who was courting should keep from each other. Even though she and Elden had not specifically spoken of it yet, once a couple was openly courting, the assumption was that their intention was to wed. Millie couldn't imagine marrying a man who wanted to leave his Amish life—and take his family with him.

"*Nay*, I've never considered it." He halted in front of her, rubbing his hands together for warmth. "I choose the life *Gott* has chosen for me." He frowned. "You?"

She shook her head emphatically. "I love my life as an Amish woman." *And I love you*, she thought. But she didn't say it out loud because what if he didn't feel the same way about her? Or what if it was too soon to say the words? For the hundredth time she wished her mother was still alive. This wasn't a subject Millie felt she could discuss with Eleanor, but she could have with her *mam*.

Elden gazed into her eyes and she felt a brush of cold on her cheek. She looked up into the sky and saw that it was filled with snowflakes slowly fluttering downward to settle on the dead grass, the wagon and Elden's eyelashes. Seeing the snow and standing so close to him as he looked down on her, she felt a little lightheaded. It was such a perfect moment, feeling the warmth of his body so close to hers, and seeing the emotion in his gray eyes, she wanted it to last forever,

"*Goot,*" Elden said softly. "We're of the same mind. I think that's important for a couple." He hooked his thumb in the direction of the greenhouse. The door to the shop was decorated in greenery, and a large sign painted in red and green read Christmas Shop Open. "Let's see if we can find Joshua or Bay and make this delivery." He headed for the door and she fell into step beside him.

An *Englisher* woman in a red coat came out the door carrying two enormous white poinsettias, with a little girl of four or five, who followed carrying a small white poinsettia.

Millie smiled as they went past, then followed Elden inside. The shop was small with a checkout counter and a passageway that led into a greenhouse that must have been thirty or forty feet long and filled with red and white poinsettias. Inside, it was warm and loud and filled with *Englishers* all trying to pay for their purchases.

"Wow, I didn't expect the place to be this busy," Elden said, gazing around. "I don't see Bay or Joshua. I'm going to go see if I can find one of them. You *oll recht* here?"

She nodded. She was enjoying the commotion. *Englishers* and their ways fascinated her. She didn't want to be one, but she certainly liked observing them. "I'll wait for you here."

Flashing a smile, her handsome beau gingerly

made his way through the crowd toward the green-house.

Millie stood where she was, looking at all the wreaths and sprays hanging on the shop walls. Some of the arrangements were simple, something she would hang on their door, and others were elaborate with sparkly ribbon and plastic birds stuck to them. One wreath that was two feet across had sparkly, white fake poinsettia leaves wired to the greenery. Another had big silver bells hanging from it. She gazed in the direction Elden had gone and spotted him talking to a pretty Amish woman who looked to be maybe twenty. She was smiling up at him, giggling.

Millie's face fell. Was that Bay, the one who had married a Mennonite? The way she was flirting with him, Millie doubted it. That was a single woman trying to catch the attention of a single man.

Millie knew she shouldn't be surprised. Elden was what her mother would have called a catch. He was handsome, well set financially, and never been married. Any girl in the county would be happy to have his attention.

Millie watched to see if Elden was flirting back. He was smiling, but he didn't do anything to encourage her. After a moment the girl pointed and Elden nodded, said something more and then headed back toward the shop.

"We're going to drive around back," he told Millie when he reached her.

Outside, where it was still snowing, they got into the wagon and he drove around the back of the greenhouse, where there was a second greenhouse. The owner Joshua, or co-owner, as Elden explained, met them along with several teenage boys, and the crates of wire frames were quickly unloaded. Joshua gifted them a huge pile of fresh greenery and soon Elden and Millie were on their way again.

They rode maybe half a mile, the snow drifting around them, making the familiar landscape appear even prettier than usual. "You're quiet," Elden said. "Feeling okay?"

Millie clasped her hands together. She'd been so happy riding over, so happy for weeks, but seeing the woman flirt with Elden had brought all her self-doubts crashing down on her. "Do you know her?" she asked.

"Know who?" They rolled to a stop at a crossroad. There were no cars coming, but he didn't urge the Clydesdale forward.

"The woman you were talking to in the greenhouse. The pretty one in the rose-colored dress."

He frowned, his eyes scrunching at the corners. She watched carefully. Was he going to deny he'd even talked to her?

"Katie?" he asked.

"Is that her name?"

Elden turned to her. "That's Katie. She works for the Millers. Sometimes she's in the harness shop, sometimes in the greenhouse."

"She's very pretty.'

He shrugged. "I suppose so."

Millie hesitated. "Is she someone you'd be interested in courting?"

He looked at her as if she had just said the silliest thing. "Millie. I'm courting you. Remember?"

She looked away, watching a blue pickup truck stop at the four-way crossroad. Christmas music floated from the driver's open window.

"She's younger than I am. Skinny and pretty. I can understand why you might be interested in a girl like that. It's only natural that a man—"

"Millie, I've told you before. I like you just as you are. In fact, I don't *just* like you, I—" He went silent, his Adam's apple bobbing, then continued. "You need to have more confidence in yourself. In us." A car pulled up behind them and he pulled into the intersection. "I think we need some hot chocolate. I brought some. And marshmallows." He tapped a paper bag at his feet. "I know your *dat* loves hot chocolate with marshmallows. How about we go back to your house and make some?"

She looked at him for a long moment. He was right. She knew he was right about having more confidence, but it was so hard when he was so handsome and so perfect.

And she wasn't.

"*Ya*," she said, watching the snow settle on the horse's back. She wasn't comfortable talking to him about why she worried she wasn't good enough for him. If she gave him all the reasons, she was afraid he'd realize she was right. He was too good for her. So instead, she ignored his comment about her self-confidence and forced a smile. "Let's have some hot chocolate. And I made some cookies. I was fiddling with recipes for the cookie exchange at my aunt's house next weekend. You're still coming, right?"

"We are. I wouldn't miss a chance to spend the evening with my sweetheart." He covered her hand with his, and Millie made the decision to stay in the moment and not worry about Katie or girls like her.

At least not today.

When Millie walked into her aunt Judy's kitchen the following Saturday, carrying her white chocolate chunk cranberry oatmeal cookies, she spotted Lavinia right away. The older woman was busy setting her rice cereal bars on a plate at the kitchen table. And if she was here, that meant that Elden was there because Lavinia rarely took the buggy out herself and she certainly didn't dare leave her property with snow on the ground. Millie must have missed him outside in the sea of buggies when her family had arrived.

"Afternoon," Millie greeted Lavinia and her aunt, who was pouring sugar into a big crockery sugar bowl. She didn't meet Lavinia's gaze as she rested the cookie tray on her hip. "Where should I put these?" she asked her aunt. "On the table?"

Looking flustered, Judy snapped the lid on the sugar canister. "We've got tables set up for the exchange in the sitting room. Those are for eating." She indicated the kitchen table with plates of cookies on them. "The Bishop insisted we be able to sample the goods." She flashed a wry smile.

It was their family's inside joke. Uncle Cyrus was turning out to be an excellent bishop, but having come to the position only recently, it was important to him that his new status be recognized by everyone, including those closest to him. Instead of referring to him by his first name, Aunt Judy had taken to calling him The Bishop as if it was his name, though not when he was within hearing distance.

Millie set her tray on the table so she could grab one of the empty serving plates. "I'll leave some here and put the others in the sitting room."

As Judy walked into the pantry, Lavinia moved to the end of the table and peeled back the foil on Millie's cookie tray. "What are these?"

Millie moved some of the cookies onto the plate. The plan was to enjoy cookies and coffee and tea and milk for the children, then they would have the cookie exchange. Everyone was supposed to bring six dozen of one kind of cookie, then you could take up to six dozen different cookies home with you. "White chocolate chunk cranberry oatmeal cookies."

Lavinia wrinkled her nose. "What's that all over them?" She pointed.

Not sure what she meant, Millie leaned over to look. "Oh, white chocolate I melted and drizzled over it." She smiled at Elden's mother. "So they look pretty. And Christmassy."

Lavinia frowned.

"I've never heard of such a cookie." Lavinia sniffed.

"I didn't exactly follow a recipe." Millie shrugged. "I thought about what would be good in an oatmeal cookie and threw it in. The dried cranberries are pretty and the white chocolate makes me think of snow. Timely with this early snowfall," she added, sounding more cheerful than she felt.

For weeks she'd been telling herself that it was her imagination that Lavinia didn't like her, but she was coming to the terrifying conclusion that it was true. Elden's mother was never outright rude to her, but Millie always felt a sense of disappointment whenever Lavinia spoke to her. She couldn't help worrying that Lavinia saw what Elden didn't. That she was fat and ugly.

"I don't care for dried cranberries." Lavinia wrinkled her nose. "Too tart. And the red is showy. Not properly Plain like an oatmeal cookie with raisins."

Millie didn't like the face Lavinia was making. If Lavinia didn't like cranberries that was one thing, but Millie got the feeling that Lavinia was trying to make her feel bad about what she'd brought for the cookie exchange.

"I don't think my Elden likes dried cranberries, either."

Millie felt her face growing warm. Her first thought was to respond, "Well, he doesn't have to eat them," but instead, she plastered on a smile, scooped up her tray of cookies and excused herself as her aunt walked back into the kitchen.

On her way to the sitting room, Millie greeted friends and neighbors and children racing through the house with a smile. As instructed, she left her tray on one of the tables laden with tins, baskets and plates of cookies. Right now, all the women, girls and small children were inside while the men chatted outside.

Aunt Judy would soon call the men in. Which meant that if Millie wanted to catch Elden alone for a few minutes, this might be her only chance.

Near the front door Millie dug through the pile of wool cloaks to find hers and went out the door. The steps were slippery and muddy from the snow and so many people going in and out of the house, and as she took the last step her feet went out from under her and she fell hard. Looking around, afraid someone had seen her, she used the handrail to pull herself up. Blessedly, while the barnyard was full of men and boys, no one seemed to have noticed her. Head down, she followed the sidewalk, brushing the snow off the back of her cloak.

Maybe she shouldn't have come at all today.

Maybe she shouldn't have made cookies that were so *showy*.

Maybe she should have told Lavinia that Lavinia didn't know what her son liked, because the previous day he had eaten seven of Millie's white chocolate chunk cranberry oatmeal cookies.

Maybe she should have—

"Millie? Are you all right?"

She looked up to see Elden striding toward her. "I saw you fall. I was afraid you'd hurt yourself."

She pressed her hand to her forehead. "*Ach.* I'm such a *doplich*." Fat *and* clumsy, she thought.

Elden stepped in front of her. "Millie, you are not. You're the most graceful—"

His voice caught in his throat and she looked up at him, surprised by the emotion she heard in his voice.

All around them, men milled about, tying up their horses, talking crops and weather. Children ran in the lane, throwing wet snowballs at each other, but the sounds of the barnyard faded as she gazed at Elden's handsome face. She waited for him to finish what he was saying.

He had been looking down at his snowy boots, but he lifted his chin now to meet her gaze. "Millie, I had this whole thing planned out but—" He glanced around and seeing several men headed their way he grabbed her hand and walked around the corner of the house, leading Millie. He followed the shoveled sidewalk until they were out of sight of the others and then stopped and turned to her, still holding her hand.

She laughed nervously, thinking he was behaving oddly. "Elden, what are you—"

"*Sigh so gude.* Please." He took an uneasy breath. "Millie, let me say this before I lose my nerve. I had planned to wait, but I can't wait any longer. And I know we haven't been courting long, but I know what I want, and I think you want the same thing." Again, he took a breath. "Millie—" He met her gaze with his beautiful eyes. "Millie, will you be my wife?"

Millie gasped, pressing her hand to her heart, afraid it might stop beating. "Will I—" Now she was the one who couldn't catch her breath.

"I know I need to talk to your father, but considering the circumstances, I thought I better ask you first because—"

"*Ya,*" Millie heard herself say in a whisper.

But he hadn't heard her and he kept talking. "If

the answer was *nay*, then there would be no need. But I hope the answer isn't no because I want to marry you. I love you, Millie, and—"

She rested her hand on his coat, feeling dizzy. He loved her. *He said he loved her.* She found her voice, speaking over him. "*Ya*, Elden. *Ya*, I'll marry you."

"And I hope that—" He halted midsentence. "You will?"

Tears filled her eyes. She couldn't believe this was happening. *Ya*, she'd been dreaming about it, but she hadn't thought it would actually happen. She'd been sure that eventually he'd see her for who she was, what she was, and realize there were too many pretty, skinny *maedels* in the world to be bothered with the likes of her.

This was the happiest moment of Millie's life.

But that was all it lasted. One moment. And then the fear came back. He was saying he loved her. That he wanted to marry her, but he was right, they hadn't been courting very long. Not long enough for him to realize that he didn't love her. That he didn't want to marry her. And when he realized how he really felt, she'd be devastated. Mortified when everyone in Honeycomb found out he had broken up with her.

Think fast, she told herself. *Think fast, Millie.*

"*Ya*, I do want to marry you, Elden," she said. Because it was true. But then she tempered it with, "But, but you're right. We haven't been courting long. And, and I think we shouldn't tell anyone yet."

His brow furrowed. "Not tell anyone?"

She gave a little laugh. "Just not…yet." He looked

so disappointed that she added, "Soon, but not yet. Our little secret to enjoy. Just until the New Year. Until Epiphany, maybe?" *Because by then you'll know what you really want*, she thought. And maybe it would be her. Maybe he did love her, but she needed him to be sure because she loved him so much. She didn't know if she could bear it if he broke up with her.

"Until Epiphany," he repeated, glancing away, then back at her. "*Oll recht.* I suppose I can wait. And enjoy the secret with you in the meantime."

"*Ya.*" She gazed up at him and he put his arms around her and again she felt dizzy. It was the first time he had ever held her this way, and the scent of him was powerful. "It will be just between us. Our little secret."

"Our little secret," he agreed, his smile as big as hers.

Chapter Eleven

Sunday, after three hours of morning church services, including a ninety-minute sermon, Millie was the first to pop up from her bench on the women's side of the Koblenz sitting room and hurry into the kitchen. She felt guilty that her mind had wandered often during the preacher's sermon, but she couldn't stop thinking about Elden and his proposal. When she'd returned from the cookie exchange, she'd been bursting at the seams to tell her sisters and *dat*, but she'd kept her mouth shut to keep from spilling the news that still didn't seem real to her. Elden Yoder had told her he loved her. He had said he wanted to marry her.

Now, almost twenty-four hours later, she was wondering if she'd made a mistake in asking Elden to keep their betrothal a secret. Thinking back, she realized that he'd shocked her by asking so soon after they began dating, and that had triggered her request. She'd said it because she was afraid he would change his mind. She feared he had asked on impulse and would think better of it later. But then, recalling his face when she'd said yes, she wondered if maybe this *was* all real. Maybe Elden *did* love her. She certainly loved him, although she hadn't told him for fear she'd start to cry and because she wasn't quite ready to give herself to the idea that he would become her husband. So many things could happen to change his mind. Wasn't it a kindness to give him a chance to think it over before they told their families and friends?

"What do you want me to do?" Millie asked Adalaide Koblenz who was stirring two pots of soup on her woodstove at the same time.

"*Ach*!" the tiny, round woman said. "I've been up since four and still everything isn't ready. You'd think as long as Amos and I have been having services in our home, I'd be better at this." She set down the wooden spoons. "There are tables set up in the parlor. While the men move the benches in the sitting room, could you put glasses at every setting and be sure there's silverware? Everything's in the pantry."

Millie grabbed the work apron she'd left on a peg in the kitchen and dropped it over her head, covering her Sunday best black dress and white cape and apron. "*Ya*. Don't worry. It will all be fine," she assured her hostess as she cut across the kitchen. "My *mam* always said that hungry men were easily pleased."

"Aggie was a woman wise beyond her years," Adalaide called as Millie walked into the pantry.

Inside the small room of floor-to-ceiling shelves, Millie found the extra silverware and glasses. Annie was there, pulling rolls out of a plastic bag and adding them to bread baskets for the tables.

"I thought that sermon would never end," Annie groaned.

Millie slid a serving tray off a shelf above her head and began loading it with glasses from a crate that had come from the church wagon full of communal tables, chairs and dishware.

She filled the tray with glasses as quickly as she could. While she and her sisters hadn't hosted church since their mother's passing, she knew how stressful it could be even for an organized woman like Adalaide, so she was eager to help her. As she grabbed another tray to load it with silverware, she realized Annie was watching. "What are you looking at?" Millie asked.

"You. I don't think I've ever seen you smile like that. And your face. You look so bright and happy." Annie moved closer. "What's going on with you?"

Millie fully intended to say, "Nothing," but that wasn't what came out of her mouth. As she turned to her best friend, she whispered, "He asked me to marry him."

Annie squealed and threw her arms around Millie. "You're getting married!"

"Shhh," Millie hushed, holding out her hand.

"Oh, Millie," Annie went on. "I'm so happy for you. When did he ask you?" She grabbed Millie's arms, squaring up to her. "I want to hear every single word he—" Her gaze moved suddenly to the pantry doorway and her eyes got round.

"What?" Millie whispered.

Before Annie could respond, Millie heard her sister Jane say, "There you are. Adalaide said to help you set tables."

Millie grabbed the closest tray of glasses and whipped around, handing it to Jane without making eye contact with her. "I'll be right in." She pretended to count silverware until her sister walked out of the pantry.

"Do you think Jane heard me?" Millie whispered, grabbing Annie's arms.

Annie stared wide-eyed at her. "I— Oh, what does it matter! You're marrying Elden Yoder!"

"Please keep your voice down," Millie hushed. "I didn't tell them yet."

"You didn't tell your family?" Annie whispered.

Millie bit down on her lower lip. "*Nay*, we agreed to wait."

"Millie!" called Adalaide from the kitchen. "When you finish with that, can you run down to the cellar and grab six jars of spiced, canned peaches?"

"*Ya!*" Millie hollered through the door. "I'll get them." She looked back at Annie. "I'll tell you everything later." She grabbed the second tray of glasses. "*Ach*, I just hope Jane didn't hear me," she groaned as she rushed out of the pantry.

Her wish was short-lived.

Later on, their family buggy was barely out of the Koblenzes' driveway when Jane declared, "Why didn't you tell us Elden asked you to marry him?"

Millie found herself barely able to speak as her sisters congratulated her. By the time they were back in their own kitchen and their father was settled in his chair in the sitting room, her sisters were making plans for the wedding. Everyone was talking at once and Millie felt overwhelmed and a little shaky. They were all firing questions at her. Offering their opinions.

"Who will be your attendants?" Willa asked.

Beth chimed in, "Will you wait until next fall to marry since the season for weddings is past?"

"I see no reason to wait," Jane said. "That's old-fashioned. I think you should have a Christmas wedding."

"Christmas! That's less than three weeks away," Cora argued. "There isn't time to meet with the bishop and have the banns read before then."

"We need more time to get ready anyway," Henry said. "The house really needs to be painted if we're having a wedding here and…"

The sisters went on and on, but their voices faded as Millie tried to wrap her head around what had happened. Was there any way she and Elden could keep their betrothal a secret now? Between Jane and Willa, they'd soon spread the news through Honeycomb and beyond. Elden would have to tell his mother. It wouldn't be right for her to hear the news at Byler's deli counter.

Millie slipped out of the kitchen and into the hall, leaning against the wall for a moment and closing her eyes. She would have to go to Elden tomorrow and tell him what had happened.

Millie heard Eleanor's footsteps coming from the

opposite end of the hall. No one could see her sister's prosthetic leg beneath her long skirts, but the rhythm of her gait was slightly different than others' and Millie recognized it at once.

"Hey," Eleanor said softly.

Millie pressed her lips together, feeling like she might cry but didn't know why. Elden wasn't going to be upset about others finding out the betrothal. He hadn't wanted to keep it a secret to begin with.

"Come on," Eleanor said gently as she looped her arm through Millie's. "Let's sit down." She led her into the parlor and indicated their mother's damask couch. "Relax a minute. I know you're excited, but I can see you're a bit overwhelmed, too."

Millie nodded, still not trusting herself to speak, and sat down. Eleanor lit two oil lamps and then dropped onto the couch beside her. Although her sister was not physically demonstrative in the way their mother had been, Millie found Eleanor's nearness comforting.

"You didn't tell us," Eleanor said quietly. "Why not, *schweschter*?"

Her hands knotted together, Millie, turning teary, told Eleanor what had happened the day before, and Eleanor listened without interrupting.

When Millie was done, Eleanor was quiet for a moment, then said, "And why did you not want us to know?" She plucked a handkerchief from her sleeve and handed it to Millie. "Did you not think we'd be happy for you?"

Millie blotted her eyes and then her face. "It's not

that I didn't want you to know. It was only that I..." She exhaled, her eyes feeling scratchy again. "I wanted to give him some more time. In case he wanted to change his mind," she managed. "Because why wouldn't he?"

"Oh, Millie," Eleanor whispered. "Why *would* he?"

"Because look at me." She gestured to her body miserably. "Why would a beautiful man like Elden want to be married to this?" She twisted the handkerchief in her hands. "Maybe I should go on a diet. Do you think I should go on a diet?"

Eleanor looked at her the way their mother had when one of them said something ridiculous. It was a kind disapproval without judgment. "You do not need to go on a diet," she said firmly. "You're healthy and this is how *Gott* made you, Millie. He also made you smart and capable and kind and such a hard worker. A woman with more faith I don't think I've ever known." She went quiet for a moment. "What's made you think you're not good enough for Elden, or that he doesn't really want this?"

Eleanor waited and when Millie didn't respond, she said, "Does this have something to do with his previous betrothal?"

Millie looked at her hands in her lap and shrugged. "I didn't really know Mary. I spoke to her a couple of times. I just know she's pretty and thin."

"Have you and Elden talked about her?"

Millie shrugged. "He's...um...mentioned her."

"Did he tell you why they broke up? Was it because of his mother?"

"I don't know," Millie admitted. "He doesn't like to talk about it."

Eleanor sat back on the couch. "That doesn't mean you don't have a right to know. I'm not saying you should talk about it all the time, or even ever again, but maybe you need to have a conversation about Mary. Once you know what happened, you'll feel more comfortable believing that Elden loves you and only you and he loves you as you are."

"I don't know if I can ask," Millie said miserably.

"I understand it will be hard, but you're going to be taking marriage vows. You need to know, Millie, so that you can be the wife you want to be to him. I think a few minutes of both of you being uncomfortable is worth it. I don't know a lot about marriage except what I saw between *Mam* and *Dat*, but I know there should never be secrets between husband and wife."

Millie knew Eleanor was right, but that didn't make it any easier. "Do you think we can ask the girls not to say anything for a few days? Until I can talk to Elden?"

"*Ya*, of course. I'll tell them now and be firm with them." Eleanor squeezed Millie's hand and stood. "And I won't pester you about this again. But believe me, you'll feel better once you talk to Elden. Once that's settled, you'll need to tell *Dat* about the betrothal and Elden should ask for your hand because *Dat* will like that. But you have my blessing, little sister." She smiled. "You deserve a husband like Elden. You need to believe that."

"*Ya*," Millie whispered when her sister was gone. "I'm trying."

* * *

Elden tossed another bale of hay down from the barn loft and leaned over to speak to his uncle, who was standing below him on the ground floor. "You think that's enough? I can come back in a few days."

"Plenty." Gabriel waved his nephew down impatiently. "I told you and Elsie that I could do this myself, but nobody seems to want to listen to me. My wrist is just sprained, my hand hasn't been amputated."

"And the doctor told you to rest it, which means no heavy lifting." Elden came down the wire-wrung ladder attached to the wall. His uncle had sprained his wrist trying to lead a spooked yearling mare into the barn. "And that means bales of hay."

"You sound like Elsie now," Gabriel grumbled.

"You're a blessed man to have such a caring wife." Elden grabbed the two bales of hay, one in each gloved hand, and carried them to the aisle between the horse stalls where his uncle could easily get to it.

"That'll be you soon enough. I'm pleased for you, nephew. I'm glad to hear you're betrothed. From what I know of Millie, the two of you will make a fine couple."

Elden walked back and grabbed another two bales of hay. He agreed, of course, that Millie was perfect for him, though he worried she might change her mind. He fretted that he'd asked her too soon.

Millie had come over to his place the day after he proposed. He'd been cutting down pine and spruce trees to sell for Christmas trees. She'd told him that her sisters had accidentally found out about their betrothal and said it was only fair that he tell his mother and aunt and uncle. However, she asked him to hold off saying anything to anyone else yet. She'd agreed to go with him to Spence's Bazaar the following day to drop off the Christmas trees to be sold, but then she'd sent her sister over to cancel right before they were supposed to leave, saying she didn't feel well. He'd tried twice more to make a date with her, but they couldn't seem to make it happen. She was busy making Christmas items to sell at a booth she and her sisters had rented at Spence's Bazaar for an Amish Christmas market the following weekend. And it was a busy time of the year for him because of all his Christmas-related side businesses.

Elden kept telling himself there was no need to worry. They were both just busy. But he couldn't help but worry. Mary had avoided him before their breakup.

"I appreciate you agreeing I made the right choice of a wife," Elden said. "I wish *Mam* felt the same way."

"Pay no attention to Lavinia." Gabriel sat down on a bale of hay, cradling his sprained wrist that was wrapped in a stretchy bandage. "Your father used to say she'd complain about a sunny day. I think she's just worried that this is too soon after Mary."

"She wouldn't have thought it was too soon if it was Willa or Beth Koffman I'd proposed to. She was pushing hard this fall for me to court one of them."

Gabriel shrugged, watching him. "What can I say? Been married forty years and I still can't figure how women think."

Elden nodded and carried two more bales of hay to the growing stack in the center of the barn.

Both men were quiet, then Gabriel asked, "Is everything *oll recht* with you?"

"I'm *goot*." Elden flashed a smile.

"You don't seem *goot*. You seem worried. Newly betrothed to a girl like Millie, you ought to be a happy man."

"I am happy."

"You know, it's normal to be nervous." Gabriel pushed his wire-frame glasses up farther on his nose. "I asked Elsie to marry me and then I was petrified. Couldn't eat, couldn't sleep. I worried how we would make it financially. Where we would live. I fretted I wouldn't be the husband she deserved."

Elden walked back to where his uncle was sitting, but instead of grabbing another bale, he just stood there, listening to the howl of the wind outside. There was more snow in the forecast. "I love Millie, Gabriel. I'll be the happiest man in the county if she marries me."

"If?" Gabriel repeated. "I thought she said yes."

Elden stared at his boots. "*Ya*, she did. But so did Mary and we know how that worked out."

"Ah," Gabriel said. "Is that what this is about?" He paused thoughtfully, then said, "Millie is not Mary."

"I know that."

"Mary wasn't right for you. I told you that when you asked me. Your mother said the same thing."

Elden pulled off one leather work glove and drew his hand across his face. He was tired. He'd worked all day in the cold clearing. He needed a good night's sleep.

"It's only natural that you have this concern, but you need to dig deep and trust yourself. You've got to put those insecurities aside. *Gott* has brought you the right match and the past is the past. You have to believe that, *sohn.* You understand what I'm saying?"

Elden slid his hand back into his glove. "I do."

"Talk to Millie, that's my advice." Gabriel held up one hand, knotty with arthritis. "You didn't ask for it, but there it is, anyway. It's hard learning to discuss what you're feeling but I'm convinced it's one of the secrets to a good marriage. It took Elsie a long time to convince me of that, but, in the end, she was right." He stood and rested a comforting hand on Elden's shoulder. "It's going to be fine. You'll figure this out. You and Millie, together."

Elden nodded determinedly and prayed that his uncle was right.

Chapter Twelve

All the way home from Gabriel's, Elden thought about what his uncle had said about the necessity of believing in himself—and believing in himself and Millie as a couple. He knew he loved her, and not in the same way he had loved Mary. With Mary, he'd been so thrilled when she expressed interest in him that his feelings had quickly become almost a worship of her. Which he could see, looking back, had been wrong on more than one level. It wasn't an excuse, but he realized now that he'd been innocent of the love between a man and a woman. He'd gotten caught up in the thrill of the romance. He and Mary hadn't had that much in common. Not like he and Millie. Millie thought like he did and laughed at the same silly things. Millie was so easy to be with, and he liked who he was when he was with her.

Gabriel was right. Elden and Millie needed to talk. He wanted to tell her that her desire to keep their betrothal a secret made him fear she wasn't sure she wanted to marry him. He would admit to her that it brought back his insecurities concerning Mary, and even if that wasn't fair, it was how he felt. He needed to confess that he wasn't as confident a man as he appeared to be.

Gott must have been thinking the same thing, because as Elden approached his farm, he spotted Millie at the end of their driveway at the mailbox. She was as pretty as ever with a blue scarf over her head, and when she saw him, she gave him a smile that made him light-headed. Because her smile was for him alone.

He eased his buggy up next to her and slid open the window. "Need a ride?" he asked.

Samson wiggled his way under Elden's feet and set his front paws on the windowsill to greet her.

Millie laughed. Her cheeks rosy from the cold, she stroked the bulldog's head. There was a light dusting of snow on her scarf and a wisp of blond hair on her cheek that was damp. He ached to touch it.

"A ride where?" Millie asked. "I've only come to our mailbox to see if *Dat*'s copy of the *Budget* arrived. It should have been here yesterday and he's in a bad way."

"You don't even have a coat on," Elden pointed out.

She tugged at her sweater. "I didn't think I needed it for such a short trip." She looked up. "But then it started snowing again."

Samson gave a little bark as if he agreed.

"All right, boy. Off," Elden ordered, pointing at the floor. The dog obeyed, making his way to his favorite place on the passenger seat so he could look out the window.

"I could give you a ride back to your house," Elden told Millie.

She held the mail against her so it wouldn't get wet, laughing. "Elden, I don't need a ride."

"Oll recht." He grinned. "It's good to see you, Millie. I got so used to seeing you every day that missing a few days makes me feel…a bit lost," he said.

She took a step closer and rested one hand on the windowsill. "I've missed you, too, Elden."

When she said it, he knew it was true and silently chastised himself for questioning her feelings for him. Maybe he hadn't been able to read Mary, but he felt like he was finding his way with Millie. "When can I see you?" he asked. "We need to talk." He didn't think this was the best place to have the conversation they needed to have. Besides, he told himself, he wanted to plan what he was going to say. He went on quickly before he lost his nerve. "Look, Millie, I know I probably should have waited to ask you to marry me until we'd been courting longer. But it just came out. You looked so beautiful that day and I've known for some time that I wanted to spend my life with you and—" He looked away, fearful he would tear up. What would she think of him, a grown man crying?

Her hand was on the sill beside his and she brushed his fingertips with his. *"Ya,* we should talk." She exhaled. "Because either we're betrothed or we're not. It's not something to hide." Now she was the one who looked away.

"Don't worry," he whispered. "We'll figure this out. Because I do love you, Millie."

She lifted her lashes to look into his eyes. "And I love you, Elden," she murmured.

"You do?" His heart fluttered and he broke into a grin. She loved him!

"*Ya*, Elden. I've loved you my whole life, I think."

"Oh, Millie." Tying up the reins, he opened the buggy door and stepped down and pulled her into his arms because he didn't think he could live another moment without holding her. She fit perfectly against him, and they stood in the falling snow with her head on his chest, her armful of mail between them.

"This is nice," she murmured.

Elden was too full of emotion to speak, so he just held her.

She was the one who came to her senses first. She gave a bubbly laugh and stepped back. "Enough of that." She looked up at him shyly. "If your mother or my father sees us, we'll both be in hot water."

"*Ya.*" He couldn't stop smiling, because everything really was going to be all right. Just as Gabriel had said. "When can I see you?"

"*Ach.*" She wiped at her face, which was wet from the snow. "We've so many projects to finish up before the Amish Christmas market on Saturday. And Jane and Beth have both caught terrible colds, so we're not getting our items to sell ready as quickly as we thought. Will you be there?"

"*Ya*, I'm selling my fresh-cut Christmas trees and some of the wreath frames. Might make some wreaths if I have time. I reserved an outside booth. You know, because of the trees." He slid his hands in his pockets, mostly so he wouldn't be tempted to hug her again. "I don't know if I'll be able to see you until it's over. JJ was going to help me but now he can't."

"We rented a table inside." She looked up at him. "We could do something after. I could ride there with my family and then you and I could go somewhere afterward."

"Good idea." He raised his eyebrows. "I think it's over at three. We could go out for an early supper. We've never eaten out together and we'll already be in town. There's this mint milkshake that's only available this time of year at one of the fast-food places. Want to go?"

Her eyes lit up. "I love mint milkshakes!" Then she grimaced. "Oh, but what about your mother? If she's going to the market? If you have to take her home first, I should go home with my family and we can leave from there."

"She may be going, I'm not sure. Knowing her, she won't want to miss it." He chuckled. "But I'll have someone else take her home. Don't worry about it." He looked into her eyes again and wished he could stand there forever with her. But she wasn't dressed for the snow in her thin sweater, and she was getting wet. "You should go in. You sure you don't want a ride?"

"No ride, Elden. I've two feet." She ran her hand down his coat sleeve. "I'll see you Saturday. *Ya?*"

"Saturday," he agreed and got into his buggy. But he didn't back out of her driveway right away. Instead, he sat there watching Millie walk up her lane, imagining what it would be like when her lane was his—

theirs—and then when he walked in the door at the end of each day, she would be waiting for him.

By noon Saturday, the Amish Christmas market was packed. Spence's Bazaar had rented out every available space inside the sprawling building as well as outside in a parking lot. Amish men and women were selling baked and canned goods, quilts, wooden toys and greenery. *Englishers* had also rented space and were selling all sorts of holiday frippery that was definitely not Plain. There were Christmas tree ornaments that flashed red, white and blue, plastic dolls in red velvet skirts, sweaters one could have their dog's name embroidered on while they waited, and so many Christmas stockings that it made Millie's head spin. There was Christmas music playing loudly from speakers and so many *Englishers* with their big voices that it was overwhelming.

Millie and her sisters were having a good sales day, which made up for all the chaos around them. Each of them had contributed in some way. They sold knitted hats, scarves and mittens, potpourri sachets from dry pine needles and jars of jam with pretty scraps of fabric and ribbons on the tops. Then they had baked goods: dozens of Christmas cookies as well as apple tarts and pecan sticky buns they'd made with the nuts they'd picked from their own trees.

At first it was fun, but as the day wore on, the Koffman sisters all began to look forward to returning home to their quieter, simpler lives. And Millie was looking forward to her date with Elden. A date with her betrothed. She had to keep reminding herself of that. She was engaged to be married. Unfortunately, she'd been so busy that she hadn't had a chance to go outside to say hello to Elden. It seemed like their line of customers never got any shorter, and without Jane and Beth, home sick, they worked nonstop selling their goods.

It wasn't until a few minutes before the market officially closed that Millie was finally able to catch her breath. She sat down on a metal chair and had a long drink of water. "My feet are so tired," she muttered, wishing now that she'd worn her leather shoes that were sturdier than the sneakers she'd chosen. "I almost wish I hadn't told Elden I'd go out with him tonight."

"Want me to go out with him instead?" Willa teased.

Millie laughed. "I think not."

"Are you leaving straight from here?" Eleanor tucked a handful of cash she'd counted into a tin box.

"I think so, but I'm not sure." Millie took another sip of water and fished a piece of gingerbread cookie from a bag of broken ones they'd brought along for snacking. The crowds had thinned out so that few shoppers were passing their table now. "I haven't gotten to talk to him yet. I saw him when I went to get our sandwiches and we waved to each other, but he was busy trimming branches off a tree for a woman carrying a dog in her pocketbook."

"I saw Lavinia earlier," Henry said. She was busy stacking empty wooden crates to take home. They'd sold nearly every single item they'd brought with them. The only items left were a few jars of pickled beets, a loaf of country white bread and a few bags of cookies. "She said something about going to the fabric store with Elsie and then home. I guess that means she's catching a ride with Gabriel."

"Why don't you go see what your plans are, Millie?" Eleanor suggested, counting another stack of money. There was relief all over their big sister's face. They had made a lot of money today.

"You sure?" Millie asked. "You don't want me to help clean up?"

"Not much to clean up, is there?" Cora looked up from a paperback book on local plants that she'd bought from a stall nearby. "We sold most everything."

The Christmas music that had been blasting for hours stopped suddenly in the middle of a song and they all seemed to sigh in unison. It felt like the sixth or seventh time they'd heard the song about a grandmother being trampled by a reindeer.

"Go on, Millie," Eleanor encouraged. "Let us know what you're doing once you know." She glanced around. "It won't take us long to finish up here. If we're not here when you return, we'll be at the buggy."

Millie snugged her black bonnet over her organza *kapp* and reached for her cloak in the pile behind them. The building that was little more than a pole shed had been warm enough when it was packed with people, but it was cool now. "Be right back," she said. She'd been so busy all day that she hadn't had time to think about her date, but now she could feel her excitement bubbling inside her.

He had mentioned the other day when they saw each other that they needed to talk. She imagined he meant about when they were going to tell others they were engaged, and she had decided she was going to tell him she was ready now. And maybe this would be a good time to ask him about his breakup with Mary. And to talk about when they should make an appointment to speak with their bishops. There was also the matter of when they wanted to marry. It wasn't the Amish way to have long courtships, but she wanted to know what he was thinking.

Millie tied her cloak as she walked away from the table, her gaze settling on an Amish woman she didn't know, cuddling a baby on her shoulder. The infant's head rested against its mother and Millie wondered what it would feel like to have her own baby. To have Elden's baby. The thought was scary, but it made her heart ache in an unfamiliar way.

Passing the woman with her child, Millie wove her way through the building where everyone else was breaking down their makeshift shops. She passed through one of the exit doors and crossed the paved parking lot toward where Elden was set up. She could see that every one of his trees was gone and the only thing left was a freestanding post he'd used to hang wreaths on.

As she walked, her eyes scanned for him and then she saw him, his back to her. She'd know him anywhere: his slender build, broad shoulders and blond hair sticking out from beneath his beanie. As she drew closer, she saw him gesturing and realized he was talking to someone. She was just about to call out to him when he moved and she recognized who it was.

Her breath was knocked from her and she froze. *It couldn't be.* Tears filled her eyes.

It was Mary. His betrothed. And even from this distance, she could hear Elden laughing. She saw him smiling down at the woman: the petite, beautiful Mary with her honey-colored hair and hazel eyes. And Mary was smiling at him the way a woman smiled at her beau. The way Millie smiled at him.

For a very brief time, Millie had thought Elden might really marry her. But, in her heart of hearts, she had known it would never happen. She had known that day when she had fallen over the fence that no matter how much she loved him, he would never be hers. She had known that men so perfect, so beautiful inside and out, didn't marry girls like her. They married perfect girls like Mary.

Millie found it difficult to catch her breath. She closed her eyes, fearing she might faint, and she hung her head, taking in great gulps of cold air.

Mary had returned for Elden.

And there he was smiling at her. Welcoming her home.

What did Millie do now? Did she walk away? She certainly wasn't going to make a scene. She cared too much for Elden to do that. And what would be the point, other than everyone talking later about how foolish Millie Koffman had been about a man who could never have been hers.

Nay, she was better than that. But she couldn't just walk away, either.

Millie took a deep, shuddering breath and forced herself to put one foot in front of the other. She walked right over to Mary and Elden, and without looking at him, she smiled at Mary and her perfect teeth and her perfect slender little face and said, "Mary, I didn't know you were back. Millie Koffman," she introduced herself.

"Good to see you again," Mary said in a melodic voice. Her eyes, however, suggested that she was trying to place Millie. She didn't seem to remember her, even though she'd lived within miles of Millie for almost a year. Of course that was because skinny girls like Mary didn't remember fat girls like Millie.

"Visiting for long?" Millie asked, afraid her face would crack from her smile.

"I—" Mary looked at Elden. "I'm not sure."

Millie turned toward Elden but didn't look at him because she couldn't bear it. "Could I speak to you?" she asked, not recognizing her own voice. This had to be one of the hardest things she had ever done in her life. As hard, as terrible, as saying goodbye to her mother.

Before Elden could respond, Millie walked to the edge of the parking lot, the wet snow slushy at her feet. The horses and cars and foot traffic had made a muck of the pristine snow and now it was soiled with dirt and manure and discarded candy wrappers and soda pop cans.

Her back was to him when he approached.

"What's wrong?"

He reached out to touch her shoulder as he walked around to face her and she pulled away. She couldn't let him touch her because if he did, surely she would shatter. And then no one would be able to pick up the pieces, not even her family who loved her.

"I release you," she said, her voice so soft that he leaned closer.

"What did you say?"

Still, she couldn't look at him. Instead, she focused on a greasy bit of snow on the toe of her boot. "I release you," she said louder. "From our betrothal agreement."

"You what?" he asked.

"I won't marry you," she said. "I… I don't want to marry you, Elden."

He just stood there, his arms at his side, and said nothing.

What was there to say?

Millie made it all the way to her buggy before she burst into tears.

Chapter Thirteen

Millie sat at the kitchen table and stared out the windows at the falling rain. The cold front that had brought the unexpected snow Thanksgiving week and continued through early December had finally passed and the temperatures had warmed up some.

She sighed and spun her ceramic mug between her hands. The peppermint tea Beth had made her had cooled, but she didn't want it anyway. The kitchen was warm with the scent of cinnamon rolls baking in the oven. At the counter, Jane was busy whipping up an orange cream cheese frosting for the top of the rolls. She'd made a batch of the frosting to try, adding orange zest to the recipe. She planned to prepare more rolls the following day to be popped into the oven Christmas morning.

By the time their family finished their morning devotionals, which would include reading the entire Christmas story from the Bible, the rolls would be ready to come out of the oven. Their mother's orange cinnamon rolls had been a Christmas tradition for as long as Millie could remember, and ordinarily, she would have been excited about the special treat. But since the day of the Christmas market, she hadn't been able to get excited about anything. That included her and Annie's annual tradition of making Christmas cards together to go along with the cookies, cakes and other treats their families would deliver on Christmas Eve. Millie was now waiting for her friend to arrive.

Continuing to stare out the window at the rivulets of rain on the glass, she listened to Jane humming a Christmas hymn as she worked. She wished she'd canceled with Annie. She wasn't in the mood for making Christmas cards. She wasn't in the mood to do anything but lie in her bed and cry, except that after ten days of crying she'd run out of tears. Now all she did was sit dry-eyed and stare, much the same way she had after their mother passed. This somehow felt worse, and she didn't know why. Maybe because her mother had gone to heaven and Elden was here in Honeycomb, in the arms of his girlfriend.

Millie lowered her head to her hands on the table. If Jane noticed, she didn't say anything, likely because she was afraid to. All her sisters tiptoed around Millie, whispering to each other, making her feel invisible. Which was okay with her because she wished she could just disappear. She hurt so badly that the pain was physical. She had so many feelings and confused thoughts in her head that it was hard sometimes for her to breathe.

The first couple of days after Millie broke up with

Elden, her sisters had tried to be helpful. They had attempted to talk to her, to make her things she liked to eat. They had even offered to do her chores so she could rest. They insisted over and over that Elden would come to her as soon as he came to his senses, that what Millie had seen with him and Mary had all been a misunderstanding.

Millie hadn't expected Elden to come to her after their breakup because there had been no misunderstanding. Mary had come back to him. The hows and whys didn't matter and there was no need for Millie to continue to analyze the situation.

Of course, she couldn't help herself. All she did was think about Elden and why he had chosen Mary over her. She even tried to place the blame elsewhere. She wondered if Lavinia had brought Mary back to Honeycomb. Maybe Lavinia had written to Mary and asked her to return to Honeycomb because she preferred her son marry her than Millie.

But what did it matter how it had happened? Elden was with Mary now. Of course a tiny part of her hoped he might come and tell her how she'd misread what she'd seen between him and Mary that day. But he hadn't come by in ten days' time, which was proof that she hadn't misunderstood anything.

Initially after the breakup, Millie's sisters thought that the relationship could still be mended. But Elden hadn't sought Millie out and Willa had heard that Mary was back in Honeycomb to stay. Then her sisters had changed their approach. They'd suggested Millie should go to him. For closure, they said. Eleanor had sat on the edge of Millie's bed one night, something she had never done in her life, and talked to her in the dark. Her oldest sister advised Millie to speak with Elden so that she could move on. So he could move on and know there were no hard feelings. Eleanor had said that no matter how painful it would be to speak to him about what had happened with Mary, talking with him would allow Millie to emotionally set Elden aside and prepare herself for the husband *Gott* had planned for her.

But Millie couldn't do it. Even though what Eleanor said made sense, Millie couldn't bring herself to confront Elden. She had all sorts of justifications, like it would only make her feel worse or he wouldn't want to speak to her anyway. And when her thoughts turned ugly, she told herself she certainly wasn't going to go to make him feel better for returning to Mary. Why did he deserve to feel better when she was in the depths of despair?

The moment ugly thoughts like those crossed her mind, Millie squeezed her eyes shut and prayed to *Gott* to take such darkness from her heart. She didn't want to be that woman. She didn't want to be a self-centered, spiteful fat girl. She just wanted to be herself again. She feared, however, that she never again would be the hopeful woman she once was.

The sound of buggy wheels caught Millie's attention and she glanced out the window.

"Looks like Annie is here," Jane said cheerfully. "Cora and Beth set everything up in the parlor on a card table for you. Cora got you some new glue and some glitter that looks like snow. And there's lots of card stock and old Christmas cards that you can cut up to make your new cards." She returned to her frosting, then spun back around to Millie. "Could you make one for Aunt Judy and Uncle Cyrus? I'm going to give them some of these rolls. So they can have something special for Christmas morning, too."

"*Ya*, we can make a card for them," Millie said without much enthusiasm. Through the window, she watched Henry come out of the barn in a rain slicker and grab the halter of Annie's horse. Once Annie was hurrying toward the door with a big basket on her arm, Henry led the horse and buggy into the barn.

There was a rap on the mudroom door and Annie let herself in. Millie's mother had often referred to Annie as her eighth daughter. When *Mam* had been in a teasing mood, she'd refer to Annie as her *favorite* daughter.

"*Hallo!*" Annie sang.

"*Ya*, in the kitchen." Millie didn't rise from her chair. She heard the rustle of Annie's coat, and her friend walked into the room.

"*Hallo*, Jane!"

"*Goot* afternoon, Annie." Jane glanced Millie's way. "Glad you're here. We all are. Millie could use some cheering up."

She was about to tell Jane that she was sorry that her heartbreak was inconveniencing others within the household, but she held her tongue. A few months ago, their preacher had talked about the evil in the world and that parishioners needed to be vigilant to recognize it. Such mean thoughts made Millie fear the devil was too close to her for comfort. Because what if he was the one putting those unkind thoughts in her head?

"I brought some more old greeting cards." Annie set down her basket. "And new envelopes. And *Mam* sent some markers in green and red and silver and gold. She bought them especially for us."

Millie slowly rose from her chair. "That was nice of her," she said, trying to sound enthusiastic.

Annie turned to her, searching her gaze. "How are you?"

Millie's lowered lip quivered and she bit down on it.

"Oh, Millie." Annie threw her arms around her friend in a generous hug. "I am so sorry. You still haven't talked to him?"

Millie shook her head. "He doesn't want to talk to me. If he did, he'd have come by now."

Annie stepped back, her brow furrowing. "You want me to go over there right now and give him a piece of my mind? Because I will. You know I will. I can't stand that he's hurt you this way."

Millie shook her head, her gaze falling to the hardwood floor between them. "What would be the sense in talking? Now that Mary's back—" She didn't finish her sentence.

"And they're definitely courting again?" Annie's gaze flitted to Jane, who was all ears. "Jane?"

"I've heard talk," Millie's little sister said, her gaze moving to Millie, then back to Annie. "But nobody knows what's going on. I do know that Mary and Elden haven't been seen out together."

"Of course not. He's not a bad person," Millie said softly. "He would keep it quiet, at least for a little while." She felt tears sting the backs of her eyelids. "He's not trying to hurt me. He's not like that."

Annie gritted her teeth. "I'll tell you one thing. I'd like to hurt him right now." She raised a pudgy fist.

Something close to a laugh burst out of Millie. She grabbed Annie's hand and lowered it to the girl's side. "Annie, we don't hit people. That's not who we are."

Annie exhaled, flexing her fingers. "I know. I didn't say I was *going* to do it. Only that I wanted to." Her tone softened. "Do you still want to make the cards, or do you not feel like it?" Her eyes filled with concern. "We don't have to do it this year if you don't want to. I'll stay and visit with you, but we don't have to do anything."

Millie stood there for a moment in indecision. She didn't feel like making the cards, but if she didn't, what was she going to do but sit around and mope? Maybe keeping her hands busy would keep her mind active and off Elden. She forced a half smile. "*Nay*. Let's do them. Come on." She headed out of the kitchen. "Beth and Cora were nice enough to get us all set up in the parlor."

"I'll bring a plate of cookies in and some hot chocolate," Jane called after them.

Her words made Millie's heavy heart a little lighter. It was true she had lost Elden, and she knew, no matter what anyone said, she would never love another man.

But Jane and Annie reminded her of how blessed she was to have so many others to love and be loved by. And she'd just have to be content with that.

Elden rested on his back, his head under the kitchen sink, and tightened the connection on the new drain-pipe he'd installed. "Could you turn the water on, *Mam*?" he asked, his voice strange in his ears. It sounded so heavy. "To be sure there's no leak."

His mother, who had been hovering over him the entire time he was making the repair, turned on the faucet, and he heard water running down the drain. He studied the new PVC pipe at the connections and deeming it didn't leak, slid out from under the sink. Rolling onto his hands and knees, he gathered his tools and the damp towel he'd used to mop up any excess water. "Good as new," he proclaimed, standing.

"*Ach*, I can't believe I was so foolish to push the compost bucket against the pipe and crack it. *Danki, sohn*. What would I do without you? Now I can make a proper Christmas Eve supper."

He returned the plumber's glue and tools to his toolbox on the counter and handed her the wet towel. "No need to cook. I'm not that hungry. We can have the leftover brats and sauerkraut from yesterday." When she didn't respond, he turned to look at her.

She'd thrown the towel over a chair and was standing behind him, arms crossed over her chest the way she had when he was a little boy and she was displeased with him. "You have to eat. You haven't eaten well since—" She stopped and started again. "I'd say it's time you saw the doctor, but I don't think he can fix what ails you."

Elden held up his hand. "Please, *Mam*. Let's not start this again. What's done is done. I'm fine." He turned from the counter, his toolbox in his hand, thinking he would return it to his workshop where he could be alone and stay there until supper.

But his mother blocked his way. "*Nay*, you're not fine, Elden. I've never seen you in a state like this. Not even after the business with Mary."

He closed his eyes for a moment, praying for patience. He opened his eyes. "Please let's not talk about this."

"We *are* going to talk about it because I'm tired of watching you mope about."

Realizing he wasn't going to be able to get away from her, he set his toolbox down hard on the counter. "I'm *not* moping," he argued, an edge to his voice.

Of course she was right; he was moping. All he did was mope. His heart was broken. Millie Koffman had broken his heart. The interesting thing about it was that he had believed that Mary had broken his heart, only to learn now that what he had experienced after that breakup was a bruised heart. The difference was vast. Without Millie, he felt lost, unmoored, and a shell of himself. Only now, in a depth of pain that he felt physically, did he understand what it meant to truly love a woman. And lose her.

"It's time you did something," his mother went on. "I don't care what you do but do something. Go talk to Millie and find out if this can be mended. The fact that you refuse to even talk to her is beyond my understanding," she fumed. "I always thought you were a bright boy, but now, I admit I may have overestimated you."

Her words almost made him laugh. This was supposed to make him feel better? "I thought you'd be happy we broke up."

"Why would I be happy?" she asked incredulously. "You're miserable. No mother wants her son to be unhappy."

"But you didn't like Millie. Not from that day we had that first supper with the Koffmans."

She planted both hands on her hips. "When did I say I didn't like Millie? I never said I didn't like Millie. She's a sweet girl."

Elden squared off with her, imitating her stance with his arms crossed over his chest. "Come to think of it, you didn't like Mary, either."

Lavinia pointed at him. "Now, *that*'s true. I didn't like Mary, at least not for you. She's a shallow, selfish girl. And she makes a terrible *hassenpfeffer*."

He laughed without humor. "You'd judge a woman's character by how well she cooks rabbit? You don't even like *hassenpfeffer*."

"We're not talking about rabbit," she quipped. "We're talking about you. You need to speak to that girl. You didn't even tell me why she broke up with you. Did you have a fight? You know quarrels are just part of two people getting to know each other. And don't think that after you're married there won't be disagreements. Your father and I never had a cross word between us until after we were married. And you of all people knew we could disagree, but we loved and respected each other."

"Millie and I didn't have a fight."

She shook her head so hard that the strings of her kapp *whipped* about. "You didn't have a fight? Then why did she break up with you?"

"I don't know," he blurted. Emotion rose in Elden's throat and he looked away.

"You don't know?" she repeated. "What do you mean you don't know? That's ridiculous. It's been nearly two weeks and you haven't bothered to march over there and ask her why?"

It wasn't that Elden had no idea. He suspected that it had something to do with Mary stopping to speak with him at the Christmas market. She'd just returned to Honeycomb to spend Christmas with her cousins and she had wanted to say hello. He had gotten the feeling that she wanted to broach the subject of them dating again, but when he told her he was betrothed, she'd seemed genuinely happy for him. That hadn't stopped her from flirting with him, but that was just how Mary was. She flirted with everyone.

The thing was, Millie hadn't asked him why Mary was there. It was a misunderstanding that could have been easily set right. But what would have been the point? The next time she thought he'd done something wrong, she'd break up with him again. And what if he did actually do something wrong, which was bound to happen at some point. After all, he was human, with human failings. He was going to make mistakes in their relationship no matter how much he loved her.

But maybe his failings were too great, he had decided. Mary had broken up with him. Millie had broken up with him. Maybe he wasn't the kind of man women wanted to marry. Maybe it was best he accept being a bachelor and focus on caring for his mother and the farm his father had left him.

"Elden? Elden! Are you listening to a word I say?" his mother asked.

Elden blinked. He hadn't been listening.

"I'm telling you, you need to go speak to Millie. I imagine she's as miserable as you are. Maybe she's changed her mind and doesn't know how to tell you that she made a terrible mistake. And if she hasn't changed her mind, at least you'll know that." She threw up her hand. "Then you can move on. And stop this moping."

"I am not moping." Elden emphasized each word. "And I'm not going to the Koffmans'."

"Fine!" His mother threw her arms up in the air in surrender, turned around and walked away.

"*Fine*," he repeated. He picked up his toolbox again. "While I have my plumbing tools, I may as well check that faucet in the upstairs bathroom." He watched her march out of the kitchen and into the laundry room, where she grabbed her wool cloak. "Where are you going?" he asked.

She threw on her cloak and began to tie it beneath her chin, her motions jerky.

"You're not going to the Koffmans', are you?" he

asked, suddenly feeling panicky. "*Mutter*, you can't go there."

"I'm going to Trudy's," she said sternly. She marched back into the kitchen and scooped up a plate of rice cereal treats she'd decorated with white chocolate and red and green sprinkles and dropped it into a basket.

"It's going to get dark before you make it home," he called after her as she strode out of the kitchen again. Her friend Trudy lived on the property behind them, but there was an old logging road they used to pass between the two farms. "Take a flashlight!"

In response, she slammed the back door on her way out.

Chapter Fourteen

Late afternoon on Christmas Eve, Millie sat at the kitchen table with her *dat*, a checkerboard between them. Behind them, Eleanor was tidying up the counter and putting away clean dishes. Millie rested her elbow on the table, her chin in her hand, as she watched him contemplate his next move. Or was he daydreaming, she wondered. He stared at the board, but his eyes were unfocused.

Millie glanced at the wall clock, which seemed to have been ticking in slow motion all day. In another hour, it would be time to begin preparing their supper. She glanced out the big windows that looked out over the barnyard. The rain had ended that morning, and according to Henry, the temperature had dropped. Jane wanted snow for Christmas Day even though it wasn't in the forecast.

Millie's attention returned to her father. "*Dat*," she said gently. "It's your move."

He pushed his round, wire-frame glasses higher on

his nose and looked at her. He'd aged five years since their mother had died. She wondered if her father's confusion was caused by the loss of his beloved wife, or because of the dementia. Either way, it was sad.

"You know that I know your mother's dead, right?" he said.

His comment surprised her. "*Ya*," she murmured, not sure she believed him. "I know."

"I just like to pretend she isn't sometimes." He sighed. "She always loved Christmas. She loved everything about it—the baking, the sewing, the visiting and the celebration of Christ's birth." He worked his jaw. "She especially loved those orange cinnamon rolls she always made for Christmas morning."

Millie covered his veined, thin hand with hers. "Jane made the rolls. We'll still have them tomorrow morning after our devotions."

He smiled tenderly, his eyes rheumy. "*Goot.* That would make my Aggie happy." He hesitated and then went on. "You know she wants her girls to be happy. She wants all of us to be happy. I try to remind myself of that when I miss her too much."

Millie couldn't help but smile as she stared at the checkerboard. "I know, *Dat*," she said, patting his hand.

"Uh-oh," he responded, his tone suddenly childish.

She looked up at him, wondering what had brought on the change. "What is it?"

"A storm blowing in."

"What?" she said, glancing out the window, then back at him. The sky was gray and cloudless, but the trees were barely bending in the breeze. "I don't think it's going to storm."

"Oh, it's going to be a storm all right. See the look on her face?" He pointed.

"What are you talking about, *Dat*?" Millie looked out the window again.

Then she saw her. A tall, thick woman in a black cloak and black bonnet striding determinedly toward the back door, a basket on her elbow. Lavinia.

Millie came out of her chair, almost knocking it over. "Ellie!" she breathed. She could barely find her voice. "It's Lavinia." She made for the hall, not even taking the time to push in her chair.

"Lavinia?" Eleanor dried her hands on a dish towel. "What's she doing here on Christmas Eve?"

"Maybe come to play checkers," their father suggested, which in any other circumstances might have made them laugh.

"She didn't come to play checkers, *Dat*." Eleanor looked to Millie, who was nearly out of the kitchen. "Where are you going?"

"I don't know. But I don't want to hear what she has to say." Millie covered her ears with her hands, panic fluttering in her chest. "I don't want to hear about Elden and Mary. She's probably here to announce their betrothal."

"Oh, Millie, stop. She wouldn't come here to tell us Elden—"

A loud rap at the back door drowned out Eleanor's last words. The knock was immediately followed by a series of bangs. "*Hallo! Hallo*, it's Lavinia! Can I come in? Coming in!" she hollered and the back door opened.

"I'm not here!" Millie whispered harshly and ran down the hallway.

"Lavinia! What a surprise," Millie heard Eleanor greet from the kitchen. "Come in and warm yourself."

When she reached the parlor door, Millie ducked in. But then, her curiosity got the better of her, and she hid out of sight, eavesdropping.

"I brought these for you, Felty. They're the ones with the sprinkles on top," Lavinia shouted. "The kind you told me you like." She was speaking louder than necessary, something Millie had noticed Lavinia had been doing frequently with her father. As if he would understand better if she said things louder. The funny thing was that his hearing was better than Lavinia's.

"Ah, more rice cereal bars," Eleanor said. "How nice. We'll have them after supper tonight."

"I'm having one now," their father announced.

"Let me take your cloak, Lavinia. Would you like a cup of tea? Coffee?"

Millie heard Lavinia removing her coat and handing it to Eleanor.

"I think I would like tea. And maybe a little snack? I know Jane's got cookies or something around here. I was expecting a nice big tin of homemade Christmas cookies from you and then my son mucked things up, didn't he?"

What was she talking about, Millie wondered. What had Elden said to her? Did Lavinia think Elden was the one who had broken up with her? The remarkable thing was that her words suggested she was *not* pleased with the breakup.

A chair scraped and Millie heard Lavinia drop heavily into it. "I've come to talk to you about Millie, Eleanor. It's time someone with a little sense butted into this mess. I think you and I both have sense, don't you?"

"*Goot*," Millie's father said, his mouth full. "Having another."

Millie heard Eleanor walk into the mudroom, then back into the kitchen. "I'm sorry, Lavinia, but I can't talk about Millie behind her back," she said carefully. "This sounds like you need to talk to her."

"Fine," Lavinia huffed. "Millie? Where are you?" she called loudly. "I know very well you're here! I saw you from the window, running to get away from me!"

Millie felt her cheeks grow hot, and she squeezed her eyes shut, embarrassed the widow had caught her.

"Why don't I find Millie?" Eleanor said.

"Or just call her to get in here. You know she's hiding in the back of the house."

Millie considered trying to sneak upstairs, but before she could make a dash for the steps, she heard Eleanor's unmistakable gait.

"Millie?" Eleanor called in a whisper.

Millie stepped into the hall, staring at her big sister, round-eyed.

"I suppose you heard all that." Eleanor stopped in front of Millie. "I don't know what's going on or what she wants from us, but I think you should talk to her."

Millie's gazed flitted toward the kitchen, then back to her sister. "I'm afraid of what she might say."

"So afraid that you won't talk to her, even if there's a chance," Eleanor whispered, "that you might be able to get Elden back?"

"I don't want him now, not after he's gone back to Mary," Millie hissed back.

"*Ach*, I see." Eleanor met her gaze with a hard stare. "How did *Mam* put it? You're willing to cut off your nose to spite your face?"

Millie hung her head and they were both quiet for a moment. She could hear Lavinia talking in the kitchen.

"Don't eat them all, Felty!" Lavinia told him. "There will be none for anyone else. Give me one."

Millie met Eleanor's gaze. "Do you think there's a chance?" she asked, her heart pounding.

"I don't know, but I think it's worth hearing what his mother has to say. Don't you?"

Millie nodded and Eleanor gave her a big hug. "Come on," Eleanor said. "Lavinia's the one who ought to be scared. Taking on the Koffman girls."

A smile came unexpectedly to Millie and she followed her big sister down the hall.

"There you are, Millie," Lavinia declared, munching on a rice cereal bar. "I thought I was going to have to play hide-and-seek with you. Sit down."

She pulled out a chair beside her and Millie felt as if she had no choice but to sit.

"I'll make tea for all of us," Eleanor offered.

"I want hot chocolate," their father declared. "With marshmallows. And don't skimp. It's Christmas Eve."

"I'm not going to futz about with you, Millie." Lavinia took a napkin from a basket on the table and wiped the sticky crumbs from her mouth. "I'm here because that ridiculous son of mine won't come." She pursed her lips. "Why did you break up with him?"

Millie was so surprised by the abrupt question that it took her a moment to respond. But, if Lavinia could be so curt, why couldn't she? "Because Mary came back to him. I saw them together and they were laughing, and it was obvious she was still in love with him."

Lavinia rolled her eyes. "The two of you belong together. Neither of you have any sense. You know she was the one who broke up with him, right? Said he wasn't good enough for her. Thought she could do better."

Millie blinked in disbelief. "I… I thought… People said you broke them up. That you didn't think she was good enough for him."

"Second part was true. She wasn't. Isn't." Lavinia waved in dismissal. "A smart girl like you, you'd think you'd have enough sense not to listen to gossip. It's rarely accurate. Though I wasn't surprised when I heard people thought I was the one responsible."

Millie's brow furrowed. "You knew people were saying you broke them up? And you didn't correct them?"

"And what? Tell people that *she* broke up with him? I knew how much he was struggling with the rejection. Why make it worse by telling people it was her and not me?" She shrugged. "What do I care what people say about me? I know the truth." She pointed heavenward. "And *Gott* knows." She met Millie's gaze. "But none of that matters. What matters is you talking some sense into my boy."

Millie's respect for Lavinia had increased tenfold in a matter of seconds. Elden had insisted his mother had a good heart, and now Millie saw it. But she still didn't understand Lavinia. "I'm confused," she said. "I thought you didn't want him to marry me. You're always watching me, criticizing me."

Lavinia snorted. "This isn't about me, but if you want to marry Elden, you best get used to my ways. I don't mean anything by my words. I just say what I'm thinking at the moment." She put her hand on Millie's. "I like you. And more importantly, you like my son. *Nay.* You love him. That Mary Yost, she never loved him. Only person she loves is herself."

Their father reached into the basket of treats and Lavinia pulled it away before he could grab another. "I told you that's enough, Felty." She looked back at Millie. "You misunderstood what you saw that day at the market. Maybe Mary did return from Kentucky hoping to find her way back to my Elden, but he only had eyes for you by then. We've not seen hide nor hair of her since the Christmas market."

Millie stared at the older woman. "You haven't?"

"*Nay*, and since you broke up with Elden, all he's done is mope around the house. Barely speaks, barely eats. Not even that dog of his can cheer him up." Lavinia sat back in her chair. "I think my son's too afraid to talk to you. And that's on me, I suppose. I should have raised him better. His father always said I spoiled him. And maybe I did." She crossed her arms. "So, what do you say? Will you at least talk to him so he knows what happened?"

Millie's heart was beating so hard in her chest that she could barely hear herself think.

"Well?" Lavinia demanded.

Millie looked at Eleanor, who was leaning against the counter. She could tell by the look on her big sister's face what she was thinking.

Before she lost her nerve, Millie got to her feet.

"That'a girl," Lavinia said. "You make this right and you and I will make a good pair. We'll handle him. He has a soft heart. He's a hard worker. But he's still a man." She pulled the basket toward her and took out two treats, handing one to Millie's father. "Practically gone now, Felty. You may as well have another."

Trembling, Millie walked over to Eleanor. All she could think of was what a terrible mistake she had made. How could she have done such a thing to Elden, to have judged him without even asking him what had taken place with Mary? Her decision, she realized, had been about herself and not him, not them. How could she have thought so little of herself as to have assumed he didn't want her?

"What are you standing there, for?" Eleanor asked, the slightest hint of a smile on her face. "Go talk to him. Lavinia will stay here with me to give you two some privacy." She looked over Millie's shoulder. "Won't you, Lavinia?" Her tone was firm.

"No need for me to go." Lavinia munched on her treat. "Already been down that road. He won't listen to me."

Eleanor grasped Millie's hands and looked into her eyes, smiling. "Talk to him," she said softly. "If your love is true, and I think it is, together you can find a way through this."

Millie whipped around, practically running for the mudroom. Behind her, she heard her father get out of his chair and a moment later, he was beside her, taking his barn coat from a peg.

"*Dat*, where are you going?"

"With you. To talk some sense into that boy."

Millie pulled on her cloak. "*Dat*, you stay here. Ellie!" she called. "Tell *Dat* he has to stay here."

Eleanor came to the doorway. "*Dat*—"

"It doesn't matter if I forget to brush my teeth sometimes," he interrupted, stepping into his boots as he slipped into his coat. "I'm still the father. And I'm still the head of this household, and I'm going."

Millie started to protest and then gave in. So what if her father went? All she wanted to do was to get to Elden now. To apologize. To tell him how sorry she was that she had made such a muck of things. "Fine." She pulled on her boots.

"Millie, if—" Eleanor said.

"*Nay*, it's all right if he comes. He can't make a bigger mess of this than I have."

Grinning, Millie's father followed her down the porch steps and ten minutes later, they walked into Elden's barnyard.

The bulldog spotted them from the barn door that was half-open and barked and raced toward them. "There's my boy! That's my good dog," *Dat* said, rushing to greet Samson.

Elden walked out of the barn. Seeing Millie, he halted, his arms hanging at his sides. He looked awful. He looked tired and so sad that she had to swallow hard to keep her tears at bay. But seeing him also made her heart swell with her love for him and she was glad she had come, no matter the outcome.

She walked toward him and when she reached him, as afraid as she was by what his reaction might be, she met his gaze bravely.

He groaned. "My mother came to your house."

She nodded.

He closed his eyes for a moment and pressed his hand to his forehead. "I'm sorry. She told me she was going to her friend Trudy's. I should have known better."

"*Nay*, I'm glad she came. We need to talk, Elden, because I made a terrible mistake. I saw you and Mary together and she was flirting with you and you were smiling and..." Against her will, the tears came anyway. "And I thought you'd rather be with her than me."

"Millie—"

"*Nay*," she interrupted, clasping her hands together. "Let me finish before I lose my nerve."

"At least come into the barn. It's cold out here." He led her inside, leaving the doors open.

Millie watched her father throw a stick for Samson to fetch, then followed Elden inside. "I broke up with

you because I had so little confidence in myself—"
she shrugged "—in your love for me, that I thought
that even if it wasn't Mary you would rather have, it
would be some other girl. The next girl who flirted
with you. It sounds silly even saying it out loud now,
Elden, but I broke our betrothal so you couldn't."

"Why would I break up with you, Millie? I told
you I loved you. I asked you to marry me." His brow
creased beneath his knit cap as he tried to comprehend. "Why would you think even for a moment that
I didn't want you?"

Her lower lip trembled. "I don't know. Because
I'm fat and ugly and...*fat*," she repeated.

"Oh, Millie." He put his arms around her and held
her tight. "I'm so sorry. I'm not good at this, at courting. This is my fault. I should have told you how beautiful you are every day. How smart and capable and
so perfect for me."

Millie clung to him, breathing in deeply the male
scent of him as her tears dampened his coat.

"This isn't your fault. It's mine." He leaned back
to look into her eyes, but he didn't let go of her. "I
knew this had to do with Mary. At least, indirectly.
I should have followed you that day and made you
talk to me. Every day since you broke up with me,
I've told myself I should go to you, but I was scared."

"Of me? Why?" she breathed.

"Because...because I didn't think I was good
enough for you, Millie. You're not the only one who
struggles with self-confidence. After Mary broke up
with me, I believed no woman would want me. I ra-

tionalized that if I wasn't good enough for her, how could I be good enough for anyone. Then I fell in love with you and dreamed of a life with you, but I worried you'd break up with me, too. And when you did—" He took a deep breath and exhaled. "When you did, I thought—I don't know what I thought. That I was unlovable?"

"Oh, Elden. What a mess we've made of this." She laughed through her tears as she hugged him tightly. "I'm so sorry my insecurities made you feel insecure. I do love you. I love you so much." She gazed into his blue-gray eyes. "And I'll marry you, if you'll have me."

"*If* I'll have you?" He laughed. "I think all I've ever wanted is you, Millie. And I think that together we can work on this, on believing in ourselves. I know I can, just knowing you believe in me." He brushed a lock of blond hair that had escaped her headscarf. "I really want to kiss you right now. Can I kiss you?"

She nodded and closed her eyes. As his mouth touched hers for the very first time, she felt as if she was melting into his arms.

"This is why a father needs to escort his daughter," her father said, startling them both.

Elden and Millie parted, both looking sheepish, and her father walked into the barn, the bulldog at his feet. "This mean we're having a wedding at my place?" he asked, looking from one to the other.

"Um…it does," Elden managed. "With your permission."

Her father smiled, lifting his shoulders with excitement. "A wedding. That's just what the Koffman family needs now." He looked upward. "Don't we, Aggie?" Then he turned to the open door. "Look! It's snowing!" He laughed like a child and rushed back outside, the dog at his heels.

"I think that was a yes," Elden said, meeting Millie's gaze again. He held out his hand and led her out of the barn and into the snow. "Merry Christmas, my love."

"Merry Christmas," she whispered, and then she rested her head on Elden's shoulder, knowing he would be her husband and that they would have as happy a marriage as she had ever dreamed of.

Epilogue

Two years later

Millie walked into the kitchen that smelled of evergreens she and Elden had cut fresh from their woods and of the cinnamon, cloves and orange peels that simmered on the back of the woodstove. Chilled, she went straight to the stove to warm her hands.

"There you are." Elden greeted her with a warm smile. He was putting away the last of the clean dishes from their Christmas Eve supper. Because they were spending all of Christmas Day with her family, they had decided to have a quiet night at home alone tonight.

"Here I am," she smiled back. Although they'd been married more than a year, she still couldn't believe this handsome man had chosen her above all the other unmarried women in Honeycomb. But she was so thankful every day that he had.

Elden carried his mother's blue onion serving platter to the dish cabinet. "How'd it go? Everything *oll recht*?"

She rubbed her hands together to warm them. She didn't know if they'd have snow for Christmas, but it was certainly bitterly cold outside. "*Oll goot.* She's tucked in for the night, a warm brick at her feet and hot water bottle under the quilts."

"No fussing?" he asked.

She grinned. "A bit, but you know how she is. I said Livie, it's bedtime." After they married, Millie hadn't been able to call Lavinia "Mother" as many married women called their mothers-in-law, so she had shortened Lavinia to Livie. Surprisingly, his mother liked Millie's pet name for her. "I said, 'You can stay up all night if you want, but we're going to bed.'" She shrugged. "I gave her the Bible and she seemed content. But she kept telling me to send you over to get her if we need her. She said she didn't care if it was the middle of the night. I told her we'd be just fine, you and I."

It had been Elden's idea to build a *grossmammi* house a short walk from the big house before he and Millie were married. Because they had chosen to wait a full year after they began courting to wed, he'd had the time to build the small one-story house for his mother. And thanks to his thoughtfulness, Millie, as a new bride, never had spent a single night under the same roof with her mother-in-law. "How are things here?"

Closing the dish cabinet door, he walked over to stand beside her in front of the stove, the scent of applewood filling the cozy kitchen to mingle with the other smells of Christmas. *"Goot."* He grinned, obviously proud of himself. "All tucked in and sound asleep last I checked."

"And David didn't give you any trouble? No fussing?" They both smiled at the little joke between them. Named after Elden's father, David was often fussy and there were times when Lavinia was able to soothe him when neither of them could. Elden believed that his son's nature was similar to his grandmother's, so the baby gravitated to her.

"No fussing," Elden confirmed. "David snuggled right in next to Aggie and they're both sound asleep. Thank you for walking *Mam* back to her house and getting her situated. By the time supper was over, I was close to being out of patience with her."

Millie gazed into his eyes, unable to stop smiling. She didn't think she'd stopped grinning since the day they were wed. "You'd run out of patience for your mother, but you still had patience for two *bopplis* barely three months old?"

He shrugged. "Not much for me to do. You'd already fed, changed them and dressed them in their sleeping gowns. All Samson and I had to do was put them to bed. Easy enough. I rocked one and Samson rocked the other."

Millie laughed and poked her husband in the side. Since they'd married, he'd filled out a bit and become more muscular. All the good food Millie cooked for him, he said. "You're not supposed to rock them to sleep every night. They need to learn to settle on their own."

"You hear that, boy?" Elden said to Samson, who lay on a rag rug beside the stove. "She doesn't want us rocking our babies."

The bulldog cocked his head as if as perplexed as his master.

Millie laughed and wagged her finger. "The two of you best not come whining to me a year from now when the babies are still not sleeping through the night."

"Speaking of sleeping through the night." Elden glanced at the clock on the wall. "We best get to bed. They'll be awake in another three hours, wanting to be fed again."

"*Ach*, you're right." Millie turned to look at the kitchen. "What's left to be done before we go upstairs?"

"Not a thing." Elden took her by the hand and led her toward the staircase. As they walked out of the kitchen, he stopped to turn off the oil lamp.

A warm, velvety darkness settled around them and Millie moved closer to her husband. "*Danki*," she whispered.

His breath was warm on her cheek. "For what?"

"For everything," she said. "For this home…our babies and for—" Emotion rose in her throat, and it took her a moment to speak again. "For loving me, Elden."

He leaned closer, his voice deep and rich and gentle. "You make it so easy to love you, Millie. Thank you for loving me. For making me a better man than I was. For helping me believe I could be a man worthy of your love."

And then her husband kissed her, and she wished the moment would last until Christmas morning. And the Christmas morning after that and beyond.

* * * * *

Get 3 FREE REWARDS!

We'll send you 2 FREE Books plus a FREE Mystery Gift.

FREE Value Over **$20**

Both the **Love Inspired®** and **Love Inspired® Suspense** series feature compelling novels filled with inspirational romance, faith, forgiveness and hope.

YES! Please send me 2 FREE novels from the Love Inspired or Love Inspired Suspense series and my FREE gift (gift is worth about $10 retail). After receiving them, if I don't wish to receive any more books, I can return the shipping statement marked "cancel." If I don't cancel, I will receive 6 brand-new Love Inspired Larger-Print books or Love Inspired Suspense Larger-Print books every month and be billed just $6.49 each in the U.S. or $6.74 each in Canada. That is a savings of at least 16% off the cover price. It's quite a bargain! Shipping and handling is just 50¢ per book in the U.S. and $1.25 per book in Canada.* I understand that accepting the 2 free books and gift places me under no obligation to buy anything. I can always return a shipment and cancel at any time by calling the number below. The free books and gift are mine to keep no matter what I decide.

Choose one: ☐ **Love Inspired Larger-Print**
(122/322 BPA GRPA)

☐ **Love Inspired Suspense Larger-Print**
(107/307 BPA GRPA)

☐ **Or Try Both!**
(122/322 & 107/307 BPA GRRP)

Name (please print)

Address _____ Apt. #

City _____ State/Province _____ Zip/Postal Code

Email: Please check this box ☐ if you would like to receive newsletters and promotional emails from Harlequin Enterprises ULC and its affiliates. You can unsubscribe anytime.

Mail to the Harlequin Reader Service:
IN U.S.A.: P.O. Box 1341, Buffalo, NY 14240-8531
IN CANADA: P.O. Box 603, Fort Erie, Ontario L2A 5X3

Want to try 2 free books from another series! Call 1-800-873-8635 or visit www.ReaderService.com.

*Terms and prices subject to change without notice. Prices do not include sales taxes, which will be charged (if applicable) based on your state or country of residence. Canadian residents will be charged applicable taxes. Offer not valid in Quebec. This offer is limited to one order per household. Books received may not be as shown. Not valid for current subscribers to the Love Inspired or Love Inspired Suspense series. All orders subject to approval. Credit or debit balances in a customer's account(s) may be offset by any other outstanding balance owed by or to the customer. Please allow 4 to 6 weeks for delivery. Offer available while quantities last.

Your Privacy—Your information is being collected by Harlequin Enterprises ULC, operating as Harlequin Reader Service. For a complete summary of the information we collect, how we use this information and to whom it is disclosed, please visit our privacy notice located at corporate.harlequin.com/privacy-notice. From time to time we may also exchange your personal information with reputable third parties. If you wish to opt out of this sharing of your personal information, please visit readerservice.com/consumerchoice or call 1-800-873-8635. **Notice to California Residents**—Under California law, you have specific rights to control and access your data. For more information on these rights and how to exercise them, visit corporate.harlequin.com/california-privacy.

LIRLIS23

Get 3 FREE REWARDS!

We'll send you 2 FREE Books plus a FREE Mystery Gift.

FREE
Value Over
$20

Both the **Harlequin®** Special Edition and **Harlequin®** Heartwarming™ series feature compelling novels filled with stories of love and strength where the bonds of friendship, family and community unite.

HARLEQUIN
PLUS

Try the best multimedia
subscription service for romance
readers like you!

Read, Watch and Play.

Experience the easiest way to get
the romance content you crave.

Start your **FREE TRIAL** at
<u>www.harlequinplus.com/freetrial</u>.